THE DUEL
AND OTHER STORIES

VOLUME TWO

THE DUEL
AND OTHER
STORIES

Anton Chekhov

Translated from the Russian by
Constance Garnett

Selected and Introduced by
Janet Malcolm

riverrun

Constance Garnett's translations of Chekhov's stories were first published
by Chatto & Windus in thirteen volumes between 1916 and 1922.

This edition published in Great Britain in 2020 by

riverrun

An imprint of

Quercus Editions Ltd
Carmelite House
50 Victoria Embankment
London EC4Y 0DZ

An Hachette UK company

A CIP catalogue record for this book is available
from the British Library

PB ISBN 978 1 78747 596 0
EBOOK ISBN 978 1 78747 597 7

This book is a work of fiction. Names, characters,
businesses, organizations, places and events are
either the product of the author's imagination
or used fictitiously. Any resemblance to
actual persons, living or dead, events or
locales is entirely coincidental.

10 9 8 7 6 5 4 3 2 1

Typeset by CC Book Production

Printed and bound in Great Britain by Clays Ltd, Elcograf S.p.A.

Contents

Preface

IN A LETTER OF July 24, 1997, Professor Gary Saul Morson of the Department of Slavic Languages at Northwestern University, wrote:

> I love Constance Garnett, and wish I had a framed picture of her on my wall, since I have often thought that what I do for a living is teach The Collected Works of Constance Garnett. She has a fine sense of English, and, especially the sort of English that appears in British fiction of the realist period, which makes her ideal for translating the Russian masterpieces. Tolstoy and Dostoevsky were constantly reading and learning from Dickens, Trollope, George Eliot and others. Every time someone else redoes one of the works, reviewers say that the new version replaces Garnett; and then another version comes out, which, apparently, replaces Garnett again and so on. She must have done something right.

The 13-volume translation of Chekhov published by Heinemann from 1916 to 1922 and reissued by the Ecco Press in 1984 as *Tales of Anton Chekhov** surely confirms Morson's estimate of Garnett – but does not answer the question that was the subject of our correspondence, namely, what is it that makes Chekhov's stories and novellas so mysteriously potent? We do not ask that question about Tolstoy and Dostoevsky. Their greatness does not mystify. It may be that the sense of mystery is intrinsic to the experience of reading Chekhov. He always leaves the meaning of a tale in some doubt, as if he were telling it precisely in order to illustrate his awareness of the pitiful incompleteness of human knowledge.

The reader will notice that the works in these volumes were all written after 1886. I have deliberately omitted the early stories. They were Chekhov's apprentice work, and some of them are remarkable, but none are in the force-field of the mature work. A number of unarguable masterpieces are missing, too. Choices had to be made to fit requirements of space, but a choice is just a choice, and I sympathize with the Chekhov-lover who would have made different ones.

Janet Malcolm

---

* The present three-volume selection is drawn from the Ecco Press edition. *The Lady with the Dog and Other Stories* contains shorter stories; *The Duel and Other Stories* and *Ward No. 6 and Other Stories* contain longer stories or novellas.

The Duel
and Other Stories

The Duel

I

IT WAS EIGHT O'CLOCK in the morning – the time when the officers, the local officials, and the visitors usually took their morning dip in the sea after the hot, stifling night, and then went into the pavilion to drink tea or coffee. Ivan Andreitch Laevsky, a thin, fair young man of twenty-eight, wearing the cap of a clerk in the Ministry of Finance and with slippers on his feet, coming down to bathe, found a number of acquaintances on the beach, and among them his friend Samoylenko, the army doctor.

With his big cropped head, short neck, his red face, his big nose, his shaggy black eyebrows and grey whiskers, his stout puffy figure and his hoarse military bass, this Samoylenko made on every newcomer the unpleasant impression of a gruff bully; but two or three days after making his acquaintance, one began to think his face extraordinarily good-natured, kind, and even

3

handsome. In spite of his clumsiness and rough manner, he was a peaceable man, of infinite kindliness and goodness of heart, always ready to be of use. He was on familiar terms with everyone in the town, lent everyone money, doctored everyone, made matches, patched up quarrels, arranged picnics at which he cooked *shashlik* and an awfully good soup of grey mullets. He was always looking after other people's affairs and trying to interest someone on their behalf, and was always delighted about something. The general opinion about him was that he was without faults of character. He had only two weaknesses: he was ashamed of his own good nature, and tried to disguise it by a surly expression and an assumed gruffness; and he liked his assistants and his soldiers to call him "Your Excellency", although he was only a civil councillor.

"Answer one question for me, Alexandr Daviditch," Laevsky began, when both he and Samoylenko were in the water up to their shoulders. "Suppose you had loved a woman and had been living with her for two or three years, and then left off caring for her, as one does, and began to feel that you had nothing in common with her. How would you behave in that case?"

"It's very simple. 'You go where you please, madam' – and that would be the end of it."

"It's easy to say that! But if she has nowhere to go? A woman with no friends or relations, without a farthing, who can't work . . ."

"Well? Five hundred roubles down or an allowance of

twenty-five roubles a month — and nothing more. It's very simple."

"Even supposing you have five hundred roubles and can pay twenty-five roubles a month, the woman I am speaking of is an educated woman and proud. Could you really bring yourself to offer her money? And how would you do it?"

Samoylenko was going to answer, but at that moment a big wave covered them both, then broke on the beach and rolled back noisily over the shingle. The friends got out and began dressing.

"Of course, it is difficult to live with a woman if you don't love her," said Samoylenko, shaking the sand out of his boots. "But one must look at the thing humanely, Vanya. If it were my case, I should never show a sign that I did not love her, and I should go on living with her till I died."

He was at once ashamed of his own words; he pulled himself up and said:

"But for aught I care, there might be no females at all. Let them all go to the devil!"

The friends dressed and went into the pavilion. There Samoylenko was quite at home, and even had a special cup and saucer. Every morning they brought him on a tray a cup of coffee, a tall cut glass of iced water, and a tiny glass of brandy. He would first drink the brandy, then the hot coffee, then the iced water, and this must have been very nice, for after drinking it his eyes looked moist with pleasure, he would stroke his whiskers with both hands, and say, looking at the sea:

"A wonderfully magnificent view!"

After a long night spent in cheerless, unprofitable thoughts which prevented him from sleeping, and seemed to intensify the darkness and sultriness of the night, Laevsky felt listless and shattered. He felt no better for the bathe and the coffee.

"Let us go on with our talk, Alexandr Daviditch," he said. "I won't make a secret of it; I'll speak to you openly as to a friend. Things are in a bad way with Nadyezhda Fyodorovna and me . . . a very bad way! Forgive me for forcing my private affairs upon you, but I must speak out."

Samoylenko, who had a misgiving of what he was going to speak about, dropped his eyes and drummed with his fingers on the table.

"I've lived with her for two years and have ceased to love her," Laevsky went on; "or, rather, I realized that I never had felt any love for her. . . . These two years have been a mistake."

It was Laevsky's habit as he talked to gaze attentively at the pink palms of his hands, to bite his nails, or to pinch his cuffs. And he did so now.

"I know very well you can't help me," he said. "But I tell you, because unsuccessful and superfluous people like me find their salvation in talking. I have to generalize about everything I do. I'm bound to look for an explanation and justification of my absurd existence in somebody else's theories, in literary types – in the idea that we, upper-class Russians, are degenerating, for instance, and so on. Last night, for example, I comforted myself by thinking all the time: 'Ah, how true Tolstoy is, how mercilessly true!' And that did me good. Yes, really, brother, he is a great writer, say what you like!"

Samoylenko, who had never read Tolstoy and was intending to do so every day of his life, was a little embarrassed, and said:

"Yes, all other authors write from imagination, but he writes straight from nature."

"My God!" sighed Laevsky; "how distorted we all are by civilization! I fell in love with a married woman and she with me. . . . To begin with, we had kisses, and calm evenings, and vows, and Spencer, and ideals, and interests in common. . . . What a deception! We really ran away from her husband, but we lied to ourselves and made out that we ran away from the emptiness of the life of the educated class. We pictured our future like this: to begin with, in the Caucasus, while we were getting to know the people and the place, I would put on the Government uniform and enter the service; then at our leisure we would pick out a plot of ground, would toil in the sweat of our brow, would have a vineyard and a field, and so on. If you were in my place, or that zoologist of yours, Von Koren, you might live with Nadyezhda Fyodorovna for thirty years, perhaps, and might leave your heirs a rich vineyard and three thousand acres of maize; but I felt like a bankrupt from the first day. In the town you have insufferable heat, boredom, and no society; if you go out into the country, you fancy poisonous spiders, scorpions, or snakes lurking under every stone and behind every bush, and beyond the fields – mountains and the desert. Alien people, an alien country, a wretched form of civilization – all that is not so easy, brother, as walking on the Nevsky Prospect in one's fur coat, arm-in-arm with Nadyezhda Fyodorovna, dreaming of the sunny South. What is needed here is a life and death struggle, and I'm not a fighting man. A wretched neurasthenic, an idle gentleman. . . . From the first day I knew that my dreams of a life of labour and of a vineyard were worthless. As for love, I ought to tell you that living with a woman who has read Spencer and has followed you to the ends of the earth is no more interesting than living with any Anfissa or Akulina. There's the same smell of ironing, of powder, and of medicines, the same curl-papers every morning, the same self-deception."

"You can't get on in the house without an iron," said Samoylenko, blushing at Laevsky's speaking to him so openly of a lady he knew. "You are out of humour today, Vanya, I notice. Nadyezhda Fyodorovna is a splendid woman, highly educated, and you are a man of the highest intellect. Of course, you are not married," Samoylenko went on, glancing round at the adjacent tables, "but that's not your fault; and besides . . . one ought to be above conventional prejudices and rise to the level of modern ideas. I believe in free love myself, yes. . . . But to my thinking, once you have settled together, you ought to go on living together all your life."

"Without love?"

"I will tell you directly," said Samoylenko. "Eight years ago there was an old fellow, an agent, here — a man of very great intelligence. Well, he used to say that the great thing in married life was patience. Do you hear, Vanya? Not love, but patience. Love cannot last long. You have lived two years in love, and now evidently your married life has reached the period when, in order to preserve equilibrium, so to speak, you ought to exercise all your patience. . . ."

"You believe in your old agent; to me his words are meaningless. Your old man could be a hypocrite; he could exercise himself in the virtue of patience, and, as he did so, look upon a person he did not love as an object indispensable for his moral exercises; but I have not yet fallen so low. If I want to exercise myself in patience, I will buy dumb-bells or a frisky horse, but I'll leave human beings alone."

Samoylenko asked for some white wine with ice. When they had drunk a glass each, Laevsky suddenly asked:

"Tell me, please, what is the meaning of softening of the brain?"

"How can I explain it to you? . . . It's a disease in which the brain becomes softer . . . as it were, dissolves."

"Is it curable?"

"Yes, if the disease is not neglected. Cold douches, blisters. . . . Something internal, too."

"Oh! . . . Well, you see my position; I can't live with her: it is more than I can do. While I'm with you I can be philosophical about it and smile, but at home I lose heart completely; I am so utterly miserable, that if I were told, for instance, that I should have to live another month with her, I should blow out my brains. At the same time, parting with her is out of the question. She has no friends or relations; she cannot work, and neither she nor I have any money. . . . What could become of her? To whom could she go? There is nothing one can think of. . . . Come, tell me, what am I to do?"

"H'm! . . ." growled Samoylenko, not knowing what to answer. "Does she love you?"

"Yes, she loves me in so far as at her age and with her temperament she wants a man. It would be as difficult for her to do without me as to do without her powder or her curl-papers. I am for her an indispensable, integral part of her boudoir."

Samoylenko was embarrassed.

"You are out of humour today, Vanya," he said. "You must have had a bad night."

"Yes, I slept badly. . . . Altogether, I feel horribly out of sorts, brother. My head feels empty; there's a sinking at my heart, a weakness. . . . I must run away."

"Run where?"

"There, to the North. To the pines and the mushrooms, to people and ideas. . . . I'd give half my life to bathe now in some little stream in the province of Moscow or Tula; to feel chilly, you know, and then to stroll for three hours even with the feeblest student, and to talk and talk endlessly. . . . And the scent of the hay! Do you remember it? And in the evening, when one walks in the garden, sounds of the piano float from the house; one hears the train passing. . . ."

Laevsky laughed with pleasure; tears came into his eyes, and to cover them, without getting up, he stretched across the next table for the matches.

"I have not been in Russia for eighteen years," said Samoylenko. "I've forgotten what it is like. To my mind, there is not a country more splendid than the Caucasus."

"Vereshtchagin has a picture in which some men condemned to death are languishing at the bottom of a very deep well. Your magnificent Caucasus strikes me as just like that well. If I were offered the choice of a chimney-sweep in Petersburg or a prince in the Caucasus, I should choose the job of chimney-sweep."

Laevsky grew pensive. Looking at his stooping figure, at his eyes fixed dreamily at one spot, at his pale, perspiring face and sunken temples, at his bitten nails, at the slipper which had dropped off his heel, displaying a badly darned sock, Samoylenko was moved to pity, and probably because Laevsky reminded him of a helpless child, he asked:

"Is your mother living?"

"Yes, but we are on bad terms. She could not forgive me for this affair."

Samoylenko was fond of his friend. He looked upon Laevsky as a good-natured fellow, a student, a man with no nonsense about him, with whom one could drink, and laugh, and talk without reserve. What he understood in him he disliked extremely. Laevsky drank a great deal and at unsuitable times; he played cards, despised his work, lived beyond his means, frequently made use of unseemly expressions in conversation, walked about the streets in his slippers, and quarrelled with Nadyezhda Fyodorovna before other people – and Samoylenko did not like this. But the fact that Laevsky had once been a student in the Faculty of Arts, subscribed to two fat reviews, often talked so cleverly that only a few people understood him, was living with a well-educated woman – all this Samoylenko did not understand, and he liked this and respected Laevsky, thinking him superior to himself.

"There is another point," said Laevsky, shaking his head. "Only it is between ourselves. I'm concealing it from Nadyezhda Fyodorovna for the time. . . . Don't let it out before her. . . . I got a letter the day before yesterday, telling me that her husband has died from softening of the brain."

"The Kingdom of Heaven be his!" sighed Samoylenko. "Why are you concealing it from her?"

"To show her that letter would be equivalent to 'Come to church to be married'. And we should first have to make our relations clear. When she understands that we can't go on living together, I will show her the letter. Then there will be no danger in it."

"Do you know what, Vanya," said Samoylenko, and a sad and imploring expression came into his face, as though he were going to ask him about something very touching and were afraid of being refused. "Marry her, my dear boy!"

"Why?"

"Do your duty to that splendid woman! Her husband is dead, and so Providence itself shows you what to do!"

"But do understand, you queer fellow, that it is impossible. To marry without love is as base and unworthy of a man as to perform mass without believing in it."

"But it's your duty to."

"Why is it my duty?" Laevsky asked irritably.

"Because you took her away from her husband and made yourself responsible for her."

"But now I tell you in plain Russian, I don't love her!"

"Well, if you've no love, show her proper respect, consider her wishes. . . ."

"'Show her respect, consider her wishes,'" Laevsky mimicked him. "As though she were some Mother Superior! . . . You are a poor psychologist and physiologist if you think that living with a woman one can get off with nothing but respect and consideration. What a woman thinks most of is her bedroom."

"Vanya, Vanya!" said Samoylenko, overcome with confusion.

"You are an elderly child, a theorist, while I am an old man in spite of my years, and practical, and we shall never understand one another. We had better drop this conversation. Mustapha!" Laevsky shouted to the waiter. "What's our bill?"

"No, no . . ." the doctor cried in dismay, clutching Laevsky's arm. "It is for me to pay. I ordered it. Make it out to me," he cried to Mustapha.

The friends got up and walked in silence along the sea-front. When they reached the boulevard, they stopped and shook hands at parting.

"You are awfully spoilt, my friend!" Samoylenko sighed. "Fate has sent you a young, beautiful, cultured woman, and you refuse the gift, while if God were to give me a crooked old woman, how pleased I should be if only she were kind and affectionate! I would live with her in my vineyard and . . ."

Samoylenko caught himself up and said:

"And she might get the samovar ready for me there, the old hag."

After parting with Laevsky he walked along the boulevard. When, bulky and majestic, with a stern expression on his face, he walked along the boulevard in his snow-white tunic and superbly polished boots, squaring his chest, decorated with the Vladimir cross on a ribbon, he was very much pleased with himself, and it seemed as though the whole world were looking at him with pleasure. Without turning his head, he looked to each side and thought that the boulevard was extremely well laid out; that the young cypress-trees, the eucalyptuses, and the ugly, anaemic palm-trees were very handsome and would in time give abundant shade; that the Circassians were an honest and hospitable people.

"It's strange that Laevsky does not like the Caucasus," he thought, "very strange."

Five soldiers, carrying rifles, met him and saluted him. On

the right side of the boulevard the wife of a local official was walking along the pavement with her son, a schoolboy.

"Good morning, Marya Konstantinovna," Samoylenko shouted to her with a pleasant smile. "Have you been to bathe? Ha, ha, ha! . . . My respects to Nikodim Alexandritch!"

And he went on, still smiling pleasantly, but seeing an assistant of the military hospital coming towards him, he suddenly frowned, stopped him, and asked:

"Is there anyone in the hospital?"

"No one, your Excellency."

"Eh?"

"No one, your Excellency."

"Very well, run along. . . ."

Swaying majestically, he made for the lemonade stall, where sat a full-bosomed old Jewess, who gave herself out to be a Georgian, and said to her as loudly as though he were giving the word of command to a regiment:

"Be so good as to give me some soda-water!"

II

Laevsky's not loving Nadyezhda Fyodorovna showed itself chiefly in the fact that everything she said or did seemed to him a lie, or equivalent to a lie, and everything he read against women and love seemed to him to apply perfectly to himself, to Nadyezhda Fyodorovna and her husband. When he returned home, she was sitting at the window, dressed and with her hair done, and with a preoccupied face was drinking coffee and turning over the leaves of a fat magazine; and he thought the drinking of coffee was not such a remarkable event that she need put on a preoccupied expression over it, and that she had been wasting her time doing her hair in a fashionable style, as there was no one here to attract and no need to be attractive. And in the magazine he saw nothing but falsity. He thought she had dressed and done her hair so as to look handsomer, and was reading in order to seem clever.

"Will it be all right for me to go to bathe today?" she said.

"Why? There won't be an earthquake whether you go or not, I suppose. . . ."

"No, I only ask in case the doctor should be vexed."

"Well, ask the doctor, then; I'm not a doctor."

On this occasion what displeased Laevsky most in Nadyezhda Fyodorovna was her white open neck and the little curls at the back of her head. And he remembered that when Anna Karenin got tired of her husband, what she disliked most of all was his ears, and thought: "How true it is, how true!"

Feeling weak and as though his head were perfectly empty, he went into his study, lay down on his sofa, and covered his face with a handkerchief that he might not be bothered by the flies. Despondent and oppressive thoughts always about the same thing trailed slowly across his brain like a long string of waggons on a gloomy autumn evening, and he sank into a state of drowsy oppression. It seemed to him that he had wronged Nadyezhda Fyodorovna and her husband, and that it was through his fault that her husband had died. It seemed to him that he had sinned against his own life, which he had ruined, against the world of lofty ideas, of learning, and of work, and he conceived that wonderful world as real and possible, not on this sea-front with hungry Turks and lazy mountaineers sauntering upon it, but there in the North, where there were operas, theatres, newspapers, and all kinds of intellectual activity. One could only there — not here — be honest, intelligent, lofty, and pure. He accused himself of having no ideal, no guiding principle in life, though he had a dim understanding now what it meant. Two years before, when he fell in love with Nadyezhda Fyodorovna, it seemed to him that he had only to go with her as his wife to the Caucasus, and he would be saved from vulgarity and emptiness; in the same way now, he was convinced that he had only to part from Nadyezhda Fyodorovna and to go to Petersburg, and he would get everything he wanted.

"Run away," he muttered to himself, sitting up and biting his nails. "Run away!"

He pictured in his imagination how he would go aboard the steamer and then would have some lunch, would drink some cold beer, would talk on deck with ladies, then would get into the train at Sevastopol and set off. Hurrah for freedom! One station after another would flash by, the air would keep growing colder and keener, then the birches and the fir-trees, then Kursk, Moscow. . . . In the restaurants cabbage soup, mutton with kasha, sturgeon, beer, no more Asiaticism, but Russia, real Russia. The passengers in the train would talk about trade, new singers, the Franco-Russian *entente*; on all sides there would be the feeling of keen, cultured, intellectual, eager life. . . . Hasten on, on! At last Nevsky Prospect, and Great Morskaya Street, and then Kovensky Place, where he used to live at one time when he was a student, the dear grey sky, the drizzling rain, the drenched cabmen. . . .

"Ivan Andreitch!" someone called from the next room. "Are you at home?"

"I'm here," Laevsky responded. "What do you want?"

"Papers."

Laevsky got up languidly, feeling giddy, walked into the other room, yawning and shuffling with his slippers. There, at the open window that looked into the street, stood one of his young fellow-clerks, laying out some government documents on the window-sill.

"One minute, my dear fellow," Laevsky said softly, and he went to look for the ink; returning to the window, he signed the papers without looking at them, and said: "It's hot!"

"Yes. Are you coming today?"

"I don't think so. . . . I'm not quite well. Tell Sheshkovsky that I will come and see him after dinner."

The clerk went away. Laevsky lay down on his sofa again and began thinking:

18

"And so I must weigh all the circumstances and reflect on them. Before I go away from here I ought to pay up my debts. I owe about two thousand roubles. I have no money. . . . Of course, that's not important; I shall pay part now, somehow, and I shall send the rest, later, from Petersburg. The chief point is Nadyezhda Fyodorovna. . . . First of all we must define our relations. . . . Yes."

A little later he was considering whether it would not be better to go to Samoylenko for advice.

"I might go," he thought, "but what use would there be in it? I shall only say something inappropriate about boudoirs, about women, about what is honest or dishonest. What's the use of talking about what is honest or dishonest, if I must make haste to save my life, if I am suffocating in this cursed slavery and am killing myself? . . . One must realize at last that to go on leading the life I do is something so base and so cruel that everything else seems petty and trivial beside it. To run away," he muttered, sitting down, "to run away."

The deserted seashore, the insatiable heat, and the monotony of the smoky lilac mountains, ever the same and silent, everlastingly solitary, overwhelmed him with depression, and, as it were, made him drowsy and sapped his energy. He was perhaps very clever, talented, remarkably honest; perhaps if the sea and the mountains had not closed him in on all sides, he might have become an excellent Zemstvo leader, a statesman, an orator, a political writer, a saint. Who knows? If so, was it not stupid to argue whether it were honest or dishonest when a gifted and useful man – an artist or musician, for instance – to escape from prison, breaks a wall and deceives his jailers? Anything is honest when a man is in such a position.

At two o'clock Laevsky and Nadyezhda Fyodorovna sat down to dinner. When the cook gave them rice and tomato soup, Laevsky said:

"The same thing every day. Why not have cabbage soup?"

"There are no cabbages."

"It's strange. Samoylenko has cabbage soup and Marya Konstantinovna has cabbage soup, and only I am obliged to eat this mawkish mess. We can't go on like this, darling."

As is common with the vast majority of husbands and wives, not a single dinner had in earlier days passed without scenes and fault-finding between Nadyezhda Fyodorovna and Laevsky; but ever since Laevsky had made up his mind that he did not love her, he had tried to give way to Nadyezhda Fyodorovna in everything, spoke to her gently and politely, smiled, and called her "darling".

"This soup tastes like liquorice," he said, smiling; he made an effort to control himself and seem amiable, but could not refrain from saying: "Nobody looks after the housekeeping. . . . If you are too ill or busy with reading, let me look after the cooking."

In earlier days she would have said to him, "Do by all means," or, "I see you want to turn me into a cook"; but now she only looked at him timidly and flushed crimson.

"Well, how do you feel today?" he asked kindly.

"I am all right today. There is nothing but a little weakness."

"You must take care of yourself, darling. I am awfully anxious about you."

Nadyezhda Fyodorovna was ill in some way. Samoylenko said she had intermittent fever, and gave her quinine; the other doctor, Ustimovitch, a tall, lean, unsociable man, who used to sit at home in the daytime, and in the evenings walk slowly up and down on the sea-front coughing, with his hands folded behind him and a cane stretched along his back, was of opinion that she had a female complaint, and prescribed warm compresses. In old days, when Laevsky loved her, Nadyezhda Fyodorovna's illness had excited his pity and terror; now he saw falsity even in her illness. Her yellow, sleepy face, her lustreless eyes, her apathetic expression, and the yawning that always followed her attacks of fever, and the fact that during them she lay under a shawl and looked more like a boy than a woman, and that it was close and stuffy in her room — all this, in his opinion, destroyed the illusion and was an argument against love and marriage.

The next dish given him was spinach with hard-boiled eggs, while Nadyezhda Fyodorovna, as an invalid, had jelly and milk. When with a preoccupied face she touched the jelly with a spoon and then began languidly eating it, sipping milk, and he heard her swallowing, he was possessed by such an overwhelming aversion that it made his head tingle. He recognized that such a feeling would be an insult even to a dog, but he was angry, not with himself but with Nadyezhda Fyodorovna, for arousing such a feeling, and he understood why lovers sometimes murder their mistresses. He would not murder her, of course, but if he had been on a jury now, he would have acquitted the murderer.

"Merci, darling," he said after dinner, and kissed Nadyezhda Fyodorovna on the forehead.

Going back into his study, he spent five minutes in walking to and fro, looking at his boots; then he sat down on his sofa and muttered:

"Run away, run away! We must define the position and run away!"

He lay down on the sofa and recalled again that Nadyezhda Fyodorovna's husband had died, perhaps, by his fault.

"To blame a man for loving a woman, or ceasing to love a woman, is stupid," he persuaded himself, lying down and raising his legs in order to put on his high boots. "Love and hatred are not under our control. As for her husband, maybe I was in an indirect way one of the causes of his death; but again, is it my fault that I fell in love with his wife and she with me?"

Then he got up, and finding his cap, set off to the lodgings of his colleague, Sheshkovsky, where the Government clerks met every day to play *vint* and drink beer.

"My indecision reminds me of Hamlet," thought Laevsky on the way. "How truly Shakespeare describes it! Ah, how truly!"

III

For the sake of sociability and from sympathy for the hard plight of newcomers without families, who, as there was not an hotel in the town, had nowhere to dine, Dr. Samoylenko kept a sort of table d'hôte. At this time there were only two men who habitually dined with him: a young zoologist called Von Koren, who had come for the summer to the Black Sea to study the embryology of the medusa, and a deacon called Pobyedov, who had only just left the seminary and been sent to the town to take the duty of the old deacon who had gone away for a cure. Each of them paid twelve roubles a month for their dinner and supper, and Samoylenko made them promise to turn up at two o'clock punctually.

Von Koren was usually the first to appear. He sat down in the drawing-room in silence, and taking an album from the table, began attentively scrutinizing the faded photographs of unknown men in full trousers and top-hats, and ladies in crinolines and caps. Samoylenko only remembered a few of them by name, and of those whom he had forgotten he said with a sigh: "A very fine fellow, remarkably intelligent!" When he had finished with the album, Von Koren took a pistol from the whatnot, and screwing up his left eye, took deliberate aim at the portrait of Prince Vorontsov, or stood still at the looking-glass and gazed a long time at his swarthy face, his big forehead, and his black hair, which curled like a negro's, and his shirt of dull-coloured cotton with big flowers on it like a Persian rug, and the broad leather belt he wore instead of a waistcoat. The contemplation of his own image seemed to afford him almost more satisfaction than looking at photographs or playing with the pistols. He was very well satisfied with his face, and his becomingly clipped beard, and the broad shoulders, which were unmistakable evidence of his excellent health and physical strength. He was satisfied, too, with his stylish get-up, from the cravat, which matched the colour of his shirt, down to his brown boots.

While he was looking at the album and standing before the glass, at that moment, in the kitchen and in the passage near, Samoylenko, without his coat and waistcoat, with his neck bare, excited and bathed in perspiration, was bustling about the tables, mixing the salad, or making some sauce, or preparing meat, cucumbers, and onion for the cold soup, while he glared fiercely at the orderly who was helping him, and brandished first a knife and then a spoon at him.

"Give me the vinegar!" he said. "That's not the vinegar — it's the salad oil!" he shouted, stamping. "Where are you off to, you brute?"

"To get the butter, your Excellency," answered the flustered orderly in a cracked voice.

"Make haste; it's in the cupboard! And tell Daria to put some fennel in the jar with the cucumbers! Fennel! Cover the cream up, gaping laggard, or the flies will get into it!"

And the whole house seemed resounding with his shouts. When it was ten or fifteen minutes to two the deacon would come in; he was a lanky young man of twenty-two, with long hair, with no beard and a hardly perceptible moustache. Going into the drawing-room, he crossed himself before the ikon, smiled, and held out his hand to Von Koren.

"Good morning," the zoologist said coldly. "Where have you been?"

"I've been catching sea-gudgeon in the harbour."

"Oh, of course. . . . Evidently, deacon, you will never be busy with work."

"Why not? Work is not like a bear; it doesn't run off into the woods," said the deacon, smiling and thrusting his hands into the very deep pockets of his white cassock.

"There's no one to whip you!" sighed the zoologist.

Another fifteen or twenty minutes passed and they were not called to dinner, and they could still hear the orderly running into the kitchen and back again, noisily treading with his boots, and Samoylenko shouting:

"Put it on the table! Where are your wits? Wash it first."

The famished deacon and Von Koren began tapping on the floor with their heels, expressing in this way their impatience like the audience at a theatre. At last the door opened and the harassed orderly announced that dinner was ready! In the dining-room they were met by Samoylenko, crimson in the face, wrathful, perspiring from the heat of the kitchen; he looked at them furiously, and with an expression of horror, took the lid off the soup tureen and helped each of them to a plateful; and only when he was convinced that they were eating it with relish and liked it, he gave a sigh of relief and settled himself in his deep arm-chair. His face looked blissful and his eyes grew moist. . . . He deliberately poured himself out a glass of vodka and said:

"To the health of the younger generation."

After his conversation with Laevsky, from early morning till dinner Samoylenko had been conscious of a load at his heart, although he was in the best of humours; he felt sorry for Laevsky and wanted to help him. After drinking a glass of vodka before the soup, he heaved a sigh and said:

"I saw Vanya Laevsky today. He is having a hard time of it, poor fellow! The material side of life is not encouraging for him, and the worst of it is all this psychology is too much for him. I'm sorry for the lad."

"Well, that is a person I am not sorry for," said Von Koren. "If that charming individual were drowning, I would push him under with a stick and say, 'Drown, brother, drown away.' . . ."

"That's untrue. You wouldn't do it."

"Why do you think that?" The zoologist shrugged his shoulders. "I'm just as capable of a good action as you are."

"Is drowning a man a good action?" asked the deacon, and he laughed.

"Laevsky? Yes."

I think there is something amiss with the soup . . ." said Samoylenko, anxious to change the conversation.

"Laevsky is absolutely pernicious and is as dangerous to society as the cholera microbe," Von Koren went on. "To drown him would be a service."

"It does not do you credit to talk like that about your neighbour. Tell us: what do you hate him for?"

"Don't talk nonsense, doctor. To hate and despise a microbe is stupid, but to look upon everybody one meets without distinction as one's neighbour, whatever happens – thanks very much, that is equivalent to giving up criticism, renouncing a straightforward attitude to people, washing one's hands of responsibility, in fact! I consider your Laevsky a blackguard; I do not conceal it, and I am perfectly conscientious in treating him as such. Well, you look upon him as your neighbour – and you may kiss him if you like: you look upon him as your neighbour, and that means that your attitude to him is the same as to me and to the deacon; that is no attitude at all. You are equally indifferent to all."

"To call a man a blackguard!" muttered Samoylenko, frowning with distaste – "that is so wrong that I can't find words for it!"

"People are judged by their actions," Von Koren continued. "Now you decide, deacon. . . . I am going to talk to you, deacon. Mr. Laevsky's career lies open before you, like a long Chinese puzzle, and you can read it from beginning to end. What has he been doing these two years that he has been living here? We will reckon his doings on our fingers. First, he has taught the inhabitants of the town to play *vint*: two years ago that game was unknown here; now they all play it from morning till late at night, even the women and the boys. Secondly, he has taught the residents to drink beer, which was not known here either; the inhabitants are indebted to him for the knowledge of various sorts of spirits, so that now they can distinguish Kospelov's vodka from Smirnov's No. 21, blindfold. Thirdly, in former days, people here made love to other men's wives in secret, from the same motives as thieves steal in secret and not openly; adultery was considered something they were ashamed to make a public display of. Laevsky has come as a pioneer in that line; he lives with another man's wife openly. . . . Fourthly . . ."

Von Koren hurriedly ate up his soup and gave his plate to the orderly.

"I understood Laevsky from the first month of our acquaintance," he went on, addressing the deacon. "We arrived here at the same time. Men like him are very fond of friendship, intimacy, solidarity, and all the rest of it, because they always want company for *vint*, drinking, and eating; besides, they are talkative and must have listeners. We made friends — that is, he turned up every day, hindered me working, and indulged in confidences in regard to his mistress. From the first he struck me by his exceptional falsity, which simply made me sick. As a friend I pitched into him, asking him why he drank too much, why he lived beyond his means and got into debt, why he did nothing and read nothing, why he had so little culture and so little knowledge; and in answer to all my questions he used to smile bitterly, sigh, and say: 'I am a failure, a superfluous man'; or: 'What do you expect, my dear fellow, from us, the debris of the serf-owning class?' or: 'We are degenerate. . . .' Or he would begin a long rigmarole about Onyegin, Petchorin, Byron's Cain, and Bazarov, of whom he would say: 'They are our fathers in flesh and in spirit.' So we are to understand that it was not his fault that Government envelopes lay unopened in his office for weeks together, and that he drank and taught others to drink, but Onyegin, Petchorin, and Turgenev, who had invented the failure and the superfluous man, were responsible for it. The cause of his extreme dissoluteness and unseemliness lies, do you see, not in himself, but somewhere outside in space. And so – an ingenious idea! – it is not only he who is dissolute, false, and disgusting, but we . . . 'we men of the eighties', 'we the spiritless, nervous offspring of the serf-owning class'; 'civilization has crippled us' . . . in fact, we are to understand that such a great man as Laevsky is great even in his fall: that his dissoluteness, his lack of culture and of moral purity, is a phenomenon of natural history, sanctified by inevitability; that the causes of it are world-wide, elemental; and that we ought to hang up a lamp before Laevsky, since he is the fated victim of the age, of influences, of heredity, and so on. All the officials and their ladies were in ecstasies when they listened to him, and I could not make out for a long time what sort of man I had to deal with, a cynic or a clever rogue. Such types as he, on the surface intellectual with a smattering of education and a great deal of talk about their own nobility, are very clever in posing as exceptionally complex natures."

"Hold your tongue!" Samoylenko flared up. "I will not allow a splendid fellow to be spoken ill of in my presence!"

"Don't interrupt, Alexandr Daviditch," said Von Koren coldly; "I am just finishing. Laevsky is by no means a complex organism. Here is his moral skeleton: in the morning, slippers, a bathe, and coffee; then till dinner-time, slippers, a constitutional, and conversation; at two o'clock slippers, dinner, and wine; at five o'clock a bathe, tea and wine, then *vint* and lying; at ten o'clock supper and wine; and after midnight sleep and *la femme*. His existence is confined within this narrow programme like an egg within its shell. Whether he walks or sits, is angry, writes, rejoices, it may all be reduced to wine, cards, slippers, and women. Woman plays a fatal, overwhelming part in his life. He tells us himself that at thirteen he was in love; that when he was a student in his first year he was living with a lady who had a good influence over him, and to whom he was indebted for his musical education. In his second year he bought a prostitute from a brothel and raised her to his level — that is, took her as his kept mistress, and she lived with him for six months and then ran away back to the brothel-keeper, and her flight caused him much spiritual suffering. Alas! his sufferings were so great that he had to leave the university and spend two years at home doing nothing. But this was all for the best. At home he made friends with a widow who advised him to leave the Faculty of Jurisprudence and go into the Faculty of Arts. And so he did. When he had taken his degree, he fell passionately in love with his present . . . what's her name? . . . married lady, and was obliged to flee with her here to the Caucasus for the sake of his ideals, he would have us believe, seeing that . . . tomorrow, if not today, he will be tired of her and flee back again to Petersburg, and that, too, will be for the sake of his ideals."

"How do you know?" growled Samoylenko, looking angrily at the zoologist. "You had better eat your dinner."

The next course consisted of boiled mullet with Polish sauce. Samoylenko helped each of his companions to a whole mullet and poured out the sauce with his own hand. Two minutes passed in silence.

"Woman plays an essential part in the life of every man," said the deacon. "You can't help that."

"Yes, but to what degree? For each of us woman means mother, sister, wife, friend. To Laevsky she is everything, and at the same time nothing but a mistress. She — that is, cohabitation with her — is the happiness and object of his life; he is gay, sad, bored, disenchanted — on account of woman; his life grows disagreeable — woman is to blame; the dawn of a new life begins to glow, ideals turn up — and again look for the woman. . . . He only derives enjoyment from books and pictures in which there is woman. Our age is, to his thinking, poor and inferior to the forties and the sixties only because we do not know how to abandon ourselves obviously to the passion and ecstasy of love. These voluptuaries must have in their brains a special growth of the nature of sarcoma, which stifles the brain and directs their whole psychology. Watch Laevsky when he is sitting anywhere in company. You notice: when one raises any general question in his presence, for instance, about the cell or instinct, he sits apart, and neither speaks nor listens; he looks languid and disillusioned; nothing has any interest for him, everything is vulgar and trivial. But as soon as you speak of male and female — for instance, of the fact that the female spider, after fertilization, devours the male — his eyes glow with curiosity, his face brightens, and the man revives, in fact. All his thoughts, however noble, lofty, or neutral they may be, they all have one point of resemblance. You walk along the street with him and meet a donkey, for instance. . . . 'Tell me, please,' he asks, 'what would happen if you mated a donkey with a camel?' And his dreams! Has he told you of his dreams? It is magnificent! First, he dreams that he is married to the moon, then that he is summoned before the police and ordered to live with a guitar . . ."

The deacon burst into resounding laughter; Samoylenko frowned and wrinkled up his face angrily so as not to laugh, but could not restrain himself, and laughed.

"And it's all nonsense!" he said, wiping his tears. "Yes, by Jove, it's nonsense!"

IV

The deacon was very easily amused, and laughed at every trifle till he got a stitch in his side, till he was helpless. It seemed as though he only liked to be in people's company because there was a ridiculous side to them, and because they might be given ridiculous nicknames. He had nicknamed Samoylenko "the tarantula", his orderly "the drake", and was in ecstasies when on one occasion Von Koren spoke of Laevsky and Nadyezhda Fyodorovna as "Japanese monkeys". He watched people's faces greedily, listened without blinking, and it could be seen that his eyes filled with laughter and his face was tense with expectation of the moment when he could let himself go and burst into laughter.

"He is a corrupt and depraved type," the zoologist continued, while the deacon kept his eyes riveted on his face, expecting he would say something funny. "It is not often one can meet with such a nonentity. In body he is inert, feeble, prematurely old, while in intellect he differs in no respect from a fat shopkeeper's wife who does nothing but eat, drink, and sleep on a feather-bed, and who keeps her coachman as a lover."

The deacon began guffawing again.

"Don't laugh, deacon," said Von Koren. "It grows stupid, at last. I should not have paid attention to his insignificance," he went on, after waiting till the deacon had left off laughing;

"I should have passed him by if he were not so noxious and dangerous. His noxiousness lies first of all in the fact that he has great success with women, and so threatens to leave descendants — that is, to present the world with a dozen Laevskys as feeble and as depraved as himself. Secondly, he is in the highest degree contaminating. I have spoken to you already of *vint* and beer. In another year or two he will dominate the whole Caucasian coast. You know how the mass, especially its middle stratum, believe in intellectuality, in a university education, in gentlemanly manners, and in literary language. Whatever filthy thing he did, they would all believe that it was as it should be, since he is an intellectual man, of liberal ideas and university education. What is more, he is a failure, a superfluous man, a neurasthenic, a victim of the age, and that means he can do anything. He is a charming fellow, a regular good sort, he is so genuinely indulgent to human weaknesses; he is compliant, accommodating, easy and not proud; one can drink with him and gossip and talk evil of people. . . . The masses, always inclined to anthropomorphism in religion and morals, like best of all the little gods who have the same weaknesses as themselves. Only think what a wide field he has for contamination! Besides, he is not a bad actor and is a clever hypocrite, and knows very well how to twist things round. Only take his little shifts and dodges, his attitude to civilization, for instance. He has scarcely sniffed at civilization, yet: 'Ah, how we have been crippled by civilization! Ah, how I envy those savages, those children of nature, who know nothing of civilization!' We are to understand, you see, that at one time, in ancient days, he has been devoted to civilization with his whole soul, has served it, has sounded it to its depths, but it has exhausted him, disillusioned him, deceived him; he is a Faust, do you see? – a second Tolstoy. . . . As for Schopenhauer and Spencer, he treats them like small boys and slaps them on the shoulder in a fatherly way: 'Well, what do you say, old Spencer?' He has not read Spencer, of course, but how charming he is when with light, careless irony he says of his lady friend: 'She has read Spencer!' And they all listen to him, and no one cares to understand that this charlatan has not the right to kiss the sole of Spencer's foot, let alone speaking about him in that tone! Sapping the foundations of civilization, of authority, of other people's altars, spattering them with filth, winking jocosely at them only to justify and conceal one's own rottenness and moral poverty is only possible for a very vain, base, and nasty creature."

"I don't know what it is you expect of him, Kolya," said Samoylenko, looking at the zoologist, not with anger now, but with a guilty air. "He is a man the same as everyone else. Of course, he has his weaknesses, but he is abreast of modern ideas, is in the service, is of use to his country. Ten years ago there was an old fellow serving as agent here, a man of the greatest intelligence . . . and he used to say . . ."

"Nonsense, nonsense!" the zoologist interrupted. "You say he is in the service; but how does he serve? Do you mean to tell

35

me that things have been done better because he is here, and the officials are more punctual, honest, and civil? On the contrary, he has only sanctioned their slackness by his prestige as an intellectual university man. He is only punctual on the 20th of the month, when he gets his salary; on the other days he lounges about at home in slippers and tries to look as if he were doing the Government a great service by living in the Caucasus. No, Alexandr Daviditch, don't stick up for him. You are insincere from beginning to end. If you really loved him and considered him your neighbour, you would above all not be indifferent to his weaknesses, you would not be indulgent to them, but for his own sake would try to make him innocuous."

"That is?"

"Innocuous. Since he is incorrigible, he can only be made innocuous in one way. . . ." Von Koren passed his finger round his throat. "Or he might be drowned . . ." he added. "In the interests of humanity and in their own interests, such people ought to be destroyed. They certainly ought."

"What are you saying?" muttered Samoylenko, getting up and looking with amazement at the zoologist's calm, cold face. "Deacon, what is he saying? Why – are you in your senses?"

"I don't insist on the death penalty," said Von Koren. "If it is proved that it is pernicious, devise something else. If we can't destroy Laevsky, why then, isolate him, make him harmless, send him to hard labour."

"What are you saying!" said Samoylenko in horror. "With

pepper, with pepper," he cried in a voice of despair, seeing that the deacon was eating stuffed aubergines without pepper. "You with your great intellect, what are you saying! Send our friend, a proud intellectual man, to penal servitude!"

"Well, if he is proud and tries to resist, put him in fetters!"

Samoylenko could not utter a word, and only twiddled his fingers; the deacon looked at his flabbergasted and really absurd face, and laughed.

"Let us leave off talking of that," said the zoologist. "Only remember one thing, Alexandr Daviditch: primitive man was preserved from such as Laevsky by the struggle for existence and by natural selection; now our civilization has considerably weakened the struggle and the selection, and we ought to look after the destruction of the rotten and worthless for ourselves; otherwise, when the Laevskys multiply, civilization will perish and mankind will degenerate utterly. It will be our fault."

"If it depends on drowning and hanging," said Samoylenko, "damnation take your civilization, damnation take your humanity! Damnation take it! I tell you what: you are a very learned and intelligent man and the pride of your country, but the Germans have ruined you. Yes, the Germans! The Germans!"

Since Samoylenko had left Dorpat, where he had studied medicine, he had rarely seen a German and had not read a single German book, but, in his opinion, every harmful idea in politics or science was due to the Germans. Where he had got this notion he could not have said himself, but he held it firmly.

"Yes, the Germans!" he repeated once more. "Come and have some tea."

All three stood up, and putting on their hats, went out into the little garden, and sat there under the shade of the light green maples, the pear-trees, and a chestnut-tree. The zoologist and the deacon sat on a bench by the table, while Samoylenko sank into a deep wicker chair with a sloping back. The orderly handed them tea, jam, and a bottle of syrup.

It was very hot, thirty degrees Réaumur in the shade. The sultry air was stagnant and motionless, and a long spider-web, stretching from the chestnut-tree to the ground, hung limply and did not stir.

The deacon took up the guitar, which was constantly lying on the ground near the table, tuned it, and began singing softly in a thin voice:

"'Gathered round the tavern were the seminary lads,'" but instantly subsided, overcome by the heat, mopped his brow and glanced upwards at the blazing blue sky. Samoylenko grew drowsy; the sultry heat, the stillness and the delicious after-dinner languor, which quickly pervaded all his limbs, made him feel heavy and sleepy; his arms dropped at his sides, his eyes grew small, his head sank on his breast. He looked with almost tearful tenderness at Von Koren and the deacon, and muttered:

"The younger generation . . . A scientific star and a luminary of the Church. . . . I shouldn't wonder if the long-skirted alleluia will be shooting up into a bishop; I dare say I may come to kissing his hand. . . . Well . . . please God. . . ."

Soon a snore was heard. Von Koren and the deacon finished their tea and went out into the street.

"Are you going to the harbour again to catch sea-gudgeon?" asked the zoologist.

"No, it's too hot."

"Come and see me. You can pack up a parcel and copy something for me. By the way, we must have a talk about what you are to do. You must work, deacon. You can't go on like this."

"Your words are just and logical," said the deacon. "But my laziness finds an excuse in the circumstances of my present life. You know yourself that an uncertain position has a great tendency to make people apathetic. God only knows whether I have been sent here for a time or permanently. I am living here in uncertainty, while my wife is vegetating at her father's and is missing me. And I must confess my brain is melting with the heat."

"That's all nonsense," said the zoologist. "You can get used to the heat, and you can get used to being without the deaconess. You mustn't be slack; you must pull yourself together."

V

Nadyezhda Fyodorovna went to bathe in the morning, and her cook, Olga, followed her with a jug, a copper basin, towels, and a sponge. In the bay stood two unknown steamers with dirty white funnels, obviously foreign cargo vessels. Some men dressed in white and wearing white shoes were walking along the harbour, shouting loudly in French, and were answered from the steamers. The bells were ringing briskly in the little church of the town.

"Today is Sunday!" Nadyezhda Fyodorovna remembered with pleasure.

She felt perfectly well, and was in a gay holiday humour. In a new loose-fitting dress of coarse thick tussore silk, and a big wide-brimmed straw hat which was bent down over her ears, so that her face looked out as though from a basket, she fancied she looked very charming. She thought that in the whole town there was only one young, pretty, intellectual woman, and that was herself, and that she was the only one who knew how to dress herself cheaply, elegantly, and with taste. That dress, for example, cost only twenty-two roubles, and yet how charming it was! In the whole town she was the only one who could be attractive, while there were numbers of men, so they must all, whether they would or not, be envious of Laevsky.

She was glad that of late Laevsky had been cold to her,

reserved and polite, and at times even harsh and rude; in the past she had met all his outbursts, all his contemptuous, cold or strange incomprehensible glances, with tears, reproaches, and threats to leave him or to starve herself to death; now she only blushed, looked guiltily at him, and was glad he was not affectionate to her. If he had abused her, threatened her, it would have been better and pleasanter, since she felt hopelessly guilty towards him. She felt she was to blame, in the first place, for not sympathizing with the dreams of a life of hard work, for the sake of which he had given up Petersburg and had come here to the Caucasus, and she was convinced that he had been angry with her of late for precisely that. When she was travelling to the Caucasus, it seemed that she would find here on the first day a cosy nook by the sea, a snug little garden with shade, with birds, with little brooks, where she could grow flowers and vegetables, rear ducks and hens, entertain her neighbours, doctor poor peasants and distribute little books amongst them. It had turned out that the Caucasus was nothing but bare mountains, forests, and huge valleys, where it took a long time and a great deal of effort to find anything and settle down; that there were no neighbours of any sort; that it was very hot and one might be robbed. Laevsky had been in no hurry to obtain a piece of land; she was glad of it, and they seemed to be in a tacit compact never to allude to a life of hard work. He was silent about it, she thought, because he was angry with her for being silent about it.

In the second place, she had without his knowledge during

41

those two years bought various trifles to the value of three hundred roubles at Atchmianov's shop. She had bought the things by degrees, at one time materials, at another time silk or a parasol, and the debt had grown imperceptibly.

"I will tell him about it today . . ." she used to decide, but at once reflected that in Laevsky's present mood it would hardly be convenient to talk to him of debts.

Thirdly, she had on two occasions in Laevsky's absence received a visit from Kirilin, the police captain: once in the morning when Laevsky had gone to bathe, and another time at midnight when he was playing cards. Remembering this, Nadyezhda Fyodorovna flushed crimson, and looked round at the cook as though she might overhear her thoughts. The long, insufferably hot, wearisome days, beautiful languorous evenings and stifling nights, and the whole manner of living, when from morning to night one is at a loss to fill up the useless hours, and the persistent thought that she was the prettiest young woman in the town, and that her youth was passing and being wasted, and Laevsky himself, though honest and idealistic, always the same, always lounging about in his slippers, biting his nails, and wearying her with his caprices, led by degrees to her becoming possessed by desire, and as though she were mad, she thought of nothing else day and night. Breathing, looking, walking, she felt nothing but desire. The sound of the sea told her she must love; the darkness of evening – the same; the mountains – the same. . . . And when Kirilin began paying her attentions, she had neither the power nor the wish to resist, and surrendered to him. . . .

Now the foreign steamers and the men in white reminded her for some reason of a huge hall; together with the shouts of French she heard the strains of a waltz, and her bosom heaved with unaccountable delight. She longed to dance and talk French.

She reflected joyfully that there was nothing terrible about her infidelity. Her soul had no part in her infidelity; she still loved Laevsky, and that was proved by the fact that she was jealous of him, was sorry for him, and missed him when he was away. Kirilin had turned out to be very mediocre, rather coarse though handsome; everything was broken off with him already and there would never be anything more. What had happened was over; it had nothing to do with anyone, and if Laevsky found it out he would not believe in it.

There was only one bathing-house for ladies on the sea-front; men bathed under the open sky. Going into the bathing-house, Nadyezhda Fyodorovna found there an elderly lady, Marya Konstantinovna Bityugov, and her daughter Katya, a schoolgirl of fifteen; both of them were sitting on a bench undressing. Marya Konstantinovna was a good-natured, enthusiastic, and genteel person, who talked in a drawling and pathetic voice. She had been a governess until she was thirty-two, and then had married Bityugov, a Government official – a bald little man with his hair combed on to his temples and with a very meek disposition.

She was still in love with him, was jealous, blushed at the word "love", and told everyone she was very happy.

"My dear," she cried enthusiastically, on seeing Nadyezhda Fyodorovna, assuming an expression which all her acquaintances called "almond-oily". "My dear, how delightful that you have come! We'll bathe together – that's enchanting!"

Olga quickly flung off her dress and chemise, and began undressing her mistress.

"It's not quite so hot today as yesterday?" said Nadyezhda Fyodorovna, shrinking at the coarse touch of the naked cook. "Yesterday I almost died of the heat."

"Oh, yes, my dear; I could hardly breathe myself. Would you believe it? I bathed yesterday three times! Just imagine, my dear, three times! Nikodim Alexandritch was quite uneasy."

"Is it possible to be so ugly?" thought Nadyezhda Fyodorovna, looking at Olga and the official's wife; she glanced at Katya and thought: "The little girl's not badly made."

"Your Nikodim Alexandritch is very charming!" she said. "I'm simply in love with him."

"Ha, ha, ha!" cried Marya Konstantinovna, with a forced laugh; "that's quite enchanting."

Free from her clothes, Nadyezhda Fyodorovna felt a desire to fly. And it seemed to her that if she were to wave her hands she would fly upwards. When she was undressed, she noticed that Olga looked scornfully at her white body. Olga, a young soldier's wife, was living with her lawful husband, and so considered herself superior to her mistress. Marya Konstantinovna and Katya were afraid of her, and did not respect her. This was disagreeable, and to raise herself in their opinion, Nadyezhda Fyodorovna said:

"At home, in Petersburg, summer villa life is at its height now. My husband and I have so many friends! We ought to go and see them."

"I believe your husband is an engineer?" said Marya Konstantinovna timidly.

"I am speaking of Laevsky. He has a great many acquaintances. But unfortunately his mother is a proud aristocrat, not very intelligent. . . ."

Nadyezhda Fyodorovna threw herself into the water without finishing; Marya Konstantinovna and Katya made their way in after her.

"There are so many conventional ideas in the world," Nadyezhda Fyodorovna went on, "and life is not so easy as it seems."

Marya Konstantinovna, who had been a governess in aristocratic families and who was an authority on social matters, said:

"Oh yes! Would you believe me, my dear, at the Garatynskys' I was expected to dress for lunch as well as for dinner, so that, like an actress, I received a special allowance for my wardrobe in addition to my salary."

She stood between Nadyezhda Fyodorovna and Katya as

though to screen her daughter from the water that washed the former.

Through the open doors looking out to the sea they could see someone swimming a hundred paces from their bathing-place.

"Mother, it's our Kostya," said Katya.

"Ach, ach!" Marya Konstantinovna cackled in her dismay. "Ach, Kostya!" she shouted, "Come back! Kostya, come back!"

Kostya, a boy of fourteen, to show off his prowess before his mother and sister, dived and swam farther, but began to be exhausted and hurried back, and from his strained and serious face it could be seen that he could not trust his own strength.

"The trouble one has with these boys, my dear!" said Marya Konstantinovna, growing calmer. "Before you can turn round, he will break his neck. Ah, my dear, how sweet it is, and yet at the same time how difficult, to be a mother! One's afraid of everything."

Nadyezhda Fyodorovna put on her straw hat and dashed out into the open sea. She swam some thirty feet and then turned on her back. She could see the sea to the horizon, the steamers, the people on the sea-front, the town; and all this, together with the sultry heat and the soft, transparent waves, excited her and whispered that she must live, live. . . . A sailing-boat darted by her rapidly and vigorously, cleaving the waves and the air; the man sitting at the helm looked at her, and she liked being looked at. . . .

After bathing, the ladies dressed and went away together.

"I have fever every alternate day, and yet I don't get thin," said Nadyezhda Fyodorovna, licking her lips, which were salt from the bathe, and responding with a smile to the bows of her acquaintances. "I've always been plump, and now I believe I'm plumper than ever."

"That, my dear, is constitutional. If, like me, one has no constitutional tendency to stoutness, no diet is of any use. . . . But you've wetted your hat, my dear."

"It doesn't matter; it will dry."

Nadyezhda Fyodorovna saw again the men in white who were walking on the sea-front and talking French; and again she felt a sudden thrill of joy, and had a vague memory of some big hall in which she had once danced, or of which, perhaps, she had once dreamed. And something at the bottom of her soul dimly and obscurely whispered to her that she was a pretty, common, miserable, worthless woman. . . .

Marya Konstantinovna stopped at her gate and asked her to come in and sit down for a little while.

"Come in, my dear," she said in an imploring voice, and at the same time she looked at Nadyezhda Fyodorovna with anxiety and hope; perhaps she would refuse and not come in!

"With pleasure," said Nadyezhda Fyodorovna, accepting. "You know how I love being with you!"

And she went into the house. Marya Konstantinovna sat her down and gave her coffee, regaled her with milk rolls, then showed her photographs of her former pupils, the Garatynskys, who were by now married. She showed her, too, the examination reports of Kostya and Katya. The reports were very good, but to make them seem even better, she complained, with a sigh, how difficult the lessons at school were now. . . . She made much of her visitor, and was sorry for her, though at the same time she was harassed by the thought that Nadyezhda Fyodorovna might have a corrupting influence on the morals of Kostya and Katya, and was glad that her Nikodim Alexandritch was not at home. Seeing that in her opinion all men are fond of "women like that", Nadyezhda Fyodorovna might have a bad effect on Nikodim Alexandritch too.

As she talked to her visitor, Marya Konstantinovna kept remembering that they were to have a picnic that evening, and that Von Koren had particularly begged her to say nothing about it to the "Japanese monkeys" – that is, Laevsky and Nadyezhda Fyodorovna; but she dropped a word about it unawares, crimsoned, and said in confusion:

"I hope you will come too!"

VI

It was agreed to drive about five miles out of town on the road to the south, to stop near a *duhan* at the junction of two streams – the Black River and the Yellow River – and to cook fish soup. They started out soon after five. Foremost of the party in a char-à-banc drove Samoylenko and Laevsky; they were followed by Marya Konstantinovna, Nadyezhda Fyodorovna, Katya and Kostya, in a coach with three horses, carrying with them the crockery and a basket with provisions. In the next carriage came the police captain, Kirilin, and the young Atchmianov, the son of the shopkeeper to whom Nadyezhda Fyodorovna owed three hundred roubles; opposite them, huddled up on the little seat with his feet tucked under him, sat Nikodim Alexandritch, a neat little man with hair combed on to his temples. Last of all came Von Koren and the deacon; at the deacon's feet stood a basket of fish.

"R-r-right!" Samoylenko shouted at the top of his voice when he met a cart or a mountaineer riding on a donkey.

"In two years' time, when I shall have the means and the people ready, I shall set off on an expedition," Von Koren was telling the deacon. "I shall go by the sea-coast from Vladivostok to the Behring Straits, and then from the Straits to the mouth of the Yenisei. We shall make the map, study the fauna and the flora, and make detailed geological, anthropological, and ethnographical researches. It depends upon you to go with me or not."

"It's impossible," said the deacon.

"Why?"

"I'm a man with ties and a family."

"Your wife will let you go; we will provide for her. Better still if you were to persuade her for the public benefit to go into a nunnery; that would make it possible for you to become a monk, too, and join the expedition as a priest. I can arrange it for you."

The deacon was silent.

"Do you know your theology well?" asked the zoologist.

"No, rather badly."

"H'm! . . . I can't give you any advice on that score, because I don't know much about theology myself. You give me a list of books you need, and I will send them to you from Petersburg in the winter. It will be necessary for you to read the notes of religious travellers, too; among them are some good ethnologists and Oriental scholars. When you are familiar with their methods, it will be easier for you to set to work. And you needn't waste your time till you get the books; come to me, and we will study the compass and go through a course of meteorology. All that's indispensable."

"To be sure . . ." muttered the deacon, and he laughed. "I was trying to get a place in Central Russia, and my uncle, the head priest, promised to help me. If I go with you I shall have troubled them for nothing."

"I don't understand your hesitation. If you go on being an ordinary deacon, who is only obliged to hold a service on holidays, and on the other days can rest from work, you will be exactly the same as you are now in ten years' time, and will have gained nothing but a beard and moustache; while on returning from this expedition in ten years' time you will be a different man, you will be enriched by the consciousness that something has been done by you."

From the ladies' carriage came shrieks of terror and delight. The carriages were driving along a road hollowed in a literally overhanging precipitous cliff, and it seemed to everyone that they were galloping along a shelf on a steep wall, and that in a moment the carriages would drop into the abyss. On the right stretched the sea; on the left was a rough brown wall with black blotches and red veins and with climbing roots; while on the summit stood shaggy fir-trees bent over, as though looking down in terror and curiosity. A minute later there were shrieks and laughter again: they had to drive under a huge overhanging rock.

"I don't know why the devil I'm coming with you," said Laevsky. "How stupid and vulgar it is! I want to go to the North, to run away, to escape; but here I am, for some reason, going to this stupid picnic."

"But look, what a view!" said Samoylenko as the horses turned to the left, and the valley of the Yellow River came into sight and the stream itself gleamed in the sunlight, yellow, turbid, frantic.

"I see nothing fine in that, Sasha," answered Laevsky. "To be in continual ecstasies over nature shows poverty of imagination. In comparison with what my imagination can give me, all these streams and rocks are trash, and nothing else."

The carriages now were by the banks of the stream. The high mountain banks gradually grew closer, the valley shrank together and ended in a gorge; the rocky mountain round which they were driving had been piled together by nature out of huge rocks, pressing upon each other with such terrible weight, that Samoylenko could not help gasping every time he looked at them. The dark and beautiful mountain was cleft in places by narrow fissures and gorges from which came a breath of dewy moisture and mystery; through the gorges could be seen other mountains, brown, pink, lilac, smoky, or bathed in vivid sunlight. From time to time as they passed a gorge they caught the sound of water falling from the heights and splashing on the stones.

"Ach, the damned mountains!" sighed Laevsky. "How sick I am of them!"

At the place where the Black River falls into the Yellow, and the water black as ink stains the yellow and struggles with it, stood the Tatar Kerbalay's *duhan*, with the Russian flag on the roof and with an inscription written in chalk: "The Pleasant *duhan*." Near it was a little garden, enclosed in a hurdle fence, with tables and chairs set out in it, and in the midst of a thicket of wretched thorn-bushes stood a single solitary cypress, dark and beautiful.

Kerbalay, a nimble little Tatar in a blue shirt and a white apron, was standing in the road, and, holding his stomach, he bowed low to welcome the carriages, and smiled, showing his glistening white teeth.

"Good evening, Kerbalay," shouted Samoylenko. "We are

driving on a little further, and you take along the samovar and chairs! Look sharp!"

Kerbalay nodded his shaven head and muttered something, and only those sitting in the last carriage could hear: "We've got trout, your Excellency."

"Bring them, bring them!" said Von Koren.

Five hundred paces from the *duhan* the carriages stopped. Samoylenko selected a small meadow round which there were scattered stones convenient for sitting on, and a fallen tree blown down by the storm with roots overgrown by moss and dry yellow needles. Here there was a fragile wooden bridge over the stream, and just opposite on the other bank there was a little barn for drying maize, standing on four low piles, and looking like the hut on hen's legs in the fairy tale; a little ladder sloped from its door.

The first impression in all was a feeling that they would never get out of that place again. On all sides wherever they looked, the mountains rose up and towered above them, and the shadows of evening were stealing rapidly, rapidly from the *duhan* and dark cypress, making the narrow winding valley of the Black River narrower and the mountains higher. They could hear the river murmuring and the unceasing chirrup of the grasshoppers.

"Enchanting!" said Marya Konstantinovna, heaving deep sighs of ecstasy. "Children, look how fine! What peace!"

"Yes, it really is fine," assented Laevsky, who liked the view, and for some reason felt sad as he looked at the sky and then at the blue smoke rising from the chimney of the *duhan*. "Yes, it is fine," he repeated.

"Ivan Andreitch, describe this view," Marya Konstantinovna said tearfully.

"Why?" asked Laevsky. "The impression is better than any description. The wealth of sights and sounds which everyone receives from nature by direct impression is ranted about by authors in a hideous and unrecognisable way."

"Really?" Von Koren asked coldly, choosing the biggest stone by the side of the water, and trying to clamber up and sit upon it. "Really?" he repeated, looking directly at Laevsky. "What of *Romeo and Juliet*? Or, for instance, Pushkin's 'Night in the Ukraine'? Nature ought to come and bow down at their feet."

"Perhaps," said Laevsky, who was too lazy to think and oppose him. "Though what is *Romeo and Juliet* after all?" he added after a short pause. "The beauty of poetry and holiness of love are simply the roses under which they try to hide its rottenness. Romeo is just the same sort of animal as all the rest of us."

"Whatever one talks to you about, you always bring it round to . . ." Von Koren glanced round at Katya and broke off.

"What do I bring it round to?" asked Laevsky.

"One tells you, for instance, how beautiful a bunch of grapes is, and you answer: 'Yes, but how ugly it is when it is chewed and digested in one's stomach!' Why say that? It's not new, and . . . altogether it is a queer habit."

Laevsky knew that Von Koren did not like him, and so was afraid of him, and felt in his presence as though everyone were constrained and someone were standing behind his back. He made no answer and walked away, feeling sorry he had come.

"Gentlemen, quick march for brushwood for the fire!" commanded Samoylenko.

They all wandered off in different directions, and no one was left but Kirilin, Atchmianov, and Nikodim Alexandritch. Kerbalay brought chairs, spread a rug on the ground, and set a few bottles of wine.

The police captain, Kirilin, a tall, good-looking man, who in all weathers wore his great-coat over his tunic, with his haughty deportment, stately carriage, and thick, rather hoarse voice, looked like a young provincial chief of police; his expression was mournful and sleepy, as though he had just been waked against his will.

"What have you brought this for, you brute?" he asked Kerbalay, deliberately articulating each word. "I ordered you to give us *kvarel*, and what have you brought, you ugly Tatar? Eh? What?"

"We have plenty of wine of our own, Yegor Alekseitch," Nikodim Alexandritch observed, timidly and politely.

"What? But I want us to have my wine, too; I'm taking part in the picnic and I imagine I have full right to contribute my share. I im-ma-gine so! Bring ten bottles of *kvarel*."

"Why so many?" asked Nikodim Alexandritch, in wonder, knowing Kirilin had no money.

"Twenty bottles! Thirty!" shouted Kirilin.

"Never mind, let him," Atchmianov whispered to Nikodim Alexandritch; "I'll pay."

Nadyezhda Fyodorovna was in a light-hearted, mischievous mood; she wanted to skip and jump, to laugh, to shout, to tease, to flirt. In her cheap cotton dress with blue pansies on it, in her red shoes and the same straw hat, she seemed to herself, little, simple, light, ethereal as a butterfly. She ran over the rickety bridge and looked for a minute into the water, in order to feel giddy; then, shrieking and laughing, ran to the other side to the drying-shed, and she fancied that all the men were admiring her, even Kerbalay. When in the rapidly falling darkness the trees began to melt into the mountains and the horses into the carriages, and a light gleamed in the windows of the *duhan*, she climbed up the mountain by the little path which zigzagged between stones and thorn-bushes and sat on a stone. Down below, the campfire was burning. Near the fire, with his sleeves tucked up, the deacon was moving to and fro, and his long black shadow kept describing a circle round it; he put on wood, and with a spoon tied to a long stick he stirred the cauldron. Samoylenko, with a copper-red face, was fussing round the fire just as though he were in his own kitchen, shouting furiously:

"Where's the salt, gentlemen? I bet you've forgotten it. Why are you all sitting about like lords while I do the work?"

Laevsky and Nikodim Alexandritch were sitting side by side on the fallen tree looking pensively at the fire. Marya

Konstantinovna, Katya, and Kostya were taking the cups, saucers, and plates out of the baskets. Von Koren, with his arms folded and one foot on a stone, was standing on a bank at the very edge of the water, thinking about something. Patches of red light from the fire moved together with the shadows over the ground near the dark human figures, and quivered on the mountain, on the trees, on the bridge, on the drying-shed; on the other side the steep, scooped-out bank was all lighted up and glimmering in the stream, and the rushing turbid water broke its reflection into little bits.

The deacon went for the fish which Kerbalay was cleaning and washing on the bank, but he stood still half-way and looked about him.

"My God, how nice it is!" he thought. "People, rocks, the fire, the twilight, a monstrous tree — nothing more, and yet how fine it is!"

On the further bank some unknown persons made their appearance near the drying-shed. The flickering light and the smoke from the camp-fire puffing in that direction made it impossible to get a full view of them all at once, but glimpses were caught now of a shaggy hat and a grey beard, now of a blue shirt, now of a figure, ragged from shoulder to knee, with a dagger across the body; then a swarthy young face with black eyebrows, as thick and bold as though they had been drawn in charcoal. Five of them sat in a circle on the ground, and the other five went into the drying-shed. One was standing at the door with his back to the fire, and with his hands behind his back was telling something, which must have been very interesting, for when Samoylenko threw on twigs and the fire flared up, and scattered sparks and threw a glaring light on the shed, two calm countenances with an expression on them of deep attention could be seen, looking out of the door, while those who were sitting in a circle turned round and began listening to the speaker. Soon after, those sitting in a circle began softly singing something slow and melodious, that sounded like Lenten Church music. . . . Listening to them, the deacon imagined how it would be with him in ten years' time, when he would come back from the expedition: he would be a young priest and monk, an author with a name and a splendid past; he would be consecrated an archimandrite, then a bishop; and he would serve mass in the cathedral; in a golden mitre he would come out into the body of the church with the ikon on his breast, and blessing the mass of the people with the triple and the double candelabra, would proclaim: "Look down from Heaven, O God, behold and visit this vineyard which Thy Hand has planted," and the children with their angel voices would sing in response: "Holy God . . ."

"Deacon, where is that fish?" he heard Samoylenko's voice.

As he went back to the fire, the deacon imagined the Church procession going along a dusty road on a hot July day; in front the peasants carrying the banners and the women and children the ikons, then the boy choristers and the sacristan with his face tied up and a straw in his hair, then in due order himself, the deacon, and behind him the priest wearing his *calotte* and carrying a cross, and behind them, tramping in the dust, a crowd of peasants — men, women, and children; in the crowd his wife and the priest's wife with kerchiefs on their heads. The choristers sing, the babies cry, the corncrakes call, the lark carols. . . . Then they make a stand and sprinkle the herd with holy water. . . . They go on again, and then kneeling pray for rain. Then lunch and talk. . . .

"And that's nice too . . ." thought the deacon.

VII

Kirilin and Atchmianov climbed up the mountain by the path. Atchmianov dropped behind and stopped, while Kirilin went up to Nadyezhda Fyodorovna.

"Good evening," he said, touching his cap.

"Good evening."

"Yes!" said Kirilin, looking at the sky and pondering.

"Why 'yes'?" asked Nadyezhda Fyodorovna after a brief pause, noticing that Atchmianov was watching them both.

"And so it seems," said the officer, slowly, "that our love has withered before it has blossomed, so to speak. How do you wish me to understand it? Is it a sort of coquetry on your part, or do you look upon me as a nincompoop who can be treated as you choose?"

"It was a mistake! Leave me alone!" Nadyezhda Fyodorovna said sharply, on that beautiful, marvellous evening, looking at him with terror and asking herself with bewilderment, could there really have been a moment when that man attracted her and had been near to her?

"So that's it!" said Kirilin; he thought in silence for a few minutes and said: "Well, I'll wait till you are in a better humour, and meanwhile I venture to assure you I am a gentleman, and I don't allow anyone to doubt it. Adieu!"

He touched his cap again and walked off, making his way between the bushes. After a short interval Atchmianov approached hesitatingly.

"What a fine evening!" he said with a slight Armenian accent.

He was nice-looking, fashionably dressed, and behaved unaffectedly like a well-bred youth, but Nadyezhda Fyodorovna did not like him because she owed his father three hundred roubles; it was displeasing to her, too, that a shopkeeper had been asked to the picnic, and she was vexed at his coming up to her that evening when her heart felt so pure.

"The picnic is a success altogether," he said, after a pause.

"Yes," she agreed, and as though suddenly remembering her debt, she said carelessly: "Oh, tell them in your shop that Ivan Andreitch will come round in a day or two and will pay three hundred roubles. . . . I don't remember exactly what it is."

"I would give another three hundred if you would not mention that debt every day. Why be prosaic?"

Nadyezhda Fyodorovna laughed; the amusing idea occurred to her that if she had been willing and sufficiently immoral she might in one minute be free from her debt. If she, for instance, were to turn the head of this handsome young fool! How amusing, absurd, wild it would be really! And she suddenly felt a longing to make him love her, to plunder him, throw him over, and then to see what would come of it.

"Allow me to give you one piece of advice," Atchmianov said timidly. "I beg you to beware of Kirilin. He says horrible things about you everywhere."

"It doesn't interest me to know what every fool says of me," Nadyezhda Fyodorovna said coldly, and the amusing thought of playing with handsome young Atchmianov suddenly lost its charm.

"We must go down," she said; "they're calling us."

The fish soup was ready by now. They were ladling it out by platefuls, and eating it with the religious solemnity with which this is only done at a picnic; and everyone thought the fish soup very good, and thought that at home they had never eaten anything so nice. As is always the case at picnics, in the mass of dinner napkins, parcels, useless greasy papers fluttering in the wind, no one knew where was his glass or where his bread. They poured the wine on the carpet and on their own knees, spilt the salt, while it was dark all round them and the fire burnt more dimly, and everyone was too lazy to get up and put wood on. They all drank wine, and even gave Kostya and Katya half a glass each. Nadyezhda Fyodorovna drank one glass and then another, got a little drunk and forgot about Kirilin.

"A splendid picnic, an enchanting evening," said Laevsky, growing lively with the wine. "But I should prefer a fine winter to all this. 'His beaver collar is silver with hoar-frost.'"

"Everyone to his taste," observed Von Koren.

Laevsky felt uncomfortable; the heat of the camp-fire was beating upon his back, and the hatred of Von Koren upon his breast and face: this hatred on the part of a decent, clever man, a feeling in which there probably lay hid a well-grounded reason, humiliated him and enervated him, and unable to stand up against it, he said in a propitiatory tone:

"I am passionately fond of nature, and I regret that I'm not a naturalist. I envy you."

"Well, I don't envy you, and don't regret it," said Nadyezhda Fyodorovna. "I don't understand how anyone can seriously interest himself in beetles and ladybirds while the people are suffering."

Laevsky shared her opinion. He was absolutely ignorant of natural science, and so could never reconcile himself to the authoritative tone and the learned and profound air of the people who devoted themselves to the whiskers of ants and the claws of beetles, and he always felt vexed that these people, relying on these whiskers, claws, and something they called protoplasm (he always imagined it in the form of an oyster), should undertake to decide questions involving the origin and life of man. But in

Nadyezhda Fyodorovna's words he heard a note of falsity, and simply to contradict her he said: "The point is not the ladybirds, but the deductions made from them."

VIII

It was late, eleven o'clock, when they began to get into the carriages to go home. They took their seats, and the only ones missing were Nadyezhda Fyodorovna and Atchmianov, who were running after one another, laughing, the other side of the stream.

"Make haste, my friends," shouted Samoylenko.

"You oughtn't to give ladies wine," said Von Koren in a low voice.

Laevsky, exhausted by the picnic, by the hatred of Von Koren, and by his own thoughts, went to meet Nadyezhda Fyodorovna, and when, gay and happy, feeling light as a feather, breathless and laughing, she took him by both hands and laid her head on his breast, he stepped back and said drily:

"You are behaving like a . . . cocotte."

It sounded horribly coarse, so that he felt sorry for her at once. On his angry, exhausted face she read hatred, pity and vexation with himself, and her heart sank at once. She realized instantly that she had gone too far, had been too free and easy in her behaviour, and overcome with misery, feeling herself heavy, stout, coarse, and drunk, she got into the first empty carriage together with Atchmianov. Laevsky got in with Kirilin, the zoologist with Samoylenko, the deacon with the ladies, and the party set off.

"You see what the Japanese monkeys are like," Von Koren began, rolling himself up in his cloak and shutting his eyes. "You heard she doesn't care to take an interest in beetles and ladybirds because the people are suffering. That's how all the Japanese monkeys look upon people like us. They're a slavish, cunning race, terrified by the whip and the fist for ten generations; they tremble and burn incense only before violence; but let the monkey into a free state where there's no one to take it by the collar, and it relaxes at once and shows itself in its true colours. Look how bold they are in picture galleries, in museums, in theatres, or when they talk of science: they puff themselves out and get excited, they are abusive and critical . . . they are bound to criticize – it's the sign of the slave. You listen: men of the liberal professions are more often sworn at than pickpockets – that's because three-quarters of society are made up of slaves, of just such monkeys. It never happens that a slave holds out his hand to you and sincerely says 'Thank you' to you for your work."

"I don't know what you want," said Samoylenko, yawning; "the poor thing, in the simplicity of her heart, wanted to talk to you of scientific subjects, and you draw a conclusion from that. You're cross with him for something or other, and with her, too, to keep him company. She's a splendid woman."

"Ah, nonsense! An ordinary kept woman, depraved and vulgar. Listen, Alexandr Daviditch; when you meet a simple peasant woman, who isn't living with her husband, who does nothing but giggle, you tell her to go and work. Why are you timid in this case and afraid to tell the truth? Simply because Nadyezhda Fyodorovna is kept, not by a sailor, but by an official."

"What am I to do with her?" said Samoylenko, getting angry. "Beat her or what?"

"Not flatter vice. We curse vice only behind its back, and that's like making a long nose at it round a corner. I am a zoologist or a sociologist, which is the same thing; you are a doctor; society believes in us; we ought to point out the terrible harm which threatens it and the next generation from the existence of ladies like Nadyezhda Ivanovna."

"Fyodorovna," Samoylenko corrected. "But what ought society to do?"

"Society? That's its affair. To my thinking the surest and most direct method is – compulsion. *Manu militari* she ought to be returned to her husband; and if her husband won't take her in, then she ought to be sent to penal servitude or some house of correction."

"Ouf!" sighed Samoylenko. He paused and asked quietly: "You said the other day that people like Laevsky ought to be destroyed. . . . Tell me, if you . . . if the State or society commissioned you to destroy him, could you . . . bring yourself to it?"

"My hand would not tremble."

IX

When they got home, Laevsky and Nadyezhda Fyodorovna went into their dark, stuffy, dull rooms. Both were silent. Laevsky lighted a candle, while Nadyezhda Fyodorovna sat down, and without taking off her cloak and hat, lifted her melancholy, guilty eyes to him.

He knew that she expected an explanation from him, but an explanation would be wearisome, useless and exhausting, and his heart was heavy because he had lost control over himself and been rude to her. He chanced to feel in his pocket the letter which he had been intending every day to read to her, and thought if he were to show her that letter now, it would turn her thoughts in another direction.

"It is time to define our relations," he thought. "I will give it her; what is to be will be."

He took out the letter and gave it her.

"Read it. It concerns you."

Saying this, he went into his own room and lay down on the sofa in the dark without a pillow. Nadyezhda Fyodorovna read the letter, and it seemed to her as though the ceiling were falling and the walls were closing in on her. It seemed suddenly dark and shut in and terrible. She crossed herself quickly three times and said:

"Give him peace, O Lord . . . give him peace. . . ."

And she began crying.

"Vanya," she called. "Ivan Andreitch!"

There was no answer. Thinking that Laevsky had come in and was standing behind her chair, she sobbed like a child, and said:

"Why did you not tell me before that he was dead? I wouldn't have gone to the picnic; I shouldn't have laughed so horribly. . . . The men said horrid things to me. What a sin, what a sin! Save me, Vanya, save me. . ,. I have been mad. . . . I am lost. . . ."

Laevsky heard her sobs. He felt stifled and his heart was beating violently. In his misery he got up, stood in the middle of the room, groped his way in the dark to an easy-chair by the table, and sat down.

"This is a prison . . ." he thought. "I must get away . . . I can't bear it."

It was too late to go and play cards; there were no restaurants in the town. He lay down again and covered his ears that he might not hear her sobbing, and he suddenly remembered that he could go to Samoylenko. To avoid going near Nadyezhda Fyodorovna, he got out of the window into the garden, climbed over the garden fence and went along the street. It was dark. A steamer, judging by its lights, a big passenger one, had just come in. He heard the clank of the anchor chain. A red light was moving rapidly from the shore in the direction of the steamer: it was the Customs boat going out to it.

"The passengers are asleep in their cabins . . ." thought Laevsky, and he envied the peace of mind of other people.

The windows in Samoylenko's house were open. Laevsky looked in at one of them, then in at another; it was dark and still in the rooms.

"Alexandr Daviditch, are you asleep?" he called. "Alexandr Daviditch!"

He heard a cough and an uneasy shout:

"Who's there? What the devil?"

"It is I, Alexandr Daviditch; excuse me."

A little later the door opened; there was a glow of soft light from the lamp, and Samoylenko's huge figure appeared all in white, with a white nightcap on his head.

"What now?" he asked, scratching himself and breathing hard from sleepiness. "Wait a minute; I'll open the door directly."

"Don't trouble; I'll get in at the window. . . ."

Laevsky climbed in at the window, and when he reached Samoylenko, seized him by the hand.

"Alexandr Daviditch," he said in a shaking voice, "save me! I beseech you, I implore you. Understand me! My position is agonizing. If it goes on for another two days I shall strangle myself like . . . like a dog."

"Wait a bit. . . . What are you talking about exactly?"

"Light a candle."

"Oh . . . oh! . . ." sighed Samoylenko, lighting a candle. "My God! My God! . . . Why, it's past one, brother."

"Excuse me, but I can't stay at home," said Laevsky, feeling great comfort from the light and the presence of Samoylenko.

"You are my best, my only friend, Alexandr Daviditch. . . .
You are my only hope. For God's sake, come to my rescue,
whether you want to or not. I must get away from here, come
what may! . . . Lend me the money!"

"Oh, my God, my God! . . . sighed Samoylenko, scratching
himself. "I was dropping asleep and I hear the whistle of the
steamer, and now you . . . Do you want much?"

"Three hundred roubles at least. I must leave her a hundred,
and I need two hundred for the journey. . . . I owe you about
four hundred already, but I will send it you all . . . all. . . ."

Samoylenko took hold of both his whiskers in one hand, and
standing with his legs wide apart, pondered.

"Yes . . ." he muttered, musing. "Three hundred. . . . Yes. . . .
But I haven't got so much. I shall have to borrow it from someone."

"Borrow it, for God's sake!" said Laevsky, seeing from
Samoylenko's face that he wanted to lend him the money and
certainly would lend it. "Borrow it, and I'll be sure to pay you
back. I will send it from Petersburg as soon as I get there. You
can set your mind at rest about that. I'll tell you what, Sasha,"
he said, growing more animated; "let us have some wine."

"Yes . . . we can have some wine, too."

They both went into the dining-room.

"And how about Nadyezhda Fyodorovna?" asked Samoylenko,
setting three bottles and a plate of peaches on the table. "Surely
she's not remaining?"

"I will arrange it all, I will arrange it all," said Laevsky, feeling an unexpected rush of joy. "I will send her the money afterwards and she will join me. . . . Then we will define our relations. To your health, friend."

"Wait a bit," said Samoylenko. "Drink this first. . . . This is from my vineyard. This bottle is from Navaridze's vineyard and this one is from Ahatulov's. . . . Try all three kinds and tell me candidly. . . . There seems a little acidity about mine. Eh? Don't you taste it?"

"Yes. You have comforted me, Alexandr Daviditch. Thank you. . . . I feel better."

"Is there any acidity?"

"Goodness only knows, I don't know. But you are a splendid, wonderful man!"

Looking at his pale, excited, good-natured face, Samoylenko remembered Von Koren's view that men like that ought to be destroyed, and Laevsky seemed to him a weak, defenceless child, whom anyone could injure and destroy.

"And when you go, make it up with your mother," he said. "It's not right."

"Yes, yes; I certainly shall."

They were silent for a while. When they had emptied the first bottle, Samoylenko said:

"You ought to make it up with Von Koren too. You are both such splendid, clever fellows, and you glare at each other like wolves."

"Yes, he's a fine, very intelligent fellow," Laevsky assented, ready now to praise and forgive everyone. "He's a remarkable man, but it's impossible for me to get on with him. No! Our natures are too different. I'm an indolent, weak, submissive nature. Perhaps in a good minute I might hold out my hand to him, but he would turn away from me . . . with contempt."

Laevsky took a sip of wine, walked from corner to corner and went on, standing in the middle of the room:

"I understand Von Koren very well. His is a resolute, strong, despotic nature. You have heard him continually talking of 'the expedition', and it's not mere talk. He wants the wilderness, the moonlit night: all around in little tents, under the open sky, lie sleeping his sick and hungry Cossacks, guides, porters, doctor, priest, all exhausted with their weary marches, while only he is awake, sitting like Stanley on a camp-stool, feeling himself the monarch of the desert and the master of these men. He goes on and on and on, his men groan and die, one after another, and he goes on and on, and in the end perishes himself, but still is monarch and ruler of the desert, since the cross upon his tomb can be seen by the caravans for thirty or forty miles over the desert. I am sorry the man is not in the army. He would have made a splendid military genius. He would not have hesitated to drown his cavalry in the river and make a bridge out of dead bodies. And such hardihood is more needed in war than any kind of fortification or strategy. Oh, I understand him perfectly! Tell me: why is he wasting his substance here? What does he want here?"

"He is studying the marine fauna."

"No, no, brother, no!" Laevsky sighed. "A scientific man who was on the steamer told me the Black Sea was poor in animal life, and that in its depths, thanks to the abundance of sulphuric hydrogen, organic life was impossible. All the serious zoologists work at the biological station at Naples or Villefranche. But Von Koren is independent and obstinate: he works on the Black Sea because nobody else is working there; he is at loggerheads with the university, does not care to know his comrades and other scientific men because he is first of all a despot and only secondly a zoologist. And you'll see he'll do something. He is already dreaming that when he comes back from his expedition he will purify our universities from intrigue and mediocrity, and will make the scientific men mind their p's and q's. Despotism is just as strong in science as in the army. And he is spending his second summer in this stinking little town because he would rather be first in a village than second in a town. Here he is a king and an eagle; he keeps all the inhabitants under his thumb and oppresses them with his authority. He has appropriated everyone, he meddles in other people's affairs; everything is of use to him, and everyone is afraid of him. I am slipping out of his clutches, he feels that and hates me. Hasn't he told you that I ought to be destroyed or sent to hard labour?"

"Yes," laughed Samoylenko.

Laevsky laughed too, and drank some wine.

"His ideals are despotic too," he said, laughing, and biting a peach. "Ordinary mortals think of their neighbour – me, you, man in fact – if they work for the common weal. To Von Koren men are puppets and nonentities, too trivial to be the object of his life. He works, will go for his expedition and break his neck there, not for the sake of love for his neighbour, but for the sake of such abstractions as humanity, future generations, an ideal race of men. He exerts himself for the improvement of the human race, and we are in his eyes only slaves, food for the cannon, beasts of burden; some he would destroy or stow away in Siberia, others he would break by discipline, would, like Araktcheev, force them to get up and go to bed to the sound of the drum; would appoint eunuchs to preserve our chastity and morality, would order them to fire at anyone who steps out of the circle of our narrow conservative morality; and all this in the name of the improvement of the human race. . . . And what is the human race? Illusion, mirage . . . despots have always been illusionists. I understand him very well, brother. I appreciate him and don't deny his importance; this world rests on men like him, and if the world were left only to such men as us, for all our good-nature and good intentions, we should make as great a mess of it as the flies have of that picture. Yes."

Laevsky sat down beside Samoylenko, and said with genuine feeling: "I'm a foolish, worthless, depraved man. The air I breathe, this wine, love, life in fact – for all that, I have given nothing in exchange so far but lying, idleness, and cowardice. Till now I have deceived myself and other people; I have been miserable about it, and my misery was cheap and common. I bow my back humbly before Von Koren's hatred because at times I hate and despise myself."

Laevsky began again pacing from one end of the room to the other in excitement, and said:

"I'm glad I see my faults clearly and am conscious of them. That will help me to reform and become a different man. My dear fellow, if only you knew how passionately, with what anguish, I long for such a change. And I swear to you I'll be a man! I will! I don't know whether it is the wine that is speaking in me, or whether it really is so, but it seems to me that it is long since I have spent such pure and lucid moments as I have just now with you."

"It's time to sleep, brother," said Samoylenko.

"Yes, yes. . . . Excuse me; I'll go directly."

Laevsky moved hurriedly about the furniture and windows, looking for his cap.

"Thank you," he muttered, sighing. "Thank you. . . . Kind and friendly words are better than charity. You have given me new life."

He found his cap, stopped, and looked guiltily at Samoylenko.

"Alexandr Daviditch," he said in an imploring voice.

"What is it?"

"Let me stay the night with you, my dear fellow!"

"Certainly. . . . Why not?"

Laevsky lay down on the sofa, and went on talking to the doctor for a long time.

X

Three days after the picnic, Marya Konstantinovna unexpectedly called on Nadyezhda Fyodorovna, and without greeting her or taking off her hat, seized her by both hands, pressed them to her breast and said in great excitement:

"My dear, I am deeply touched and moved: our dear kind-hearted doctor told my Nikodim Alexandritch yesterday that your husband was dead. Tell me, my dear . . . tell me, is it true?"

"Yes, it's true; he is dead," answered Nadyezhda Fyodorovna.

"That is awful, awful, my dear! But there's no evil without some compensation; your husband was no doubt a noble, wonderful, holy man, and such are more needed in Heaven than on earth."

Every line and feature in Marya Konstantinovna's face began quivering as though little needles were jumping up and down under her skin; she gave an almond-oily smile and said, breathlessly, enthusiastically:

"And so you are free, my dear. You can hold your head high now, and look people boldly in the face. Henceforth God and man will bless your union with Ivan Andreitch. It's enchanting. I am trembling with joy, I can find no words. My dear, I will give you away. . . . Nikodim Alexandritch and I have been so fond of you, you will allow us to give our blessing to your pure, lawful union. When, when do you think of being married?"

"I haven't thought of it," said Nadyezhda Fyodorovna, freeing her hands.

"That's impossible, my dear. You have thought of it, you have."

"Upon my word, I haven't," said Nadyezhda Fyodorovna, laughing. "What should we be married for? I see no necessity for it. We'll go on living as we have lived."

"What are you saying!" cried Marya Konstantinovna in horror. "For God's sake, what are you saying!"

"Our getting married won't make things any better. On the contrary, it will make them even worse. We shall lose our freedom."

"My dear, my dear, what are you saying!" exclaimed Marya Konstantinovna, stepping back and flinging up her hands. "You are talking wildly! Think what you are saying. You must settle down!"

"'Settle down.' How do you mean? I have not lived yet, and you tell me to settle down."

Nadyezhda Fyodorovna reflected that she really had not lived. She had finished her studies in a boarding-school and had been married to a man she did not love; then she had thrown in her lot with Laevsky, and had spent all her time with him on this empty, desolate coast, always expecting something better. Was that life?

"I ought to be married though," she thought, but remembering Kirilin and Atchmianov she flushed and said:

"No, it's impossible. Even if Ivan Andreitch begged me to on his knees — even then I would refuse."

Marya Konstantinovna sat on the sofa for a minute in silence, grave and mournful, gazing fixedly into space; then she got up and said coldly:

"Goodbye, my dear! Forgive me for having troubled you. Though it's not easy for me, it's my duty to tell you that from this day all is over between us, and, in spite of my profound respect for Ivan Andreitch, the door of my house is closed to you henceforth."

She uttered these words with great solemnity and was herself overwhelmed by her solemn tone. Her face began quivering again; it assumed a soft almond-oily expression. She held out both hands to Nadyezhda Fyodorovna, who was overcome with alarm and confusion, and said in an imploring voice:

"My dear, allow me if only for a moment to be a mother or an elder sister to you! I will be as frank with you as a mother."

Nadyezhda Fyodorovna felt in her bosom warmth, gladness, and pity for herself, as though her own mother had really risen up and were standing before her. She impulsively embraced Marya Konstantinovna and pressed her face to her shoulder.

Both of them shed tears. They sat down on the sofa and for a few minutes sobbed without looking at one another or being able to utter a word.

"My dear child," began Marya Konstantinovna, "I will tell you some harsh truths, without sparing you."

"For God's sake, for God's sake, do!"

"Trust me, my dear. You remember of all the ladies here, I was the only one to receive you. You horrified me from the very first day, but I had not the heart to treat you with disdain like all the rest. I grieved over dear, good Ivan Andreitch as though he were my son — a young man in a strange place, inexperienced, weak, with no mother; and I was worried, dreadfully worried. . . . My husband was opposed to our making his acquaintance, but I talked him over . . . persuaded him. . . . We began receiving Ivan Andreitch, and with him, of course, you. If we had not, he would have been insulted. I have a daughter, a son. . . . You understand the tender mind, the pure heart of childhood . . . 'who so offendeth one of these little ones.' . . . I received you into my house and trembled for my children. Oh, when you become a mother, you will understand my fears. And everyone was surprised at my receiving you, excuse my saying so, as a respectable woman, and hinted to me . . . well, of course, slanders, suppositions. . . . At the bottom of my heart I blamed you, but you were unhappy, flighty, to be pitied, and my heart was wrung with pity for you."

"But why, why?" asked Nadyezhda Fyodorovna, trembling all over. "What harm have I done anyone?"

"You are a terrible sinner. You broke the vow you made your husband at the altar. You seduced a fine young man, who perhaps had he not met you might have taken a lawful partner for life from a good family in his own circle, and would have been like everyone else now. You have ruined his youth. Don't speak, don't speak, my dear! I never believe that man is to blame for our sins. It is always the woman's fault. Men are frivolous in domestic life; they are guided by their minds, and not by their hearts. There's a great deal they don't understand; woman understands it all. Everything depends on her. To her much is given and from her much will be required. Oh, my dear, if she had been more foolish or weaker than man on that side, God would not have entrusted her with the education of boys and girls. And then, my dear, you entered on the path of vice, forgetting all modesty; any other woman in your place would have hidden herself from people, would have sat shut up at home, and would only have been seen in the temple of God, pale, dressed all in black and weeping, and everyone would have said in genuine compassion: 'O Lord, this erring angel is coming back again to Thee. . . .' But you, my dear, have forgotten all discretion; have lived openly, extravagantly; have seemed to be proud of your sin; you have been gay and laughing, and I, looking at you, shuddered with horror, and have been afraid that thunder from Heaven would strike our house while you were sitting with us. My dear, don't speak, don't speak," cried Marya Konstantinovna, observing that Nadyezhda Fyodorovna wanted to speak. "Trust me, I will not deceive you, I will not hide one truth from the eyes of your soul. Listen to me, my dear. . . . God marks great sinners, and you have been marked out: only think — your costumes have always been appalling."

Nadyezhda Fyodorovna, who had always had the highest opinion of her costumes, left off crying and looked at her with surprise.

"Yes, appalling," Marya Konstantinovna went on. "Anyone could judge of your behaviour from the elaboration and gaudiness of your attire. People laughed and shrugged their shoulders as they looked at you, and I grieved, I grieved. . . . And forgive me, my dear; you are not nice in your person! When we met in the bathing-place, you made me tremble. Your outer clothing was decent enough, but your petticoat, your chemise. . . . My dear, I blushed! Poor Ivan Andreitch! No one ever ties his cravat properly, and from his linen and his boots, poor fellow! one can see he has no one at home to look after him. And he is always hungry, my darling, and of course, if there is no one at home to think of the samovar and the coffee, one is forced to spend half one's salary at the pavilion. And it's simply awful, awful in your home! No one else in the town has flies, but there's no getting rid of them in your rooms: all the plates and dishes are black with them. If you look at the windows and the chairs, there's nothing but dust, dead flies, and glasses. . . . What do you want glasses standing about for? And, my dear, the table's not cleared till this time in the day. And one's ashamed to go into your bedroom: underclothes flung about everywhere, india-rubber tubes hanging on the walls, pails and basins standing about. . . . My dear! A husband ought to know nothing, and his wife ought to be as neat as a little angel in his presence. I wake up every morning before it is light, and wash my face with cold water that my Nikodim Alexandritch may not see me looking drowsy."

"That's all nonsense," Nadyezhda Fyodorovna sobbed. "If only I were happy, but I am so unhappy!"

"Yes, yes; you are very unhappy!" Marya Konstantinovna sighed, hardly able to restrain herself from weeping. "And there's terrible grief in store for you in the future! A solitary old age, ill-health; and then you will have to answer at the dread judgment seat . . . It's awful, awful. Now fate itself holds out to you a helping hand, and you madly thrust it from you. Be married, make haste and be married!"

"Yes, we must, we must," said Nadyezhda Fyodorovna; "but it's impossible!"

"Why?"

"It's impossible. Oh, if only you knew!"

Nadyezhda Fyodorovna had an impulse to tell her about Kirilin, and how the evening before she had met handsome young Atchmianov at the harbour, and how the mad, ridiculous idea had occurred to her of cancelling her debt for three hundred; it had amused her very much, and she returned home late in the evening feeling that she had sold herself and was irrevocably lost. She did not know herself how it had happened. And she longed to swear to Marya Konstantinovna that she would certainly pay that debt, but sobs and shame prevented her from speaking.

"I am going away," she said. "Ivan Andreitch may stay, but I am going."

"Where?"

"To Russia."

"But how will you live there? Why, you have nothing."

"I will do translation, or . . . or I will open a library . . . ."

"Don't let your fancy run away with you, my dear. You must have money for a library. Well, I will leave you now, and you calm yourself and think things over, and tomorrow come and see me, bright and happy. That will be enchanting! Well, goodbye, my angel. Let me kiss you."

Marya Konstantinovna kissed Nadyezhda Fyodorovna on the forehead, made the sign of the cross over her, and softly withdrew. It was getting dark, and Olga lighted up in the kitchen. Still crying, Nadyezhda Fyodorovna went into the bedroom and lay down on the bed. She began to be very feverish. She undressed without getting up, crumpled up her clothes at her feet, and curled herself up under the bedclothes. She was thirsty, and there was no one to give her something to drink.

"I'll pay it back!" she said to herself, and it seemed to her in delirium that she was sitting beside some sick woman, and recognized her as herself. "I'll pay it back. It would be stupid to imagine that it was for money I . . . I will go away and send him the money from Petersburg. At first a hundred . . . then another hundred . . . and then the third hundred. . . ."

It was late at night when Laevsky came in.

"At first a hundred . . ." Nadyezhda Fyodorovna said to him, "then another hundred . . ."

"You ought to take some quinine," he said, and thought, "Tomorrow is Wednesday; the steamer goes and I am not going in it. So I shall have to go on living here till Saturday."

Nadyezhda Fyodorovna knelt up in bed.

"I didn't say anything just now, did I?" she asked, smiling and screwing up her eyes at the light.

"No, nothing. We shall have to send for the doctor tomorrow morning. Go to sleep."

He took his pillow and went to the door. Ever since he had finally made up his mind to go away and leave Nadyezhda Fyodorovna, she had begun to raise in him pity and a sense of guilt; he felt a little ashamed in her presence, as though in the presence of a sick or old horse whom one has decided to kill. He stopped in the doorway and looked round at her.

"I was out of humour at the picnic and said something rude to you. Forgive me, for God's sake!"

Saying this, he went off to his study, lay down, and for a long while could not get to sleep.

Next morning when Samoylenko, attired, as it was a holiday, in full-dress uniform with epaulettes on his shoulders and decorations on his breast, came out of the bedroom after feeling Nadyezhda Fyodorovna's pulse and looking at her tongue, Laevsky, who was standing in the doorway, asked him anxiously: "Well? Well?"

There was an expression of terror, of extreme uneasiness, and of hope on his face.

"Don't worry yourself; there's nothing dangerous," said Samoylenko; "it's the usual fever."

"I don't mean that." Laevsky frowned impatiently. "Have you got the money?"

"My dear soul, forgive me," he whispered, looking round at the door and overcome with confusion.

"For God's sake, forgive me! No one has anything to spare, and I've only been able to collect by five- and by ten-rouble notes. . . . Only a hundred and ten in all. Today I'll speak to some one else. Have patience."

"But Saturday is the latest date," whispered Laevsky, trembling with impatience. "By all that's sacred, get it by Saturday! If I don't get away by Saturday, nothing's any use, nothing! I can't understand how a doctor can be without money!"

"Lord have mercy on us!" Samoylenko whispered rapidly and intensely, and there was positively a breaking note in his throat. "I've been stripped of everything; I am owed seven thousand, and I'm in debt all round. Is it my fault?"

"Then you'll get it by Saturday? Yes?"

"I'll try."

"I implore you, my dear fellow! So that the money may be in my hands by Friday morning!"

Samoylenko sat down and prescribed solution of quinine and kalii bromati and tincture of rhubarb, tincturae gentianae, aquae foeniculi – all in one mixture, added some pink syrup to sweeten it, and went away.

XI

"You look as though you were coming to arrest me," said Von Koren, seeing Samoylenko coming in, in his full-dress uniform.

"I was passing by and thought: 'Suppose I go in and pay my respects to zoology,'" said Samoylenko, sitting down at the big table, knocked together by the zoologist himself out of plain boards. "Good morning, holy father," he said to the deacon, who was sitting in the window, copying something. "I'll stay a minute and then run home to see about dinner. It's time. . . . I'm not hindering you?"

"Not in the least," answered the zoologist, laying out over the table slips of paper covered with small writing. "We are busy copying."

"Ah! . . . Oh, my goodness, my goodness! . . ." sighed Samoylenko. He cautiously took up from the table a dusty book on which there was lying a dead dried spider, and said: "Only fancy, though; some little green beetle is going about its business, when suddenly a monster like this swoops down upon it. I can fancy its terror."

"Yes, I suppose so."

"Is poison given it to protect it from its enemies?"

"Yes, to protect it and enable it to attack."

"To be sure, to be sure. . . . And everything in nature, my dear fellows, is consistent and can be explained," sighed Samoylenko; "only I tell you what I don't understand. You're a man of very great intellect, so explain it to me, please. There are, you know, little beasts no bigger than rats, rather handsome to look at, but nasty and immoral in the extreme, let me tell you. Suppose such a little beast is running in the woods. He sees a bird; he catches it and devours it. He goes on and sees in the grass a nest of eggs; he does not want to eat them — he is not hungry, but yet he tastes one egg and scatters the others out of the nest with his paw. Then he meets a frog and begins to play with it; when he has tormented the frog he goes on licking himself and meets a beetle; he crushes the beetle with his paw . . . and so he spoils and destroys everything on his way. . . . He creeps into other beasts' holes, tears up the anthills, cracks the snail's shell. If he meets a rat, he fights with it; if he meets a snake or a mouse, he must strangle it; and so the whole day long. Come, tell me: what is the use of a beast like that? Why was he created?"

"I don't know what animal you are talking of," said Von Koren; "most likely one of the insectivora. Well, he got hold of the bird because it was incautious; he broke the nest of eggs because the bird was not skilful, had made the nest badly and did not know how to conceal it. The frog probably had some defect in its colouring or he would not have seen it, and so on. Your little beast only destroys the weak, the unskilful, the careless – in fact, those who have defects which nature does not think fit to hand on to posterity. Only the cleverer, the stronger, the more careful and developed survive; and so your little beast, without suspecting it, is serving the great ends of perfecting creation."

"Yes, yes, yes. . . . By the way, brother," said Samoylenko carelessly, "lend me a hundred roubles."

"Very good. There are some very interesting types among the insectivorous mammals. For instance, the mole is said to be useful because he devours noxious insects. There is a story that some German sent William I a fur coat made of moleskins, and the Emperor ordered him to be reproved for having destroyed so great a number of useful animals. And yet the mole is not a bit less cruel than your little beast, and is very mischievous besides, as he spoils meadows terribly."

Von Koren opened a box and took out a hundred-rouble note.

"The mole has a powerful thorax, just like the bat," he went on, shutting the box; "the bones and muscles are tremendously developed, the mouth is extraordinarily powerfully furnished. If it had the proportions of an elephant, it would be an all-destructive, invincible animal. It is interesting when two moles meet underground; they begin at once as though by agreement digging a little platform; they need the platform in order to have a battle more conveniently. When they have made it they enter upon a ferocious struggle and fight till the weaker one falls. Take the hundred roubles," said Von Koren, dropping his voice, "but only on condition that you're not borrowing it for Laevsky."

"And if it were for Laevsky," cried Samoylenko, flaring up, "what is that to you?"

"I can't give it to you for Laevsky. I know you like lending people money. You would give it to Kerim, the brigand, if he were to ask you; but, excuse me, I can't assist you in that direction."

"Yes, it is for Laevsky I am asking it," said Samoylenko, standing up and waving his right arm. "Yes! For Laevsky! And no one, fiend or devil, has a right to dictate to me how to dispose of my own money. It doesn't suit you to lend it me? No?"

The deacon began laughing.

"Don't get excited, but be reasonable," said the zoologist. "To shower benefits on Mr. Laevsky is, to my thinking, as senseless as to water weeds or to feed locusts."

"To my thinking, it is our duty to help our neighbours!" cried Samoylenko.

"In that case, help that hungry Turk who is lying under the fence! He is a workman and more useful and indispensable than your Laevsky. Give him that hundred-rouble note! Or subscribe a hundred roubles to my expedition!"

"Will you give me the money or not? I ask you!"

"Tell me openly: what does he want money for?

"It's not a secret; he wants to go to Petersburg on Saturday."

"So that is it!" Von Koren drawled out. "Aha! . . . We understand. And is she going with him, or how is it to be?"

"She's staying here for the time. He'll arrange his affairs in Petersburg and send her the money, and then she'll go."

"That's smart!" said the zoologist, and he gave a short tenor laugh. "Smart, well planned."

He went rapidly up to Samoylenko, and standing face to face with him, and looking him in the eyes, asked: "Tell me now honestly: is he tired of her? Yes? tell me: is he tired of her? Yes?"

"Yes," Samoylenko articulated, beginning to perspire.

"How repulsive it is!" said Von Koren, and from his face it could be seen that he felt repulsion. "One of two things, Alexandr Daviditch: either you are in the plot with him, or, excuse my saying so, you are a simpleton. Surely you must see that he is taking you in like a child in the most shameless way? Why, it's as clear as day that he wants to get rid of her and abandon her here. She'll be left a burden on you. It is as clear as day that you will have to send her to Petersburg at your expense. Surely your fine friend can't have so blinded you by his dazzling qualities that you can't see the simplest thing?"

"That's all supposition," said Samoylenko, sitting down.

"Supposition? But why is he going alone instead of taking her with him? And ask him why he doesn't send her off first. The sly beast!"

Overcome with sudden doubts and suspicions about his friend, Samoylenko weakened and took a humbler tone.

"But it's impossible," he said, recalling the night Laevsky had spent at his house. "He is so unhappy!"

"What of that? Thieves and incendiaries are unhappy too!"

"Even supposing you are right . . ." said Samoylenko, hesitating. "Let us admit it. . . . Still, he's a young man in a strange place . . . a student. We have been students, too, and there is no one but us to come to his assistance."

"To help him to do abominable things, because he and you at different times have been at universities, and neither of you did anything there! What nonsense!"

"Stop; let us talk it over coolly. I imagine it will be possible to make some arrangement. . . ." Samoylenko reflected, twiddling his fingers. "I'll give him the money, you see, but make him promise on his honour that within a week he'll send Nadyezhda Fyodorovna the money for the journey."

"And he'll give you his word of honour – in fact, he'll shed tears and believe in it himself; but what's his word of honour worth? He won't keep it, and when in a year or two you meet him on the Nevsky Prospect with a new mistress on his arm, he'll excuse himself on the ground that he has been crippled by civilization, and that he is made after the pattern of Rudin. Drop him, for God's sake! Keep away from the filth; don't stir it up with both hands!"

Samoylenko thought for a minute and said resolutely:

"But I shall give him the money all the same. As you please. I can't bring myself to refuse a man simply on an assumption."

"Very fine, too. You can kiss him if you like."

"Give me the hundred roubles, then," Samoylenko asked timidly.

"I won't."

A silence followed. Samoylenko was quite crushed; his face wore a guilty, abashed, and ingratiating expression, and it was strange to see this pitiful, childish, shamefaced countenance on a huge man wearing epaulettes and orders of merit.

"The bishop here goes the round of his diocese on horse-back instead of in a carriage," said the deacon, laying down his pen. "It's extremely touching to see him sit on his horse. His simplicity and humility are full of Biblical grandeur."

"Is he a good man?" asked Von Koren, who was glad to change the conversation.

"Of course! If he hadn't been a good man, do you suppose he would have been consecrated a bishop?"

"Among the bishops are to be found good and gifted men," said Von Koren. "The only drawback is that some of them have the weakness to imagine themselves statesmen. One busies himself with Russification, another criticizes the sciences. That's not their business. They had much better look into their consistory a little."

"A layman cannot judge of bishops."

"Why so, deacon? A bishop is a man just the same as you or I."

"The same, but not the same." The deacon was offended and took up his pen. "If you had been the same, the Divine Grace would have rested upon you, and you would have been bishop yourself; and since you are not bishop, it follows you are not the same."

"Don't talk nonsense, deacon," said Samoylenko dejectedly. "Listen to what I suggest," he said, turning to Von Koren. "Don't give me that hundred roubles. You'll be having your dinners with me for three months before the winter, so let me have the money beforehand for three months."

"I won't."

Samoylenko blinked and turned crimson; he mechanically drew towards him the book with the spider on it and looked at it, then he got up and took his hat.

Von Koren felt sorry for him.

"What it is to have to live and do with people like this," said the zoologist, and he kicked a paper into the corner with indignation. "You must understand that this is not kindness, it is not love, but cowardice, slackness, poison! What's gained by reason is lost by your flabby good-for-nothing hearts! When I was ill with typhoid as a schoolboy, my aunt in her sympathy gave me pickled mushrooms to eat, and I very nearly died. You, and my aunt too, must understand that love for man is not to be found in the heart or the stomach or the bowels, but here!"

Von Koren slapped himself on the forehead.

"Take it," he said, and thrust a hundred-rouble note into his hand.

"You've no need to be angry, Kolya," said Samoylenko mildly, folding up the note. "I quite understand you, but . . . you must put yourself in my place."

"You are an old woman, that's what you are."

The deacon burst out laughing.

"Hear my last request, Alexandr Daviditch," said Von Koren hotly. "When you give that scoundrel the money, make it a condition that he takes his lady with him, or sends her on ahead, and don't give it him without. There's no need to stand on ceremony with him. Tell him so, or, if you don't, I give you my word I'll go to his office and kick him downstairs, and I'll break off all acquaintance with you. So you'd better know it."

"Well! To go with her or send her on beforehand will be more convenient for him," said Samoylenko. "He'll be delighted indeed. Well, goodbye."

He said goodbye affectionately and went out, but before shutting the door after him, he looked round at Von Koren and, with a ferocious face, said:

"It's the Germans who have ruined you, brother! Yes! The Germans!"

XII

Next day, Thursday, Marya Konstantinovna was celebrating the birthday of her Kostya. All were invited to come at midday and eat pies, and in the evening to drink chocolate. When Laevsky and Nadyezhda Fyodorovna arrived in the evening, the zoologist, who was already sitting in the drawing-room, drinking chocolate, asked Samoylenko:

"Have you talked to him?"

"Not yet."

"Mind now, don't stand on ceremony. I can't understand the insolence of these people! Why, they know perfectly well the view taken by this family of their cohabitation, and yet they force themselves in here."

"If one is to pay attention to every prejudice," said Samoylenko, "one could go nowhere."

"Do you mean to say that the repugnance felt by the masses for illicit love and moral laxity is a prejudice?"

"Of course it is. It's prejudice and hate. When the soldiers see a girl of light behaviour, they laugh and whistle; but just ask them what they are themselves."

"It's not for nothing they whistle. The fact that girls strangle their illegitimate children and go to prison for it, and that Anna Karenin flung herself under the train, and that in the villages they smear the gates with tar, and that you and I, without knowing why, are pleased by Katya's purity, and that every one of us feels a vague craving for pure love, though he knows there is no such love – is all that prejudice? That is the one thing, brother, which has survived intact from natural selection, and, if it were not for that obscure force regulating the relations of the sexes, the Laevskys would have it all their own way, and mankind would degenerate in two years."

Laevsky came into the drawing-room, greeted everyone, and shaking hands with Von Koren, smiled ingratiatingly. He waited for a favourable moment and said to Samoylenko:

"Excuse me, Alexandr Daviditch, I must say two words to you."

Samoylenko got up, put his arm round Laevsky's waist, and both of them went into Nikodim Alexandritch's study.

"Tomorrow's Friday," said Laevsky, biting his nails. "Have you got what you promised?"

"I've only got two hundred. I'll get the rest today or tomorrow. Don't worry yourself."

"Thank God . . ." sighed Laevsky, and his hands began trembling with joy. "You are saving me, Alexandr Daviditch, and I swear to you by God, by my happiness and anything you like, I'll send you the money as soon as I arrive. And I'll send you my old debt too."

"Look here, Vanya . . ." said Samoylenko, turning crimson and taking him by the button. "You must forgive my meddling in your private affairs, but . . . why shouldn't you take Nadyezhda Fyodorovna with you?"

"You queer fellow. How is that possible? One of us must stay, or our creditors will raise an outcry. You see, I owe seven hundred or more to the shops. Only wait, and I will send them the money. I'll stop their mouths, and then she can come away."

"I see. . . . But why shouldn't you send her on first?"

"My goodness, as though that were possible!" Laevsky was horrified. "Why, she's a woman; what would she do there alone? What does she know about it? That would only be a loss of time and a useless waste of money."

"That's reasonable . . ." thought Samoylenko, but remembering his conversation with Von Koren, he looked down and said sullenly: "I can't agree with you. Either go with her or send her first; otherwise . . . otherwise I won't give you the money. Those are my last words . . ."

He staggered back, lurched backwards against the door, and went into the drawing-room, crimson, and overcome with confusion.

"Friday . . . Friday," thought Laevsky, going back into the drawing-room. "Friday. . . ."

He was handed a cup of chocolate; he burnt his lips and tongue with the scalding chocolate and thought: "Friday . . . Friday. . . ."

For some reason he could not get the word "Friday" out of his head; he could think of nothing but Friday, and the only thing that was clear to him, not in his brain but somewhere in his heart, was that he would not get off on Saturday. Before him

96

stood Nikodim Alexandritch, very neat, with his hair combed over his temples, saying:

"Please take something to eat. . . ."

Marya Konstantinovna showed the visitors Katya's school report and said, drawling:

"It's very, very difficult to do well at school nowadays! So much is expected . . ."

"Mamma!" groaned Katya, not knowing where to hide her confusion at the praises of the company.

Laevsky, too, looked at the report and praised it. Scripture, Russian language, conduct, fives and fours, danced before his eyes, and all this, mixed with the haunting refrain of "Friday", with the carefully combed locks of Nikodim Alexandritch and the red cheeks of Katya, produced on him a sensation of such immense overwhelming boredom that he almost shrieked with despair and asked himself: "Is it possible, is it possible I shall not get away?"

They put two card tables side by side and sat down to play post. Laevsky sat down too.

"Friday . . . Friday . . ." he kept thinking, as he smiled and took a pencil out of his pocket. "Friday. . . ."

He wanted to think over his position, and was afraid to think. It was terrible to him to realize that the doctor had detected him in the deception which he had so long and carefully concealed from himself. Every time he thought of his future he would not let his thoughts have full rein. He would get into the train and set off, and thereby the problem of his life would be solved, and he did not let his thoughts go farther. Like a far-away dim light in the fields, the thought sometimes flickered in his mind that in one of the side-streets of Petersburg, in the remote future, he would have to have recourse to a tiny lie in order to get rid of Nadyezhda Fyodorovna and pay his debts; he would tell a lie only once, and then a completely new life would begin. And that was right: at the price of a small lie he would win so much truth.

Now when by his blunt refusal the doctor had crudely hinted at his deception, he began to understand that he would need deception not only in the remote future, but today, and tomorrow, and in a month's time, and perhaps up to the very end of his life. In fact, in order to get away he would have to lie to Nadyezhda Fyodorovna, to his creditors, and to his superiors in the Service; then, in order to get money in Petersburg, he would have to lie to his mother, to tell her that he had already broken with Nadyezhda Fyodorovna; and his mother would not give him more than five hundred roubles, so he had already deceived the doctor, as he would not be in a position to pay him back the money within a short time. Afterwards, when Nadyezhda Fyodorovna came to Petersburg, he would have to resort to a regular series of deceptions, little and big, in order to get free of her; and again there would be tears, boredom, a disgusting existence, remorse, and so there would be no new life. Deception and nothing more. A whole mountain of lies rose before Laevsky's imagination. To leap over it at one bound and not to do his lying piecemeal, he would have to bring himself to stern, uncompromising action; for instance, to getting up without saying a word, putting on his hat, and at once setting off without money and without explanation. But Laevsky felt that was impossible for him.

"Friday, Friday . . ." he thought. "Friday. . . ."

They wrote little notes, folded them in two, and put them in Nikodim Alexandritch's old top-hat. When there were a sufficient heap of notes, Kostya, who acted the part of postman, walked round the table and delivered them. The deacon, Katya, and Kostya, who received amusing notes and tried to write as funnily as they could, were highly delighted.

"We must have a little talk," Nadyezhda Fyodorovna read in a little note; she glanced at Marya Konstantinovna, who gave her an almond-oily smile and nodded.

"Talk of what?" thought Nadyezhda Fyodorovna. "If one can't tell the whole, it's no use talking."

Before going out for the evening she had tied Laevsky's cravat for him, and that simple action filled her soul with tenderness and sorrow. The anxiety in his face, his absent-minded looks, his pallor, and the incomprehensible change that had taken place in him of late, and the fact that she had a terrible revolting secret from him, and the fact that her hands trembled when she tied his cravat — all this seemed to tell her that they had not long left to be together. She looked at him as though he were an ikon, with terror and penitence, and thought: "Forgive, forgive."

Opposite her was sitting Atchmianov, and he never took his black, love-sick eyes off her. She was stirred by passion; she was ashamed of herself, and afraid that even her misery and sorrow would not prevent her from yielding to impure desire tomorrow, if not today – and that, like a drunkard, she would not have the strength to stop herself.

She made up her mind to go away that she might not continue this life, shameful for herself, and humiliating for Laevsky. She would beseech him with tears to let her go; and if he opposed her, she would go away secretly. She would not tell him what had happened; let him keep a pure memory of her.

"I love you, I love you, I love you," she read. It was from Atchmianov.

She would live in some far remote place, would work and send Laevsky, "anonymously", money, embroidered shirts, and tobacco, and would return to him only in old age or if he were dangerously ill and needed a nurse. When in his old age he learned what were her reasons for leaving him and refusing to be his wife, he would appreciate her sacrifice and forgive.

"You've got a long nose." That must be from the deacon or Kostya.

Nadyezhda Fyodorovna imagined how, parting from Laevsky, she would embrace him warmly, would kiss his hand, and would swear to love him all her life, all her life, and then, living in obscurity among strangers, she would every day think that somewhere she had a friend, someone she loved – a pure, noble, lofty man who kept a pure memory of her.

"If you don't give me an interview today, I shall take measures, I assure you on my word of honour. You can't treat decent people like this; you must understand that." That was from Kirilin.

XIII

Laevsky received two notes; he opened one and read: "Don't go away, my darling."

"Who could have written that?" he thought. "Not Samoylenko, of course. And not the deacon, for he doesn't know I want to go away. Von Koren, perhaps?"

The zoologist bent over the table and drew a pyramid. Laevsky fancied that his eyes were smiling.

"Most likely Samoylenko . . . has been gossiping," thought Laevsky.

In the other note, in the same disguised angular handwriting with long tails to the letters, was written: "Somebody won't go away on Saturday."

"A stupid gibe," thought Laevsky. "Friday, Friday. . . ."

Something rose in his throat. He touched his collar and coughed, but instead of a cough a laugh broke from his throat.

"Ha-ha-ha!" he laughed. "Ha-ha-ha! What am I laughing at? Ha-ha-ha!"

He tried to restrain himself, covered his mouth with his hand, but the laugh choked his chest and throat, and his hand could not cover his mouth.

"How stupid it is!" he thought, rolling with laughter. "Have I gone out of my mind?"

The laugh grew shriller and shriller, and became something like the bark of a lap-dog. Laevsky tried to get up from the table, but his legs would not obey him and his right hand was strangely, without his volition, dancing on the table, convulsively clutching and crumpling up the bits of paper. He saw looks of wonder, Samoylenko's grave, frightened face, and the eyes of the zoologist full of cold irony and disgust, and realized that he was in hysterics.

"How hideous, how shameful!" he thought, feeling the warmth of tears on his face. ". . . Oh, oh, what a disgrace! It has never happened to me. . . ."

They took him under his arms, and supporting his head from behind, led him away; a glass gleamed before his eyes and knocked against his teeth, and the water was spilt on his breast; he was in a little room, with two beds in the middle, side by side, covered by two snow-white quilts. He dropped on one of the beds and sobbed.

"It's nothing, it's nothing," Samoylenko kept saying; "it does happen . . . it does happen. . . ."

Chill with horror, trembling all over and dreading something awful, Nadyezhda Fyodorovna stood by the bedside and kept asking:

"What is it? What is it? For God's sake, tell me."

"Can Kirilin have written him something?" she thought.

"It's nothing," said Laevsky, laughing and crying; "go away, darling."

His face expressed neither hatred nor repulsion: so he knew nothing; Nadyezhda Fyodorovna was somewhat reassured, and she went into the drawing-room.

"Don't agitate yourself, my dear!" said Marya Konstantinovna, sitting down beside her and taking her hand. "It will pass. Men are just as weak as we poor sinners. You are both going through a crisis. . . . One can so well understand it! Well, my dear, I am waiting for an answer. Let us have a little talk."

"No, we are not going to talk," said Nadyezhda Fyodorovna, listening to Laevsky's sobs. "I feel depressed. . . . You must allow me to go home."

"What do you mean, what do you mean, my dear?" cried Marya Konstantinovna in alarm. "Do you think I could let you go without supper? We will have something to eat, and then you may go with my blessing."

"I feel miserable . . ." whispered Nadyezhda Fyodorovna, and she caught at the arm of the chair with both hands to avoid falling.

"He's got a touch of hysterics," said Von Koren gaily, coming into the drawing-room, but seeing Nadyezhda Fyodorovna, he was taken aback and retreated.

When the attack was over, Laevsky sat on the strange bed and thought.

"Disgraceful! I've been howling like some wretched girl! I must have been absurd and disgusting. I will go away by the back stairs. . . . But that would seem as though I took my hysterics too seriously. I ought to take it as a joke. . . ."

He looked in the looking-glass, sat there for some time, and went back into the drawing-room.

"Here I am," he said, smiling; he felt agonizingly ashamed, and he felt others were ashamed in his presence. "Fancy such a thing happening," he said, sitting down. "I was sitting here, and all of a sudden, do you know, I felt a terrible piercing pain in my side . . . unendurable, my nerves could not stand it, and . . . and it led to this silly performance. This is the age of nerves; there is no help for it."

At supper he drank some wine, and, from time to time, with an abrupt sigh rubbed his side as though to suggest that he still felt the pain. And no one, except Nadyezhda Fyodorovna, believed him, and he saw that.

After nine o'clock they went for a walk on the boulevard. Nadyezhda Fyodorovna, afraid that Kirilin would speak to her, did her best to keep all the time beside Marya Konstantinovna and the children. She felt weak with fear and misery, and felt she was going to be feverish; she was exhausted and her legs would hardly move, but she did not go home, because she felt sure that she would be followed by Kirilin or Atchmianov or both at once. Kirilin walked behind her with Nikodim Alexandritch, and kept humming in an undertone:

"I don't al-low people to play with me! I don't al-low it."

From the boulevard they went back to the pavilion and walked along the beach, and looked for a long time at the phosphorescence on the water. Von Koren began telling them why it looked phosphorescent.

XIV

"It's time I went to my *vint.* . . . They will be waiting for me," said Laevsky. "Goodbye, my friends."

"I'll come with you; wait a minute," said Nadyezhda Fyodorovna, and she took his arm.

They said goodbye to the company and went away. Kirilin took leave too, and saying that he was going the same way, went along beside them.

"What will be, will be," thought Nadyezhda Fyodorovna. "So be it. . . ."

And it seemed to her that all the evil memories in her head had taken shape and were walking beside her in the darkness, breathing heavily, while she, like a fly that had fallen into the inkpot, was crawling painfully along the pavement and smirching Laevsky's side and arm with blackness.

If Kirilin should do anything horrid, she thought, not he but she would be to blame for it. There was a time when no man would have talked to her as Kirilin had done, and she had torn up her security like a thread and destroyed it irrevocably – who was to blame for it? Intoxicated by her passions she had smiled at a complete stranger, probably just because he was tall and a fine figure. After two meetings she was weary of him, had thrown him over, and did not that, she thought now, give him the right to treat her as he chose?

"Here I'll say goodbye to you, darling," said Laevsky. "Ilya Mihalitch will see you home."

He nodded to Kirilin, and, quickly crossing the boulevard, walked along the street to Sheshkovsky's, where there were lights in the windows, and then they heard the gate bang as he went in.

"Allow me to have an explanation with you," said Kirilin. "I'm not a boy, not some Atchkasov or Latchkasov, Zatchkasov. . . . I demand serious attention."

Nadyezhda Fyodorovna's heart began beating violently. She made no reply.

"The abrupt change in your behaviour to me I put down at first to coquetry," Kirilin went on; "now I see that you don't know how to behave with gentlemanly people. You simply wanted to play with me, as you are playing with that wretched

Armenian boy; but I'm a gentleman and I insist on being treated like a gentleman. And so I am at your service. . . ."

"I'm miserable," said Nadyezhda Fyodorovna beginning to cry, and to hide her tears she turned away.

"I'm miserable too," said Kirilin, "but what of that?"

Kirilin was silent for a space, then he said distinctly and emphatically:

"I repeat, madam, that if you do not give me an interview this evening, I'll make a scandal this very evening."

"Let me off this evening," said Nadyezhda Fyodorovna, and she did not recognize her own voice, it was so weak and pitiful.

"I must give you a lesson. . . . Excuse me for the roughness of my tone, but it's necessary to give you a lesson. Yes, I regret to say I must give you a lesson. I insist on two interviews — today and tomorrow. After tomorrow you are perfectly free and can go wherever you like with anyone you choose. Today and tomorrow."

Nadyezhda Fyodorovna went up to her gate and stopped.

"Let me go," she murmured, trembling all over and seeing nothing before her in the darkness but his white tunic. "You're right: I'm a horrible woman. . . . I'm to blame, but let me go . . . I beg you." She touched his cold hand and shuddered. "I beseech you. . . ."

"Alas!" sighed Kirilin, "alas! it's not part of my plan to let you go; I only mean to give you a lesson and make you realize. And what's more, madam, I've too little faith in women."

"I'm miserable. . . ."

Nadyezhda Fyodorovna listened to the even splash of the sea, looked at the sky studded with stars, and longed to make haste and end it all, and get away from the cursed sensation of life, with its sea, stars, men, fever.

"Only not in my home," she said coldly. "Take me somewhere else."

"Come to Muridov's. That's better."

"Where's that?"

"Near the old wall."

She walked quickly along the street and then turned into the side-street that led towards the mountains. It was dark. There were pale streaks of light here and there on the pavement, from the lighted windows, and it seemed to her that, like a fly, she kept falling into the ink and crawling out into the light again. At one point he stumbled, almost fell down and burst out laughing.

"He's drunk," thought Nadyezhda Fyodorovna. "Never mind. . . . Never mind. . . . So be it."

Atchmianov, too, soon took leave of the party and followed Nadyezhda Fyodorovna to ask her to go for a row. He went to her house and looked over the fence: the windows were wide open, there were no lights.

"Nadyezhda Fyodorovna!" he called.

A moment passed, he called again.

"Who's there?" he heard Olga's voice.

"Is Nadyezhda Fyodorovna at home?"

"No, she has not come in yet."

"Strange . . . very strange," thought Atchmianov, feeling very uneasy. "She went home. . . ."

He walked along the boulevard, then along the street, and glanced in at the windows of Sheshkovsky's. Laevsky was sitting at the table without his coat on, looking attentively at his cards.

"Strange, strange," muttered Atchmianov, and remembering Laevsky's hysterics, he felt ashamed. "If she is not at home, where is she?"

He went to Nadyezhda Fyodorovna's lodgings again, and looked at the dark windows.

"It's a cheat, a cheat . . ." he thought, remembering that, meeting him at midday at Marya Konstantinovna's, she had promised to go in a boat with him that evening.

The windows of the house where Kirilin lived were dark, and there was a policeman sitting asleep on a little bench at the gate. Everything was clear to Atchmianov when he looked at the windows and the policeman. He made up his mind to go home, and set off in that direction, but somehow found himself near Nadyezhda Fyodorovna's lodgings again. He sat down on the bench near the gate and took off his hat, feeling that his head was burning with jealousy and resentment.

The clock in the town church only struck twice in the twenty-four hours — at midday and midnight. Soon after it struck midnight he heard hurried footsteps.

"Tomorrow evening, then, again at Muridov's," Atchmianov heard, and he recognized Kirilin's voice. "At eight o'clock; goodbye!"

Nadyezhda Fyodorovna made her appearance near the garden. Without noticing that Atchmianov was sitting on the bench, she passed beside him like a shadow, opened the gate, and leaving it open, went into the house. In her own room she lighted the candle and quickly undressed, but instead of getting into bed, she sank on her knees before a chair, flung her arms round it, and rested her head on it.

It was past two when Laevsky came home.

XV

Having made up his mind to lie, not all at once but piecemeal, Laevsky went soon after one o'clock next day to Samoylenko to ask for the money that he might be sure to get off on Saturday. After his hysterical attack, which had added an acute feeling of shame to his depressed state of mind, it was unthinkable to remain in the town. If Samoylenko should insist on his conditions, he thought it would be possible to agree to them and take the money, and next day, just as he was starting, to say that Nadyezhda Fyodorovna refused to go. He would be able to persuade her that evening that the whole arrangement would be for her benefit. If Samoylenko, who was obviously under the influence of Von Koren, should refuse the money altogether or make fresh conditions, then he, Laevsky, would go off that very evening in a cargo vessel, or even in a sailing-boat, to Novy Athon or Novorossiisk, would send from there an humiliating telegram, and would stay there till his mother sent him the money for the journey.

When he went into Samoylenko's, he found Von Koren in the drawing-room. The zoologist had just arrived for dinner, and, as usual, was turning over the album and scrutinizing the gentlemen in top-hats and the ladies in caps.

"How very unlucky!" thought Laevsky, seeing him. "He may be in the way. Good morning."

"Good morning," answered Von Koren, without looking at him.

"Is Alexandr Daviditch at home?"

"Yes, in the kitchen."

Laevsky went into the kitchen, but seeing from the door that Samoylenko was busy over the salad, he went back into the drawing-room and sat down. He always had a feeling of awkwardness in the zoologist's presence, and now he was afraid there would be talk about his attack of hysterics. There was more than a minute of silence. Von Koren suddenly raised his eyes to Laevsky and asked:

"How do you feel after yesterday?"

"Very well indeed," said Laevsky, flushing. "It really was nothing much. . . ."

"Until yesterday I thought it was only ladies who had hysterics, and so at first I thought you had St. Vitus's dance."

Laevsky smiled ingratiatingly, and thought:

"How indelicate on his part! He knows quite well how unpleasant it is for me. . . ."

"Yes, it was a ridiculous performance," he said, still smiling. "I've been laughing over it the whole morning. What's so curious in an attack of hysterics is that you know it is absurd, and are laughing at it in your heart, and at the same time you sob. In our neurotic age we are the slaves of our nerves; they are our masters and do as they like with us. Civilization has done us a bad turn in that way. . . ."

As Laevsky talked, he felt it disagreeable that Von Koren listened to him gravely, and looked at him steadily and attentively as though studying him; and he was vexed with himself that in spite of his dislike of Von Koren, he could not banish the ingratiating smile from his face.

"I must admit, though," he added, "that there were immediate causes for the attack, and quite sufficient ones too. My health has been terribly shaky of late. To which one must add boredom, constantly being hard up . . . the absence of people and general interests. . . . My position is worse than a governor's."

"Yes, your position is a hopeless one," answered Von Koren.

These calm, cold words, implying something between a jeer and an uninvited prediction, offended Laevsky. He recalled the zoologist's eyes the evening before, full of mockery and disgust. He was silent for a space and then asked, no longer smiling:

"How do you know anything of my position?"

"You were only just speaking of it yourself. Besides, your friends take such a warm interest in you, that I am hearing about you all day long."

"What friends? Samoylenko, I suppose?"

"Yes, he too."

"I would ask Alexandr Daviditch and my friends in general not to trouble so much about me."

"Here is Samoylenko; you had better ask him not to trouble so much about you."

"I don't understand your tone," Laevsky muttered, suddenly feeling as though he had only just realized that the zoologist hated and despised him, and was jeering at him, and was his bitterest and most inveterate enemy.

"Keep that tone for someone else," he said softly, unable to speak aloud for the hatred with which his chest and throat were choking, as they had been the night before with laughter.

Samoylenko came in in his shirt-sleeves, crimson and perspiring from the stifling kitchen.

"Ah, you here?" he said. "Good morning, my dear boy. Have you had dinner? Don't stand on ceremony. Have you had dinner?"

"Alexandr Daviditch," said Laevsky, standing up, "though I did appeal to you to help me in a private matter, it did not follow that I released you from the obligation of discretion and respect for other people's private affairs."

"What's this?" asked Samoylenko, in astonishment.

"If you have no money," Laevsky went on, raising his voice and shifting from one foot to the other in his excitement, "don't give it; refuse it. But why spread abroad in every back street that my position is hopeless, and all the rest of it? I can't endure such benevolence and friend's assistance where there's a shilling-worth of talk for a ha'p'orth of help! You can boast of your benevolence as much as you please, but no one has given you the right to gossip about my private affairs!"

"What private affairs?" asked Samoylenko, puzzled and beginning to be angry. "If you've come here to be abusive, you had better clear out. You can come again afterwards!"

He remembered the rule that when one is angry with one's neighbour, one must begin to count a hundred, and one will grow calm again; and he began rapidly counting.

"I beg you not to trouble yourself about me," Laevsky went on. "Don't pay any attention to me, and whose business is it what I do and how I live? Yes, I want to go away. Yes, I get into debt, I drink, I am living with another man's wife, I'm hysterical, I'm ordinary. I am not so profound as some people, but whose business is that? Respect other people's privacy."

"Excuse me, brother," said Samoylenko, who had counted up to thirty-five, "but . . ."

"Respect other people's individuality!" interrupted Laevsky.

"This continual gossip about other people's affairs, this sighing and groaning and everlasting prying, this eavesdropping, this friendly sympathy . . . damn it all! They lend me money and make conditions as though I were a schoolboy! I am treated as the devil knows what! I don't want anything," shouted Laevsky, staggering with excitement and afraid that it might end in another attack of hysterics. "I shan't get away on Saturday, then," flashed through his mind. "I want nothing. All I ask of you is to spare me your protecting care. I'm not a boy, and I'm not mad, and I beg you to leave off looking after me."

The deacon came in, and seeing Laevsky pale and gesticulating, addressing his strange speech to the portrait of Prince Vorontsov, stood still by the door as though petrified.

"This continual prying into my soul," Laevsky went on, "is insulting to my human dignity, and I beg these volunteer detectives to give up their spying! Enough!"

"What's that . . . what did you say?" said Samoylenko, who had counted up to a hundred. He turned crimson and went up to Laevsky.

"It's enough," said Laevsky, breathing hard and snatching up his cap.

"I'm a Russian doctor, a nobleman by birth, and a civil councillor," said Samoylenko emphatically. "I've never been a spy, and I allow no one to insult me!" he shouted in a breaking voice, emphasizing the last word. "Hold your tongue!"

The deacon, who had never seen the doctor so majestic,

so swelling with dignity, so crimson and so ferocious, shut his mouth, ran out into the entry and there exploded with laughter.

As though through a fog, Laevsky saw Von Koren get up and, putting his hands in his trouser-pockets, stand still in an attitude of expectancy, as though waiting to see what would happen. This calm attitude struck Laevsky as insolent and insulting to the last degree.

"Kindly take back your words," shouted Samoylenko.

Laevsky, who did not by now remember what his words were, answered:

"Leave me alone! I ask for nothing. All I ask is that you and German upstarts of Jewish origin should let me alone! Or I shall take steps to make you! I will fight you!"

"Now we understand," said Von Koren, coming from behind the table. "Mr. Laevsky wants to amuse himself with a duel before he goes away. I can give him that pleasure. Mr. Laevsky, I accept your challenge."

"A challenge," said Laevsky, in a low voice, going up to the zoologist and looking with hatred at his swarthy brow and curly hair. "A challenge? By all means! I hate you! I hate you!"

"Delighted. Tomorrow morning early near Kerbalay's. I leave all details to your taste. And now, clear out!"

"I hate you," Laevsky said softly, breathing hard. "I have hated you a long while! A duel! Yes!"

"Get rid of him, Alexandr Daviditch, or else I'm going," said Von Koren. "He'll bite me."

Von Koren's cool tone calmed the doctor; he seemed suddenly to come to himself, to recover his reason; he put both arms round Laevsky's waist, and, leading him away from the zoologist, muttered in a friendly voice that shook with emotion:

"My friends . . . dear, good . . . you've lost your tempers and that's enough . . . and that's enough, my friends."

Hearing his soft, friendly voice, Laevsky felt that something unheard of, monstrous, had just happened to him, as though he had been nearly run over by a train; he almost burst into tears, waved his hand, and ran out of the room.

"To feel that one is hated, to expose oneself before the man who hates one, in the most pitiful, contemptible, helpless state. My God, how hard it is!" he thought a little while afterwards as he sat in the pavilion, feeling as though his body were scarred by the hatred of which he had just been the object.

"How coarse it is, my God!"

Cold water with brandy in it revived him. He vividly pictured Von Koren's calm, haughty face; his eyes the day before, his shirt like a rug, his voice, his white hand; and heavy, passionate, hungry hatred rankled in his breast and clamoured for satisfaction. In his thoughts he felled Von Koren to the ground, and trampled him underfoot. He remembered to the minutest detail all that had happened, and wondered how he could have smiled ingratiatingly to that insignificant man, and how he could care for the opinion of wretched petty people whom nobody knew, living in a miserable little town which was not, it seemed, even on the map, and of which not one decent person in Petersburg had heard. If this wretched little town suddenly fell into ruins or caught fire, the telegram with the news would be read in Russia with no more interest than an advertisement of the sale of second-hand furniture. Whether he killed Von Koren next day or left him alive, it would be just the same, equally useless and uninteresting. Better to shoot him in the leg or hand, wound him, then laugh at him, and let him, like an insect with a broken leg lost in the grass – let him be lost with his obscure sufferings in the crowd of insignificant people like himself.

Laevsky went to Sheshkovsky, told him all about it, and asked him to be his second; then they both went to the superintendent of the postal telegraph department, and asked him, too, to be a second, and stayed to dinner with him. At dinner there was a great deal of joking and laughing. Laevsky made jests at his own expense, saying he hardly knew how to fire off a pistol, calling himself a royal archer and William Tell.

"We must give this gentleman a lesson . . ." he said.

After dinner they sat down to cards. Laevsky played, drank wine, and thought that duelling was stupid and senseless, as it did not decide the question but only complicated it, but that it was sometimes impossible to get on without it. In the given case, for instance, one could not, of course, bring an action against Von Koren. And this duel was so far good in that it made it impossible for Laevsky to remain in the town afterwards. He got a little drunk and interested in the game, and felt at ease.

But when the sun had set and it grew dark, he was possessed by a feeling of uneasiness. It was not fear at the thought of death, because while he was dining and playing cards, he had for some reason a confident belief that the duel would end in nothing; it was dread at the thought of something unknown which was to happen next morning for the first time in his life, and dread of the coming night. . . . He knew that the night would be long and sleepless, and that he would have to think not only of Von Koren and his hatred, but also of the mountain of lies which he had to get through, and which he had not strength or ability to dispense with. It was as though he had been taken suddenly ill; all at once he lost all interest in the cards and in people, grew restless, and began asking them to let him go home. He was eager to get into bed, to lie without moving, and to prepare his thoughts for the night. Sheshkovsky and the postal superintendent saw him home and went on to Von Koren's to arrange about the duel.

Near his lodgings Laevsky met Atchmianov. The young man was breathless and excited.

"I am looking for you, Ivan Andreitch," he said. "I beg you to come quickly. . . ."

"Where?"

"Someone wants to see you, someone you don't know, about very important business; he earnestly begs you to come for a minute. He wants to speak to you of something. . . . For him it's a question of life and death. . . ." In his excitement Atchmianov spoke in a strong Armenian accent.

"Who is it?" asked Laevsky.

"He asked me not to tell you his name."

"Tell him I'm busy; tomorrow, if he likes. . . ."

"How can you!" Atchmianov was aghast. "He wants to tell you something very important for you . . . very important! If you don't come, something dreadful will happen."

"Strange . . ." muttered Laevsky, unable to understand why Atchmianov was so excited and what mysteries there could be in this dull, useless little town.

"Strange," he repeated in hesitation. "Come along, though; I don't care."

Atchmianov walked rapidly on ahead and Laevsky followed him. They walked down a street, then turned into an alley.

"What a bore this is!" said Laevsky.

"One minute, one minute . . . it's near."

Near the old rampart they went down a narrow alley between two empty enclosures, then they came into a sort of large yard and went towards a small house.

"That's Muridov's, isn't it?" asked Laevsky.

"Yes."

"But why we've come by the back yards I don't understand. We might have come by the street; it's nearer. . . ."

"Never mind, never mind. . . ."

It struck Laevsky as strange, too, that Atchmianov led him to a back entrance, and motioned to him as though bidding him go quietly and hold his tongue.

"This way, this way . . ." said Atchmianov, cautiously opening the door and going into the passage on tiptoe. "Quietly, quietly, I beg you . . . they may hear."

He listened, drew a deep breath and said in a whisper:

"Open that door, and go in . . . don't be afraid."

Laevsky, puzzled, opened the door and went into a room with a low ceiling and curtained windows.

There was a candle on the table.

"What do you want?" asked someone in the next room. "Is it you, Muridov?"

Laevsky turned into that room and saw Kirilin, and beside him Nadyezhda Fyodorovna.

He didn't hear what was said to him; he staggered back, and did not know how he found himself in the street. His hatred for Von Koren and his uneasiness – all had vanished from his soul. As he went home he waved his right arm awkwardly and looked carefully at the ground under his feet, trying to step where it was smooth. At home in his study he walked backwards and forwards, rubbing his hands, and awkwardly shrugging his shoulders and neck, as though his jacket and shirt were too tight; then he lighted a candle and sat down to the table. . . .

XVI

"The 'humane studies' of which you speak will only satisfy human thought when, as they advance, they meet the exact sciences and progress side by side with them. Whether they will meet under a new microscope, or in the monologues of a new Hamlet, or in a new religion, I do not know, but I expect the earth will be covered with a crust of ice before it comes to pass. Of all humane learning the most durable and living is, of course, the teaching of Christ; but look how differently even that is interpreted! Some teach that we must love all our neighbours but make an exception of soldiers, criminals, and lunatics. They allow the first to be killed in war, the second to be isolated or executed, and the third they forbid to marry. Other interpreters teach that we must love all our neighbours without exception, with no distinction of *plus* or *minus*. According to their teaching, if a consumptive or a murderer or an epileptic asks your daughter in marriage, you must let him have her. If *crétins* go to war against the physically and mentally healthy, don't defend yourselves. This advocacy of love for love's sake, like art for art's sake, if it could have power, would bring mankind in the long run to complete extinction, and so would become the vastest crime that has ever been committed upon earth. There are very many interpretations, and since there are many of them, serious thought is not satisfied by any one of them, and hastens to add its own individual interpretation to the mass. For that reason you should never put a question on a philosophical or so-called Christian basis; by so doing you only remove the question further from solution."

The deacon listened to the zoologist attentively, thought a little, and asked:

"Have the philosophers invented the moral law which is innate in every man, or did God create it together with the body?"

"I don't know. But that law is so universal among all peoples and all ages that I fancy we ought to recognize it as organically connected with man. It is not invented, but exists and will exist. I don't tell you that one day it will be seen under the microscope, but its organic connection is shown, indeed, by evidence: serious affections of the brain and all so-called mental diseases, to the best of my belief, show themselves first of all in the perversion of the moral law."

"Good. So then, just as our stomach bids us eat, our moral sense bids us love our neighbours. Is that it? But our natural man through self-love opposes the voice of conscience and reason, and this gives rise to many brain-racking questions. To whom ought we to turn for the solution of those questions if you forbid us to put them on the philosophic basis?"

"Turn to what little exact science we have. Trust to evidence and the logic of facts. It is true it is but little, but, on the other hand, it is less fluid and shifting than philosophy. The moral law, let us suppose, demands that you love your neighbour. Well? Love ought to show itself in the removal of everything which in one way or another is injurious to men and threatens them with danger in the present or in the future. Our knowledge and the evidence tells us that the morally and physically abnormal are a menace to humanity. If so you must struggle against the abnormal; if you are not able to raise them to the normal standard you must have strength and ability to render them harmless — that is, to destroy them."

"So love consists in the strong overcoming the weak."

"Undoubtedly."

"But you know the strong crucified our Lord Jesus Christ," said the deacon hotly.

"The fact is that those who crucified Him were not the strong but the weak. Human culture weakens and strives to nullify the struggle for existence and natural selection; hence the rapid advancement of the weak and their predominance over the strong. Imagine that you succeeded in instilling into bees humanitarian ideas in their crude and elementary form. What would come of it? The drones who ought to be killed would remain alive, would devour the honey, would corrupt and stifle the bees, resulting in the predominance of the weak over the strong and the degeneration of the latter. The same process is taking place now with humanity; the weak are oppressing the strong. Among savages untouched by civilization the strongest, cleverest, and most moral takes the lead; he is the chief and the master. But we civilized men have crucified Christ, and we go on crucifying Him, so there is something lacking in us. . . . And that something one ought to raise up in ourselves, or there will be no end to these errors."

"But what criterion have you to distinguish the strong from the weak?"

"Knowledge and evidence. The tuberculous and the scrofulous are recognized by their diseases, and the insane and the immoral by their actions."

"But mistakes may be made!"

"Yes, but it's no use to be afraid of getting your feet wet when you are threatened with the deluge!"

"That's philosophy," laughed the deacon.

"Not a bit of it. You are so corrupted by your seminary philosophy that you want to see nothing but fog in everything. The abstract studies with which your youthful head is stuffed are called abstract just because they abstract your minds from what is obvious. Look the devil straight in the eye, and if he's the devil, tell him he's the devil, and don't go calling to Kant or Hegel for explanations."

The zoologist paused and went on:

"Twice two's four, and a stone's a stone. Here tomorrow we have a duel. You and I will say it's stupid and absurd, that the duel is out of date, that there is no real difference between the aristocratic duel and the drunken brawl in the pot-house, and yet we shall not stop, we shall go there and fight. So there is some force stronger than our reasoning. We shout that war is plunder, robbery, atrocity, fratricide; we cannot look upon blood without fainting; but the French or the Germans have only to insult us for us to feel at once an exaltation of spirit; in the most genuine way we shout 'Hurrah!' and rush to attack the foe. You will invoke the blessing of God on our weapons, and our valour will arouse universal and general enthusiasm. Again it follows that there is a force, if not higher, at any rate stronger, than us and our philosophy. We can no more stop it than that cloud which is moving upwards over the sea. Don't be hypocritical, don't make a long nose at it on the sly; and don't say, 'Ah, old-fashioned, stupid! Ah, it's inconsistent with Scripture!' but look it straight in the face, recognize its rational lawfulness, and when, for instance, it wants to destroy a rotten, scrofulous, corrupt race, don't hinder it with your pilules and misunderstood quotations from the Gospel. Leskov has a story of a conscientious Danila who found a leper outside the town, and fed and warmed him in the name of love and of Christ. If that Danila had really loved humanity, he would have dragged the leper as far as possible from the town, and would have flung him in a pit, and would have gone to save the healthy. Christ, I hope, taught us a rational, intelligent, practical love."

"What a fellow you are!" laughed the deacon. "You don't believe in Christ. Why do you mention His name so often?"

"Yes, I do believe in Him. Only, of course, in my own way,

not in yours. Oh, deacon, deacon!" laughed the zoologist; he put his arm round the deacon's waist, and said gaily: "Well? Are you coming with us to the duel tomorrow?"

"My orders don't allow it, or else I should come."

"What do you mean by 'orders'?"

"I have been consecrated. I am in a state of grace."

"Oh, deacon, deacon," repeated Von Koren, laughing, "I love talking to you."

"You say you have faith," said the deacon. "What sort of faith is it? Why, I have an uncle, a priest, and he believes so that when in time of drought he goes out into the fields to pray for rain, he takes his umbrella and leather overcoat for fear of getting wet through on his way home. That's faith! When he speaks of Christ, his face is full of radiance, and all the peasants, men and women, weep floods of tears. He would stop that cloud and put all those forces you talk about to flight. Yes . . . faith moves mountains."

The deacon laughed and slapped the zoologist on the shoulder.

"Yes . . ." he went on; "here you are teaching all the time, fathoming the depths of the ocean, dividing the weak and the strong, writing books and challenging to duels – and everything remains as it is; but, behold! some feeble old man will mutter just one word with a holy spirit, or a new Mahomet, with a sword, will gallop from Arabia, and everything will be topsy-turvy, and in Europe not one stone will be left standing upon another."

"Well, deacon, that's on the knees of the gods."

"Faith without works is dead, but works without faith are worse still – mere waste of time and nothing more."

The doctor came into sight on the sea-front. He saw the deacon and the zoologist, and went up to them.

"I believe everything is ready," he said, breathing hard. "Govorovsky and Boyko will be the seconds. They will start at five o'clock in the morning. How it has clouded over," he said, looking at the sky. "One can see nothing; there will be rain directly."

"I hope you are coming with us?" said the zoologist.

"No, God preserve me; I'm worried enough as it is. Ustimovitch is going instead of me. I've spoken to him already."

Far over the sea was a flash of lightning, followed by a hollow roll of thunder.

"How stifling it is before a storm!" said Von Koren. "I bet you've been to Laevsky already and have been weeping on his bosom."

"Why should I go to him?" answered the doctor in confusion. "What next?"

Before sunset he had walked several times along the boulevard and the street in the hope of meeting Laevsky. He was ashamed of his hastiness and the sudden outburst of friendliness which had followed it. He wanted to apologize to Laevsky in a joking tone, to give him a good talking to, to soothe him and to tell him that the duel was a survival of mediaeval barbarism, but that Providence itself had brought them to the duel as a means of reconciliation; that the next day, both being splendid and highly intelligent people, they would, after exchanging shots, appreciate each other's noble qualities and would become friends. But he could not come across Laevsky.

"What should I go and see him for?" repeated Samoylenko. "I did not insult him; he insulted me. Tell me, please, why he attacked me. What harm had I done him? I go into the drawing-room, and, all of a sudden, without the least provocation: 'Spy!' There's a nice thing! Tell me, how did it begin? What did you say to him?"

"I told him his position was hopeless. And I was right. It is only honest men or scoundrels who can find an escape from any position, but one who wants to be at the same time an honest man and a scoundrel — it is a hopeless position. But it's eleven o'clock, gentlemen, and we have to be up early tomorrow."

There was a sudden gust of wind; it blew up the dust on the sea-front, whirled it round in eddies, with a howl that drowned the roar of the sea.

"A squall," said the deacon. "We must go in, our eyes are getting full of dust."

As they went, Samoylenko sighed and, holding his hat, said:

"I suppose I shan't sleep tonight."

"Don't you agitate yourself," laughed the zoologist. "You can set your mind at rest; the duel will end in nothing. Laevsky will magnanimously fire into the air — he can do nothing else;

and I daresay I shall not fire at all. To be arrested and lose my time on Laevsky's account — the game's not worth the candle. By the way, what is the punishment for duelling?"

"Arrest, and in the case of the death of your opponent a maximum of three years' imprisonment in the fortress."

"The fortress of St. Peter and St. Paul?"

"No, in a military fortress, I believe."

"Though this fine gentleman ought to have a lesson!"

Behind them on the sea, there was a flash of lightning, which for an instant lighted up the roofs of the houses and the mountains. The friends parted near the boulevard. When the doctor disappeared in the darkness and his steps had died away, Von Koren shouted to him:

"I only hope the weather won't interfere with us tomorrow!"

"Very likely it will! Please God it may!"

"Good-night!"

"What about the night? What do you say?"

In the roar of the wind and the sea and the crashes of thunder, it was difficult to hear.

"It's nothing," shouted the zoologist, and hurried home.

XVII

"Upon my mind, weighed down with woe,
Crowd thoughts, a heavy multitude:
In silence memory unfolds
Her long, long scroll before my eyes.
Loathing and shuddering I curse
And bitterly lament in vain,
And bitter though the tears I weep
I do not wash those lines away."

PUSHKIN

Whether they killed him next morning, or mocked at him — that is, left him his life — he was ruined, anyway. Whether this disgraced woman killed herself in her shame and despair, or dragged on her pitiful existence, she was ruined anyway.

So thought Laevsky as he sat at the table late in the evening, still rubbing his hands. The windows suddenly blew open with a bang; a violent gust of wind burst into the room, and the papers fluttered from the table. Laevsky closed the windows and bent down to pick up the papers. He was aware of something new in his body, a sort of awkwardness he had not felt before, and his movements were strange to him. He moved timidly, jerking with his elbows and shrugging his shoulders; and when he sat down to the table again, he again began rubbing his hands. His body had lost its suppleness.

On the eve of death one ought to write to one's nearest relation. Laevsky thought of this. He took a pen and wrote with a tremulous hand:

"Mother!"

He wanted to write to beg his mother, for the sake of the merciful God in whom she believed, that she would give shelter and bring a little warmth and kindness into the life of the unhappy woman who, by his doing, had been disgraced and was in solitude, poverty, and weakness, that she would forgive and forget everything, everything, everything, and by her sacrifice atone to some extent for her son's terrible sin. But he remembered how his mother, a stout, heavily-built old woman in a lace cap, used to go out into the garden in the morning, followed by her companion with the lap-dog; how she used to shout in a peremptory way to the gardener and the servants, and how proud and haughty her face was – he remembered all this and scratched out the word he had written.

There was a vivid flash of lightning at all three windows, and it was followed by a prolonged, deafening roll of thunder, beginning with a hollow rumble and ending with a crash so violent that all the window-panes rattled. Laevsky got up, went to the window, and pressed his forehead against the pane. There was a fierce, magnificent storm. On the horizon lightning-flashes were flung in white streams from the storm-clouds into the sea, lighting up the high, dark waves over the far-away expanse.

And to right and to left, and, no doubt, over the house too, the lightning flashed.

"The storm!" whispered Laevsky; he had a longing to pray to someone or to something, if only to the lightning or the storm-clouds. "Dear storm!"

He remembered how as a boy he used to run out into the garden without a hat on when there was a storm, and how two fair-haired girls with blue eyes used to run after him, and how they got wet through with the rain; they laughed with delight, but when there was a loud peal of thunder, the girls used to nestle up to the boy confidingly, while he crossed himself and made haste to repeat: "Holy, holy, holy. . . ." Oh, where had they vanished to! In what sea were they drowned, those dawning days of pure, fair life? He had no fear of the storm, no love of nature now; he had no God. All the confiding girls he had ever known had by now been ruined by him and those like him. All his life he had not planted one tree in his own garden, nor grown one blade of grass; and living among the living, he had not saved one fly; he had done nothing but destroy and ruin, and lie, lie. . . .

"What in my past was not vice?" he asked himself, trying to clutch at some bright memory as a man falling down a precipice clutches at the bushes.

School? The university? But that was a sham. He had neglected his work and forgotten what he had learned. The service of his country? That, too, was a sham, for he did nothing in the Service, took a salary for doing nothing, and it was an abominable swindling of the State for which one was not pun-ished.

He had no craving for truth, and had not sought it; spellbound by vice and lying, his conscience had slept or been silent. Like a stranger, like an alien from another planet, he had taken no part in the common life of men, had been indifferent to their sufferings, their ideas, their religion, their sciences, their striv-ings, and their struggles. He had not said one good word, not written one line that was not useless and vulgar; he had not done his fellows one ha'p'orth of service, but had eaten their bread, drunk their wine, seduced their wives, lived on their thoughts, and to justify his contemptible, parasitic life in their eyes and in his own, he had always tried to assume an air of being higher and better than they. Lies, lies, lies. . . .

He vividly remembered what he had seen that evening at Muridov's, and he was in an insufferable anguish of loathing and misery. Kirilin and Atchmianov were loathsome, but they were only continuing what he had begun; they were his accomplices and his disciples. This young weak woman had trusted him more than a brother, and he had deprived her of her husband, of her friends and of her country, and had brought her here — to the heat, to fever, and to boredom; and from day to day she was bound to reflect, like a mirror, his idleness, his viciousness and falsity — and that was all she had had to fill her weak, listless, pitiable life. Then he had grown sick of her, had begun to hate her, but had not had the pluck to abandon her, and he had tried to entangle her more and more closely in a web of lies. . . . These men had done the rest.

Laevsky sat at the table, then got up and went to the window; at one minute he put out the candle and then he lighted it again. He cursed himself aloud, wept and wailed, and asked forgiveness; several times he ran to the table in despair, and wrote:

"Mother!"

Except his mother, he had no relations or near friends; but how could his mother help him? And where was she? He had an impulse to run to Nadyezhda Fyodorovna, to fall at her feet, to kiss her hands and feet, to beg her forgiveness; but she was his victim, and he was afraid of her as though she were dead.

"My life is ruined," he repeated, rubbing his hands. "Why am I still alive, my God! . . ."

He had cast out of heaven his dim star; it had fallen, and its track was lost in the darkness of night. It would never return to the sky again, because life was given only once and never came a second time. If he could have turned back the days and years of the past, he would have replaced the falsity with truth, the idleness with work, the boredom with happiness; he would have given back purity to those whom he had robbed of it. He would have found God and goodness, but that was as impossible as to put back the fallen star into the sky, and because it was impossible he was in despair.

When the storm was over, he sat by the open window and thought calmly of what was before him. Von Koren would most likely kill him. The man's clear, cold theory of life justified the destruction of the rotten and the useless; if it changed at the crucial moment, it would be the hatred and the repugnance that Laevsky inspired in him that would save him. If he missed his aim or, in mockery of his hated opponent, only wounded him, or fired in the air, what could he do then? Where could he go?

"Go to Petersburg?" Laevsky asked himself. But that would mean beginning over again the old life which he cursed. And the man who seeks salvation in change of place like a migrating bird would find nothing anywhere, for all the world is alike to him. Seek salvation in men? In whom and how? Samoylenko's kindness and generosity could no more save him than the deacon's laughter or Von Koren's hatred. He must look for salvation in himself alone, and if there were no finding it, why waste time? He must kill himself, that was all. . . .

He heard the sound of a carriage. It was getting light. The carriage passed by, turned, and crunching on the wet sand, stopped near the house. There were two men in the carriage.

"Wait a minute; I'm coming directly," Laevsky said to them out of the window. "I'm not asleep. Surely it's not time yet?"

"Yes, it's four o'clock. By the time we get there . . . ."

Laevsky put on his overcoat and cap, put some cigarettes in his pocket, and stood still hesitating. He felt as though there was something else he must do. In the street the seconds talked in low voices and the horses snorted, and this sound in the damp, early morning, when everybody was asleep and light was hardly dawning in the sky, filled Laevsky's soul with a disconsolate feeling which was like a presentiment of evil. He stood for a little, hesitating, and went into the bedroom.

Nadyezhda Fyodorovna was lying stretched out on the bed, wrapped from head to foot in a rug. She did not stir, and her whole appearance, especially her head, suggested an Egyptian mummy. Looking at her in silence, Laevsky mentally asked her forgiveness, and thought that if the heavens were not empty and there really were a God, then He would save her; if there were no God, then she had better perish – there was nothing for her to live for.

All at once she jumped up, and sat up in bed. Lifting her pale face and looking with horror at Laevsky, she asked:

"Is it you? Is the storm over?"

"Yes."

She remembered; put both hands to her head and shuddered all over.

"How miserable I am!" she said. "If only you knew how miserable I am! I expected," she went on, half closing her eyes, "that you would kill me or turn me out of the house into the rain and storm, but you delay . . . delay . . ."

Warmly and impulsively he put his arms round her and covered her knees and hands with kisses. Then when she muttered something and shuddered with the thought of the past, he stroked her hair, and looking into her face, realized that this unhappy, sinful woman was the one creature near and dear to him, whom no one could replace.

When he went out of the house and got into the carriage he wanted to return home alive.

XVIII

The deacon got up, dressed, took his thick, gnarled stick and slipped quietly out of the house. It was dark, and for the first minute when he went into the street, he could not even see his white stick. There was not a single star in the sky, and it looked as though there would be rain again. There was a smell of wet sand and sea.

"It's to be hoped that the mountaineers won't attack us," thought the deacon, hearing the tap of the stick on the pavement, and noticing how loud and lonely the taps sounded in the stillness of the night.

When he got out of town, he began to see both the road and his stick. Here and there in the black sky there were dark cloudy patches, and soon a star peeped out and timidly blinked its one eye. The deacon walked along the high rocky coast and did not see the sea; it was slumbering below, and its unseen waves broke languidly and heavily on the shore, as though sighing "Ouf!" and how slowly! One wave broke – the deacon had time to count eight steps; then another broke, and six steps; later a third. As before, nothing could be seen, and in the darkness one could hear the languid, drowsy drone of the sea. One could hear the infinitely far-away, inconceivable time when God moved above chaos.

The deacon felt uncanny. He hoped God would not punish him for keeping company with infidels, and even going to look at their duels. The duel would be nonsensical, bloodless, absurd, but however that might be, it was a heathen spectacle, and it was altogether unseemly for an ecclesiastical person to be present at it. He stopped and wondered – should he go back? But an intense, restless curiosity triumphed over his doubts, and he went on.

"Though they are infidels they are good people, and will be saved," he assured himself. "They are sure to be saved," he said aloud, lighting a cigarette.

By what standard must one measure men's qualities, to judge rightly of them? The deacon remembered his enemy, the inspector of the clerical school, who believed in God, lived in chastity, and did not fight duels; but he used to feed the deacon on bread with sand in it, and on one occasion almost pulled off the deacon's ear. If human life was so artlessly constructed that everyone respected this cruel and dishonest inspector who stole the Government flour, and his health and salvation were prayed for in the schools, was it just to shun such men as Von Koren and Laevsky, simply because they were unbelievers? The deacon was weighing this question, but he recalled how absurd Samoylenko had looked yesterday, and that broke the thread of his ideas. What fun they would have next day! The deacon imagined how he would sit under a bush and look on, and when Von Koren began boasting next day at dinner, he, the deacon, would begin laughing and telling him all the details of the duel.

"How do you know all about it?" the zoologist would ask.

"Well, there you are! I stayed at home, but I know all about it."

It would be nice to write a comic description of the duel. His father-in-law would read it and laugh. A good story, told or written, was more than meat and drink to his father-in-law.

The valley of the Yellow River opened before him. The stream was broader and fiercer for the rain, and instead of murmuring as before, it was raging. It began to get light. The grey, dingy morning, and the clouds racing towards the west to overtake the storm-clouds, the mountains girt with mist, and the wet trees, all struck the deacon as ugly and sinister. He washed at the brook, repeated his morning prayer, and felt a longing for tea and hot rolls, with sour cream, which were served every morning at his father-in-law's. He remembered his wife and the "Days past Recall", which she played on the piano. What sort of woman was she? His wife had been introduced, betrothed, and married to him all in one week: he had lived with her less than a month when he was ordered here, so that he had not had time to find out what she was like. All the same, he rather missed her.

"I must write her a nice letter . . ." he thought. The flag on the *duhan* hung limp, soaked by the rain, and the *duhan* itself with its wet roof seemed darker and lower than it had been before. Near the door was standing a cart; Kerbalay, with two mountaineers and a young Tatar woman in trousers — no doubt Kerbalay's wife or daughter — were bringing sacks of something out of the *duhan*, and putting them on maize straw in the cart.

Near the cart stood a pair of asses hanging their heads. When they had put in all the sacks, the mountaineers and the Tatar woman began covering them over with straw, while Kerbalay began hurriedly harnessing the asses.

"Smuggling, perhaps," thought the deacon.

Here was the fallen tree with the dried pine-needles, here was the blackened patch from the fire. He remembered the picnic and all its incidents, the fire, the singing of the mountaineers, his sweet dreams of becoming a bishop, and of the Church procession. . . . The Black River had grown blacker and broader with the rain. The deacon walked cautiously over the narrow bridge, which by now was reached by the topmost crests of the dirty water, and went up through the little copse to the drying-shed.

"A splendid head," he thought, stretching himself on the straw, and thinking of Von Koren. "A fine head — God grant him health; only there is cruelty in him. . . ."

Why did he hate Laevsky and Laevsky hate him? Why were they going to fight a duel? If from their childhood they had known poverty as the deacon had; if they had been brought up among ignorant, hard-hearted, grasping, coarse and ill-mannered people who grudged you a crust of bread, who spat on the floor and hiccoughed at dinner and at prayers; if they had not been spoilt from childhood by the pleasant surroundings and the select circle of friends they lived in – how they would have rushed at each other, how readily they would have overlooked each other's shortcomings and would have prized each other's strong points! Why, how few even outwardly decent people there were in the world! It was true that Laevsky was flighty, dissipated, queer, but he did not steal, did not spit loudly on the floor; he did not abuse his wife and say, "You'll eat till you burst, but you don't want to work"; he would not beat a child with reins, or give his servants stinking meat to eat – surely this was reason enough to be indulgent to him? Besides, he was the chief sufferer from his failings, like a sick man from his sores. Instead of being led by boredom and some sort of misunderstanding to look for degeneracy, extinction, heredity, and other such incomprehensible things in each other, would they not do better to stoop a little lower and turn their hatred and anger where whole streets resounded with moanings from coarse ignorance, greed, scolding, impurity, swearing, the shrieks of women. . . .

The sound of a carriage interrupted the deacon's thoughts. He glanced out of the door and saw a carriage and in it three persons: Laevsky, Sheshkovsky, and the superintendent of the post-office.

"Stop!" said Sheshkovsky.

All three got out of the carriage and looked at one another.

"They are not here yet," said Sheshkovsky, shaking the mud

off. "Well? Till the show begins, let us go and find a suitable spot; there's not room to turn round here."

They went further up the river and soon vanished from sight. The Tatar driver sat in the carriage with his head resting on his shoulder and fell asleep. After waiting ten minutes the deacon came out of the drying-shed, and taking off his black hat that he might not be noticed, he began threading his way among the bushes and strips of maize along the bank, crouching and looking about him. The grass and maize were wet, and big drops fell on his head from the trees and bushes. "Disgraceful!" he muttered, picking up his wet and muddy skirt. "Had I realized it, I would not have come."

Soon he heard voices and caught sight of them. Laevsky was walking rapidly to and fro in the small glade with bowed back and hands thrust in his sleeves; his seconds were standing at the water's edge, rolling cigarettes.

"Strange," thought the deacon, not recognizing Laevsky's walk; "he looks like an old man. . . ."

"How rude it is of them!" said the superintendent of the post-office, looking at his watch. "It may be learned manners to be late, but to my thinking it's hoggish."

Sheshkovsky, a stout man with a black beard, listened and said:

"They're coming!"

XIX

"It's the first time in my life I've seen it! How glorious!" said Von Koren, pointing to the glade and stretching out his hands to the east. "Look: green rays!"

In the east behind the mountains rose two green streaks of light, and it really was beautiful. The sun was rising.

"Good morning!" the zoologist went on, nodding to Laevsky's seconds. "I'm not late, am I?"

He was followed by his seconds, Boyko and Govorovsky, two very young officers of the same height, wearing white tunics, and Ustimovitch, the thin, unsociable doctor; in one hand he had a bag of some sort, and in the other hand, as usual, a cane which he held behind him. Laying the bag on the ground and greeting no one, he put the other hand, too, behind his back and began pacing up and down the glade.

Laevsky felt the exhaustion and awkwardness of a man who is soon perhaps to die, and is for that reason an object of general attention. He wanted to be killed as soon as possible or taken home. He saw the sunrise now for the first time in his life; the early morning, the green rays of light, the dampness, and the men in wet boots, seemed to him to have nothing to do with his life, to be superfluous and embarrassing. All this had no connection with the night he had been through, with his thoughts and his feeling of guilt, and so he would have gladly gone away without waiting for the duel.

Von Koren was noticeably excited and tried to conceal it, pretending that he was more interested in the green light than anything. The seconds were confused, and looked at one another as though wondering why they were here and what they were to do.

"I imagine, gentlemen, there is no need for us to go further," said Sheshkovsky. "This place will do."

"Yes, of course," Von Koren agreed.

A silence followed. Ustimovitch, pacing to and fro, suddenly turned sharply to Laevsky and said in a low voice, breathing into his face:

"They have very likely not told you my terms yet. Each side is to pay me fifteen roubles, and in the case of the death of one party, the survivor is to pay thirty."

Laevsky was already acquainted with the man, but now for the first time he had a distinct view of his lustreless eyes, his stiff moustaches, and wasted, consumptive neck; he was a money-grubber, not a doctor; his breath had an unpleasant smell of beef.

"What people there are in the world!" thought Laevsky, and answered: "Very good."

The doctor nodded and began pacing to and fro again, and it was evident he did not need the money at all, but simply asked for it from hatred. Everyone felt it was time to begin, or to end what had been begun, but instead of beginning or ending, they stood about, moved to and fro and smoked. The young officers, who were present at a duel for the first time in their lives, and even now hardly believed in this civilian and, to their thinking, unnecessary duel, looked critically at their tunics and stroked their sleeves. Sheshkovsky went up to them and said softly: "Gentlemen, we must use every effort to prevent this duel; they ought to be reconciled."

He flushed crimson and added:

"Kirilin was at my rooms last night complaining that Laevsky had found him with Nadyezhda Fyodorovna, and all that sort of thing."

"Yes, we know that too," said Boyko.

"Well, you see, then . . . Laevsky's hands are trembling and all that sort of thing . . . he can scarcely hold a pistol now. To fight with him is as inhuman as to fight a man who is drunk or who has typhoid. If a reconciliation cannot be arranged, we ought to put off the duel, gentlemen, or something. . . . It's such a sickening business, I can't bear to see it."

"Talk to Von Koren."

"I don't know the rules of duelling, damnation take them, and I don't want to either; perhaps he'll imagine Laevsky funks it and has sent me to him, but he can think what he likes – I'll speak to him."

Sheshkovsky hesitatingly walked up to Von Koren with a slight limp, as though his leg had gone to sleep; and as he went towards him, clearing his throat, his whole figure was a picture of indolence.

"There's something I must say to you, sir," he began, carefully scrutinizing the flowers on the zoologist's shirt. "It's confidential. I don't know the rules of duelling, damnation take them, and I don't want to, and I look on the matter not as a second and that sort of thing, but as a man, and that's all about it."

"Yes. Well?"

"When seconds suggest reconciliation they are usually not listened to; it is looked upon as a formality. *Amour propre* and all that. But I humbly beg you to look carefully at Ivan Andreitch. He's not in a normal state, so to speak, today — not in his right mind, and a pitiable object. He has had a misfortune. I can't endure gossip. . . ."

Sheshkovsky flushed crimson and looked round.

"But in view of the duel, I think it necessary to inform you, Laevsky found his madam last night at Muridov's with . . . another gentleman."

"How disgusting!" muttered the zoologist; he turned pale, frowned, and spat loudly. "Tfoo!"

His lower lip quivered, he walked away from Sheshkovsky, unwilling to hear more, and as though he had accidentally tasted something bitter, spat loudly again, and for the first time that morning looked with hatred at Laevsky. His excitement and awkwardness passed off; he tossed his head and said aloud:

"Gentlemen, what are we waiting for, I should like to know? Why don't we begin?"

Sheshkovsky glanced at the officers and shrugged his shoulders.

"Gentlemen," he said aloud, addressing no one in particular. "Gentlemen, we propose that you should be reconciled."

"Let us make haste and get the formalities over," said Von Koren. "Reconciliation has been discussed already. What is the next formality? Make haste, gentlemen, time won't wait for us."

"But we insist on reconciliation all the same," said Sheshkovsky in a guilty voice, as a man compelled to interfere in another man's business; he flushed, laid his hand on his heart, and went on: "Gentlemen, we see no grounds for associating the offence with the duel. There's nothing in common between duelling and offences against one another of which we are sometimes guilty through human weakness. You are university men and men of culture, and no doubt you see in the duel nothing but a foolish and out-of-date formality, and all that sort of thing. That's how we look at it ourselves, or we shouldn't have come, for we cannot allow that in our presence men should fire at one another, and all that." Sheshkovsky wiped the perspiration off his face and went on: "Make an end to your misunderstanding, gentlemen; shake hands, and let us go home and drink to peace. Upon my honour, gentlemen!"

Von Koren did not speak. Laevsky, seeing that they were looking at him, said:

"I have nothing against Nikolay Vassilitch; if he considers I'm to blame, I'm ready to apologize to him."

Von Koren was offended.

"It is evident, gentlemen," he said, "you want Mr. Laevsky to return home a magnanimous and chivalrous figure, but I cannot give you and him that satisfaction. And there was no need to get up early and drive eight miles out of town simply to drink to peace, to have breakfast, and to explain to me that the duel is an out-of-date formality. A duel is a duel, and there is no need to make it more false and stupid than it is in reality. I want to fight!"

A silence followed. Boyko took a pair of pistols out of a box; one was given to Von Koren and one to Laevsky, and then there followed a difficulty which afforded a brief amusement to the zoologist and the seconds. It appeared that of all the people present not one had ever in his life been at a duel, and no one knew precisely how they ought to stand, and what the seconds ought to say and do. But then Boyko remembered and began, with a smile, to explain.

"Gentlemen, who remembers the description in Lermontov?" asked Von Koren, laughing. "In Turgenev, too, Bazarov had a duel with someone. . . ."

"There's no need to remember," said Ustimovitch impatiently. "Measure the distance, that's all."

And he took three steps as though to show how to measure it. Boyko counted out the steps while his companion drew his sabre and scratched the earth at the extreme points to mark the barrier. In complete silence the opponents took their places.

"Moles," the deacon thought, sitting in the bushes.

Sheshkovsky said something, Boyko explained something again, but Laevsky did not hear — or rather heard, but did not understand. He cocked his pistol when the time came to do so, and raised the cold, heavy weapon with the barrel upwards. He forgot to unbutton his overcoat, and it felt very tight over his shoulder and under his arm, and his arm rose as awkwardly as though the sleeve had been cut out of tin. He remembered the hatred he had felt the night before for the swarthy brow and curly hair, and felt that even yesterday at the moment of intense hatred and anger he could not have shot a man. Fearing that the bullet might somehow hit Von Koren by accident, he raised the pistol higher and higher, and felt that this too obvious magnanimity was indelicate and anything but magnanimous, but he did not know how else to do and could do nothing else. Looking at the pale, ironically smiling face of Von Koren, who evidently had been convinced from the beginning that his opponent would fire in the air, Laevsky thought that, thank God, everything would be over directly, and all that he had to do was to press the trigger rather hard. . . .

He felt a violent shock on the shoulder; there was the sound of a shot and an answering echo in the mountains: ping-ting!

Von Koren cocked his pistol and looked at Ustimovitch, who was pacing as before with his hands behind his back, taking no notice of anyone.

"Doctor," said the zoologist, "be so good as not to move to and fro like a pendulum. You make me dizzy."

The doctor stood still. Von Koren began to take aim at Laevsky.

"It's all over!" thought Laevsky.

The barrel of the pistol aimed straight at his face, the expression of hatred and contempt in Von Koren's attitude and whole figure, and the murder just about to be committed by a decent man in broad daylight, in the presence of decent men, and the stillness and the unknown force that compelled Laevsky to stand still and not to run — how mysterious it all was, how incomprehensible and terrible!

The moment while Von Koren was taking aim seemed to Laevsky longer than a night: he glanced imploringly at the seconds; they were pale and did not stir.

"Make haste and fire," thought Laevsky, and felt that his pale, quivering, and pitiful face must arouse even greater hatred in Von Koren.

"I'll kill him directly," thought Von Koren, aiming at his forehead, with his finger already on the catch. "Yes, of course I'll kill him."

"He'll kill him!" A despairing shout was suddenly heard somewhere very close at hand.

A shot rang out at once. Seeing that Laevsky remained standing where he was and did not fall, they all looked in the direction from which the shout had come, and saw the deacon. With pale face and wet hair sticking to his forehead and his cheeks, wet through and muddy, he was standing in the maize on the further bank, smiling rather queerly and waving his wet hat. Sheshkovsky laughed with joy, burst into tears, and moved away. . . .

XX

A little while afterwards, Von Koren and the deacon met near the little bridge. The deacon was excited; he breathed hard, and avoided looking in people's faces. He felt ashamed both of his terror and his muddy, wet garments.

"I thought you meant to kill him . . ." he muttered. "How contrary to human nature it is! How utterly unnatural it is!"

"But how did you come here?" asked the zoologist.

"Don't ask," said the deacon, waving his hand. "The evil one tempted me, saying: 'Go, go. . . .' So I went and almost died of fright in the maize. But now, thank God, thank God. . . . I am awfully pleased with you," muttered the deacon. "Old Grandad Tarantula will be glad. . . . It's funny, it's too funny! Only I beg of you most earnestly don't tell anybody I was there, or I may get into hot water with the authorities. They will say: 'The deacon was a second.'"

"Gentlemen," said Von Koren, "the deacon asks you not to tell anyone you've seen him here. He might get into trouble."

"How contrary to human nature it is!" sighed the deacon.

"Excuse my saying so, but your face was so dreadful that I thought you were going to kill him."

"I was very much tempted to put an end to that scoundrel," said Von Koren, "but you shouted close by, and I missed my aim. The whole procedure is revolting to anyone who is not used to it, and it has exhausted me, deacon. I feel awfully tired. Come along. . . ."

"No, you must let me walk back. I must get dry, for I am wet and cold."

"Well, as you like," said the zoologist, in a weary tone, feeling dispirited, and, getting into the carriage, he closed his eyes. "As you like. . . ."

While they were moving about the carriages and taking their seats, Kerbalay stood in the road, and, laying his hands on his stomach, he bowed low, showing his teeth; he imagined that the gentry had come to enjoy the beauties of nature and drink tea, and could not understand why they were getting into the carriages. The party set off in complete silence and only the deacon was left by the *duhan*.

"Come to the *duhan*, drink tea," he said to Kerbalay. "Me wants to eat."

Kerbalay spoke good Russian, but the deacon imagined that the Tatar would understand him better if he talked to him in broken Russian. "Cook omelette, give cheese. . . ."

"Come, come, father," said Kerbalay, bowing. "I'll give you everything. . . . I've cheese and wine. . . . Eat what you like."

"What is 'God' in Tatar?" asked the deacon, going into the *duhan*.

"Your God and my God are the same," said Kerbalay, not understanding him. "God is the same for all men, only men are different. Some are Russian, some are Turks, some are English — there are many sorts of men, but God is one."

"Very good. If all men worship the same God, why do you Mohammedans look upon Christians as your everlasting enemies?"

"Why are you angry?" said Kerbalay, laying both hands on his stomach. "You are a priest; I am a Mussulman: you say, 'I want to eat' — I give it you. . . . Only the rich man distinguishes your God from my God; for the poor man it is all the same. If you please, it is ready."

While this theological conversation was taking place at the *duhan*, Laevsky was driving home thinking how dreadful it had been driving there at daybreak, when the roads, the rocks, and the mountains were wet and dark, and the uncertain future seemed like a terrible abyss, of which one could not see the bottom; while now the raindrops hanging on the grass and on the stones were sparkling in the sun like diamonds, nature was smiling joyfully, and the terrible future was left behind. He looked at Sheshkovsky's sullen, tear-stained face, and at the two carriages ahead of them in which Von Koren, his seconds, and the doctor were sitting, and it seemed to him as though they were all coming back from a graveyard in which a wearisome, insufferable man who was a burden to others had just been buried.

"Everything is over," he thought of his past, cautiously touching his neck with his fingers.

On the right side of his neck was a small swelling, of the length and breadth of his little finger, and he felt a pain, as though someone had passed a hot iron over his neck. The bullet had bruised it.

Afterwards, when he got home, a strange, long, sweet day began for him, misty as forgetfulness. Like a man released from prison or from hospital, he stared at the long-familiar objects and wondered that the tables, the windows, the chairs, the light, and the sea stirred in him a keen, childish delight such as he had not known for long, long years. Nadyezhda Fyodorovna, pale and haggard, could not understand his gentle voice and strange movements; she made haste to tell him everything that had happened to her. . . . It seemed to her that very likely he scarcely heard and did not understand her, and that if he did know everything he would curse her and kill her, but he listened to her, stroked her face and hair, looked into her eyes and said:

"I have nobody but you. . . ."

Then they sat a long while in the garden, huddled close together, saying nothing, or dreaming aloud of their happy life in the future, in brief, broken sentences, while it seemed to him that he had never spoken at such length or so eloquently.

XXI

More than three months had passed.

The day came that Von Koren had fixed on for his departure. A cold, heavy rain had been falling from early morning, a north-east wind was blowing, and the waves were high on the sea. It was said that the steamer would hardly be able to come into the harbour in such weather. By the time-table it should have arrived at ten o'clock in the morning, but Von Koren, who had gone on to the sea-front at midday and again after dinner, could see nothing through the field-glass but grey waves and rain covering the horizon.

Towards the end of the day the rain ceased and the wind began to drop perceptibly. Von Koren had already made up his mind that he would not be able to get off that day, and had settled down to play chess with Samoylenko; but after dark the orderly announced that there were lights on the sea and that a rocket had been seen.

Von Koren made haste. He put his satchel over his shoulder, and kissed Samoylenko and the deacon. Though there was not the slightest necessity, he went through the rooms again, said goodbye to the orderly and the cook, and went out into the street, feeling that he had left something behind, either at the doctor's or his lodging. In the street he walked beside Samoylenko, behind them came the deacon with a box, and last of all the orderly with two portmanteaus. Only Samoylenko and the orderly could distinguish the dim lights on the sea. The others gazed into the darkness and saw nothing. The steamer had stopped a long way from the coast.

"Make haste, make haste," Von Koren hurried them. "I am afraid it will set off."

As they passed the little house with three windows, into which Laevsky had moved soon after the duel, Von Koren could not resist peeping in at the window. Laevsky was sitting, writing, bent over the table, with his back to the window.

"I wonder at him!" said the zoologist softly. "What a screw he has put on himself!"

"Yes, one may well wonder," said Samoylenko. "He sits from morning till night, he's always at work. He works to pay off his debts. And he lives, brother, worse than a beggar!"

Half a minute of silence followed. The zoologist, the doctor, and the deacon stood at the window and went on looking at Laevsky.

"So he didn't get away from here, poor fellow," said Samoylenko. "Do you remember how hard he tried?"

"Yes, he has put a screw on himself," Von Koren repeated. "His marriage, the way he works all day long for his daily bread, a new expression in his face, and even in his walk – it's all so extraordinary that I don't know what to call it."

The zoologist took Samoylenko's sleeve and went on with emotion in his voice:

"You tell him and his wife that when I went away I was full of admiration for them and wished them all happiness . . . and I beg him, if he can, not to remember evil against me. He knows me. He knows that if I could have foreseen this change, then I might have become his best friend."

"Go in and say goodbye to him."

"No, that wouldn't do."

"Why? God knows, perhaps you'll never see him again."

The zoologist reflected, and said:

"That's true."

Samoylenko tapped softly at the window. Laevsky started and looked round.

"Vanya, Nikolay Vassilitch wants to say goodbye to you," said Samoylenko. "He is just going away."

Laevsky got up from the table, and went into the passage to open the door. Samoylenko, the zoologist, and the deacon went into the house.

"I can only come for one minute," began the zoologist, taking off his goloshes in the passage, and already wishing he had not given way to his feelings and come in, uninvited. "It is as though I were forcing myself on him," he thought, "and that's stupid."

"Forgive me for disturbing you," he said as he went into the room with Laevsky, "but I'm just going away, and I had an impulse to see you. God knows whether we shall ever meet again."

"I am very glad to see you. . . . Please come in," said Laevsky, and he awkwardly set chairs for his visitors as though he wanted to bar their way, and stood in the middle of the room, rubbing his hands.

"I should have done better to have left my audience in the street," thought Von Koren, and he said firmly: "Don't remember evil against me, Ivan Andreitch. To forget the past is, of course, impossible — it is too painful, and I've not come here to apologize or to declare that I was not to blame. I acted sincerely, and I have not changed my convictions since then. . . . It is true that I see, to my great delight, that I was mistaken in regard to you, but it's easy to make a false step even on a smooth road, and, in fact, it's the natural human lot: if one is not mistaken in the main, one is mistaken in the details. Nobody knows the real truth."

"No, no one knows the truth," said Laevsky.

"Well, goodbye. . . . God give you all happiness."

Von Koren gave Laevsky his hand; the latter took it and bowed.

"Don't remember evil against me," said Von Koren. "Give my greetings to your wife, and say I am very sorry not to say goodbye to her."

"She is at home."

Laevsky went to the door of the next room, and said:

"Nadya, Nikolay Vassilitch wants to say goodbye to you."

Nadyezhda Fyodorovna came in; she stopped near the doorway and looked shyly at the visitors. There was a look of guilt and dismay on her face, and she held her hands like a schoolgirl receiving a scolding.

"I'm just going away, Nadyezhda Fyodorovna," said Von Koren, "and have come to say goodbye."

She held out her hand uncertainly, while Laevsky bowed.

"What pitiful figures they are, though!" thought Von Koren. "The life they are living does not come easy to them. I shall be in Moscow and Petersburg; can I send you anything?" he asked.

"Oh!" said Nadyezhda Fyodorovna, and she looked anxiously at her husband. "I don't think there's anything. . . ."

"No, nothing . . ." said Laevsky, rubbing his hands. "Our greetings."

Von Koren did not know what he could or ought to say, though as he went in he thought he would say a very great deal that would be warm and good and important. He shook hands with Laevsky and his wife in silence, and left them with a depressed feeling.

"What people!" said the deacon in a low voice, as he walked behind them. "My God, what people! Of a truth, the right hand of God has planted this vine! Lord! Lord! One man vanquishes thousands and another tens of thousands. Nikolay Vassilitch," he said ecstatically, "let me tell you that today you have conquered the greatest of man's enemies – pride."

"Hush, deacon! Fine conquerors we are! Conquerors ought to look like eagles, while he's a pitiful figure, timid, crushed; he bows like a Chinese idol, and I, I am sad. . . ."

They heard steps behind them. It was Laevsky, hurrying after them to see him off. The orderly was standing on the quay with the two portmanteaus, and at a little distance stood four boatmen.

"There is a wind, though. . . . Brrr!" said Samoylenko. "There must be a pretty stiff storm on the sea now! You are not going off at a nice time, Koyla."

"I'm not afraid of sea-sickness."

"That's not the point. . . . I only hope these rascals won't upset you. You ought to have crossed in the agent's sloop. Where's the agent's sloop?" he shouted to the boatmen.

"It has gone, your Excellency."

"And the Customs-house boat?"

"That's gone, too."

"Why didn't you let us know?" said Samoylenko angrily. "You dolts!"

"It's all the same, don't worry yourself . . ." said Von Koren. "Well, goodbye. God keep you."

Samoylenko embraced Von Koren and made the sign of the cross over him three times.

"Don't forget us, Kolya. . . . Write. . . . We shall look out for you next spring."

"Goodbye, deacon," said Von Koren, shaking hands with the deacon. "Thank you for your company and for your pleasant conversation. Think about the expedition."

"Oh Lord, yes! to the ends of the earth," laughed the deacon. "I've nothing against it."

Von Koren recognized Laevsky in the darkness, and held out his hand without speaking. The boatmen were by now below, holding the boat, which was beating against the piles, though the breakwater screened it from the breakers. Von Koren went down the ladder, jumped into the boat, and sat at the helm.

"Write!" Samoylenko shouted to him. "Take care of yourself."

"No one knows the real truth," thought Laevsky, turning up the collar of his coat and thrusting his hands into his sleeves.

The boat turned briskly out of the harbour into the open sea. It vanished in the waves, but at once from a deep hollow glided up on to a high breaker, so that they could distinguish the men and even the oars. The boat moved three yards forward and was sucked two yards back.

"Write!" shouted Samoylenko; "it's devilish weather for you to go in."

"Yes, no one knows the real truth . . ." thought Laevsky, looking wearily at the dark, restless sea.

"It flings the boat back," he thought; "she makes two steps forward and one step back; but the boatmen are stubborn, they work the oars unceasingly, and are not afraid of the high waves. The boat goes on and on. Now she is out of sight, but in half an hour the boatmen will see the steamer lights distinctly, and within an hour they will be by the steamer ladder. So it is in life. . . . In the search for truth man makes two steps forward and one step back. Suffering, mistakes, and weariness of life thrust them back, but the thirst for truth and stubborn will drive them on and on. And who knows? Perhaps they will reach the real truth at last."

"Go—o—od—by—e," shouted Samoylenko.

"There's no sight or sound of them," said the deacon. "Good luck on the journey!"

It began to spot with rain.

A Dreary Story

From the Notebook of an Old Man

I

THERE IS IN RUSSIA an emeritus Professor Nikolay Stepanovitch, a chevalier and privy councillor; he has so many Russian and
foreign decorations that when he has occasion to put them on the
students nickname him "The Ikonstand". His acquaintances are of
the most aristocratic; for the last twenty-five or thirty years, at any
rate, there has not been one single distinguished man of learning
in Russia with whom he has not been intimately acquainted. There
is no one for him to make friends with nowadays; but if we turn
to the past, the long list of his famous friends winds up with such
names as Pirogov, Kavelin, and the poet Nekrasov, all of whom
bestowed upon him a warm and sincere affection. He is a member
of all the Russian and of three foreign universities. And so on, and
so on. All that and a great deal more that might be said makes up
what is called my "name".

That is my name as known to the public. In Russia it is known to every educated man, and abroad it is mentioned in the lecture-room with the addition "honoured and distinguished". It is one of those fortunate names to abuse which or to take which in vain, in public or in print, is considered a sign of bad taste. And that is as it should be. You see, my name is closely associated with the conception of a highly distinguished man of great gifts and unquestionable usefulness. I have the industry and power of endurance of a camel, and that is important, and I have talent, which is even more important. Moreover, while I am on this subject, I am a well-educated, modest, and honest fellow. I have never poked my nose into literature or politics; I have never sought popularity in polemics with the ignorant; I have never made speeches either at public dinners or at the funerals of my friends. . . . In fact, there is no slur on my learned name, and there is no complaint one can make against it. It is fortunate.

The bearer of that name, that is I, see myself as a man of sixty-two, with a bald head, with false teeth, and with an incurable tic douloureux. I am myself as dingy and unsightly as my name is brilliant and splendid. My head and my hands tremble with weakness; my neck, as Turgenev says of one of his heroines, is like the handle of a double bass; my chest is hollow; my shoulders narrow; when I talk or lecture, my mouth turns down at one corner; when I smile, my whole face is covered with aged-looking, deathly wrinkles. There is nothing impressive about my pitiful figure; only, perhaps, when I have an attack of tic douloureux my face wears a peculiar expression, the sight of which must have roused in everyone the grim and impressive thought, "Evidently that man will soon die."

I still, as in the past, lecture fairly well; I can still, as in the past, hold the attention of my listeners for a couple of hours. My fervour, the literary skill of my exposition, and my humour, almost efface the defects of my voice, though it is harsh, dry, and monotonous as a praying beggar's. I write poorly. That bit of my brain which presides over the faculty of authorship refuses to work. My memory has grown weak; there is a lack of sequence in my ideas, and when I put them on paper it always seems to me that I have lost the instinct for their organic connection; my construction is monotonous; my language is poor and timid. Often I write what I do not mean; I have forgotten the beginning when I am writing the end. Often I forget ordinary words, and I always have to waste a great deal of energy in avoiding superfluous phrases and unnecessary parentheses in my letters, both unmistakable proofs of a decline in mental activity. And it is noteworthy that the simpler the letter the more painful the effort to write it. At a scientific article I feel far more intelligent and at ease than at a letter of congratulation or a minute of proceedings. Another point: I find it easier to write German or English than to write Russian.

As regards my present manner of life, I must give a foremost place to the insomnia from which I have suffered of late. If I were asked what constituted the chief and fundamental feature of my existence now, I should answer, Insomnia. As in the past, from habit I undress and go to bed exactly at midnight. I fall asleep quickly, but before two o'clock I wake up and feel as though I had not slept at all. Sometimes I get out of bed and light a lamp. For an hour or two I walk up and down the room looking at the familiar photographs and pictures. When I am weary of walking about, I sit down to my table. I sit motionless, thinking of nothing, conscious of no inclination; if a book is lying before me, I mechanically move it closer and read it without any interest – in that way not long ago I mechanically read through in one night a whole novel, with the strange title *The Song the Lark was Singing*; or to occupy my attention I force myself to count to a thousand; or I imagine the face of one of my colleagues and begin trying to remember in what year and under what circumstances he entered the service. I like listening to sounds. Two rooms away from me my daughter Liza says something rapidly in her sleep, or my wife crosses the drawing-room with a candle and invariably drops the matchbox; or a warped cupboard creaks; or the burner of the lamp suddenly begins to hum – and all these sounds, for some reason, excite me.

To lie awake at night means to be at every moment conscious of being abnormal, and so I look forward with impatience to the morning and the day when I have a right to be awake. Many wearisome hours pass before the cock crows in the yard. He is my first bringer of good tidings. As soon as he crows I know that within an hour the porter will wake up below, and, coughing angrily, will go upstairs to fetch something. And then a pale light will begin gradually glimmering at the windows, voices will sound in the street. . . .

The day begins for me with the entrance of my wife. She comes in to me in her petticoat, before she has done her hair, but after she has washed, smelling of flower-scented eau-de-Cologne, looking as though she had come in by chance. Every time she says exactly the same thing: "Excuse me, I have just come in for a minute. . . . Have you had a bad night again?"

Then she puts out the lamp, sits down near the table, and begins talking. I am no prophet, but I know what she will talk about. Every morning it is exactly the same thing. Usually, after anxious inquiries concerning my health, she suddenly mentions our son who is an officer serving at Warsaw. After the twentieth of each month we send him fifty roubles, and that serves as the chief topic of our conversation.

"Of course it is difficult for us," my wife would sigh, "but until he is completely on his own feet it is our duty to help him. The boy is among strangers, his pay is small. . . . However, if you like, next month we won't send him fifty, but forty. What do you think?"

Daily experience might have taught my wife that constantly talking of our expenses does not reduce them, but my wife refuses to learn by experience, and regularly every morning discusses our officer son, and tells me that bread, thank God, is cheaper, while sugar is a halfpenny dearer — with a tone and an air as though she were communicating interesting news.

I listen, mechanically assent, and probably because I have had a bad night, strange and inappropriate thoughts intrude themselves upon me. I gaze at my wife and wonder like a child. I ask myself in perplexity, is it possible that this old, very stout, ungainly woman, with her dull expression of petty anxiety and alarm about daily bread, with eyes dimmed by continual brooding over debts and money difficulties, who can talk of nothing but expenses and who smiles at nothing but things getting cheaper — is it possible that this woman is no other than the slender Varya whom I fell in love with so passionately for her fine, clear intelligence, for her pure soul, her beauty, and, as Othello his Desdemona, for her "sympathy" for my studies? Could that woman be no other than the Varya who had once borne me a son?

I look with strained attention into the face of this flabby, spiritless, clumsy old woman, seeking in her my Varya, but of her past self nothing is left but her anxiety over my health and her manner of calling my salary "our salary", and my cap "our cap". It is painful for me to look at her, and, to give her what little comfort I can, I let her say what she likes, and say nothing even when she passes unjust criticisms on other people or pitches into me for not having a private practice or not publishing textbooks.

Our conversation always ends in the same way. My wife

suddenly remembers with dismay that I have not had my tea.

"What am I thinking about, sitting here?" she says, getting up. "The samovar has been on the table ever so long, and here I stay gossiping. My goodness! how forgetful I am growing!"

She goes out quickly, and stops in the doorway to say:

"We owe Yegor five months' wages. Did you know it? You mustn't let the servants' wages run on; how many times I have said it! It's much easier to pay ten roubles a month than fifty roubles every five months!"

As she goes out, she stops to say:

"The person I am sorriest for is our Liza. The girl studies at the Conservatoire, always mixes with people of good position, and goodness knows how she is dressed. Her fur coat is in such a state she is ashamed to show herself in the street. If she were somebody else's daughter it wouldn't matter, but of course everyone knows that her father is a distinguished professor, a privy councillor."

And having reproached me with my rank and reputation, she goes away at last. That is how my day begins. It does not improve as it goes on.

As I am drinking my tea, my Liza comes in wearing her fur coat and her cap, with her music in her hand, already quite ready to go to the Conservatoire. She is two-and-twenty. She looks younger, is pretty, and rather like my wife in her young days. She kisses me tenderly on my forehead and on my hand, and says:

"Good morning, papa; are you quite well?"

As a child she was very fond of ice-cream, and I used often to take her to a confectioner's. Ice-cream was for her the type of everything delightful. If she wanted to praise me she would say: "You are as nice as cream, papa." We used to call one of her little fingers "pistachio ice", the next, "cream ice", the third "raspberry", and so on. Usually when she came in to say good morning to me I used to sit her on my knee, kiss her little fingers, and say:

"Creamy ice . . . pistachio . . . lemon. . . ."

And now, from old habit, I kiss Liza's fingers and mutter: "Pistachio . . . cream . . . lemon . . ." but the effect is utterly different. I am cold as ice and I am ashamed. When my daughter comes in to me and touches my forehead with her lips I start as though a bee had stung me on the head, give a forced smile, and turn my face away. Ever since I have been suffering from sleeplessness, a question sticks in my brain like a nail. My daughter often sees me, an old man and a distinguished man, blush painfully at being in debt to my footman; she sees how often anxiety over petty debts forces me to lay aside my work and to walk up and down the room for hours together, thinking; but why is it she never comes to me in secret to whisper in my ear: "Father, here is my watch, here are my bracelets, my earrings, my dresses. . . . Pawn them all; you want money . . ."? How is it that, seeing how her mother and I are placed in a false position and do our utmost to hide our poverty from people, she does not give up her expensive pleasure of music lessons? I would not accept her watch nor her bracelets, nor the sacrifice of her lessons — God forbid! That isn't what I want.

I think at the same time of my son, the officer at Warsaw. He is a clever, honest, and sober fellow. But that is not enough for me. I think if I had an old father, and if I knew there were moments when he was put to shame by his poverty, I should give up my officer's commission to somebody else, and should go out to earn my living as a workman. Such thoughts about my children poison me. What is the use of them? It is only a narrow-minded or embittered man who can harbour evil thoughts about ordinary people because they are not heroes. But enough of that!

At a quarter to ten I have to go and give a lecture to my dear boys. I dress and walk along the road which I have known for thirty years, and which has its history for me. Here is the big grey house with the chemist's shop; at this point there used to stand a little house, and in it was a beershop; in that beershop I thought out my thesis and wrote my first love-letter to Varya. I wrote it in pencil, on a page headed "Historia morbi". Here there is a grocer's shop; at one time it was kept by a little Jew, who sold me cigarettes on credit; then by a fat peasant woman, who liked the students because "every one of them has a mother"; now there is a red-haired shopkeeper sitting in it, a very stolid man who drinks tea from a copper teapot. And here are the gloomy gates of the University, which have long needed doing up; I see the bored porter in his sheep-skin, the broom, the drifts of snow. . . . On a boy coming fresh from the provinces and imagining that the temple of science must really be a temple, such gates cannot make a healthy impression. Altogether the dilapidated condition of the University buildings, the gloominess of the corridors, the griminess of the walls, the lack of light, the dejected aspect of the steps, the hat-stands and the benches, take a prominent position among predisposing causes in the history of Russian pessimism. . . . Here is our garden . . . I fancy it has grown neither better nor worse since I was a student. I don't like it. It would be far more sensible if there were tall pines and fine oaks growing here instead of sickly-looking lime-trees, yellow acacias, and skimpy pollard lilacs. The student whose state of mind is in the majority of cases created by his surroundings, ought in the place where he is studying to see facing him at every turn nothing but what is lofty, strong and elegant. . . . God preserve him from gaunt trees, broken windows, grey walls, and doors covered with torn American leather!

When I go to my own entrance the door is flung wide open, and I am met by my colleague, contemporary, and namesake, the porter Nikolay. As he lets me in he clears his throat and says:

"A frost, your Excellency!"

Or, if my great-coat is wet:

"Rain, your Excellency!"

Then he runs on ahead of me and opens all the doors on my way. In my study he carefully takes off my fur coat, and while doing so manages to tell me some bit of University news. Thanks to the close intimacy existing between all the University porters and beadles, he knows everything that goes on in the four faculties, in the office, in the rector's private room, in the library. What does he not know? When in an evil day a rector or dean, for instance, retires, I hear him in conversation with the young porters mention the candidates for the post, explain that such a one would not be confirmed by the minister, that another would himself refuse to accept it, then drop into fantastic details concerning mysterious papers received in the office, secret conversations alleged to have taken place between the minister and the trustee, and so on. With the exception of these details, he almost always turns out to be right. His estimates of the candidates, though original, are very correct, too. If one wants to know in what year someone read his thesis, entered the service, retired, or died, then summon to your assistance the vast memory of that soldier, and he will not only tell you the year, the month and the day, but will furnish you also with the details that accompanied this or that event. Only one who loves can remember like that.

He is the guardian of the University traditions. From the porters who were his predecessors he has inherited many legends of University life, has added to that wealth much of his own gained during his time of service, and if you care to hear he will tell you many long and intimate stories. He can tell one about extraordinary sages who knew *everything*, about remarkable students who did not sleep for weeks, about numerous martyrs and victims of science; with him good triumphs over evil, the weak always vanquishes the strong, the wise man the fool, the humble the proud, the young the old. There is no need to take all these fables and legends for sterling coin; but filter them, and you will have left what is wanted: our fine traditions and the names of real heroes, recognized as such by all.

In our society the knowledge of the learned world consists of anecdotes of the extraordinary absent-mindedness of certain old professors, and two or three witticisms variously ascribed to Gruber, to me, and to Babukin. For the educated public that is not much. If it loved science, learned men, and students, as Nikolay does, its literature would long ago have contained whole epics, records of sayings and doings such as, unfortunately, it cannot boast of now.

After telling me a piece of news, Nikolay assumes a severe expression, and conversation about business begins. If any outsider could at such times overhear Nikolay's free use of our terminology, he might perhaps imagine that he was a learned man disguised as a soldier. And, by the way, the rumours of the erudition of the University porters are greatly exaggerated. It is true that Nikolay knows more than a hundred Latin words, knows how to put the skeleton together, sometimes prepares the apparatus and amuses the students by some long, learned quotation, but the by no means complicated theory of the circulation of the blood, for instance, is as much a mystery to him now as it was twenty years ago.

At the table in my study, bending low over some book or preparation, sits Pyotr Ignatyevitch, my demonstrator, a modest and industrious but by no means clever man of five-and-thirty, already bald and corpulent; he works from morning to night, reads a lot, remembers well everything he has read – and in that way he is not a man, but pure gold; in all else he is a carthorse or, in other words, a learned dullard. The carthorse characteristics that show his lack of talent are these: his outlook is narrow and sharply limited by his specialism; outside his special branch he is simple as a child.

"Fancy! what a misfortune! They say Skobelev is dead."

Nikolay crosses himself, but Pyotr Ignatyevitch turns to me and asks:

"What Skobelev is that?"

Another time – somewhat earlier – I told him that Professor Perov was dead. Good Pyotr Ignatyevitch asked:

"What did he lecture on?"

I believe if Patti had sung in his very ear, if a horde of Chinese had invaded Russia, if there had been an earthquake, he would not have stirred a limb, but screwing up his eye, would have gone on calmly looking through his microscope. What is he to Hecuba or Hecuba to him, in fact? I would give a good deal to see how this dry stick sleeps with his wife at night.

Another characteristic is his fanatical faith in the infallibility of science, and, above all, of everything written by the Germans. He believes in himself, in his preparations; knows the object of life, and knows nothing of the doubts and disappointments that turn the hair of talent grey. He has a slavish reverence for authorities and a complete lack of any desire for independent thought. To change his convictions is difficult, to argue with him impossible. How is one to argue with a man who is firmly persuaded that medicine is the finest of sciences, that doctors are the best of men, and that the traditions of the medical profession are superior to those of any other? Of the evil past of medicine only one tradition has been preserved – the white tie still worn by doctors; for a learned – in fact, for any educated man the only traditions that can exist are those of the University as a whole, with no distinction between medicine, law, etc. But it would be hard for Pyotr Ignatyevitch to accept these facts, and he is ready to argue with you till the day of judgment.

I have a clear picture in my mind of his future. In the course of his life he will prepare many hundreds of chemicals of exceptional purity; he will write a number of dry and very accurate memoranda, will make some dozen conscientious translations, but he won't do anything striking. To do that one must have imagination, inventiveness, the gift of insight, and Pyotr Ignatyevitch has nothing of the kind. In short, he is not a master in science, but a journeyman.

Pyotr Ignatyevitch, Nikolay, and I, talk in subdued tones. We are not quite ourselves. There is always a peculiar feeling when one hears through the doors a murmur as of the sea from the lecture-theatre. In the course of thirty years I have not grown accustomed to this feeling, and I experience it every morning. I nervously button up my coat, ask Nikolay unnecessary questions, lose my temper. . . . It is just as though I were frightened; it is not timidity, though, but something different which I can neither describe nor find a name for.

Quite unnecessarily, I look at my watch and say: "Well, it's time to go in."

And we march into the room in the following order: foremost goes Nikolay, with the chemicals and apparatus or with a chart; after him I come; and then the carthorse follows humbly, with hanging head; or, when necessary, a dead body is carried in first on a stretcher, followed by Nikolay, and so on. On my entrance the students all stand up, then they sit down, and the sound as of the sea is suddenly hushed. Stillness reigns.

I know what I am going to lecture about, but I don't know how I am going to lecture, where I am going to begin or with what I am going to end. I haven't a single sentence ready in my head. But I have only to look round the lecture-hall (it is built in the form of an amphitheatre) and utter the stereotyped phrase, "Last lecture we stopped at . . ." when sentences spring up from my soul in a long string, and I am carried away by my own eloquence. I speak with irresistible rapidity and passion, and it seems as though there were no force which could check the flow of my words. To lecture well — that is, with profit to the listeners and without boring them – one must have, besides talent, experience and a special knack; one must possess a clear conception of one's own powers, of the audience to which one is lecturing, and of the subject of one's lecture. Moreover, one must be a man who knows what he is doing; one must keep a sharp lookout, and not for one second lose sight of what lies before one.

A good conductor, interpreting the thought of the composer, does twenty things at once: reads the score, waves his baton, watches the singer, makes a motion sideways, first to the drum then to the wind-instruments, and so on. I do just the same when I lecture. Before me a hundred and fifty faces, all unlike one another; three hundred eyes all looking straight into my face. My object is to dominate this many-headed monster. If every moment as I lecture I have a clear vision of the degree of its attention and its power of comprehension, it is in my power. The other foe I have to overcome is in myself. It is the infinite variety of forms, phenomena, laws, and the multitude of ideas of my own and other people's conditioned by them. Every moment I must have the skill to snatch out of that vast mass of material what is most important and necessary, and, as rapidly as my words flow, clothe my thought in a form in which it can be grasped by the monster's intelligence, and may arouse its attention, and at the same time one must keep a sharp lookout that one's thoughts are conveyed, not just as they come, but in a certain order, essential for the correct composition of the picture I wish to sketch. Further, I endeavour to make my diction literary, my definitions brief and precise, my wording, as far as possible, simple and eloquent. Every minute I have to pull myself up and remember that I have only an hour and forty minutes at my disposal. In short, one has one's work cut out. At one and the same minute one has to play the part of savant and teacher and orator, and it's a bad thing if the orator gets the upper hand of the savant or of the teacher in one, or *vice versa*.

You lecture for a quarter of an hour, for half an hour, when you notice that the students are beginning to look at the ceiling, at Pyotr Ignatyevitch; one is feeling for his handkerchief, another shifts in his seat, another smiles at his thoughts. . . . That means that their attention is flagging. Something must be done. Taking advantage of the first opportunity, I make some pun. A broad grin comes on to a hundred and fifty faces, the eyes shine brightly, the sound of the sea is audible for a brief moment. . . . I laugh too. Their attention is refreshed, and I can go on.

No kind of sport, no kind of game or diversion, has ever given me such enjoyment as lecturing. Only at lectures have I been able to abandon myself entirely to passion, and have understood that inspiration is not an invention of the poets, but exists in real life, and I imagine Hercules after the most piquant of his exploits felt just such voluptuous exhaustion as I experience after every lecture.

That was in old times. Now at lectures I feel nothing but torture. Before half an hour is over I am conscious of an overwhelming weakness in my legs and my shoulders. I sit down in my chair, but I am not accustomed to lecture sitting down; a minute later I get up and go on standing, then sit down again. There is a dryness in my mouth, my voice grows husky, my head begins to go round. . . . To conceal my condition from my audience I continually drink water, cough, often blow my nose as though I were hindered by a cold, make puns inappropriately, and in the end break off earlier than I ought to. But above all I am ashamed.

My conscience and my intelligence tell me that the very best thing I could do now would be to deliver a farewell lecture to the boys, to say my last word to them, to bless them, and give up my post to a man younger and stronger than me. But, God, be my judge, I have not manly courage enough to act according to my conscience.

Unfortunately, I am not a philosopher and not a theologian. I know perfectly well that I cannot live more than another six months; it might be supposed that I ought now to be chiefly concerned with the question of the shadowy life beyond the grave, and the visions that will visit my slumbers in the tomb. But for some reason my soul refuses to recognize these questions, though my mind is fully alive to their importance. Just as twenty, thirty years ago, so now, on the threshold of death, I am interested in nothing but science. As I yield up my last breath

I shall still believe that science is the most important, the most splendid, the most essential thing in the life of man; that it always has been and will be the highest manifestation of love, and that only by means of it will man conquer himself and nature. This faith is perhaps naïve and may rest on false assumptions, but it is not my fault that I believe that and nothing else; I cannot overcome in myself this belief.

But that is not the point. I only ask people to be indulgent to my weakness, and to realize that to tear from the lecture-theatre and his pupils a man who is more interested in the history of the development of the bone medulla than in the final object of creation would be equivalent to taking him and nailing him up in his coffin without waiting for him to be dead.

Sleeplessness and the consequent strain of combating increasing weakness leads to something strange in me. In the middle of my lecture tears suddenly rise in my throat, my eyes begin to smart, and I feel a passionate, hysterical desire to stretch out my hands before me and break into loud lamentation. I want to cry out in a loud voice that I, a famous man, have been sentenced by fate to the death penalty, that within some six months another man will be in control here in the lecture-theatre. I want to shriek that I am poisoned; new ideas such as I have not known before have poisoned the last days of my life, and are still stinging my brain like mosquitoes. And at that moment my position seems to me so awful that I want all my listeners to be horrified, to leap up from their seats and to rush in panic terror, with desperate screams, to the exit.

It is not easy to get through such moments.

II

After my lecture I sit at home and work. I read journals and monographs, or prepare my next lecture; sometimes I write something. I work with interruptions, as I have from time to time to see visitors.

There is a ring at the bell. It is a colleague come to discuss some business matter with me. He comes in to me with his hat and his stick, and, holding out both these objects to me, says:

"Only for a minute! Only for a minute! Sit down, *collega*! Only a couple of words."

To begin with, we both try to show each other that we are extraordinarily polite and highly delighted to see each other. I make him sit down in an easy-chair, and he makes me sit down; as we do so, we cautiously pat each other on the back, touch each other's buttons, and it looks as though we were feeling each other and afraid of scorching our fingers. Both of us laugh, though we say nothing amusing. When we are seated we bow our heads towards each other and begin talking in subdued voices. However affectionately disposed we may be to one another, we cannot help adorning our conversation with all sorts of Chinese mannerisms, such as "As you so justly observed", or "I have already had the honour to inform you"; we cannot help laughing if one of us makes a joke, however unsuccessfully. When we have finished with business my colleague gets up impulsively and, waving his hat in the direction of my work, begins to say goodbye. Again we paw one another and laugh. I see him into the hall; when I assist my colleague to put on his coat, he does all he can to decline this high honour. Then when Yegor opens the door my colleague declares that I shall catch cold, while I make a show of being ready to go even into the street with him. And when at last I go back into my study my face still goes on smiling, I suppose from inertia.

A little later another ring at the bell. Somebody comes into the hall, and is a long time coughing and taking off his things. Yegor announces a student. I tell him to ask him in. A minute later a young man of agreeable appearance comes in. For the last year he and I have been on strained relations; he answers me disgracefully at the examinations, and I mark him one. Every year I have some seven such hopefuls whom, to express it in the students' slang, I "chivy" or "floor". Those of them who fail in their examination through incapacity or illness usually bear their cross patiently and do not haggle with me; those who come to the house and haggle with me are always youths of sanguine temperament, broad natures, whose failure at examinations spoils their appetites and hinders them from visiting the opera with their usual regularity. I let the first class off easily, but the second I chivy through a whole year.

"Sit down," I say to my visitor; "what have you to tell me?"

"Excuse me, professor, for troubling you," he begins, hesitating, and not looking me in the face. "I would not have ventured to trouble you if it had not been . . . I have been up for your examination five times, and have been ploughed. . . . I beg you, be so good as to mark me for a pass, because . . ."

The argument which all the sluggards bring forward on their own behalf is always the same; they have passed well in all their subjects and have only come to grief in mine, and that is the more surprising because they have always been particularly interested in my subject and knew it so well; their failure has always been entirely owing to some incomprehensible misunderstanding.

"Excuse me, my friend," I say to the visitor; "I cannot mark you for a pass. Go and read up the lectures and come to me again. Then we shall see."

A pause. I feel an impulse to torment the student a little for liking beer and the opera better than science, and I say, with a sigh:

"To my mind, the best thing you can do now is to give up medicine altogether. If, with your abilities, you cannot succeed in passing the examination, it's evident that you have neither the desire nor the vocation for a doctor's calling."

The sanguine youth's face lengthens.

"Excuse me, professor," he laughs, "but that would be odd

of me, to say the least of it. After studying for five years, all at once to give it up."

"Oh, well! Better to have lost your five years than have to spend the rest of your life in doing work you do not care for."

But at once I feel sorry for him, and I hasten to add:

"However, as you think best. And so read a little more and come again."

"When?" the idle youth asks in a hollow voice.

"When you like. Tomorrow if you like."

And in his good-natured eyes I read:

"I can come all right, but of course you will plough me again, you beast!"

"Of course," I say, "you won't know more science for going in for my examination another fifteen times, but it is training your character, and you must be thankful for that."

Silence follows. I get up and wait for my visitor to go, but he stands and looks towards the window, fingers his beard, and thinks. It grows boring.

The sanguine youth's voice is pleasant and mellow, his eyes are clever and ironical, his face is genial, though a little bloated from frequent indulgence in beer and overlong lying on the sofa; he looks as though he could tell me a lot of interesting things about the opera, about his affairs of the heart, and about comrades whom he likes. Unluckily, it is not the thing to discuss these subjects, or else I should have been glad to listen to him.

"Professor, I give you my word of honour that if you mark me for a pass I . . . I'll . . ."

As soon as we reach the "word of honour" I wave my hands and sit down to the table. The student ponders a minute longer, and says dejectedly:

"In that case, goodbye . . . I beg your pardon."

"Goodbye, my friend. Good luck to you."

He goes irresolutely into the hall, slowly puts on his outdoor things, and, going out into the street, probably ponders for some time longer; unable to think of anything, except "old devil", inwardly addressed to me, he goes into a wretched restaurant to dine and drink beer, and then home to bed. "Peace be to thy ashes, honest toiler."

A third ring at the bell. A young doctor, in a pair of new black trousers, gold spectacles, and of course a white tie, walks in. He introduces himself. I beg him to be seated, and ask what I can do for him. Not without emotion, the young devotee of science begins telling me that he has passed his examination as a doctor of medicine, and that he has now only to write his dissertation. He would like to work with me under my guidance, and he would be greatly obliged to me if I would give him a subject for his dissertation.

"Very glad to be of use to you, colleague," I say, "but just let us come to an understanding as to the meaning of a dissertation. That word is taken to mean a composition which is a product of independent creative effort. Is that not so? A work written on another man's subject and under another man's guidance is called something different. . . ."

The doctor says nothing. I fly into a rage and jump up from my seat.

"Why is it you all come to me?" I cry angrily. "Do I keep a shop? I don't deal in subjects. For the thousand and oneth time I ask you all to leave me in peace! Excuse my brutality, but I am quite sick of it!"

The doctor remains silent, but a faint flush is apparent on his cheek-bones. His face expresses a profound reverence for my fame and my learning, but from his eyes I can see he feels a contempt for my voice, my pitiful figure, and my nervous gesticulation. I impress him in my anger as a queer fish.

"I don't keep a shop," I go on angrily. "And it is a strange thing! Why don't you want to be independent? Why have you such a distaste for independence?"

I say a great deal, but he still remains silent. By degrees I calm down, and of course give in. The doctor gets a subject from me for his theme not worth a halfpenny, writes under my supervision a dissertation of no use to anyone, with dignity defends it in a dreary discussion, and receives a degree of no use to him.

The rings at the bell may follow one another endlessly, but I will confine my description here to four of them. The bell rings for the fourth time, and I hear familiar footsteps, the rustle of a dress, a dear voice. . . .

Eighteen years ago a colleague of mine, an oculist, died

leaving a little daughter Katya, a child of seven, and sixty thousand roubles. In his will he made me the child's guardian. Till she was ten years old Katya lived with us as one of the family, then she was sent to a boarding-school, and only spent the summer holidays with us. I never had time to look after her education. I only superintended it at leisure moments, and so I can say very little about her childhood.

The first thing I remember, and like so much in remembrance, is the extraordinary trustfulness with which she came into our house and let herself be treated by the doctors, a trustfulness which was always shining in her little face. She would sit somewhere out of the way, with her face tied up, invariably watching something with attention; whether she watched me writing or turning over the pages of a book, or watched my wife bustling about, or the cook scrubbing a potato in the kitchen, or the dog playing, her eyes invariably expressed the same thought – that is, "Everything that is done in this world is nice and sensible." She was curious, and very fond of talking to me. Sometimes she would sit at the table opposite me, watching my movements and asking questions. It interested her to know what I was reading, what I did at the University, whether I was not afraid of the dead bodies, what I did with my salary.

"Do the students fight at the University?" she would ask.

"They do, dear."

"And do you make them go down on their knees?"

"Yes, I do."

And she thought it funny that the students fought and I made them go down on their knees, and she laughed. She was a gentle, patient, good child. It happened not infrequently that I saw something taken away from her, saw her punished without reason, or her curiosity repressed; at such times a look of sadness was mixed with the invariable expression of trustfulness on her face — that was all. I did not know how to take her part; only when I saw her sad I had an inclination to draw her to me and to commiserate her like some old nurse: "My poor little orphan one!"

I remember, too, that she was fond of fine clothes and of sprinkling herself with scent. In that respect she was like me. I, too, am fond of pretty clothes and nice scent.

I regret that I had not time nor inclination to watch over the rise and development of the passion which took complete possession of Katya when she was fourteen or fifteen. I mean her passionate love for the theatre. When she used to come from boarding-school and stay with us for the summer holidays, she talked of nothing with such pleasure and such warmth as of plays and actors. She bored us with her continual talk of the theatre. My wife and children would not listen to her. I was the only one who had not the courage to refuse to attend to her. When she had a longing to share her transports, she used to come into my study and say in an imploring tone:

"Nikolay Stepanovitch, do let me talk to you about the theatre!"

I pointed to the clock, and said:

"I'll give you half an hour – begin."

Later on she used to bring with her dozens of portraits of actors and actresses which she worshipped; then she attempted several times to take part in private theatricals, and the upshot of it all was that when she left school she came to me and announced that she was born to be an actress.

I had never shared Katya's inclinations for the theatre. To my mind, if a play is good there is no need to trouble the actors in order that it may make the right impression; it is enough to read it. If the play is poor, no acting will make it good.

In my youth I often visited the theatre, and now my family takes a box twice a year and carries me off for a little distraction. Of course, that is not enough to give me the right to judge of the theatre. In my opinion the theatre has become no better than it was thirty or forty years ago. Just as in the past, I can never find a glass of clean water in the corridors or foyers of the theatre. Just as in the past, the attendants fine me twenty kopecks for my fur coat, though there is nothing reprehensible in wearing a warm coat in winter. As in the past, for no sort of reason, music is played in the intervals, which adds something new and uncalled-for to the impression made by the play. As in the past, men go in the intervals and drink spirits in the buffet. If no progress can be seen in trifles, I should look for it in vain in what is more important. When an actor wrapped from head to foot in stage traditions and conventions tries to recite a simple ordinary speech, "To be or not to be", not simply, but invariably with the accompaniment of hissing and convulsive movements all over his body, or when he tries to convince me at all costs that Tchatsky, who talks so much with fools and is so fond of folly, is a very clever man, and that *Woe from Wit* is not a dull play, the stage gives me the same feeling of conventionality which bored me so much forty years ago when I was regaled with the classical howling and beating on the breast. And every time I come out of the theatre more conservative than I go in.

The sentimental and confiding public may be persuaded that the stage, even in its present form, is a school; but anyone who is familiar with a school in its true sense will not be caught with that bait. I cannot say what will happen in fifty or a hundred years, but in its actual condition the theatre can serve only as an entertainment. But this entertainment is too costly to be frequently enjoyed. It robs the state of thousands of healthy and talented young men and women, who, if they had not devoted themselves to the theatre, might have been good doctors, farmers, schoolmistresses, officers; it robs the public of the evening hours – the best time for intellectual work and social intercourse. I say nothing of the waste of money and the moral damage to the spectator when he sees murder, fornication, or false witness unsuitably treated on the stage.

Katya was of an entirely different opinion. She assured me that the theatre, even in its present condition, was superior to the lecture-hall, to books, or to anything in the world. The stage was a power that united in itself all the arts, and actors were missionaries. No art nor science was capable of producing so strong and so certain an effect on the soul of man as the stage, and it was with good reason that an actor of medium quality enjoys greater popularity than the greatest savant or artist. And no sort of public service could provide such enjoyment and gratification as the theatre.

And one fine day Katya joined a troupe of actors, and went off, I believe to Ufa, taking away with her a good supply of money, a store of rainbow hopes, and the most aristocratic views of her work.

Her first letters on the journey were marvellous. I read them, and was simply amazed that those small sheets of paper could contain so much youth, purity of spirit, holy innocence, and at the same time subtle and apt judgments which would have done credit to a fine masculine intellect. It was more like a rapturous paean of praise she sent me than a mere description of the Volga, the country, the towns she visited, her companions, her failures and successes; every sentence was fragrant with that confiding trustfulness I was accustomed to read in her face – and at the same time there were a great many grammatical mistakes, and there was scarcely any punctuation at all.

Before six months had passed I received a highly poetical and enthusiastic letter beginning with the words, "I have come to love . . ." This letter was accompanied by a photograph representing a young man with a shaven face, a wide-brimmed hat, and a plaid flung over his shoulder. The letters that followed were as splendid as before, but now commas and stops made their appearance in them, the grammatical mistakes disappeared, and there was a distinctly masculine flavour about them. Katya began writing to me how splendid it would be to build a great theatre somewhere on the Volga, on a cooperative system, and to attract to the enterprise the rich merchants and the steamer owners; there would be a great deal of money in it; there would be vast audiences; the actors would play on co-operative terms. . . . Possibly all this was really excellent, but it seemed to me that such schemes could only originate from a man's mind.

However that may have been, for a year and a half everything seemed to go well: Katya was in love, believed in her work, and was happy; but then I began to notice in her letters unmistakable signs of falling off. It began with Katya's complaining of her companions – this was the first and most ominous symptom; if a young scientific or literary man begins his career with bitter complaints of scientific and literary men, it is a sure sign that he is worn out and not fit for his work. Katya wrote to me that her companions did not attend the rehearsals and never knew their parts; that one could see in every one of them an utter disrespect for the public in the production of absurd plays, and in their behaviour on the stage; that for the benefit of the Actors' Fund, which they only talked about, actresses of the serious drama demeaned themselves by singing chansonettes, while tragic actors sang comic songs making fun of deceived husbands and the pregnant condition of unfaithful wives, and so on. In fact, it was amazing that all this had not yet ruined the provincial stage, and that it could still maintain itself on such a rotten and unsubstantial footing.

In answer I wrote Katya a long and, I must confess, a very boring letter. Among other things, I wrote to her:

"I have more than once happened to converse with old actors, very worthy men, who showed a friendly disposition towards me; from my conversations with them I could understand that their work was controlled not so much by their own intelligence and free choice as by fashion and the mood of the public. The best of them had had to play in their day in tragedy, in operetta, in Parisian farces, and in extravaganzas, and they always seemed equally sure that they were on the right path and that they were of use. So, as you see, the cause of the evil must be sought, not in the actors, but, more deeply, in the art itself and in the attitude of the whole of society to it."

This letter of mine only irritated Katya. She answered me:

"You and I are singing parts out of different operas. I wrote to you, not of the worthy men who showed a friendly disposition to you, but of a band of knaves who have nothing worthy about them. They are a horde of savages who have got on the stage simply because no one would have taken them elsewhere, and who call themselves artists simply because they are impudent. There are numbers of dull-witted creatures, drunkards, intriguing schemers and slanderers, but there is not one person of talent among them. I cannot tell you how bitter it is to me that the art I love has fallen into the hands of people I detest; how bitter it is that the best men look on at evil from afar, not caring to come closer, and, instead of intervening, write ponderous commonplaces and utterly useless sermons. . . ." And so on, all in the same style.

A little time passed, and I got this letter: "I have been brutally deceived. I cannot go on living. Dispose of my money as you think best. I loved you as my father and my only friend. Goodbye."

It turned out that *he*, too, belonged to the "horde of savages". Later on, from certain hints, I gathered that there had been an attempt at suicide. I believe Katya tried to poison herself. I imagine that she must have been seriously ill afterwards, as the next letter I got was from Yalta, where she had most probably been sent by the doctors. Her last letter contained a request to send her a thousand roubles to Yalta as quickly as possible, and ended with these words:

"Excuse the gloominess of this letter; yesterday I buried my child." After spending about a year in the Crimea, she returned home.

She had been about four years on her travels, and during those four years, I must confess, I had played a rather strange and unenviable part in regard to her. When in earlier days she had told me she was going on the stage, and then wrote to me of her love; when she was periodically overcome by extravagance, and I continually had to send her first one and then two thousand roubles; when she wrote to me of her intention of suicide, and then of the death of her baby, every time I lost my head, and all my sympathy for her sufferings found no expression except that, after prolonged reflection, I wrote long, boring letters which I might just as well not have written. And yet I took a father's place with her and loved her like a daughter!

Now Katya is living less than half a mile off. She has taken a flat of five rooms, and has installed herself fairly comfortably and in the taste of the day. If anyone were to undertake to describe her surroundings, the most characteristic note in the picture would be indolence. For the indolent body there are soft lounges, soft stools; for indolent feet soft rugs; for indolent eyes faded, dingy, or flat colours; for the indolent soul the walls are hung with a number of cheap fans and trivial pictures, in which the originality of the execution is more conspicuous than the subject; and the room contains a multitude of little tables and shelves filled with utterly useless articles of no value, and shapeless rags in place of curtains. . . . All this, together with the dread of bright colours, of symmetry, and of empty space, bears witness not only to spiritual indolence, but also to a corruption of natural taste. For days together Katya lies on the lounge reading, principally novels and stories. She only goes out of the house once a day, in the afternoon, to see me.

I go on working while Katya sits silent not far from me on the sofa, wrapping herself in her shawl, as though she were cold.

Either because I find her sympathetic or because I was used to her frequent visits when she was a little girl, her presence does not prevent me from concentrating my attention. From time to time I mechanically ask her some question; she gives very brief replies; or, to rest for a minute, I turn round and watch her as she looks dreamily at some medical journal or review. And at such moments I notice that her face has lost the old look of confiding trustfulness. Her expression now is cold, apathetic, and absent-minded, like that of passengers who had to wait too long for a train. She is dressed, as in old days, simply and beautifully, but carelessly; her dress and her hair show visible traces of the sofas and rocking-chairs in which she spends whole days at a stretch. And she has lost the curiosity she had in old days. She has ceased to ask me questions now, as though she had experienced everything in life and looked for nothing new from it.

Towards four o'clock there begins to be sounds of movement in the hall and in the drawing-room. Liza has come back from the Conservatoire, and has brought some girl-friends in with her. We hear them playing on the piano, trying their voices and laughing; in the dining-room Yegor is laying the table, with the clatter of crockery.

"Goodbye," said Katya. "I won't go in and see your people today. They must excuse me. I haven't time. Come and see me."

While I am seeing her to the door, she looks me up and down grimly, and says with vexation:

"You are getting thinner and thinner! Why don't you consult

a doctor? I'll call at Sergey Fyodorovitch's and ask him to have a look at you."

"There's no need, Katya."

"I can't think where your people's eyes are! They are a nice lot, I must say!"

She puts on her fur coat abruptly, and as she does so two or three hairpins drop unnoticed on the floor from her carelessly arranged hair. She is too lazy and in too great a hurry to do her hair up; she carelessly stuffs the falling curls under her hat, and goes away.

When I go into the dining-room my wife asks me:

"Was Katya with you just now? Why didn't she come in to see us? It's really strange . . ."

"Mamma," Liza says to her reproachfully, "let her alone, if she doesn't want to. We are not going down on our knees to her."

"It's very neglectful, anyway. To sit for three hours in the study without remembering our existence! But of course she must do as she likes."

Varya and Liza both hate Katya. This hatred is beyond my comprehension, and probably one would have to be a woman in order to understand it. I am ready to stake my life that of the hundred and fifty young men I see every day in the lecture-theatre, and of the hundred elderly ones I meet every week, hardly one could be found capable of understanding their hatred and aversion for Katya's past – that is, for her having been a mother without being a wife, and for her having had an illegitimate child; and at the same time I cannot recall one woman or girl of my acquaintance who would not consciously or unconsciously harbour such feelings. And this is not because woman is purer or more virtuous than man: why, virtue and purity are not very different from vice if they are not free from evil feeling. I attribute this simply to the backwardness of woman. The mournful feeling of compassion and the pang of conscience experienced by a modern man at the sight of suffering is, to my mind, far greater proof of culture and moral elevation than hatred and aversion. Woman is as tearful and as coarse in her feelings now as she was in the Middle Ages, and to my thinking those who advise that she should be educated like a man are quite right.

My wife also dislikes Katya for having been an actress, for ingratitude, for pride, for eccentricity, and for the numerous vices which one woman can always find in another.

Besides my wife and daughter and me, there are dining with us two or three of my daughter's friends and Alexandr Adolfovitch Gnekker, her admirer and suitor. He is a fair-haired young man under thirty, of medium height, very stout and broad-shouldered, with red whiskers near his ears, and little waxed moustaches which make his plump smooth face look like a toy. He is dressed in a very short reefer jacket, a flowered waistcoat, breeches very full at the top and very narrow at the ankle, with a large check pattern on them, and yellow boots without heels. He has prominent eyes like a crab's, his cravat is like a crab's neck, and I even fancy there is a smell of crab soup about the young man's whole person. He visits us every day, but no one in my family knows anything of his origin nor of the place of his education, nor of his means of livelihood. He neither plays nor sings, but has some connection with music and singing, sells somebody's pianos somewhere, is frequently at the Conservatoire, is acquainted with all the celebrities, and is a steward at the concerts; he criticizes music with great authority, and I have noticed that people are eager to agree with him.

Rich people always have dependants hanging about them; the arts and sciences have the same. I believe there is not an art nor a science in the world free from "foreign bodies" after the style of this Mr. Gnekker. I am not a musician, and possibly I am mistaken in regard to Mr. Gnekker, of whom, indeed, I know very little. But his air of authority and the dignity with which he takes his stand beside the piano when anyone is playing or singing strike me as very suspicious.

You may be ever so much of a gentleman and a privy councillor, but if you have a daughter you cannot be secure of immunity from that petty bourgeois atmosphere which is so often brought into your house and into your mood by the attentions of suitors, by matchmaking and marriage. I can never reconcile myself, for instance, to the expression of triumph on my wife's face every time Gnekker is in our company, nor can I reconcile myself to the bottles of Lafitte, port and sherry which are only brought out on his account, that he may see with his own eyes the liberal and luxurious way in which we live. I cannot tolerate the habit of spasmodic laughter Liza has picked up at the Conservatoire, and her way of screwing up her eyes whenever there are men in the room. Above all, I cannot understand why a creature utterly alien to my habits, my studies, my whole manner of life, completely different from the people I like, should come and see me every day, and every day should dine with me. My wife and my servants mysteriously whisper that he is a suitor, but still I don't understand his presence; it rouses in me the same wonder and perplexity as if they were to set a Zulu beside me at the table. And it seems strange to me, too, that my daughter, whom I am used to thinking of as a child, should love that cravat, those eyes, those soft cheeks. . . .

In the old days I used to like my dinner, or at least was indifferent about it; now it excites in me no feeling but weariness and irritation. Ever since I became an "Excellency" and one of the Deans of the Faculty my family has for some reason found it necessary to make a complete change in our menu and dining habits. Instead of the simple dishes to which I was accustomed when I was a student and when I was in practice, now they feed me with a purée with little white things like circles floating about in it, and kidneys stewed in madeira. My rank as a general and my fame have robbed me for ever of cabbage soup and savoury pies, and goose with apple-sauce, and bream with boiled grain. They have robbed me of our maid-servant Agasha, a chatty and laughter-loving old woman, instead of whom Yegor, a dull-witted and conceited fellow with a white glove on his right hand, waits at dinner. The intervals between the courses are short, but they seem immensely long because there is nothing to occupy them. There is none of the gaiety of the old days, the spontaneous talk, the jokes, the laughter; there is nothing of mutual affection and the joy which used to animate the children, my wife, and me when in old days we met together at meals. For me, the celebrated man of science, dinner was a time of rest and reunion, and for my wife and children a fête – brief indeed, but bright and joyous – in which they knew that for half an hour I belonged, not to science, not to students, but to them alone. Our real exhilaration from one glass of wine is gone for ever, gone is Agasha, gone the bream with boiled grain, gone the uproar that greeted every little startling incident at dinner, such as the cat and dog fighting under the table, or Katya's bandage falling off her face into her soup-plate.

To describe our dinner nowadays is as uninteresting as to eat it. My wife's face wears a look of triumph and affected dignity, and her habitual expression of anxiety. She looks at our plates and says, "I see you don't care for the joint. Tell me; you don't like it, do you?" and I am obliged to answer: "There is no need for you to trouble, my dear; the meat is very nice." And she will say: "You always stand up for me, Nikolay Stepanovitch, and you never tell the truth. Why is Alexandr Adolfovitch eating so little?" And so on in the same style all through dinner. Liza laughs spasmodically and screws up her eyes. I watch them both, and it is only now at dinner that it becomes absolutely evident to me that the inner life of these two has slipped away out of my ken. I have a feeling as though I had once lived at home with a real wife and children and that now I am dining with visitors, in the house of a sham wife who is not the real one, and am looking at a Liza who is not the real Liza. A startling change has taken place in both of them; I have missed the long process by which that change was effected, and it is no wonder that I can make nothing of it. Why did that change take place? I don't know. Perhaps the whole trouble is that God has not given my wife and daughter the same strength of character as me. From childhood I have been accustomed to resisting external influences, and have steeled myself pretty thoroughly. Such catastrophes in life as fame, the rank of a general, the transition from comfort to living beyond our means, acquaintance with celebrities, etc., have scarcely affected me, and I have remained intact and un-ashamed; but on my wife and Liza, who have not been through the same hardening process and are weak, all this has fallen like an avalanche of snow, overwhelming them. Gnekker and the young ladies talk of fugues, of counterpoint, of singers and pianists, of Bach and Brahms, while my wife, afraid of their suspecting her of ignorance of music, smiles to them sympathetically and mutters: "That's exquisite . . . really! You don't say so! . . ." Gnekker eats with solid dignity, jests with solid dignity, and condescendingly listens to the remarks of the young ladies. From time to time he is moved to speak in bad French, and then, for some reason or other, he thinks it necessary to address me as "*Votre Excellence*".

And I am glum. Evidently I am a constraint to them and they are a constraint to me. I have never in my earlier days had a close knowledge of class antagonism, but now I am tormented by something of that sort. I am on the lookout for nothing but bad qualities in Gnekker; I quickly find them, and am fretted at the thought that a man not of my circle is sitting here as my daughter's suitor. His presence has a bad influence on me in other ways, too. As a rule, when I am alone or in the society of people I like, never think of my own achievements, or, if I do recall them, they seem to me as trivial as though I had only completed my studies yesterday; but in the presence of people like Gnekker my achievements in science seem to be a lofty mountain the top of which vanishes into the clouds, while at its foot Gnekkers are running about scarcely visible to the naked eye.

After dinner I go into my study and there smoke my pipe, the only one in the whole day, the sole relic of my old bad habit of smoking from morning till night. While I am smoking my wife comes in and sits down to talk to me. Just as in the morning, I know beforehand what our conversation is going to be about.

"I must talk to you seriously, Nikolay Stepanovitch," she begins. "I mean about Liza. . . . Why don't you pay attention to it?"

"To what?"

"You pretend to notice nothing. But that is not right. We can't shirk responsibility. . . . Gnekker has intentions in regard to Liza. . . . What do you say?"

"That he is a bad man I can't say, because I don't know him, but that I don't like him I have told you a thousand times already."

"But you can't . . . you can't!"

She gets up and walks about in excitement.

"You can't take up that attitude to a serious step," she says. "When it is a question of our daughter's happiness we must lay aside all personal feeling. I know you do not like him. . . . Very good . . . if we refuse him now, if we break it all off, how can you be sure that Liza will not have a grievance against us all her life? Suitors are not plentiful nowadays, goodness knows, and it may happen that no other match will turn up. . . . He is very much in love with Liza, and she seems to like him. . . . Of course, he has no settled position, but that can't be helped. Please God, in time he will get one. He is of good family and well off."

"Where did you learn that?"

"He told us so. His father has a large house in Harkov and an estate in the neighbourhood. In short, Nikolay Stepanovitch, you absolutely must go to Harkov."

"What for?"

"You will find out all about him there. . . . You know the professors there; they will help you. I would go myself, but I am a woman. I cannot. . . ."

"I am not going to Harkov," I say morosely.

My wife is frightened, and a look of intense suffering comes into her face.

"For God's sake, Nikolay Stepanovitch," she implores me, with tears in her voice — "for God's sake, take this burden off me! I am so worried!"

It is painful for me to look at her.

"Very well, Varya," I say affectionately, "if you wish it, then certainly I will go to Harkov and do all you want."

She presses her handkerchief to her eyes and goes off to her room to cry, and I am left alone.

A little later lights are brought in. The arm-chair and the lamp-shade cast familiar shadows that have long grown wearisome on the walls and on the floor, and when I look at them I feel as though the night had come and with it my accursed sleeplessness. I lie on my bed, then get up and walk about the room, then lie down again. As a rule it is after dinner, at the approach of evening, that my nervous excitement reaches its highest pitch. For no reason I begin crying and burying my head in the pillow. At such times I am afraid that someone may come in; I am afraid of suddenly dying; I am ashamed of my tears, and altogether there is something insufferable in my soul. I feel that I can no longer bear the sight of my lamp, of my books, of the shadows on the floor. I cannot bear the sound of the voices coming from the drawing-room. Some force unseen, uncomprehended, is roughly thrusting me out of my flat. I leap up hurriedly, dress, and cautiously, that my family may not notice, slip out into the street. Where am I to go?

The answer to that question has long been ready in my brain. To Katya.

III

As a rule she is lying on the sofa or in a lounge-chair reading. Seeing me, she raises her head languidly, sits up, and shakes hands.

"You are always lying down," I say, after pausing and taking breath. "That's not good for you. You ought to occupy yourself with something."

"What?"

"I say you ought to occupy yourself in some way."

"With what? A woman can be nothing but a simple work-woman or an actress."

"Well, if you can't be a workwoman, be an actress."

She says nothing.

"You ought to get married," I say, half in jest.

"There is no one to marry. There's no reason to, either."

"You can't live like this."

"Without a husband? Much that matters; I could have as many men as I like if I wanted to."

"That's ugly, Katya."

"What is ugly?"

"Why, what you have just said."

Noticing that I am hurt and wishing to efface the disagreeable impression, Katya says:

"Let us go; come this way."

She takes me into a very snug little room, and says, pointing to the writing-table:

"Look . . . I have got that ready for you. You shall work here. Come here every day and bring your work with you. They only hinder you there at home. Will you work here? Will you like to?"

Not to wound her by refusing, I answer that I will work here, and that I like the room very much. Then we both sit down in the snug little room and begin talking.

The warm, snug surroundings and the presence of a sympathetic person does not, as in old days, arouse in me a feeling of pleasure, but an intense impulse to complain and grumble. I feel for some reason that if I lament and complain I shall feel better.

"Things are in a bad way with me, my dear – very bad. . . ."

"What is it?"

"You see how it is, my dear; the best and holiest right of kings is the right of mercy. And I have always felt myself a king, since I have made unlimited use of that right. I have never judged, I have been indulgent, I have readily forgiven everyone, right and left. Where others have protested and expressed indignation, I have only advised and persuaded. All my life it has been my endeavour that my society should not be a burden to my family, to my students, to my colleagues, to my servants. And I know that this attitude to people has had a good influence on all who have chanced to come into contact with me. But now I am not a king. Something is happening to me that is only excusable in a slave; day and night my brain is haunted by evil thoughts, and feelings such as I never knew before are brooding in my soul. I am full of hatred, and contempt, and indignation, and loathing, and dread. I have become excessively severe, exacting, irritable, ungracious, suspicious. Even things that in old days would have provoked me only to an unnecessary jest and a good-natured laugh now arouse an oppressive feeling in me. My reasoning, too, has undergone a change: in old days I despised money; now I harbour an evil feeling, not towards money, but towards the rich as though they were to blame: in old days I hated violence and tyranny, but now I hate the men who make use of violence, as though they were alone to blame, and not all of us who do not know how to educate each other. What is the meaning of it? If these new ideas and new feelings have come from a change of convictions, what is that change due to? Can the world have grown worse and I better, or was I blind before and indifferent? If this change is the result of a general decline of physical and intellectual powers – I am ill, you know, and every day I am losing weight – my position is pitiable; it means that my new ideas are morbid and abnormal; I ought to be ashamed of them and think them of no consequence. . . ."

"Illness has nothing to do with it," Katya interrupts me; "it's simply that your eyes are opened, that's all. You have seen what in old days, for some reason, you refused to see. To my thinking, what you ought to do first of all, is to break with your family for good, and go away."

"You are talking nonsense."

"You don't love them; why should you force your feelings? Can you call them a family? Nonentities! If they died today, no one would notice their absence tomorrow."

Katya despises my wife and Liza as much as they hate her. One can hardly talk at this date of people's having a right to despise one another. But if one looks at it from Katya's standpoint and recognizes such a right, one can see she has as much right to despise my wife and Liza as they have to hate her.

"Nonentities," she goes on. "Have you had dinner today? How was it they did not forget to tell you it was ready? How is it they still remember your existence?"

"Katya," I say sternly, "I beg you to be silent."

"You think I enjoy talking about them? I should be glad not to know them at all. Listen, my dear: give it all up and go away. Go abroad. The sooner the better."

"What nonsense! What about the University?"

"The University, too. What is it to you? There's no sense in it, anyway. You have been lecturing for thirty years, and where are your pupils? Are many of them celebrated scientific men? Count them up! And to multiply the doctors who exploit ignorance and pile up hundreds of thousands for themselves, there is no need to be a good and talented man. You are not wanted."

"Good heavens! how harsh you are!" I cry in horror. "How harsh you are! Be quiet or I will go away! I don't know how to answer the harsh things you say!"

The maid comes in and summons us to tea. At the samovar our conversation, thank God, changes. After having had my grumble out, I have a longing to give way to another weakness of old age, reminiscences. I tell Katya about my past, and to my great astonishment tell her incidents which, till then, I did not suspect of being still preserved in my memory, and she listens to me with tenderness, with pride, holding her breath. I am particularly fond of telling her how I was educated in a seminary and dreamed of going to the University.

"At times I used to walk about our seminary garden . . ." I would tell her. "If from some far-away tavern the wind floated sounds of a song and the squeaking of an accordion, or a sledge with bells dashed by the garden-fence, it was quite enough to send a rush of happiness, filling not only my heart, but even my stomach, my legs, my arms. . . . I would listen to the accordion or the bells dying away in the distance and imagine myself a doctor, and paint pictures, one better than another. And here, as you see, my dreams have come true. I have had more than I dared to dream of. For thirty years I have been the favourite professor, I have had splendid comrades, I have enjoyed fame and honour. I have loved, married from passionate love, have had children. In fact, looking back upon it, I see my whole life as a fine composition arranged with talent. Now all that is left to me is not to spoil the end. For that I must die like a man. If death is really a thing to dread, I must meet it as a teacher, a man of science, and a citizen of a Christian country ought to meet it, with courage and untroubled soul. But I am spoiling the end; I am sinking, I fly to you, I beg for help, and you tell me 'Sink; that is what you ought to do.'"

But here there comes a ring at the front-door. Katya and I recognize it, and say:

"It must be Mihail Fyodorovitch."

And a minute later my colleague, the philologist Mihail Fyodorovitch, a tall, well-built man of fifty, clean-shaven, with thick grey hair and black eyebrows, walks in. He is a good-natured man and an excellent comrade. He comes of a fortunate and talented old noble family which has played a prominent part in the history of literature and enlightenment. He is himself intelligent, talented, and very highly educated, but has his oddities. To a certain extent we are all odd and all queer fish, but in his oddities there is something exceptional, apt to cause anxiety among his acquaintances. I know a good many people for whom his oddities completely obscure his good qualities.

Coming in to us, he slowly takes off his gloves and says in his velvety bass:

"Good evening. Are you having tea? That's just right. It's diabolically cold."

Then he sits down to the table, takes a glass, and at once begins talking. What is most characteristic in his manner of talking is the continually jesting tone, a sort of mixture of philosophy and drollery as in Shakespeare's gravediggers. He is always talking about serious things, but he never speaks seriously. His judgments are always harsh and railing, but, thanks to his soft, even, jesting tone, the harshness and abuse do not jar upon the ear, and one soon grows used to them. Every evening he brings with him five or six anecdotes from the University, and he usually begins with them when he sits down to table.

"Oh, Lord!" he sighs, twitching his black eyebrows ironically. "What comic people there are in the world!"

"Well?" asks Katya.

"As I was coming from my lecture this morning I met that old idiot N. N— on the stairs. . . . He was going along as usual, sticking out his chin like a horse, looking for someone to listen to his grumblings at his migraine, at his wife, and his students who won't attend his lectures. 'Oh,' I thought, 'he has seen me – I am done for now; it is all up. . . .'"

And so on in the same style. Or he will begin like this:

"I was yesterday at our friend Z. Z—'s public lecture. I wonder how it is our alma mater – don't speak of it after dark – dare display in public such noodles and patent dullards as that Z. Z—. Why, he is a European fool! Upon my word, you could not find another like him all over Europe! He lectures – can you imagine? – as though he were sucking a sugar-stick – sue,

sue, sue; . . . he is in a nervous funk; he can hardly decipher his own manuscript; his poor little thoughts crawl along like a bishop on a bicycle, and, what's worse, you can never make out what he is trying to say. The deadly dullness is awful, the very flies expire. It can only be compared with the boredom in the assembly-hall at the yearly meeting when the traditional address is read – damn it!"

And at once an abrupt transition:

"Three years ago – Nikolay Stepanovitch here will remember it – I had to deliver that address. It was hot, stifling, my uniform cut me under the arms – it was deadly! I read for half an hour, for an hour, for an hour and a half, for two hours. . . . 'Come,' I thought; 'thank God, there are only ten pages left!' And at the end there were four pages that there was no need to read, and I reckoned to leave them out. 'So there are only six really,' I thought; 'that is, only six pages left to read.' But, only fancy, I chanced to glance before me, and, sitting in the front row, side by side, were a general with a ribbon on his breast and a bishop. The poor beggars were numb with boredom; they were staring with their eyes wide open to keep awake, and yet they were trying to put on an expression of attention and to pretend that they understood what I was saying and liked it. 'Well,' I thought, 'since you like it you shall have it! I'll pay you out;' so I just gave them those four pages too."

As is usual with ironical people, when he talks nothing in his face smiles but his eyes and eyebrows. At such times there is no trace of hatred or spite in his eyes, but a great deal of humour, and that peculiar fox-like slyness which is only to be noticed in very observant people. Since I am speaking about his eyes, I notice another peculiarity in them. When he takes a glass from Katya, or listens to her speaking, or looks after her as she goes out of the room for a moment, I notice in his eyes something gentle, beseeching, pure. . . .

The maid-servant takes away the samovar and puts on the table a large piece of cheese, some fruit, and a bottle of Crimean champagne – a rather poor wine of which Katya had grown fond in the Crimea. Mihail Fyodorovitch takes two packs of cards off the whatnot and begins to play patience. According to him, some varieties of patience require great concentration and attention, yet while he lays out the cards he does not leave off distracting his attention with talk. Katya watches his cards attentively, and more by gesture than by words helps him in his play. She drinks no more than a couple of wine-glasses of wine the whole evening; I drink four glasses, and the rest of the bottle falls to the share of Mihail Fyodorovitch, who can drink a great deal and never get drunk.

Over our patience we settle various questions, principally of the higher order, and what we care for most of all – that is, science and learning – is more roughly handled than anything.

"Science, thank God, has outlived its day," says Mihail Fyodorovitch emphatically. "Its song is sung. Yes, indeed. Mankind begins to feel impelled to replace it by something different. It has grown on the soil of superstition, been nourished by superstition, and is now just as much the quintessence of superstition as its defunct granddames, alchemy, metaphysics, and philosophy. And, after all, what has it given to mankind? Why, the difference between the learned Europeans and the Chinese who have no science is trifling, purely external. The Chinese know nothing of science, but what have they lost thereby?"

"Flies know nothing of science, either," I observe, "but what of that?"

"There is no need to be angry, Nikolay Stepanovitch. I only say this here between ourselves . . . I am more careful than you think, and I am not going to say this in public — God forbid! The superstition exists in the multitude that the arts and sciences are superior to agriculture, commerce, superior to handicrafts. Our sect is maintained by that superstition, and it is not for you and me to destroy it. God forbid!"

After patience the younger generation comes in for a dressing too.

"Our audiences have degenerated," sighs Mihail Fyodorovitch. "Not to speak of ideals and all the rest of it, if only they were capable of work and rational thought! In fact, it's a case of 'I look with mournful eyes on the young men of today'."

"Yes; they have degenerated horribly," Katya agrees. "Tell me, have you had one man of distinction among them for the last five or ten years?"

"I don't know how it is with the other professors, but I can't remember any among mine."

"I have seen in my day many of your students and young scientific men and many actors — well, I have never once been so fortunate as to meet — I won't say a hero or a man of talent, but even an interesting man. It's all the same grey mediocrity, puffed up with self-conceit."

All this talk of degeneration always affects me as though I had accidentally overheard offensive talk about my own daughter. It offends me that these charges are wholesale, and rest on such worn-out commonplaces, on such wordy vapourings as degeneration and absence of ideals, or on references to the splendours of the past. Every accusation, even if it is uttered in ladies' society, ought to be formulated with all possible definiteness, or it is not an accusation, but idle disparagement, unworthy of decent people.

I am an old man, I have been lecturing for thirty years, but I notice neither degeneration nor lack of ideals, and I don't find that the present is worse than the past. My porter Nikolay, whose experience of this subject has its value, says that the students of today are neither better nor worse than those of the past.

If I were asked what I don't like in my pupils of today, I should answer the question, not straight off and not at length, but with sufficient definiteness. I know their failings, and so have no need to resort to vague generalities. I don't like their smoking, using spirituous beverages, marrying late, and often being so irresponsible and careless that they will let one of their number be starving in their midst while they neglect to pay their subscriptions to the Students' Aid Society. They don't know modern languages, and they don't express themselves correctly in Russian; no longer ago than yesterday my colleague, the professor of hygiene, complained to me that he had to give twice as many lectures, because the students had a very poor knowledge of physics and were utterly ignorant of meteorology. They are readily carried away by the influence of the last new writers, even when they are not first-rate, but they take absolutely no interest in classics such as Shakespeare, Marcus Aurelius, Epictetus, or Pascal, and this inability to distinguish the great from the small betrays their ignorance of practical life more than anything. All difficult questions that have more or less a social character (for instance the migration question) they settle by studying monographs on the subject, but not by way of scientific investigation or experiment, though that method is at their disposal and is more in keeping with their calling. They gladly become ward-surgeons, assistants, demonstrators, external teachers, and are ready to fill such posts until they are forty, though independence, a sense of freedom and personal initiative, are no less necessary in science than, for instance, in art or commerce. I have pupils and listeners, but no successors and helpers, and so I love them and am touched by them, but am not proud of them. And so on, and so on. . . .

Such shortcomings, however numerous they may be, can

only give rise to a pessimistic or fault-finding temper in a faint-hearted and timid man. All these failings have a casual, transitory character, and are completely dependent on conditions of life; in some ten years they will have disappeared or given place to other fresh defects, which are all inevitable and will in their turn alarm the faint-hearted. The students' sins often vex me, but that vexation is nothing in comparison with the joy I have been experiencing now for the last thirty years when I talk to my pupils, lecture to them, watch their relations, and compare them with people not of their circle.

Mihail Fyodorovitch speaks evil of everything. Katya listens, and neither of them notices into what depths the apparently innocent diversion of finding fault with their neighbours is gradually drawing them. They are not conscious how by degrees simple talk passes into malicious mockery and jeering, and how they are both beginning to drop into the habits and methods of slander.

"Killing types one meets with," says Mihail Fyodorovitch. "I went yesterday to our friend Yegor Petrovitch's, and there I found a studious gentleman, one of your medicals in his third year, I believe. Such a face! . . . in the Dobrolubov style, the imprint of profound thought on his brow; we got into talk. 'Such doings, young man,' said I. 'I've read,' said I, 'that some German — I've forgotten his name — has created from the human brain a new kind of alkaloid, idiotine.' What do you think? He believed it, and there was positively an expression of respect on his face, as though to say, 'See what we fellows can do!'

And the other day I went to the theatre. I took my seat. In the next row directly in front of me were sitting two men: one of 'us fellows' and apparently a law student, the other a shaggy-looking figure, a medical student. The latter was as drunk as a cobbler. He did not look at the stage at all. He was dozing with his nose on his shirt-front. But as soon as an actor begins loudly reciting a monologue, or simply raises his voice, our friend starts, pokes his neighbour in the ribs, and asks, 'What is he saying? Is it elevating?' 'Yes,' answers one of our fellows. 'B-r-r-ravo!' roars the medical student. 'Elevating! Bravo!' He had gone to the theatre, you see, the drunken blockhead, not for the sake of art, the play, but for elevation! He wanted noble sentiments."

Katya listens and laughs. She has a strange laugh; she catches her breath in rhythmically regular gasps, very much as though she were playing the accordion, and nothing in her face is laughing but her nostrils. I grow depressed and don't know what to say. Beside myself, I fire up, leap up from my seat, and cry:

"Do leave off! Why are you sitting here like two toads, poisoning the air with your breath? Give over!"

And without waiting for them to finish their gossip I prepare to go home. And, indeed, it is high time: it is past ten.

"I will stay a little longer," says Mihail Fyodorovitch. "Will you allow me, Ekaterina Vladimirovna?"

"I will," answers Katya.

"*Bene!* In that case have up another little bottle."

They both accompany me with candles to the hall, and while I put on my fur coat, Mihail Fyodorovitch says:

"You have grown dreadfully thin and older looking, Nikolay Stepanovitch. What's the matter with you? Are you ill?"

"Yes; I am not very well."

"And you are not doing anything for it . . ." Katya puts in grimly.

"Why don't you? You can't go on like that! God helps those who help themselves, my dear fellow. Remember me to your wife and daughter, and make my apologies for not having been to see them. In a day or two, before I go abroad, I shall come to say goodbye. I shall be sure to. I am going away next week."

I come away from Katya, irritated and alarmed by what has been said about my being ill, and dissatisfied with myself. I ask myself whether I really ought not to consult one of my colleagues. And at once I imagine how my colleague, after listening to me, would walk away to the window without speaking, would think a moment, then would turn round to me and, trying to prevent my reading the truth in his face, would say in a careless tone: "So far I see nothing serious, but at the same time, *collega*, I advise you to lay aside your work. . . ." And that would deprive me of my last hope.

Who is without hope? Now that I am diagnosing my illness and prescribing for myself, from time to time I hope that I am deceived by my own illness, that I am mistaken in regard to the albumen and the sugar I find, and in regard to my heart, and in regard to the swellings I have twice noticed in the mornings; when with the fervour of the hypochondriac I look through the textbooks of therapeutics and take a different medicine every day, I keep fancying that I shall hit upon something comforting. All that is petty.

Whether the sky is covered with clouds or the moon and the stars are shining, I turn my eyes towards it every evening and think that death is taking me soon. One would think that my thoughts at such times ought to be deep as the sky, brilliant, striking. . . . But no! I think about myself, about my wife, about Liza, Gnekker, the students, people in general; my thoughts are evil, petty, I am insincere with myself, and at such times my theory of life may be expressed in the words the celebrated Araktcheev said in one of his intimate letters: "Nothing good can exist in the world without evil, and there is more evil than good." That is, everything is disgusting; there is nothing to live for, and the sixty-two years I have already lived must be reckoned as wasted. I catch myself in these thoughts, and try to persuade myself that they are accidental, temporary, and not deeply rooted in me, but at once I think:

"If so, what drives me every evening to those two toads?"

And I vow to myself that I will never go to Katya's again, though I know I shall go next evening.

Ringing the bell at the door and going upstairs, I feel that I have no family now and no desire to bring it back again. It is clear that the new Araktcheev thoughts are not casual, temporary visitors, but have possession of my whole being. With my conscience ill at ease, dejected, languid, hardly able to move my limbs, feeling as though tons were added to my weight, I get into bed and quickly drop asleep.

And then — insomnia!

IV

Summer comes on and life is changed.

One fine morning Liza comes in to me and says in a jesting tone:

"Come, your Excellency! We are ready."

My Excellency is conducted into the street, and seated in a cab. As I go along, having nothing to do, I read the signboards from right to left. The word "Traktir" reads "Ritkart"; that would just suit some baron's family: Baroness Ritkart. Farther on I drive through fields, by the graveyard, which makes absolutely no impression on me, though I shall soon lie in it; then I drive by forests and again by fields. There is nothing of interest. After two hours of driving, my Excellency is conducted into the lower storey of a summer villa and installed in a small, very cheerful little room with light blue hangings.

At night there is sleeplessness as before, but in the morning I do not put a good face upon it and listen to my wife, but lie in bed. I do not sleep, but lie in the drowsy, half-conscious condition in which you know you are not asleep, but dreaming. At midday I get up and from habit sit down at my table, but I do not work now; I amuse myself with French books in yellow covers, sent me by Katya. Of course, it would be more patriotic to read Russian authors, but I must confess I cherish no particular liking for them. With the exception of two or three of the older writers, all our literature of today strikes me as not being literature, but a special sort of home industry, which exists simply in order to be encouraged, though people do not readily make use of its products. The very best of these home products cannot be called remarkable and cannot be sincerely praised without qualification. I must say the same of all the literary novelties I have read during the last ten or fifteen years; not one of them is remarkable, and not one of them can be praised without a "but". Cleverness, a good tone, but no talent; talent, a good tone, but no cleverness; or talent, cleverness, but not a good tone.

I don't say the French books have talent, cleverness, and a good tone. They don't satisfy me, either. But they are not so tedious as the Russian, and it is not unusual to find in them the chief element of artistic creation – the feeling of personal freedom which is lacking in the Russian authors. I don't remember one new book in which the author does not try from the first page to entangle himself in all sorts of conditions and contracts with his conscience. One is afraid to speak of the naked body; another ties himself up hand and foot in psychological analysis; a third must have a "warm attitude to man"; a fourth purposely scrawls whole descriptions of nature that he may not be suspected of writing with a purpose. . . . One is bent upon being middle-class in his work, another must be a nobleman, and so on. There is intentionalness, circumspection, and self-will, but they have neither the independence nor the manliness to write as they like, and therefore there is no creativeness.

All this applies to what is called belles-lettres.

As for serious treatises in Russian on sociology, for instance, on art, and so on, I do not read them simply from timidity. In my childhood and early youth I had for some reason a terror of doorkeepers and attendants at the theatre, and that terror has remained with me to this day. I am afraid of them even now. It is said that we are only afraid of what we do not understand. And, indeed, it is very difficult to understand why doorkeepers and theatre attendants are so dignified, haughty, and majestically rude. I feel exactly the same terror when I read serious articles. Their extraordinary dignity, their bantering lordly tone, their familiar manner to foreign authors, their ability to split straws with dignity — all that is beyond my understanding; it is intimidating and utterly unlike the quiet, gentlemanly tone to which I am accustomed when I read the works of our medical and scientific writers. It oppresses me to read not only the articles written by serious Russians, but even works translated or edited by them. The pretentious, edifying tone of the preface; the redundancy of remarks made by the translator, which prevent me from concentrating my attention; the question marks and "sic" in parenthesis scattered all over the book or article by the liberal translator, are to my mind an outrage on the author and on my independence as a reader.

Once I was summoned as an expert to a circuit court; in an interval one of my fellow-experts drew my attention to the rudeness of the public prosecutor to the defendants, among whom there were two ladies of good education. I believe I did not exaggerate at all when I told him that the prosecutor's manner was no ruder than that of the authors of serious articles to one another. Their manners are, indeed, so rude that I cannot speak of them without distaste. They treat one another and the writers they criticize either with superfluous respect, at the sacrifice of their own dignity, or, on the contrary, with far more ruthlessness than I have shown in my notes and my thoughts in regard to my future son-in-law Gnekker. Accusations of irrationality, of evil intentions, and, indeed, of every sort of crime, form an habitual ornament of serious articles. And that, as young medical men are fond of saying in their monographs, is the *ultima ratio*! Such ways must infallibly have an effect on the morals of the younger generation of writers, and so I am not at all surprised that in the new works with which our literature has been enriched during the last ten or fifteen years the heroes drink too much vodka and the heroines are not over-chaste.

I read French books, and I look out of the window which is open; I can see the spikes of my garden-fence, two or three scraggy trees, and beyond the fence the road, the fields, and beyond them a broad stretch of pine-wood. Often I admire a boy and girl, both flaxen-headed and ragged, who clamber on the fence and laugh at my baldness. In their shining little eyes I read, "Go up, go up, thou baldhead!" They are almost the only people who care nothing for my celebrity or my rank.

Visitors do not come to me every day now. I will only mention the visits of Nikolay and Pyotr Ignatyevitch. Nikolay usually comes to me on holidays, with some pretext of business, though really to see me. He arrives very much exhilarated, a thing which never occurs to him in the winter.

"What have you to tell me?" I ask, going out to him in the hall.

"Your Excellency!" he says, pressing his hand to his heart and looking at me with the ecstasy of a lover – "your Excellency! God be my witness! Strike me dead on the spot! *Gaudeamus egitur juventus!*"

And he greedily kisses me on the shoulder, on the sleeve, and on the buttons.

"Is everything going well?" I ask him.

"Your Excellency! So help me God! . . ."

He persists in grovelling before me for no sort of reason, and soon bores me, so I send him away to the kitchen, where they give him dinner.

Pyotr Ignatyevitch comes to see me on holidays, too, with the special object of seeing me and sharing his thoughts with me. He usually sits down near my table, modest, neat, and reasonable, and does not venture to cross his legs or put his elbows on the table. All the time, in a soft, even, little voice, in rounded bookish phrases, he tells me various, to his mind, very interesting and piquant items of news which he has read in the magazines and journals. They are all alike and may be reduced to this type: "A Frenchman has made a discovery; someone else, a German, has denounced him, proving that the discovery was made in 1870 by some American; while a third person, also a German, trumps them both by proving they both had made fools of themselves, mistaking bubbles of air for dark pigment under the microscope. Even when he wants to amuse me, Pyotr Ignatyevitch tells me things in the same lengthy, circumstantial manner as though he were defending a thesis, enumerating in detail the literary sources from which he is deriving his narrative, doing his utmost to be accurate as to the date and number of the journals and the name of everyone concerned, invariably mentioning it in full – Jean Jacques Petit, never simply Petit. Sometimes he stays to dinner with us, and then during the whole of dinner-time he goes on telling me the same sort of piquant anecdotes, reducing everyone at table to a state of dejected boredom. If Gnekker and Liza begin talking before him of fugues and counterpoint, Brahms and Bach, he drops his eyes modestly, and is overcome with embarrassment; he is ashamed that such trivial subjects should be discussed before such serious people as him and me.

In my present state of mind five minutes of him is enough to sicken me as though I had been seeing and hearing him for an eternity. I hate the poor fellow. His soft, smooth voice and bookish language exhaust me, and his stories stupefy me. . . . He cherishes the best of feelings for me, and talks to me simply in order to give me pleasure, and I repay him by looking at him as though I wanted to hypnotize him, and think, "Go, go, go! . . ." But he is not amenable to thought-suggestion, and sits on and on and on. . . .

While he is with me I can never shake off the thought, "It's possible when I die he will be appointed to succeed me," and my poor lecture-hall presents itself to me as an oasis in which the spring is died up; and I am ungracious, silent, and surly with Pyotr Ignatyevitch, as though he were to blame for such thoughts, and not I myself. When he begins, as usual, praising up the German savants, instead of making fun of him good-humouredly, as I used to do, I mutter sullenly:

"Asses, your Germans! . . ."

That is like the late Professor Nikita Krylov, who once, when he was bathing with Pirogov at Revel and vexed at the water's being very cold, burst out with, "Scoundrels, these Germans!" I behave badly with Pyotr Ignatyevitch, and only when he is going away, and from the window I catch a glimpse of his grey hat behind the garden-fence, I want to call out and say, "Forgive me, my dear fellow!"

Dinner is even drearier than in the winter. Gnekker, whom now I hate and despise, dines with us almost every day. I used to endure his presence in silence, now I aim biting remarks at him which make my wife and daughter blush. Carried away by evil feeling, I often say things that are simply stupid, and I don't know why I say them. So on one occasion it happened that I stared a long time at Gnekker, and, *à propos* of nothing, I fired off:

"An eagle may perchance swoop down below a cock,

But never will the fowl soar upwards to the clouds. . . ."

And the most vexatious thing is that the fowl Gnekker shows himself much cleverer than the eagle professor. Knowing that my wife and daughter are on his side, he takes up the line of meeting my gibes with condescending silence, as though to say:

"The old chap is in his dotage; what's the use of talking to him?"

Or he makes fun of me good-naturedly. It is wonderful how petty a man may become! I am capable of dreaming all dinner-time of how Gnekker will turn out to be an adventurer, how my wife and Liza will come to see their mistake, and how I will taunt them — and such absurd thoughts at the time when I am standing with one foot in the grave!

There are now, too, misunderstandings of which in the old days I had no idea except from hearsay. Though I am ashamed of it, I will describe one that occurred the other day after dinner.

I was sitting in my room smoking a pipe; my wife came in as usual, sat down, and began saying what a good thing it would be for me to go to Harkov now while it is warm and I have free time, and there find out what sort of person our Gnekker is.

"Very good; I will go," I assented.

My wife, pleased with me, got up and was going to the door, but turned back and said:

"By the way, I have another favour to ask of you. I know you will be angry, but it is my duty to warn you. . . . Forgive my saying it, Nikolay Stepanovitch, but all our neighbours and acquaintances have begun talking about your being so often at Katya's. She is clever and well-educated; I don't deny that her company may be agreeable; but at your age and with your social position it seems strange that you should find pleasure in her society. . . . Besides, she has such a reputation that . . ."

All the blood suddenly rushed to my brain, my eyes flashed fire, I leaped up and, clutching at my head and stamping my feet, shouted in a voice unlike my own:

"Let me alone! let me alone! let me alone!"

Probably my face was terrible, my voice was strange, for my wife suddenly turned pale and began shrieking aloud in a despairing voice that was utterly unlike her own. Liza, Gnekker, then Yegor, came running in at our shouts. . . .

"Let me alone!" I cried; "let me alone! Go away!"

My legs turned numb as though they had ceased to exist; I felt myself falling into someone's arms; for a little while I still heard weeping, then sank into a swoon which lasted two or three hours.

Now about Katya; she comes to see me every day towards evening, and of course neither the neighbours nor our acquaintances can avoid noticing it. She comes in for a minute and carries me off for a drive with her. She has her own horse and a new chaise bought this summer. Altogether she lives in an expensive style; she has taken a big detached villa with a large garden, and has taken all her town retinue with her – two maids, a coachman . . . I often ask her:

"Katya, what will you live on when you have spent your father's money?"

"Then we shall see," she answers.

"That money, my dear, deserves to be treated more seriously. It was earned by a good man, by honest labour."

"You have told me that already. I know it."

At first we drive through the open country, then through the pine-wood which is visible from my window. Nature seems to me as beautiful as it always has been, though some evil spirit whispers to me that these pines and fir-trees, birds, and white clouds on the sky, will not notice my absence when in three or four months I am dead. Katya loves driving, and she is pleased that it is fine weather and that I am sitting beside her. She is in good spirits and does not say harsh things.

"You are a very good man, Nikolay Stepanovitch," she says. "You are a rare specimen, and there isn't an actor who would understand how to play you. Me or Mihail Fyodorovitch, for instance, any poor actor could do, but not you. And I envy you, I envy you horribly! Do you know what I stand for? What?"

She ponders for a minute, and then asks me:

"Nikolay Stepanovitch, I am a negative phenomenon! Yes?"

"Yes," I answer.

"H'm! what am I to do?"

What answer was I to make her? It is easy to say "work", or "give your possessions to the poor", or "know yourself", and because it is so easy to say that, I don't know what to answer.

My colleagues when they teach therapeutics advise "the individual study of each separate case". One has but to obey this advice to gain the conviction that the methods recommended in the textbooks as the best and as providing a safe basis for treatment turn out to be quite unsuitable in individual cases. It is just the same in moral ailments.

But I must make some answer, and I say:

"You have too much free time, my dear; you absolutely must take up some occupation. After all, why shouldn't you be an actress again if it is your vocation?"

"I cannot!"

"Your tone and manner suggest that you are a victim. I don't like that, my dear; it is your own fault. Remember, you began with falling out with people and methods, but you have done nothing to make either better. You did not struggle with evil, but were cast down by it, and you are not the victim of the struggle, but of your own impotence. Well, of course you were young and inexperienced then; now it may all be different. Yes, really, go on the stage. You will work, you will serve a sacred art."

"Don't pretend, Nikolay Stepanovitch," Katya interrupts me. "Let us make a compact once for all; we will talk about

234

actors, actresses, and authors, but we will let art alone. You are a splendid and rare person, but you don't know enough about art sincerely to think it sacred. You have no instinct or feeling for art. You have been hard at work all your life, and have not had time to acquire that feeling. Altogether . . . I don't like talk about art," she goes on nervously. "I don't like it! And, my goodness, how they have vulgarized it!"

"Who has vulgarized it?"

"They have vulgarized it by drunkenness, the newspapers by their familiar attitude, clever people by philosophy."

"Philosophy has nothing to do with it."

"Yes, it has. If anyone philosophizes about it, it shows he does not understand it."

To avoid bitterness I hasten to change the subject, and then sit a long time silent. Only when we are driving out of the wood and turning towards Katya's villa I go back to my former question, and say:

"You have still not answered me, why you don't want to go on the stage."

"Nikolay Stepanovitch, this is cruel!" she cries, and suddenly flushes all over. "You want me to tell you the truth aloud? Very well, if . . . if you like it! I have no talent! No talent and . . . and a great deal of vanity! So there!"

After making this confession she turns her face away from me, and to hide the trembling of her hands tugs violently at the reins.

As we are driving towards her villa we see Mihail Fyodoro-vitch walking near the gate, impatiently awaiting us.

"That Mihail Fyodorovitch again!" says Katya with vex-ation. "Do rid me of him, please! I am sick and tired of him . . . bother him!"

Mihail Fyodorovitch ought to have gone abroad long ago, but he puts off going from week to week. Of late there have been certain changes in him. He looks, as it were, sunken, has taken to drinking until he is tipsy, a thing which never used to happen to him, and his black eyebrows are beginning to turn grey. When our chaise stops at the gate he does not conceal his joy and his impatience. He fussily helps me and Katya out, hurriedly asks questions, laughs, rubs his hands, and that gentle, imploring, pure expression, which I used to notice only in his eyes, is now suffused all over his face. He is glad and at the same time he is ashamed of his gladness, ashamed of his habit of spending every evening with Katya. And he thinks it necessary to explain his visit by some obvious absurdity such as: "I was driving by, and I thought I would just look in for a minute."

We all three go indoors; first we drink tea, then the familiar packs of cards, the big piece of cheese, the fruit, and the bottle of Crimean champagne are put upon the table. The subjects of our conversation are not new; they are just the same as in the winter. We fall foul of the University, the students, and liter-ature and the theatre; the air grows thick and stifling with evil speaking, and poisoned by the breath, not of two toads as in the winter, but of three. Besides the velvety baritone laugh and the giggle like the gasp of a concertina, the maid who waits upon us hears an unpleasant cracked "He, he!" like the chuckle of a general in a vaudeville.

V

There are terrible nights with thunder, lightning, rain, and wind, such as are called among the people "sparrow nights". There has been one such night in my personal life.

I woke up after midnight and leaped suddenly out of bed. It seemed to me for some reason that I was just immediately going to die. Why did it seem so? I had no sensation in my body that suggested my immediate death, but my soul was oppressed with terror, as though I had suddenly seen a vast menacing glow of fire.

I rapidly struck a light, drank some water straight out of the decanter, then hurried to the open window. The weather outside was magnificent. There was a smell of hay and some other very sweet scent. I could see the spikes of the fence, the gaunt, drowsy trees by the window, the road, the dark streak of woodland, there was a serene, very bright moon in the sky and not a single cloud, perfect stillness, not one leaf stirring. I felt that everything was looking at me and waiting for me to die. . . .

It was uncanny. I closed the window and ran to my bed. I

felt for my pulse, and not finding it in my wrist, tried to find it in my temple, then in my chin, and again in my wrist, and everything I touched was cold and clammy with sweat. My breathing came more and more rapidly, my body was shivering, all my inside was in commotion; I had a sensation on my face and on my bald head as though they were covered with spiders' webs.

What should I do? Call my family? No; it would be no use. I could not imagine what my wife and Liza would do when they came in to me.

I hid my head under the pillow, closed my eyes, and waited and waited. . . . My spine was cold; it seemed to be drawn inwards, and I felt as though death were coming upon me stealthily from behind . . . .

"Kee-vee! kee-vee!" I heard a sudden shriek in the night's stillness, and did not know where it was — in my breast or in the street — "Kee-vee! kee-vee!"

"My God, how terrible!" I would have drunk some more water, but by then it was fearful to open my eyes and I was afraid to raise my head. I was possessed by unaccountable animal terror, and I cannot understand why I was so frightened: was it that I wanted to live, or that some new unknown pain was in store for me?

Upstairs, overhead, someone moaned or laughed. I listened. Soon afterwards there was a sound of footsteps on the stairs. Someone came hurriedly down, then went up again. A minute later there was a sound of steps downstairs again; someone stopped near my door and listened.

"Who is there?" I cried.

The door opened. I boldly opened my eyes, and saw my wife. Her face was pale and her eyes were tear-stained.

"You are not asleep, Nikolay Stepanovitch?" she asked.

"What is it?"

"For God's sake, go up and have a look at Liza; there is something the matter with her. . . ."

"Very good, with pleasure," I muttered, greatly relieved at not being alone. "Very good, this minute. . . ."

I followed my wife, heard what she said to me, and was too agitated to understand a word. Patches of light from her candle danced about the stairs, our long shadows trembled. My feet caught in the skirts of my dressing-gown; I gasped for breath, and felt as though something were pursuing me and trying to catch me from behind.

"I shall die on the spot, here on the staircase," I thought. "On the spot. . . ." But we passed the staircase, the dark corridor with the Italian windows, and went into Liza's room. She was sitting on the bed in her nightdress, with her bare feet hanging down, and she was moaning.

"Oh, my God! Oh, my God!" she was muttering, screwing up her eyes at our candle. "I can't bear it."

"Liza, my child," I said, "what is it?"

Seeing me, she began crying out, and flung herself on my neck.

"My kind papa! . . ." she sobbed – "my dear, good papa . . . my darling, my pet, I don't know what is the matter with me. . . . I am miserable!"

She hugged me, kissed me, and babbled fond words I used to hear from her when she was a child.

"Calm yourself, my child. God be with you," I said. "There is no need to cry. I am miserable, too."

I tried to tuck her in; my wife gave her water, and we awkwardly stumbled by her bedside; my shoulder jostled against her shoulder, and meanwhile I was thinking how we used to give our children their bath together.

"Help her! help her!" my wife implored me. "Do something!"

What could I do? I could do nothing. There was some load on the girl's heart; but I did not understand, I knew nothing about it, and could only mutter:

"It's nothing, it's nothing; it will pass. Sleep, sleep!"

To make things worse, there was a sudden sound of dogs howling, at first subdued and uncertain, then loud, two dogs howling together. I had never attached significance to such omens as the howling of dogs or the shrieking of owls, but on that occasion it sent a pang to my heart, and I hastened to explain the howl to myself.

"It's nonsense," I thought, "the influence of one organism on another. The intensely strained condition of my nerves has infected my wife, Liza, the dog – that is all. . . . Such infection explains presentiments, forebodings. . . ."

When a little later I went back to my room to write a prescription for Liza, I no longer thought I should die at once, but only had such a weight, such a feeling of oppression in my soul that I felt actually sorry that I had not died on the spot. For a long time I stood motionless in the middle of the room, pondering what to prescribe for Liza. But the moans overhead ceased, and I decided to prescribe nothing, and yet I went on standing there. . . .

There was a deathlike stillness, such a stillness, as some author has expressed it, "it rang in one's ears". Time passed slowly; the streaks of moonlight on the window-sill did not shift their position, but seemed as though frozen. . . . It was still some time before dawn.

But the gate in the fence creaked, someone stole in and, breaking a twig from one of those scraggy trees, cautiously tapped on the window with it.

"Nikolay Stepanovitch," I heard a whisper. "Nikolay Stepanovitch."

I opened the window, and fancied I was dreaming: under the window, huddled against the wall, stood a woman in a black dress, with the moonlight bright upon her, looking at me with great eyes. Her face was pale, stern, and weird-looking in the moonlight, like marble, her chin was quivering.

"It is I," she said — "I . . . Katya."

In the moonlight all women's eyes look big and black, all people look taller and paler, and that was probably why I had not recognized her for the first minute.

"What is it?"

"Forgive me!" she said. "I suddenly felt unbearably miserable . . . I couldn't stand it, so came here. There was a light in your window and . . . and I ventured to knock. . . . I beg your pardon. Ah! if you knew how miserable I am! What are you doing just now?"

"Nothing. . . . I can't sleep."

"I had a feeling that there was something wrong, but that is nonsense."

Her brows were lifted, her eyes shone with tears, and her whole face was lighted up with the familiar look of trustfulness which I had not seen for so long.

"Nikolay Stepanovitch," she said imploringly, stretching out both hands to me, "my precious friend, I beg you, I implore you. . . . If you don't despise my affection and respect for you, consent to what I ask of you."

"What is it?"

"Take my money from me!"

"Come! what an idea! What do I want with your money?"

"You'll go away somewhere for your health. . . . You ought to go for your health. Will you take it? Yes? Nikolay Stepanovitch darling, yes?"

She looked greedily into my face and repeated: "Yes, you will take it?"

"No, my dear, I won't take it . . ." I said. "Thank you."

She turned her back upon me and bowed her head. Probably

I refused her in a tone which made further conversation about money impossible.

"Go home to bed," I said. "We will see each other tomorrow."

"So you don't consider me your friend?" she asked dejectedly.

"I don't say that. But your money would be no use to me now."

"I beg your pardon . . ." she said, dropping her voice a whole octave. "I understand you . . . to be indebted to a person like me . . . a retired actress. . . . But, goodbye. . . ."

And she went away so quickly that I had not time even to say goodbye.

VI

I am in Harkov.

As it would be useless to contend against my present mood and, indeed, beyond my power, I have made up my mind that the last days of my life shall at least be irreproachable externally. If I am unjust in regard to my wife and daughter, which I fully recognize, I will try and do as she wishes; since she wants me to go to Harkov, I go to Harkov. Besides, I have become of late so indifferent to everything that it is really all the same to me where I go, to Harkov, or to Paris, or to Berditchev.

I arrived here at midday, and have put up at the hotel not far from the cathedral. The train was jolting, there were draughts, and now I am sitting on my bed, holding my head and expecting tic douloureux. I ought to have gone today to see some professors of my acquaintance, but I have neither strength nor inclination.

The old corridor attendant comes in and asks whether I have brought my bed-linen. I detain him for five minutes, and put several questions to him about Gnekker, on whose account I have come here. The attendant turns out to be a native of Harkov; he knows the town like the fingers of his hand, but does not remember any household of the surname of Gnekker. I question him about the estate – the same answer.

The clock in the corridor strikes one, then two, then three. . . . These last months in which I am waiting for death seem much longer than the whole of my life. And I have never before been so ready to resign myself to the slowness of time as now. In the old days, when one sat in the station and waited for a train, or presided in an examination-room, a quarter of an hour would seem an eternity. Now I can sit all night on my bed without moving, and quite unconcernedly reflect that tomorrow will be followed by another night as long and colourless, and the day after tomorrow.

In the corridor it strikes five, six, seven. . . . It grows dark.

There is a dull pain in my cheek, the tic beginning. To occupy myself with thoughts, I go back to my old point of view, when I was not so indifferent, and ask myself why I, a distinguished man, a privy councillor, am sitting in this little hotel room, on this bed with the unfamiliar grey quilt. Why am I looking at that cheap tin washing-stand and listening to the whirr of the wretched clock in the corridor? Is all this in keeping with my fame and my lofty position? And I answer these questions with a jeer. I am amused by the naïveté with which I used in my youth to exaggerate the value of renown and of the exceptional position which celebrities are supposed to enjoy. I am famous, my name is pronounced with reverence, my portrait has been both in the *Niva* and in the *Illustrated News of the World*; I have read my biography even in a German magazine. And what of all that? Here I am sitting utterly alone in a strange town, on a strange bed, rubbing my aching cheek with my hand. . . . Domestic worries, the hard-heartedness of creditors, the rudeness of the railway servants, the inconveniences of the passport system, the expensive and unwholesome food in the refreshment-rooms, the general rudeness and coarseness in social intercourse – all this, and a great deal more which would take too long to reckon up, affects me as much as any working man who is famous only in his alley. In what way does my exceptional position find expression? Admitting that I am celebrated a thousand times over, that I am a hero of whom my country is proud. They publish bulletins of my illness in every paper, letters of sympathy come to me by post from my colleagues, my pupils, the general public; but all that does not prevent me from dying in a strange bed, in misery, in utter loneliness. Of course, no one is to blame for that; but I in my foolishness dislike my popularity. I feel as though it had cheated me.

At ten o'clock I fall asleep, and in spite of the tic I sleep soundly, and should have gone on sleeping if I had not been awakened. Soon after one came a sudden knock at the door.

"Who is there?"

"A telegram."

"You might have waited till tomorrow," I say angrily, taking the telegram from the attendant. "Now I shall not get to sleep again."

"I am sorry. Your light was burning, so I thought you were not asleep."

I tear open the telegram and look first at the signature. From my wife.

"What does she want?"

"Gnekker was secretly married to Liza yesterday. Return."

I read the telegram, and my dismay does not last long. I am dismayed, not by what Liza and Gnekker have done, but by the indifference with which I hear of their marriage. They say philosophers and the truly wise are indifferent. It is false: indifference is the paralysis of the soul; it is premature death.

I go to bed again, and begin trying to think of something to occupy my mind. What am I to think about? I feel as though everything had been thought over already and there is nothing which could hold my attention now.

When daylight comes I sit up in bed with my arms round my knees, and to pass the time I try to know myself. "Know thyself" is excellent and useful advice; it is only a pity that the ancients never thought to indicate the means of following this precept.

When I have wanted to understand somebody or myself I have considered, not the actions, in which everything is relative, but the desires.

"Tell me what you want, and I will tell you what manner of man you are."

And now I examine myself: what do I want?

I want our wives, our children, our friends, our pupils, to love in us, not our fame, not the brand and not the label, but to love us as ordinary men. Anything else? I should like to have had helpers and successors. Anything else? I should like to wake up in a hundred years' time and to have just a peep out of one eye at what is happening in science. I should have liked to have lived another ten years . . . What further? Why, nothing further. I think and think, and can think of nothing more. And however much I might think, and however far my thoughts might travel, it is clear to me that there is nothing vital, nothing of great importance in my desires. In my passion for science, in my desire to live, in this sitting on a strange bed, and in this striving to know myself – in all the thoughts, feelings, and ideas I form about everything, there is no common bond to connect it all into one whole. Every feeling and every thought exists apart in me; and in all my criticisms of science, the theatre, literature, my pupils, and in all the pictures my imagination draws, even the most skilful analyst could not find what is called a general idea, or the god of a living man.

And if there is not that, then there is nothing.

In a state so poverty-stricken, a serious ailment, the fear of death, the influences of circumstance and men were enough to turn upside down and scatter in fragments all which I had once looked upon as my theory of life, and in which I had seen the meaning and joy of my existence. So there is nothing surprising in the fact that I have over-shadowed the last months of my life with thoughts and feelings only worthy of a slave and barbarian, and that now I am indifferent and take no heed of the dawn. When a man has not in him what is loftier and mightier than all external impressions a bad cold is really enough to upset his equilibrium and make him begin to see an owl in every bird, to hear a dog howling in every sound. And all his pessimism or optimism with his thoughts great and small have at such times significance as symptoms and nothing more.

I am vanquished. If it is so, it is useless to think, it is useless to talk. I will sit and wait in silence for what is to come.

In the morning the corridor attendant brings me tea and a copy of the local newspaper. Mechanically I read the advertisements on the first page, the leading article, the extracts from the newspapers and journals, the chronicle of events. . . . In the latter I find, among other things, the following paragraph: "Our distinguished savant, Professor Nikolay Stepanovitch So-and-so, arrived yesterday in Harkov, and is staying in the So-and-so Hotel."

Apparently, illustrious names are created to live on their own account, apart from those that bear them. Now my name is promenading tranquilly about Harkov; in another three months, printed in gold letters on my monument, it will shine bright as the sun itself, while I shall be already under the moss.

A light tap at the door. Somebody wants me.

"Who is there? Come in."

The door opens, and I step back surprised and hurriedly wrap my dressing-gown round me. Before me stands Katya.

"How do you do?" she says, breathless with running upstairs. "You didn't expect me? I have come here, too. . . . I have come, too!"

She sits down and goes on, hesitating and not looking at me.

"Why don't you speak to me? I have come, too . . . today. . . . I found out that you were in this hotel, and have come to you."

"Very glad to see you," I say, shrugging my shoulders, "but I am surprised. You seem to have dropped from the skies. What have you come for?"

"Oh . . . I've simply come."

Silence. Suddenly she jumps up impulsively and comes to me.

"Nikolay Stepanovitch," she says, turning pale and pressing her hands on her bosom – "Nikolay Stepanovitch, I cannot go on living like this! I cannot! For God's sake tell me quickly, this minute, what I am to do! Tell me, what am I to do?"

"What can I tell you?" I ask in perplexity. "I can do nothing."

"Tell me, I beseech you," she goes on, breathing hard and trembling all over. "I swear that I cannot go on living like this. It's too much for me!"

She sinks on a chair and begins sobbing. She flings her head back, wrings her hands, taps with her feet; her hat falls off and hangs bobbing on its elastic; her hair is ruffled.

"Help me! help me! "she implores me. "I cannot go on!"

She takes her handkerchief out of her travelling-bag, and with it pulls out several letters, which fall from her lap to the floor. I pick them up, and on one of them I recognize the handwriting of Mihail Fyodorovitch and accidentally read a bit of a word "passionat . . ."

"There is nothing I can tell you, Katya," I say.

"Help me!" she sobs, clutching at my hand and kissing it. "You are my father, you know, my only friend! You are clever, educated; you have lived so long; you have been a teacher! Tell me, what am I to do?"

"Upon my word, Katya, I don't know. . . ."

I am utterly at a loss and confused, touched by her sobs, and hardly able to stand.

"Let us have lunch, Katya," I say, with a forced smile. "Give over crying."

And at once I add in a sinking voice:

"I shall soon be gone, Katya. . . ."

"Only one word, only one word!" she weeps, stretching out her hands to me.

"What am I to do?"

"You are a queer girl, really . . ." I mutter. "I don't understand it! So sensible, and all at once crying your eyes out. . . ."

A silence follows. Katya straightens her hair, puts on her hat, then crumples up the letters and stuffs them in her bag — and all this deliberately, in silence. Her face, her bosom, and her gloves are wet with tears, but her expression now is cold and forbidding. . . . I look at her, and feel ashamed that I am happier than she. The absence of what my philosophic colleagues call a general idea I have detected in myself only just before death, in the decline of my days, while the soul of this poor girl has known and will know no refuge all her life, all her life!

"Let us have lunch, Katya," I say.

"No, thank you," she answers coldly. Another minute passes in silence. "I don't like Harkov," I say; "it's so grey here — such a grey town."

"Yes, perhaps. . . . It's ugly. I am here not for long, passing through. I am going on today."

"Where?"

"To the Crimea . . . that is, to the Caucasus."

"Oh! For long?"

"I don't know."

Katya gets up, and, with a cold smile, holds out her hand without looking at me.

I want to ask her, "Then, you won't be at my funeral?" but she does not look at me; her hand is cold and, as it were, strange.

I escort her to the door in silence. She goes out, walks down the long corridor without looking back; she knows that I am looking after her, and most likely she will look back at the turn.

No, she did not look back. I've seen her black dress for the last time: her steps have died away. Farewell, my treasure!

In the Ravine

I

THE VILLAGE OF UKLEEVO lay in a ravine so that only the belfry and the chimneys of the printed cottons factories could be seen from the high road and the railway-station. When visitors asked what village this was, they were told:

"That's the village where the deacon ate all the caviare at the funeral."

It had happened at the dinner at the funeral of Kostukov that the old deacon saw among the savouries some large-grained caviare and began eating it greedily; people nudged him, tugged at his arm, but he seemed petrified with enjoyment: felt nothing, and only went on eating. He ate up all the caviare, and there were four pounds in the jar. And years had passed since then, the deacon had long been dead, but the caviare was still remembered. Whether life was so poor here or people had not been clever enough to notice anything but that unimportant incident that had occurred ten years before, anyway the people had nothing else to tell about the village Ukleevo.

The village was never free from fever, and there was boggy mud there even in the summer, especially under the fences over which hung old willow-trees that gave deep shade. Here there was always a smell from the factory refuse and the acetic acid which was used in the finishing of the cotton print.

The three cotton factories and the tanyard were not in the village itself, but a little way off. They were small factories, and not more than four hundred workmen were employed in all of them. The tanyard often made the water in the little river stink; the refuse contaminated the meadows, the peasants' cattle suffered from Siberian plague, and orders were given that the factory should be closed. It was considered to be closed, but went on working in secret with the connivance of the local police officer and the district doctor, who was paid ten roubles a month by the owner. In the whole village there were only two decent houses built of brick with iron roofs; one of them was the local court, in the other, a two-storeyed house just opposite the church, there lived a shopkeeper from Epifan called Grigory Petrovitch Tsybukin.

Grigory kept a grocer's shop, but that was only for appearance' sake: in reality he sold vodka, cattle, hides, grain, and pigs; he traded in anything that came to hand, and when, for instance, magpies were wanted abroad for ladies' hats, he made some thirty kopecks on every pair of birds; he bought timber for felling, lent money at interest, and altogether was a sharp old man, full of resources.

He had two sons. The elder, Anisim, was in the police in the detective department and was rarely at home. The younger, Stepan, had gone in for trade and helped his father: but no great help was expected from him as he was weak in health and deaf; his wife Aksinya, a handsome woman with a good figure, who wore a hat and carried a parasol on holidays, got up early and went to bed late, and ran about all day long, picking up her skirts and jingling her keys, going from the granary to the cellar and from there to the shop, and old Tsybukin looked at her good-humouredly while his eyes glowed, and at such moments he regretted she had not been married to his elder son instead of to the younger one, who was deaf, and who evidently knew very little about female beauty.

The old man had always an inclination for family life, and he loved his family more than anything on earth, especially his elder son, the detective, and his daughter-in-law. Aksinya had no sooner married the deaf son than she began to display an extraordinary gift for business, and knew who could be allowed to run up a bill and who could not: she kept the keys and would not trust them even to her husband; she kept the accounts by means of the reckoning beads, looked at the horses' teeth like a peasant, and was always laughing or shouting; and whatever she did or said the old man was simply delighted and muttered:

"Well done, daughter-in-law! You are a smart wench!"

He was a widower, but a year after his son's marriage he could not resist getting married himself. A girl was found for him, living twenty miles from Ukleevo, called Varvara Nikolaevna, no longer quite young, but good-looking, comely, and belonging to a decent family. As soon as she was installed into the upper-storey room everything in the house seemed to brighten up as though new glass had been put into all the windows. The lamps gleamed before the ikons, the tables were covered with snow-white cloths, flowers with red buds made their appearance in the windows and in the front garden, and at dinner, instead of eating from a single bowl, each person had a separate plate set for him. Varvara Nikolaevna had a pleasant, friendly smile, and it seemed as though the whole house were smiling, too. Beggars and pilgrims, male and female, began to come into the yard, a thing which had never happened in the past; the plaintive sing-song voices of the Ukleevo peasant women and the apologetic coughs of weak, seedy-looking men who had been dismissed from the factory for drunkenness were heard under the windows. Varvara helped them with money, with bread, with old clothes, and afterwards, when she felt more at home, began taking things out of the shop. One day the deaf man saw her take four ounces of tea and that disturbed him.

"Here, mother's taken four ounces of tea," he informed his father afterwards; "where is that to be entered?"

The old man made no reply but stood still and thought a

moment, moving his eyebrows, and then went upstairs to his wife.

"Varvarushka, if you want anything out of the shop," he said affectionately, "take it, my dear. Take it and welcome; don't hesitate."

And the next day the deaf man, running across the yard, called to her:

"If there is anything you want, mother, take it."

There was something new, something gay and light-hearted in her giving of alms, just as there was in the lamps before the ikons and in the red flowers. When at Carnival or at the church festival, which lasted for three days, they sold the peasants tainted salt meat, smelling so strong it was hard to stand near the tub of it, and took scythes, caps, and their wives' kerchiefs in pledge from the drunken men; when the factory hands stupefied with bad vodka lay rolling in the mud, and sin seemed to hover thick like a fog in the air, then it was a relief to think that up there in the house there was a gentle, neatly dressed woman who had nothing to do with salt meat or vodka; her charity had in those burdensome, murky days the effect of a safety valve in a machine.

The days in Tsybukin's house were spent in business cares. Before the sun had risen in the morning Aksinya was panting and puffing as she washed in the outer room, and the samovar was boiling in the kitchen with a hum that boded no good. Old Grigory Petrovitch, dressed in a long black coat, cotton breeches and shiny top boots, looking a dapper little figure, walked about the rooms, tapping with his little heels like the father-in-law in a well-known song. The shop was opened. When it was daylight a racing droshky was brought up to the front door and the old man got jauntily on to it, pulling his big cap down to his ears; and, looking at him, no one would have said he was fifty-six. His wife and daughter-in-law saw him off, and at such times when he had on a good, clean coat, and had in the droshky a huge black horse that had cost three hundred roubles, the old man did not like the peasants to come up to him with their complaints and petitions; he hated the peasants and disdained them, and if he saw some peasants waiting at the gate, he would shout angrily:

"Why are you standing there? Go further off."

Or if it were a beggar, he would say:

"God will provide!"

He used to drive off on business; his wife, in a dark dress and a black apron, tidied the rooms or helped in the kitchen. Aksinya attended to the shop, and from the yard could be heard the clink of bottles and of money, her laughter and loud talk, and the anger of customers whom she had offended; and at the same time it could be seen that the secret sale of vodka was already going on in the shop. The deaf man sat in the shop, too, or walked about the street bare-headed, with his hands in his pockets looking absent-mindedly now at the huts, now at the sky overhead. Six times a day they had tea; four times a day they sat down to meals; and in the evening they counted over their takings, put them down, went to bed, and slept soundly.

All the three cotton factories in Ukleevo and the houses of the factory owners – Hrymin Seniors, Hrymin Juniors, and Kostukov – were on a telephone. The telephone was laid on in the local court, too, but it soon ceased to work as bugs and beetles bred there. The elder of the rural district had had little education and wrote every word in the official documents in capitals. But when the telephone was spoiled he said:

"Yes, now we shall be badly off without a telephone."

The Hrymin Seniors were continually at law with the Juniors, and sometimes the Juniors quarrelled among themselves and began going to law, and their factory did not work for a month or two till they were reconciled again, and this was an entertainment for the people of Ukleevo, as there was a great deal of talk and gossip on the occasion of each quarrel. On holidays Kostukov and the Juniors used to get up races, used to dash about Ukleevo and run over calves. Aksinya, rustling her starched petticoats, used to promenade in a low-necked dress up and down the street near her shop; the Juniors used to snatch her up and carry her off as though by force. Then old Tsybukin would drive out to show his new horse and take Varvara with him.

In the evening, after the races, when people were going to bed, an expensive concertina was played in the Juniors' yard and, if it were a moonlight night, those sounds sent a thrill of delight to the heart, and Ukleevo no longer seemed a wretched hole.

II

The elder son Anisim came home very rarely, only on great holidays, but he often sent by a returning villager presents and letters written in very good writing by some other hand, always on a sheet of foolscap in the form of a petition. The letters were full of expressions that Anisim never made use of in conversation: "Dear papa and mamma, I send you a pound of flower tea for the satisfaction of your physical needs."

At the bottom of every letter was scratched, as though with a broken pen: "Anisim Tsybukin", and again in the same excellent hand: "Agent."

The letters were read aloud several times, and the old father, touched, red with emotion, would say:

"Here he did not care to stay at home, he has gone in for an intellectual line. Well, let him! Every man to his own job!"

It happened just before Carnival there was a heavy storm of rain mixed with hail; the old man and Varvara went to the window to look at it, and lo and behold! Anisim drove up in a sledge from the station. He was quite unexpected. He came indoors, looking anxious and troubled about something, and he remained the same all the time; there was something free and easy in his manner. He was in no haste to go away, it seemed, as though he had been dismissed from the service. Varvara was pleased at his arrival; she looked at him with a sly expression, sighed, and shook her head.

"How is this, my friends?" she said. "Tut, tut, the lad's in his twenty-eighth year, and he is still leading a gay bachelor life; tut, tut, tut. . . ."

From the other room her soft, even speech sounded like tut, tut, tut. She began whispering with her husband and Aksinya, and their faces wore the same sly and mysterious expression as though they were conspirators.

It was decided to marry Anisim.

"Oh, tut, tut . . . the younger brother has been married long ago," said Varvara, "and you are still without a helpmate like a cock at a fair. What is the meaning of it? Tut, tut, you will be married, please God, then as you choose – you will go into the service and your wife will remain here at home to help us. There is no order in your life, young man, and I see you have forgotten how to live properly. Tut, tut, it's the same trouble with all you townspeople."

When the Tsybukins married, the most handsome girls were chosen as brides for them as rich men. For Anisim, too, they found a handsome one. He was himself of an uninteresting and inconspicuous appearance; of a feeble, sickly build and short stature; he had full, puffy cheeks which looked as though he were blowing them out; his eyes looked with a keen, unblinking stare; his beard was red and scanty, and when he was thinking he always put it into his mouth and bit it; moreover he often drank too much, and that was noticeable from his face and his walk. But when he was informed that they had found a very beautiful bride for him, he said:

"Oh well, I am not a fright myself. All of us Tsybukins are handsome, I may say."

The village of Torguevo was near the town. Half of it had lately been incorporated into the town, the other half remained a village. In the first — the town half — there was a widow living in her own little house; she had a sister living with her who was quite poor and went out to work by the day, and this sister had a daughter called Lipa, a girl who went out to work, too. People in Torguevo were already talking about Lipa's good looks, but her terrible poverty put everyone off; people opined that some widower or elderly man would marry her regardless of her poverty, or would perhaps take her to himself without marriage, and that her mother would get enough to eat living with her. Varvara heard about Lipa from the matchmakers, and she drove over to Torguevo.

Then a visit of inspection was arranged at the aunt's, with lunch and wine all in due order, and Lipa wore a new pink dress made on purpose for this occasion, and a crimson ribbon like a flame gleamed in her hair. She was pale-faced, thin, and frail, with soft, delicate features sunburnt from working in the open air; a shy, mournful smile always hovered about her face, and there was a childlike look in her eyes, trustful and curious.

She was young, quite a little girl, her bosom still scarcely perceptible, but she could be married because she had reached the legal age. She really was beautiful, and the only thing that might be thought unattractive was her big masculine hands which hung idle now like two big claws.

"There is no dowry — and we don't think much of that," said Tsybukin to the aunt. "We took a wife from a poor family for our son Stepan, too, and now we can't say too much for her. In house and in business alike she has hands of gold."

Lipa stood in the doorway and looked as though she would say: "Do with me as you will, I trust you," while her mother Praskovya the workwoman hid herself in the kitchen numb with shyness. At one time in her youth a merchant whose floors she was scrubbing stamped at her in a rage; she went chill with terror and there always was a feeling of fear at the bottom of her heart. When she was frightened her arms and legs trembled and her cheeks twitched. Sitting in the kitchen she tried to hear what the visitors were saying, and she kept crossing herself, pressing her fingers to her forehead, and gazing at the ikons. Anisim, slightly drunk, opened the door into the kitchen and said in a free-and-easy way:

"Why are you sitting in here, precious mamma? We are dull without you."

And Praskovya, overcome with timidity, pressing her hands to her lean, wasted bosom, said:

"Oh, not at all. . . . It's very kind of you."

After the visit of inspection the wedding day was fixed. Then Anisim walked about the rooms at home whistling, or suddenly thinking of something, would fall to brooding and would look at the floor fixedly, silently, as though he would probe to the depths of the earth. He expressed neither pleasure that he was to be married, married so soon, on Low Sunday, nor a desire to see his bride, but simply went on whistling. And it was evident he was only getting married because his father and stepmother wished him to, and because it was the custom in the village to marry the son in order to have a woman to help in the house. When he went away he seemed in no haste, and behaved altogether not as he had done on previous visits – was particularly free and easy, and talked inappropriately.

III

In the village Shikalovo lived two dressmakers, sisters, belonging to the Flagellant sect. The new clothes for the wedding were ordered from them, and they often came to try them on, and stayed a long while drinking tea. They were making Varvara a brown dress with black lace and bugles on it, and Aksinya a light green dress with a yellow front, with a train. When the dressmakers had finished their work Tsybukin paid them not in money but in goods from the shop, and they went away depressed, carrying parcels of tallow candles and tins of sardines which they did not in the least need, and when they got out of the village into the open country they sat down on a hillock and cried.

Anisim arrived three days before the wedding, rigged out in new clothes from top to toe. He had dazzling india-rubber goloshes, and instead of a cravat wore a red cord with little balls on it, and over his shoulder he had hung an overcoat, also new, without putting his arms into the sleeves.

After crossing himself sedately before the ikon, he greeted his father and gave him ten silver roubles and ten half-roubles; to Varvara he gave as much, and to Aksinya twenty quarter-roubles. The chief charm of the present lay in the fact that all the coins, as though carefully matched, were new and glittered in the sun. Trying to seem grave and sedate he pursed up his face and puffed out his cheeks, and he smelt of spirits. Probably he had visited the refreshment bar at every station. And again there was a free-and-easiness about the man – something superfluous and out of place. Then Anisim had lunch and drank tea with the old man, and Varvara turned the new coins over in her hand and inquired about villagers who had gone to live in the town.

"They are all right, thank God, they get on quite well," said Anisim. "Only something has happened to Ivan Yegorov: his old wife Sofya Nikiforovna is dead. From consumption. They ordered the memorial dinner for the peace of her soul at the confectioner's at two and a half roubles a head. And there was real wine. Those who were peasants from our village – they paid two and a half roubles for them, too. They ate nothing, as though a peasant would understand sauce!"

"Two and a half," said his father, shaking his head.

"Well, it's not like the country there, you go into a restaurant to have a snack of something, you ask for one thing and another, others join till there is a party of us, one has a drink — and before you know where you are it is daylight and you've three or four roubles each to pay. And when one is with Samorodov he likes to have coffee with brandy in it after everything, and brandy is sixty kopecks for a little glass."

"And he is making it all up," said the old man enthusiastically; "he is making it all up, lying!"

"I am always with Samorodov now. It is Samorodov who writes my letters to you. He writes splendidly. And if I were to tell you, mamma," Anisim went on gaily, addressing Varvara, "the sort of fellow that Samorodov is, you would not believe me. We call him Muhtar, because he is black like an Armenian. I can see through him, I know all his affairs like the five fingers of my hand, and he feels that, and he always follows me about, we are regular inseparables. He seems not to like it in a way, but he can't get on without me. Where I go he goes. I have a correct, trustworthy eye, mamma. One sees a peasant selling a shirt in the market place. 'Stay, that shirt's stolen.' And really it turns out it is so: the shirt was a stolen one."

"What do you tell from?" asked Varvara.

"Not from anything, I have just an eye for it. I know nothing about the shirt, only for some reason I seem drawn to it: it's stolen, and that's all I can say. Among us detectives it's come to their saying, 'Oh, Anisim has gone to shoot snipe!' That means looking for stolen goods. Yes. . . . Anybody can steal, but it is another thing to keep! The earth is wide, but there is nowhere to hide stolen goods."

"In our village a ram and two ewes were carried off last week," said Varvara, and she heaved a sigh, and there is no one to try and find them. . . . Oh, tut, tut. . . ."

"Well, I might have a try. I don't mind."

The day of the wedding arrived. It was a cool but bright, cheerful April day. People were driving about Ukleevo from early morning with pairs or teams of three horses decked with many-coloured ribbons on their yokes and manes, with a jingle of bells. The rooks, disturbed by this activity, were cawing noisily in the willows, and the starlings sang their loudest unceasingly as though rejoicing that there was a wedding at the Tsybukins'.

Indoors the tables were already covered with long fish, smoked hams, stuffed fowls, boxes of sprats, pickled savouries of various sorts, and a number of bottles of vodka and wine; there was a smell of smoked sausage and of sour tinned lobster. Old Tsybukin walked about near the tables, tapping with his heels and sharpening the knives against each other. They kept calling Varvara and asking for things, and she was constantly with a distracted face running breathlessly into the kitchen, where the man cook from Kostukov's and the woman cook from Hrymin Juniors' had been at work since early morning. Aksinya, with her hair curled, in her stays without her dress on, in new creaky boots, flew about the yard like a whirlwind showing glimpses of her bare knees and bosom.

It was noisy, there was a sound of scolding and oaths; passers-by stopped at the wide-open gates, and in everything there was a feeling that something extraordinary was happening.

"They have gone for the bride!"

The bells began jingling and died away far beyond the village. . . . Between two and three o'clock people ran up: again there was a jingling of bells: they were bringing the bride! The church was full, the candelabra were lighted, the choir were singing from music books as old Tsybukin had wished it. The glare of the lights and the bright coloured dresses dazzled Lipa; she felt as though the singers with their loud voices were hitting her on the head with a hammer. Her boots and the stays, which she had put on for the first time in her life, pinched her, and her face looked as though she had only just come to herself after fainting; she gazed about without understanding. Anisim, in his black coat with a red cord instead of a tie, stared at the same spot lost in thought, and when the singers shouted loudly he hurriedly crossed himself. He felt touched and disposed to weep. This church was familiar to him from earliest childhood; at one time his dead mother used to bring him here to take the sacrament; at one time he used to sing in the choir; every ikon he remembered so well, every corner. Here he was being married, he had to take a wife for the sake of doing the proper thing, but he was not thinking of that now, he had forgotten his wedding completely. Tears dimmed his eyes so that he could not see the ikons, he felt heavy at heart; he prayed and besought God that the misfortunes that threatened him, that were ready to burst upon him tomorrow, if not today, might somehow pass him by as storm-clouds in time of drought pass over the village without yielding one drop of rain. And so many sins were heaped up in the past, so many sins, all getting away from them or setting them right was so beyond hope that it seemed incongruous even to ask forgiveness. But he did ask forgiveness, and even gave a loud sob, but no one took any notice of that, since they all supposed he had had a drop too much.

There was a sound of a fretful childish wail:

"Take me away, mamma darling!"

"Quiet there!" cried the priest.

When they returned from the church people ran after them; there were crowds, too, round the shop, round the gates, and in the yard under the windows. The peasant women came in to sing songs of congratulation to them. The young couple had scarcely crossed the threshold when the singers, who were already standing in the outer room with their music books, broke into a loud chant at the top of their voices; a band ordered expressly from the town began playing. Foaming Don wine was brought in tall wine-glasses, and Elizarov, a carpenter who did jobs by contract, a tall, gaunt old man with eyebrows so bushy that his eyes could scarcely be seen, said, addressing the happy pair:

"Anisim and you, my child, love one another, live in God's way, little children, and the Heavenly Mother will not abandon you."

He leaned his face on the old father's shoulder and gave a sob.

"Grigory Petrovitch, let us weep, let us weep with joy!" he said in a thin voice, and then at once burst out laughing in a loud bass guffaw. "Ho-ho-ho! This is a fine daughter-in-law for you too! Everything is in its place in her; all runs smoothly, no creaking, the mechanism works well, lots of screws in it."

He was a native of the Yegoryevsky district, but had worked in the factories in Ukleevo and the neighbourhood from his youth up, and had made it his home. He had been a familiar figure for years as old and gaunt and lanky as now, and for years he had been nicknamed "Crutch". Perhaps because he had been for forty years occupied in repairing the factory machinery he judged everybody and everything by its soundness or its need of repair. And before sitting down to the table he tried several chairs to see whether they were solid, and he touched the smoked fish also.

After the Don wine, they all sat down to the table. The visitors talked, moving their chairs. The singers were singing in the outer room. The band was playing, and at the same time the peasant women in the yard were singing their songs all in chorus – and there was an awful, wild medley of sounds which made one giddy.

Crutch turned round in his chair and prodded his neighbours

with his elbows, prevented people from talking, and laughed and cried alternately.

"Little children, little children, little children," he muttered rapidly. "Aksinya my dear, Varvara darling, we will live all in peace and harmony, my dear little axes. . . ."

He drank little and was now only drunk from one glass of English bitters. The revolting bitters, made from nobody knows what, intoxicated everyone who drank it as though it had stunned them. Their tongues began to falter.

The local clergy, the clerks from the factories with their wives, the tradesmen and tavern-keepers from the other villages were present. The clerk and the elder of the rural district who had served together for fourteen years, and who had during all that time never signed a single document for anybody nor let a single person out of the local court without deceiving or insulting him, were sitting now side by side, both fat and well-fed, and it seemed as though they were so saturated in injustice and falsehood that even the skin of their faces was somehow peculiar, fraudulent. The clerk's wife, a thin woman with a squint, had brought all her children with her, and like a bird of prey looked aslant at the plates and snatched anything she could get hold of to put in her own or her children's pockets.

Lipa sat as though turned to stone, still with the same expression as in church. Anisim had not said a single word to her since he had made her acquaintance, so that he did not yet know the sound of her voice; and now, sitting beside her, he remained mute and went on drinking bitters, and when he got drunk he began talking to the aunt who was sitting opposite:

"I have a friend called Samorodov. A peculiar man. He is by rank an honorary citizen, and he can talk. But I know him through and through, auntie, and he feels it. Pray join me in drinking to the health of Samorodov, auntie!"

Varvara, worn out and distracted, walked round the table pressing the guests to eat, and was evidently pleased that there were so many dishes and that everything was so lavish – no one could disparage them now. The sun set, but the dinner went on: the guests were beyond knowing what they were eating or drinking, it was impossible to distinguish what was said, and only from time to time when the band subsided some peasant woman could be heard shouting:

"They have sucked the blood out of us, the Herods; a pest on them!"

In the evening they danced to the band. The Hrymin Juniors came, bringing their wine, and one of them, when dancing a quadrille, held a bottle in each hand and a wineglass in his mouth, and that made everyone laugh. In the middle of the quadrille they suddenly crooked their knees and danced in a squatting position; Aksinya in green flew by like a flash, stirring up a wind with her train. Someone trod on her flounce and Crutch shouted:

"Aie, they have torn off the panel! Children!"

Aksinya had naïve grey eyes which rarely blinked, and a naïve smile played continually on her face. And in those unblinking eyes, and in that little head on the long neck, and in her slenderness there was something snake-like; all in green but for the yellow on her bosom, she looked with a smile on her face as a viper looks out of the young rye in the spring at the passers-by, stretching itself and lifting its head. The Hrymins were free in their behaviour to her, and it was very noticeable that she was on intimate terms with the elder of them. But her deaf husband saw nothing, he did not look at her; he sat with his legs crossed and ate nuts, cracking them so loudly that it sounded like pistol shots.

But, behold, old Tsybukin himself walked into the middle of the room and waved his handkerchief as a sign that he, too, wanted to dance the Russian dance, and all over the house and from the crowd in the yard rose a roar of approbation:

"*He's* going to dance! *He* himself!"

Varvara danced, but the old man only waved his handkerchief and kicked up his heels, but the people in the yard, propped against one another, peeping in at the windows, were in raptures, and for the moment forgave him everything – his wealth and the wrongs he had done them.

"Well done, Grigory Petrovitch!" was heard in the crowd. "That's right, do your best! You can still play your part! Ha-ha!"

It was kept up till late, till two o'clock in the morning. Anisim, staggering, went to take leave of the singers and bandsmen, and gave each of them a new half-rouble. His father, who was not staggering but still seemed to be standing on one leg, saw his guests off, and said to each of them:

"The wedding has cost two thousand."

As the party was breaking up, someone took the Shikalovo innkeeper's good coat instead of his own old one, and Anisim suddenly flew into a rage and began shouting:

"Stop, I'll find it at once; I know who stole it, stop."

He ran out into the street and pursued someone. He was caught, brought back home and shoved, drunken, red with anger, and wet, into the room where the aunt was undressing Lipa, and was locked in.

IV

Five days had passed. Anisim, who was preparing to go, went upstairs to say goodbye to Varvara. All the lamps were burning before the ikons, there was a smell of incense, while she sat at the window knitting a stocking of red wool.

"You have not stayed with us long," she said. "You've been dull, I dare say. Oh, tut, tut. We live comfortably; we have plenty of everything. We celebrated your wedding properly, in good style; your father says it came to two thousand. In fact we live like merchants, only it's dreary. We treat the people very badly. My heart aches, my dear; how we treat them, my goodness! Whether we exchange a horse or buy something or hire a labourer — it's cheating in everything. Cheating and cheating. The Lenten oil in the shop is bitter, rancid, the people have pitch that is better. But surely, tell me pray, couldn't we sell good oil?"

"Every man to his job, mamma."

"But you know we all have to die? Oy, oy, really you ought to talk to your father . . . !"

"Why, you should talk to him yourself."

"Well, well, I did put in my word, but he said just what you do: 'Every man to his own job.' Do you suppose in the next world they'll consider what job you have been put to? God's judgment is just."

"Of course no one will consider," said Anisim, and he heaved a sigh. "There is no God, anyway, you know, mamma, so what considering can there be?"

Varvara looked at him with surprise, burst out laughing, and clasped her hands. Perhaps because she was so genuinely surprised at his words and looked at him as though he were a queer person, he was confused.

"Perhaps there is a God, only there is no faith. When I was being married I was not myself. Just as you may take an egg from under a hen and there is a chicken chirping in it, so my conscience was beginning to chirp in me, and while I was being married I thought all the time there was a God! But when I left the church it was nothing. And indeed, how can I tell whether there is a God or not? We are not taught right from childhood, and while the babe is still at his mother's breast he is only taught 'every man to his own job.' Father does not believe in

God, either. You were saying that Guntorev had some sheep stolen. . . . I have found them; it was a peasant at Shikalovo stole them; he stole them, but father's got the fleeces . . . so that's all his faith amounts to."

Anisim winked and wagged his head.

"The elder does not believe in God, either," he went on. "And the clerk and the deacon, too. And as for their going to church and keeping the fasts, that is simply to prevent people talking ill of them, and in case it really may be true that there will be a Day of Judgment. Nowadays people say that the end of the world has come because people have grown weaker, do not honour their parents, and so on. All that is nonsense. My idea, mamma, is that all our trouble is because there is so little conscience in people. I see through things, mamma, and I understand. If a man has a stolen shirt I see it. A man sits in a tavern and you fancy he is drinking tea and no more, but to me the tea is neither here nor there; I see further, he has no conscience. You can go about the whole day and not meet one man with a conscience. And the whole reason is that they don't know whether there is a God or not. . . . Well, goodbye, mamma, keep alive and well, don't remember evil against me."

Anisim bowed down at Varvara's feet.

"I thank you for everything, mamma," he said. "You are a great gain to our family. You are a very ladylike woman, and I am very pleased with you."

Much moved, Anisim went out, but returned again and said:

"Samorodov has got me mixed up in something: I shall either make my fortune or come to grief. If anything happens, then you must comfort my father, mamma."

"Oh, nonsense, don't you worry, tut, tut, tut . . . God is merciful. And, Anisim, you should be affectionate to your wife, instead of giving each other sulky looks as you do; you might smile at least."

"Yes, she is rather a queer one," said Anisim, and he gave a sigh. "She does not understand anything, she never speaks. She is very young, let her grow up."

A tall, sleek white stallion was already standing at the front door, harnessed to the chaise.

Old Tsybukin jumped in jauntily with a run and took the reins. Anisim kissed Varvara, Aksinya, and his brother. On the steps Lipa, too, was standing; she was standing motionless, looking away, and it seemed as though she had not come to see him off but just by chance for some unknown reason. Anisim went up to her and just touched her cheek with his lips.

"Goodbye," he said.

And without looking at him she gave a strange smile; her face began to quiver, and everyone for some reason felt sorry for her. Anisim, too, leaped into the chaise with a bound and put his arms jauntily akimbo, for he considered himself a good-looking fellow.

When they drove up out of the ravine Anisim kept looking back towards the village. It was a warm, bright day. The cattle were being driven out for the first time, and the peasant girls and women were walking by the herd in their holiday dresses. The dun-coloured bull bellowed, glad to be free, and pawed the ground with his forefeet. On all sides, above and below, the larks were singing. Anisim looked round at the elegant white church – it had only lately been whitewashed – and he thought how he had been praying in it five days before; he looked round at the school with its green roof, at the little river in which he used once to bathe and catch fish, and there was a stir of joy in his heart, and he wished that walls might rise up from the ground and prevent him from going further, and that he might be left with nothing but the past.

At the station they went to the refreshment room and drank a glass of sherry each. His father felt in his pocket for his purse to pay.

"I will stand treat," said Anisim. The old man, touched and delighted, slapped him on the shoulder, and winked to the waiter as much as to say, "See what a fine son I have got."

"You ought to stay at home in the business, Anisim," he said; "you would be worth any price to me! I would shower gold on you from head to foot, my son."

"It can't be done, papa."

The sherry was sour and smelt of sealing-wax, but they had another glass.

When old Tsybukin returned home from the station, for the first moment he did not recognize his younger daughter-in-law.

As soon as her husband had driven out of the yard, Lipa was transformed and suddenly brightened up. Wearing a threadbare old petticoat, with her feet bare and her sleeves tucked up to the shoulders, she was scrubbing the stairs in the entry and singing in a silvery little voice, and when she brought out a big tub of dirty water and looked up at the sun with her childlike smile it seemed as though she, too, were a lark.

An old labourer who was passing by the door shook his head and cleared his throat.

"Yes, indeed, your daughters-in-law, Grigory Petrovitch, are a blessing from God," he said. "Not women, but treasures!"

V

On Friday the 8th of July, Elizarov, nicknamed Crutch, and Lipa were returning from the village of Kazanskoe, where they had been to a service on the occasion of a church holiday in the honour of the Holy Mother of Kazan. A good distance after them walked Lipa's mother Praskovya, who always fell behind, as she was ill and short of breath. It was drawing towards evening.

"A-a-a . . ." said Crutch, wondering as he listened to Lipa. "A-a! . . . We-ell!"

"I am very fond of jam, Ilya Makaritch," said Lipa. "I sit down in my little corner and drink tea and eat jam. Or I drink it with Varvara Nikolaevna, and she tells some story full of feeling. We have a lot of jam — four jars. 'Have some, Lipa; eat as much as you like.'"

"A-a-a, four jars!"

"They live very well. We have white bread with our tea; and meat, too, as much as one wants. They live very well, only I am frightened with them, Ilya Makaritch. Oh, oh, how frightened I am!"

"Why are you frightened, child?" asked Crutch, and he looked back to see how far Praskovya was behind.

"To begin with, when the wedding had been celebrated I was afraid of Anisim Grigoritch. Anisim Grigoritch did nothing, he didn't ill-treat me, only when he comes near me a cold shiver runs all over me, through all my bones. And I did not sleep one night, I trembled all over and kept praying to God. And now I am afraid of Aksinya, Ilya Makaritch. It's not that she does anything, she is always laughing, but sometimes she glances at the window, and her eyes are so fierce and there is a gleam of green in them — like the eyes of the sheep in the shed. The Hrymin Juniors are leading her astray: 'Your old man,' they tell her, 'has a bit of land at Butyokino, a hundred and twenty acres,' they say, 'and there is sand and water there, so you, Aksinya,' they say, 'build a brickyard there and we will go shares in it.' Bricks now are twenty roubles the thousand, it's a profitable business. Yesterday at dinner Aksinya said to my father-in-law: 'I want to build a brickyard at Butyokino; I'm going into business on my own account.' She laughed as she said it. And Grigory

Petrovitch's face darkened, one could see he did not like it. 'As long as I live,' he said, 'the family must not break up, we must go on altogether.' She gave a look and gritted her teeth. . . . Fritters were served, she would not eat them."

"A-a-a! . . ." Crutch was surprised.

"And tell me, if you please, when does she sleep?" said Lipa. "She sleeps for half an hour, then jumps up and keeps walking and walking about to see whether the peasants have not set fire to something, have not stolen something. . . . I am frightened with her, Ilya Makaritch. And the Hrymin Juniors did not go to bed after the wedding, but drove to the town to go to law with each other; and folks do say it is all on account of Aksinya. Two of the brothers have promised to build her a brickyard, but the third is offended, and the factory has been at a standstill for a month, and my uncle Prohor is without work and goes about from house to house getting crusts. 'Hadn't you better go working on the land or sawing up wood, meanwhile, uncle?' I tell him; 'why disgrace yourself?' 'I've got out of the way of it,' he says; 'I don't know how to do any sort of peasant's work now, Lipinka.' . . ."

They stopped to rest and wait for Praskovya near a copse of young aspen-trees. Elizarov had long been a contractor in a small way, but he kept no horses, going on foot all over the district with nothing but a little bag in which there was bread and onions, and stalking along with big strides, swinging his arms. And it was difficult to walk with him.

At the entrance to the copse stood a milestone. Elizarov touched it; read it. Praskovya reached them out of breath. Her wrinkled and always scared-looking face was beaming with happiness; she had been at church today like anyone else, then she had been to the fair and there had drunk pear cider. For her this was unusual, and it even seemed to her now that she had lived for her own pleasure that day for the first time in her life. After resting they all three walked on side by side. The sun had already set, and its beams filtered through the copse, casting a light on the trunks of the trees. There was a faint sound of voices ahead. The Ukleevo girls had long before pushed on ahead but had lingered in the copse, probably gathering mushrooms.

"Hey, wenches!" cried Elizarov. "Hey, my beauties!"

There was a sound of laughter in response.

"Crutch is coming! Crutch! The old horseradish."

And the echo laughed, too. And then the copse was left behind. The tops of the factory chimneys came into view. The cross on the belfry glittered: this was the village: "the one at which the deacon ate all the caviare at the funeral." Now they were almost home; they only had to go down into the big ravine. Lipa and Praskovya, who had been walking barefooted, sat down on the grass to put on their boots; Elizarov sat down with them. If they looked down from above Ukleevo looked beautiful and peaceful with its willow-trees, its white church, and its little river, and the only blot on the picture was the roof of the factories, painted for the sake of cheapness a gloomy ashen grey.

On the slope on the further side they could see the rye — some in stacks and sheaves here and there as though strewn about by the storm, and some freshly cut lying in swathes; the oats, too, were ripe and glistened now in the sun like mother-of-pearl. It was harvest-time. Today was a holiday, tomorrow they would harvest the rye and carry the hay, and then Sunday a holiday again; every day there were mutterings of distant thunder. It was misty and looked like rain, and, gazing now at the fields, everyone thought, God grant we get the harvest in in time; and everyone felt gay and joyful and anxious at heart.

"Mowers ask a high price nowadays," said Praskovya. "One rouble and forty kopecks a day."

People kept coming and coming from the fair at Kazanskoe: peasant women, factory workers in new caps, beggars, children. . . . Here a cart would drive by stirring up the dust and behind it would run an unsold horse, and it seemed glad it had not been sold; then a cow was led along by the horns, resisting stubbornly; then a cart again, and in it drunken peasants swinging their legs. An old woman led a little boy in a big cap and big boots; the boy was tired out with the heat and the heavy boots which prevented his bending his legs at the knees, but yet blew unceasingly with all his might at a tin trumpet. They had gone down the slope and turned into the street, but the trumpet could still be heard.

"Our factory owners don't seem quite themselves . . ." said Elizarov. "There's trouble. Kostukov is angry with me. 'Too many boards have gone on the cornices.' 'Too many? As many have gone on it as were needed, Vassily Danilitch; I don't eat them with my porridge.' 'How can you speak to me like that?' said he, 'you good-for-nothing blockhead! Don't forget yourself! It was I made you a contractor.' 'That's nothing so wonderful,' said I. 'Even before I was a contractor I used to have tea every day.' 'You are a rascal . . .' he said. I said nothing. 'We are rascals in this world,' thought I, 'and you will be rascals in the next. . . .' Ha-ha-ha! The next day he was softer. 'Don't you bear malice against me for my words, Makaritch,' he said. 'If I said too much,' says he, 'what of it? I am a merchant of the first guild, your superior – you ought to hold your tongue.' 'You,' said I, 'are a merchant of the first guild and I am a carpenter, that's correct. And Saint Joseph was a carpenter, too. Ours is a righteous calling and pleasing to God, and if you are pleased to be my superior you are very welcome to it, Vassily Danilitch.' And later on, after that conversation I mean, I thought: 'Which was the superior? A merchant of the first guild or a carpenter?' The carpenter must be, my child!"

Crutch thought a minute and added:

"Yes, that's how it is, child. He who works, he who is patient is the superior."

By now the sun had set and a thick mist as white as milk was rising over the river, in the church enclosure, and in the open spaces round the factories. Now when the darkness was coming on rapidly, when lights were twinkling below, and when it seemed as though the mists were hiding a fathomless abyss, Lipa and her mother who were born in poverty and prepared to live so till the end, giving up to others everything except their frightened, gentle souls, may have fancied for a minute perhaps that in the vast, mysterious world, among the endless series of lives, they, too, counted for something, and they, too, were superior to someone; they liked sitting here at the top, they smiled happily and forgot that they must go down below again all the same.

At last they went home again. The mowers were sitting on the ground at the gates near the shop. As a rule the Ukleevo peasants did not go to Tsybukin's to work, and they had to hire strangers, and now in the darkness it seemed as though there were men sitting there with long black beards. The shop was open, and through the doorway they could see the deaf man playing draughts with a boy. The mowers were singing softly, scarcely audibly, or loudly demanding their wages for the previous day, but they were not paid for fear they should go away before tomorrow. Old Tsybukin, with his coat off, was sitting in his waistcoat with Aksinya under the birch-tree, drinking tea; a lamp was burning on the table.

"I say, grandfather," a mower called from outside the gates, as though taunting him, "pay us half anyway! Hey, grandfather."

And at once there was the sound of laughter, and then again they sang hardly audibly. . . . Crutch, too, sat down to have some tea.

"We have been at the fair, you know," he began telling them. "We have had a walk, a very nice walk, my children, praise the Lord. But an unfortunate thing happened: Sashka the blacksmith bought some tobacco and gave the shopman half a rouble to be sure. And the half rouble was a false one" —Crutch went on, and he meant to speak in a whisper, but he spoke in a smothered husky voice which was audible to everyone. "The half-rouble turned out to be a bad one. He was asked where he got it. 'Anisim Tsybukin gave it me,' he said. 'When I went to his wedding,' he said. They called the police inspector, took the man away. . . . Look out, Grigory Petrovitch, that nothing comes of it, no talk. . . ."

"Gra-ndfather!" the same voice called tauntingly outside the gates. "Gra-andfather!"

A silence followed.

"Ah, little children, little children, little children . . ." Crutch muttered rapidly, and he got up. He was overcome with drowsiness. "Well, thank you for the tea, for the sugar, little children. It is time to sleep. I am like a bit of rotten timber nowadays, my beams are crumbling under me. Ho-ho-ho! I suppose it's time I was dead."

And he gave a gulp. Old Tsybukin did not finish his tea but sat on a little, pondering; and his face looked as though he were listening to the footsteps of Crutch, who was far away down the street.

"Sashka the blacksmith told a lie, I expect," said Aksinya, guessing his thoughts.

He went into the house and came back a little later with a parcel; he opened it, and there was the gleam of roubles — perfectly new coins. He took one, tried it with his teeth, flung it on the tray; then flung down another.

"The roubles really are false . . ." he said, looking at Aksinya and seeming perplexed. "These are those Anisim brought, his present. Take them, daughter," he whispered, and thrust the parcel into her hands. "Take them and throw them into the well . . . confound them! And mind there is no talk about it. Harm might come of it. . . . Take away the samovar, put out the light."

Lipa and her mother sitting in the barn saw the lights go out one after the other; only overhead in Varvara's room there were blue and red lamps gleaming, and a feeling of peace, content, and happy ignorance seemed to float down from there. Praskovya could never get used to her daughter's being married to a rich man, and when she came she huddled timidly in the outer room with a deprecating smile on her face, and tea and sugar were sent out to her. And Lipa, too, could not get used to it either, and after her husband had gone away she did not sleep in her bed, but lay down anywhere to sleep, in the kitchen or the barn, and every day she scrubbed the floor or washed the clothes, and felt as though she were hired by the day. And now, on coming back from the service, they drank tea in the kitchen with the cook, then they went into the barn and lay down on the ground between the sledge and the wall. It was dark here and smelt of harness.

The lights went out about the house, then they could hear the deaf man shutting up the shop, the mowers settling themselves about the yard to sleep. In the distance at the Hrymin Juniors' they were playing on the expensive concertina. . . . Praskovya and Lipa began to go to sleep.

And when they were awakened by somebody's steps it was bright moonlight; at the entrance of the barn stood Aksinya with her bedding in her arms.

"Maybe it's a bit cooler here," she said; then she came in and lay down almost in the doorway so that the moonlight fell full upon her.

She did not sleep, but breathed heavily, tossing from side to side with the heat, throwing off almost all the bedclothes. And in the magic moonlight what a beautiful, what a proud animal she was! A little time passed, and then steps were heard again: the old father, white all over, appeared in the doorway.

"Aksinya," he called, "are you here?"

"Well?" she responded angrily.

"I told you just now to throw the money into the well, have you done so?"

"What next, throwing property into the water! I gave them to the mowers. . . ."

"Oh my God!" cried the old man, dumbfounded and alarmed. "Oh my God! you wicked woman. . . ."

He flung up his hands and went out, and he kept saying something as he went away. And a little later Aksinya sat up and sighed heavily with annoyance, then got up and, gathering up her bedclothes in her arms, went out.

"Why did you marry me into this family, mother?" said Lipa.

"One has to be married, daughter. It was not us who ordained it."

And a feeling of inconsolable woe was ready to take possession of them. But it seemed to them that someone was looking down from the height of the heavens, out of the blue from where the stars were seeing everything that was going on in Ukleevo, watching over them. And however great was wickedness, still the night was calm and beautiful, and still in God's world there is and will be truth and justice as calm and beautiful, and everything on earth is only waiting to be made one with truth and justice, even as the moonlight is blended with the night.

And both, huddling close to one another, fell asleep comforted.

VI

News had come long before that Anisim had been put in prison for coining and passing bad money. Months passed, more than half a year passed, the long winter was over, spring had begun, and everyone in the house and the village had grown used to the fact that Anisim was in prison. And when anyone passed by the house or the shop at night he would remember that Anisim was in prison; and when they rang at the churchyard for some reason, that, too, reminded them that he was in prison awaiting trial.

It seemed as though a shadow had fallen upon the house. The house looked darker, the roof was rustier, the heavy, iron-bound door into the shop, which was painted green, was covered with cracks, or, as the deaf man expressed it, "blisters"; and old Tsybukin seemed to have grown dingy, too. He had given up cutting his hair and beard, and looked shaggy. He no longer sprang jauntily into his chaise, nor shouted to beggars: "God will provide!" His strength was on the wane, and that was evident in everything. People were less afraid of him now, and the police officer drew up a formal charge against him in the shop though he received his regular bribe as before; and three times the old man was called up to the town to be tried for illicit dealing in spirits, and the case was continually adjourned owing to the non-appearance of witnesses, and old Tsybukin was worn out with worry.

He often went to see his son, hired somebody, handed in a petition to somebody else, presented a holy banner to some church. He presented the governor of the prison in which Anisim was confined with a silver glass stand with a long spoon and the inscription: "The soul knows its right measure."

"There is no one to look after things for us," said Varvara. "Tut, tut. . . . You ought to ask someone of the gentlefolks, they would write to the head officials. . . . At least they might let him out on bail! Why wear the poor fellow out?"

She, too, was grieved, but had grown stouter and whiter; she lighted the lamps before the ikons as before, and saw that everything in the house was clean, and regaled the guests with jam and apple cheese. The deaf man and Aksinya looked after the shop. A new project was in progress – a brickyard in Butyokino – and Aksinya went there almost every day in the chaise. She drove herself, and when she met acquaintances she stretched out her neck like a snake out of the young rye, and smiled naïvely and enigmatically. Lipa spent her time playing with the baby which had been born to her before Lent. It was a tiny, thin, pitiful little baby, and it was strange that it should cry and gaze about and be considered a human being, and even be called Nikifor. He lay in his swinging cradle, and Lipa would walk away towards the door and say, bowing to him:

"Good-day, Nikifor Anisimitch!"

And she would rush at him and kiss him. Then she would walk away to the door, bow again, and say:

"Good-day, Nikifor Anisimitch!"

And he kicked up his little red legs, and his crying was mixed with laughter like the carpenter Elizarov's.

At last the day of the trial was fixed. Tsybukin went away five days before. Then they heard that the peasants called as witnesses had been fetched; their old workman who had received a notice to appear went too.

The trial was on a Thursday. But Sunday had passed, and Tsybukin was still not back, and there was no news. Towards the evening on Tuesday Varvara was sitting at the open window, listening for her husband to come. In the next room Lipa was playing with her baby. She was tossing him up in her arms and saying enthusiastically:

"You will grow up ever so big, ever so big. You will be a peasant, we shall go out to work together! We shall go out to work together!"

"Come, come," said Varvara, offended. "Go out to work, what an idea, you silly girl! He will be a merchant . . . !"

Lipa sang softly, but a minute later she forgot and again:

"You will grow ever so big, ever so big. You will be a peasant, we'll go out to work together."

"There she is at it again!"

Lipa, with Nikifor in her arms, stood still in the doorway and asked:

"Why do I love him so much, mamma? Why do I feel so sorry for him?" she went on in a quivering voice, and her eyes glistened with tears. "Who is he? What is he like? As light as a little feather, as a little crumb, but I love him; I love him like a real person. Here he can do nothing, he can't talk, and yet I know what he wants with his little eyes."

Varvara was listening; the sound of the evening train coming in to the station reached her. Had her husband come? She did not hear and she did not heed what Lipa was saying, she had no idea how the time passed, but only trembled all over — not from dread, but intense curiosity. She saw a cart full of peasants roll quickly by with a rattle. It was the witnesses coming back from the station. When the cart passed the shop the old workman jumped out and walked into the yard. She could hear him being greeted in the yard and being asked some questions. . . .

"Deprivation of rights and all his property," he said loudly, "and six years' penal servitude in Siberia."

She could see Aksinya come out of the shop by the back way; she had just been selling kerosene, and in one hand held a bottle and in the other a can, and in her mouth she had some silver coins.

"Where is father?" she asked, lisping.

"At the station," answered the labourer. "'When it gets a little darker,' he said, 'then I shall come.'"

And when it became known all through the household that Anisim was sentenced to penal servitude, the cook in the kitchen suddenly broke into a wail as though at a funeral, imagining that this was demanded by the proprieties:

"There is no one to care for us now you have gone, Anisim Grigoritch, our bright falcon. . . ."

The dogs began barking in alarm. Varvara ran to the window, and rushing about in distress, shouted to the cook with all her might, straining her voice:

"Sto-op, Stepanida, sto-op! Don't harrow us, for Christ's sake!"

They forgot to set the samovar, they could think of nothing.

Only Lipa could not make out what it was all about and went on playing with her baby.

When the old father arrived from the station they asked him no questions. He greeted them and walked through all the rooms in silence; he had no supper.

"There was no one to see about things . . ." Varvara began when they were alone. "I said you should have asked some of the gentry, you would not heed me at the time. . . . A petition would . . ."

"I saw to things," said her husband with a wave of his hand. "When Anisim was condemned I went to the gentleman who was defending him. 'It's no use now,' he said, 'it's too late'; and Anisim said the same; it's too late. But all the same as I came out of the court I made an agreement with a lawyer, I paid him something in advance. I'll wait a week and then I will go again. It is as God wills."

Again the old man walked through all the rooms, and when he went back to Varvara he said:

"I must be ill. My head's in a sort of . . . fog. My thoughts are in a maze."

He closed the door that Lipa might not hear, and went on softly:

"I am unhappy about my money. Do you remember on Low Sunday before his wedding Anisim's bringing me some new roubles and half-roubles? One parcel I put away at the time, but the others I mixed with my own money. When my uncle

Dmitri Filatitch – the Kingdom of Heaven be his – was alive, he used constantly to go journeys to Moscow and to the Crimea to buy goods. He had a wife, and this same wife, when he was away buying goods, used to take up with other men. She had half a dozen children. And when uncle was in his cups he would laugh and say: 'I never can make out,' he used to say, 'which are my children and which are other people's.' An easy-going disposition, to be sure; and so I now can't distinguish which are genuine roubles and which are false ones. And it seems to me that they are all false."

"Nonsense, God bless you."

"I take a ticket at the station, I give the man three roubles, and I keep fancying they are false. And I am frightened. I must be ill."

"There's no denying it, we are all in God's hands. . . . Oh dear, dear . . ." said Varvara, and she shook her head. "You ought to think about this, Grigory Petrovitch: you never know, anything may happen, you are not a young man. See they don't wrong your grandchild when you are dead and gone. Oy, I am afraid they will be unfair to Nikifor! He has as good as no father, his mother's young and foolish . . . you ought to secure something for him, poor little boy, at least the land, Butyokino, Grigory Petrovitch, really! Think it over!" Varvara went on persuading him. "The pretty boy, one is sorry for him! You go tomorrow and make out a deed; why put it off?"

"I'd forgotten about my grandson," said Tsybukin. "I must

go and have a look at him. So you say the boy is all right? Well, let him grow up, please God."

He opened the door and, crooking his finger, beckoned to Lipa. She went up to him with the baby in her arms.

"If there is anything you want, Lipinka, you ask for it," he said. "And eat anything you like, we don't grudge it, so long as it does you good. . . ." He made the sign of the cross over the baby. "And take care of my grandchild. My son is gone, but my grandson is left."

Tears rolled down his cheeks; he gave a sob and went away. Soon afterwards he went to bed and slept soundly after seven sleepless nights.

VII

Old Tsybukin went to the town for a short time. Someone told Aksinya that he had gone to the notary to make his will and that he was leaving Butyokino, the very place where she had set up a brickyard, to Nikifor, his grandson. She was informed of this in the morning when old Tsybukin and Varvara were sitting near the steps under the birch-tree, drinking their tea. She closed the shop in the front and at the back, gathered together all the keys she had, and flung them at her father-in-law's feet.

"I am not going on working for you," she began in a loud voice, and suddenly broke into sobs. "It seems I am not your daughter-in-law, but a servant! Everybody's jeering and saying, 'See what a servant the Tsybukins have got hold of!' I did not come to you for wages! I am not a beggar, I am not a slave, I have a father and mother."

She did not wipe away her tears, she fixed upon her father-in-law eyes full of tears, vindictive, squinting with wrath; her face and neck were red and tense, and she was shouting at the top of her voice.

"I don't mean to go on being a slave!" she went on. "I am worn out. When it is work, when it is sitting in the shop day in and day out, scurrying out at night for vodka – then it is my share, but when it is giving away the land then it is for that convict's wife and her imp. She is mistress here, and I am her servant. Give her everything, the convict's wife, and may it choke her! I am going home! Find yourselves some other fool, you damned Herods!"

Tsybukin had never in his life scolded or punished his children, and had never dreamed that one of his family could speak to him rudely or behave disrespectfully; and now he was very much frightened; he ran into the house and there hid behind the cupboard. And Varvara was so much flustered that she could not get up from her seat, and only waved her hands before her as though she were warding off a bee.

"Oh, Holy Saints! what's the meaning of it?" she muttered in horror. "What is she shouting? Oh, dear, dear! . . . People will hear! Hush. Oh, hush!"

"He has given Butyokino to the convict's wife," Aksinya went on bawling. "Give her everything now, I don't want anything from you! Let me alone! You are all a gang of thieves here! I have seen my fill of it, I have had enough! You have robbed folks coming in and going out; you have robbed old and young alike, you brigands! And who has been selling vodka without a licence? And false money? You've filled boxes full of false coins, and now I am no more use!"

A crowd had by now collected at the open gate and was staring into the yard.

"Let the people look," bawled Aksinya. "I will shame you all! You shall burn with shame! You shall grovel at my feet. Hey! Stepan," she called to the deaf man, "let us go home this minute! Let us go to my father and mother; I don't want to live with convicts. Get ready!"

Clothes were hanging on lines stretched across the yard; she snatched off her petticoats and blouses still wet and flung them into the deaf man's arms. Then in her fury she dashed about the yard by the linen, tore down all of it, and what was not hers she threw on the ground and trampled upon.

"Holy Saints, take her away," moaned Varvara. "What a woman! Give her Butyokino! Give it her, for the Lord's sake!"

"Well! Wha-at a woman!" people were saying at the gate. "She's a wo-oman! She's going it — something like!"

Aksinya ran into the kitchen where washing was going on. Lipa was washing alone, the cook had gone to the river to rinse the clothes. Steam was rising from the trough and from the cauldron on the side of the stove, and the kitchen was thick and stifling from the steam. On the floor was a heap of unwashed clothes, and Nikifor, kicking up his little red legs, had been put down on a bench near them, so that if he fell he should not hurt himself. Just as Aksinya went in Lipa took the former's chemise out of the heap and put it in the trough, and was just stretching out her hand to a big ladle of boiling water which was standing on the table.

"Give it here," said Aksinya, looking at her with hatred, and snatching the chemise out of the trough; "it is not your business to touch my linen! You are a convict's wife, and ought to know your place and who you are."

Lipa gazed at her, taken aback, and did not understand, but suddenly she caught the look Aksinya turned upon the child, and at once she understood and went numb all over.

"You've taken my land, so here you are!" Saying this Aksinya snatched up the ladle with the boiling water and flung it over Nikifor.

After this there was heard a scream such as had never been heard before in Ukleevo, and no one would have believed that a little weak creature like Lipa could scream like that. And it was suddenly silent in the yard.

Aksinya walked into the house with her old naïve smile. . . . The deaf man kept moving about the yard with his arms full of linen, then he began hanging it up again, in silence, without haste.

And until the cook came back from the river no one ventured to go into the kitchen and see what was there.

VIII

Nikifor was taken to the district hospital, and towards evening he died there. Lipa did not wait for them to come for her, but wrapped the dead baby in its little quilt and carried it home.

The hospital, a new one recently built, with big windows, stood high up on a hill; it was glittering from the setting sun and looked as though it were on fire from inside. There was a little village below. Lipa went down along the road, and before reaching the village sat down by a pond. A woman brought a horse down to drink and the horse did not drink.

"What more do you want?" said the woman to it softly. "What do you want?"

A boy in a red shirt, sitting at the water's edge, was washing his father's boots. And not another soul was in sight either in the village or on the hill.

"It's not drinking," said Lipa, looking at the horse.

Then the woman with the horse and the boy with the boots walked away, and there was no one left at all. The sun went to bed wrapped in cloth of gold and purple, and long clouds, red and lilac, stretched across the sky, guarded its slumbers. Some-where far away a bittern cried, a hollow, melancholy sound like a cow shut up in a barn. The cry of that mysterious bird was heard every spring, but no one knew what it was like or where it lived. At the top of the hill by the hospital, in the bushes close to the pond, and in the fields the nightingales were trilling. The cuckoo kept reckoning someone's years and losing count and beginning again. In the pond the frogs called angrily to one another, straining themselves to bursting, and one could even make out the words: "That's what you are! That's what you are!" What a noise there was! It seemed as though all these creatures were singing and shouting so that no one might sleep on that spring night, so that all, even the angry frogs, might appreciate and enjoy every minute: life is given only once.

A silver half-moon was shining in the sky; there were many stars. Lipa had no idea how long she sat by the pond, but when she got up and walked on everybody was asleep in the little village, and there was not a single light. It was probably about nine miles' walk home, but she had not the strength, she had not the power to think how to go: the moon gleamed now in front, now on the right, and the same cuckoo kept calling in a voice grown husky, with a chuckle as though gibing at her: "Oy, look out, you'll lose your way!" Lipa walked rapidly; she lost the kerchief from her head . . . she looked at the sky and wondered where her baby's soul was now: was it following her, or floating aloft yonder among the stars and thinking nothing now of his mother? Oh, how lonely it was in the open country at night, in the midst of that singing when one cannot sing oneself; in the midst of the incessant cries of joy when one cannot oneself be joyful, when the moon, which cares not whether it is spring or winter, whether men are alive or dead, looks down as lonely, too. . . . When there is grief in the heart it is hard to be without people. If only her mother, Praskovya, had been with her, or Crutch, or the cook, or some peasant!

"Boo-oo!" cried the bittern. "Boo-oo!"

And suddenly she heard clearly the sound of human speech: "Put the horses in, Vavila!"

By the wayside a camp-fire was burning ahead of her: the flames had died down, there were only red embers. She could hear the horses munching. In the darkness she could see the outlines of two carts, one with a barrel, the other, a lower one with sacks in it, and the figures of two men; one was leading a horse to put it into the shafts, the other was standing motionless by the fire with his hands behind his back. A dog growled by the carts. The one who was leading the horse stopped and said:

"It seems as though someone were coming along the road."

"Sharik, be quiet!" the other called to the dog.

And from the voice one could tell that the second was an old man. Lipa stopped and said:

"God help you."

The old man went up to her and answered not immediately:

"Good evening!"

"Your dog does not bite, grandfather?"

"No, come along, he won't touch you."

"I have been at the hospital," said Lipa after a pause. "My little son died there. Here I am carrying him home."

It must have been unpleasant for the old man to hear this, for he moved away and said hurriedly:

"Never mind, my dear. It's God's will. You are very slow, lad," he added, addressing his companion; "look alive!"

"Your yoke's nowhere," said the young man; "it is not to be seen."

"You are a regular Vavila."

The old man picked up an ember, blew on it – only his eyes and nose were lighted up – then, when they had found the yoke, he went with the light to Lipa and looked at her, and his look expressed compassion and tenderness.

"You are a mother," he said; "every mother grieves for her child."

And he sighed and shook his head as he said it. Vavila threw something on the fire, stamped on it – and at once it was very dark; the vision vanished, and as before there were only the fields, the sky with the stars, and the noise of the birds hindering each other from sleep. And the landrail called, it seemed, in the very place where the fire had been.

But a minute passed, and again she could see the two carts and the old man and lanky Vavila. The carts creaked as they went out on the road.

"Are you holy men?" Lipa asked the old man.

"No. We are from Firsanovo."

"You looked at me just now and my heart was softened. And the young man is so gentle. I thought you must be holy men."

"Are you going far?"

"To Ukleevo."

"Get in, we will give you a lift as far as Kuzmenki, then you go straight on and we turn off to the left."

Vavila got into the cart with the barrel and the old man and Lipa got into the other. They moved at a walking pace, Vavila in front.

"My baby was in torment all day," said Lipa. "He looked at me with his little eyes and said nothing; he wanted to speak and could not. Holy Father, Queen of Heaven! In my grief I kept falling down on the floor. I stood up and fell down by the bedside. And tell me, grandfather, why a little thing should be tormented before his death? When a grown-up person, a man or woman, are in torment their sins are forgiven, but why a little thing, when he has no sins? Why?"

"Who can tell?" answered the old man.

They drove on for half an hour in silence.

"We can't know everything, how and wherefore," said the old man. "It is ordained for the bird to have not four wings but two because it is able to fly with two; and so it is ordained for man not to know everything but only a half or a quarter. As much as he needs to know so as to live, so much he knows."

"It is better for me to go on foot, grandfather. Now my heart is all of a tremble."

"Never mind, sit still."

The old man yawned and made the sign of the cross over his mouth.

"Never mind," he repeated. "Yours is not the worst of sorrows. Life is long, there will be good and bad to come, there will be everything. Great is mother Russia," he said, and looked round on each side of him. "I have been all over Russia, and I have seen everything in her, and you may believe my words, my dear. There will be good and there will be bad. I went as a delegate from my village to Siberia, and I have been to the Amur River and the Altai Mountains and I settled in Siberia; I worked the land there, then I was homesick for mother Russia and I came back to my native village. We came back to Russia on foot; and I remember we went on a steamer, and I was thin as thin, all in rags, barefoot, freezing with cold, and gnawing a crust, and a gentleman who was on the steamer — the Kingdom of Heaven be his if he is dead — looked at me pitifully, and the tears came into his eyes. 'Ah,' he said, 'your bread is black, your days are black. . . .' And when I got home, as the saying is, there was neither stick nor stall; I had a wife, but I left her behind in Siberia, she was buried there. So I am living as a day labourer. And yet I tell you: since then I have had good as well as bad. Here I do not want to die, my dear, I would be glad to live another twenty years; so there has been more of the good. And great is our mother Russia!" and again he gazed to each side and looked round.

"Grandfather," Lipa asked, "when anyone dies, how many days does his soul walk the earth?"

"Who can tell! Ask Vavila here, he has been to school. Now they teach them everything. Vavila!" the old man called to him.

"Yes!"

"Vavila, when anyone dies how long does his soul walk the earth?"

Vavila stopped the horse and only then answered:

"Nine days. My uncle Kirilla died and his soul lived in our hut thirteen days after."

"How do you know?"

"For thirteen days there was a knocking in the stove."

"Well, that's all right. Go on," said the old man, and it could be seen that he did not believe a word of all that.

Near Kuzmenki the cart turned into the high road while Lipa went straight on. It was by now getting light. As she went down into the ravine the Ukleevo huts and the church were hidden in fog. It was cold, and it seemed to her that the same cuckoo was calling still.

When Lipa reached home the cattle had not yet been driven out; everyone was asleep. She sat down on the steps and waited. The old man was the first to come out; he understood all that had happened from the first glance at her, and for a long time he could not articulate a word, but only moved his lips without a sound.

"Ech, Lipa," he said, "you did not take care of my grandchild. . . ."

306

Varvara was awakened. She clasped her hands and broke into sobs, and immediately began laying out the baby.

"And he was a pretty child . . ." she said. "Oh, dear, dear. . . . You only had the one child, and you did not take care enough of him, you silly girl. . . ."

There was a requiem service in the morning and the evening. The funeral took place the next day, and after it the guests and the priests ate a great deal, and with such greed that one might have thought that they had not tasted food for a long time. Lipa waited at table, and the priest, lifting his fork on which there was a salted mushroom, said to her:

"Don't grieve for the babe. For of such is the Kingdom of Heaven."

And only when they had all separated Lipa realized fully that there was no Nikifor and never would be, she realized it and broke into sobs. And she did not know what room to go into to sob, for she felt that now that her child was dead there was no place for her in the house, that she had no reason to be here, that she was in the way; and the others felt it, too.

"Now what are you bellowing for?" Aksinya shouted, suddenly appearing in the doorway; in honour of the funeral she was dressed all in new clothes and had powdered her face. "Shut up!"

Lipa tried to stop but could not, and sobbed louder than ever.

"Do you hear?" shouted Aksinya, and she stamped her foot in violent anger. "Who is it I am speaking to? Go out of the yard and don't set foot here again, you convict's wife. Get away."

"There, there, there," the old man put in fussily. "Aksinya, don't make such an outcry, my girl. . . . She is crying, it is only natural . . . her child is dead. . . ."

"'It's only natural,'" Aksinya mimicked him. "Let her stay the night here, and don't let me see a trace of her here tomorrow! 'It's only natural!' . . ." she mimicked him again, and, laughing, she went into the shop.

Early the next morning Lipa went off to her mother at Torguevo.

IX

At the present time the steps and the front door of the shop have been repainted and are as bright as though they were new, there are gay geraniums in the windows as of old, and what happened in Tsybukin's house and yard three years ago is almost forgotten.

Grigory Petrovitch is looked upon as the master as he was in old days, but in reality everything has passed into Aksinya's hands; she buys and sells, and nothing can be done without her consent. The brickyard is working well; and as bricks are wanted for the railway the price has gone up to twenty-four roubles a thousand; peasant women and girls cart the bricks to the station and load them up in the trucks and earn a quarter-rouble a day for the work.

Aksinya has gone into partnership with the Hrymin Juniors,

and their factory is now called Hrymin Juniors and Co. They have opened a tavern near the station, and now the expensive concertina is played not at the factory but at the tavern, and the head of the post-office often goes there, and he, too, is engaged in some sort of traffic, and the stationmaster, too. Hrymin Juniors have presented the deaf man Stepan with a gold watch, and he is constantly taking it out of his pocket and putting it to his ear.

People say of Aksinya that she has become a person of power; and it is true that when she drives in the morning to her brick-yard, handsome and happy, with the naïve smile on her face, and afterwards when she is giving orders there, one is aware of great power in her. Everyone is afraid of her in the house and in the village and in the brickyard. When she goes to the post the head of the postal department jumps up and says to her:

"I humbly beg you to be seated, Aksinya Abramovna!"

A certain landowner, middle-aged but foppish, in a tunic of fine cloth and patent leather high boots, sold her a horse, and was so carried away by talking to her that he knocked down the price to meet her wishes. He held her hand a long time and, looking into her merry, sly, naïve eyes, said:

"For a woman like you, Aksinya Abramovna, I should be ready to do anything you please. Only say when we can meet where no one will interfere with us?"

"Why, when you please."

And since then the elderly fop drives up to the shop almost every day to drink beer. And the beer is horrid, bitter as wormwood. The landowner shakes his head, but he drinks it.

Old Tsybukin does not have anything to do with the business now at all. He does not keep any money because he cannot distinguish between the good and the false, but he is silent, he says nothing of this weakness. He has become forgetful, and if they don't give him food he does not ask for it. They have grown used to having dinner without him, and Varvara often says:

"He went to bed again yesterday without any supper."

And she says it unconcernedly because she is used to it. For some reason, summer and winter alike, he wears a fur coat, and only in very hot weather he does not go out but sits at home. As a rule putting on his fur coat, wrapping it round him and turning up his collar, he walks about the village, along the road to the station, or sits from morning till night on the seat near the church gates. He sits there without stirring. Passers-by bow to him, but he does not respond, for as of old he dislikes the peasants. If he is asked a question he answers quite rationally and politely, but briefly.

There is a rumour going about in the village that his daughter-in-law turns him out of the house and gives him nothing to eat, and that he is fed by charity; some are glad, others are sorry for him.

Varvara has grown even fatter and whiter, and as before she is active in good works, and Aksinya does not interfere with her.

There is so much jam now that they have not time to eat

it before the fresh fruit comes in; it goes sugary, and Varvara almost sheds tears, not knowing what to do with it.

They have begun to forget about Anisim. A letter has come from him written in verse on a big sheet of paper as though it were a petition, all in the same splendid handwriting. Evidently his friend Samorodov was sharing his punishment. Under the verses in an ugly, scarcely legible handwriting there was a single line: "I am ill here all the time; I am wretched, for Christ's sake help me!"

Towards evening – it was a fine autumn day – old Tsybukin was sitting near the church gates, with the collar of his fur coat turned up and nothing of him could be seen but his nose and the peak of his cap. At the other end of the long seat was sitting Elizarov the contractor, and beside him Yakov the school watchman, a toothless old man of seventy. Crutch and the watchman were talking.

"Children ought to give food and drink to the old. . . . Honour thy father and mother . . ." Yakov was saying with irritation, "while she, this daughter-in-law, has turned her father-in-law out of his own house; the old man has neither food nor drink, where is he to go? He has not had a morsel for these three days."

"Three days!" said Crutch, amazed.

"Here he sits and does not say a word. He has grown feeble. And why be silent? He ought to prosecute her, they wouldn't flatter her in the police court."

"Wouldn't flatter whom?" asked Crutch, not hearing.

"What?"

"The woman's all right, she does her best. In their line of business they can't get on without that . . . without sin, I mean. . . ."

"From his own house," Yakov went on with irritation. "Save up and buy your own house, then turn people out of it! She is a nice one, to be sure! A pla-ague!"

Tsybukin listened and did not stir.

"Whether it is your own house or others' it makes no difference so long as it is warm and the women don't scold . . ." said Crutch, and he laughed. "When I was young I was very fond of my Nastasya. She was a quiet woman. And she used to be always at it: 'Buy a house, Makaritch! Buy a house, Makaritch! Buy a house, Makaritch!' She was dying and yet she kept on saying, 'Buy yourself a racing droshky, Makaritch, that you may not have to walk.' And I bought her nothing but gingerbread."

"Her husband's deaf and stupid," Yakov went on, not hearing Crutch; "a regular fool, just like a goose. He can't understand anything. Hit a goose on the head with a stick and even then it does not understand."

Crutch got up to go home to the factory. Yakov also got up, and both of them went off together, still talking. When they had gone fifty paces old Tsybukin got up, too, and walked after them, stepping uncertainly as though on slippery ice.

The village was already plunged in the dusk of evening and the sun only gleamed on the upper part of the road which ran wriggling like a snake up the slope. Old women were coming back from the woods and children with them; they were bringing baskets of mushrooms. Peasant women and girls came in a crowd from the station where they had been loading the trucks with bricks, and their noses and their cheeks under their eyes were covered with red brick-dust. They were singing. Ahead of them all was Lipa singing in a high voice, with her eyes turned upwards to the sky, breaking into trills as though triumphant and ecstatic that at last the day was over and she could rest. In the crowd was her mother Praskovya, who was walking with a bundle in her arms and breathless as usual.

"Good evening, Makaritch!" cried Lipa, seeing Crutch. "Good evening, darling!"

"Good evening, Lipinka," cried Crutch delighted. "Dear girls and women, love the rich carpenter! Ho-ho! My little children, my little children. (Crutch gave a gulp.) My dear little axes!"

Crutch and Yakov went on further and could still be heard talking. Then after them the crowd was met by old Tsybukin and there was a sudden hush. Lipa and Praskovya had dropped a little behind, and when the old man was on a level with them Lipa bowed down low and said:

"Good evening, Grigory Petrovitch."

Her mother, too, bowed down. The old man stopped and, saying nothing, looked at the two in silence; his lips were quivering and his eyes full of tears. Lipa took out of her mother's bundle a piece of savoury turnover and gave it him. He took it and began eating.

The sun had by now set: its glow died away on the road above. It grew dark and cool. Lipa and Praskovya walked on and for some time they kept crossing themselves.

Three Years

I

IT WAS DARK, and already lights had begun to gleam here and there in the houses, and a pale moon was rising behind the barracks at the end of the street. Laptev was sitting on a bench by the gate waiting for the end of the evening service at the Church of St. Peter and St. Paul. He was reckoning that Yulia Sergeyevna would pass by on her way from the service, and then he would speak to her, and perhaps spend the whole evening with her.

He had been sitting there for an hour and a half already, and all that time his imagination had been busy picturing his Moscow rooms, his Moscow friends, his man Pyotr, and his writing-table. He gazed half wonderingly at the dark, motionless trees, and it seemed strange to him that he was living now, not in his summer villa at Sokolniki, but in a provincial town in a house by which a great herd of cattle was driven every morning and evening, accompanied by terrible clouds of dust and the blowing of a horn. He thought of long conversations in which he had taken part quite lately in Moscow — conversations in which it had been maintained that one could live without love, that passionate love was an obsession, that finally there is no such love, but only a physical attraction between the sexes — and so on, in the same style; he remembered them and thought mournfully that if he were asked now what love was, he could not have found an answer.

The service was over, the people began to appear. Laptev strained his eyes gazing at the dark figures. The bishop had been driven by in his carriage, the bells had stopped ringing, and the red and green lights in the belfry were one after another extinguished — there had been an illumination, as it was dedication day — but the people were still coming out, lingering, talking, and standing under the windows. But at last Laptev heard a familiar voice, his heart began beating violently, and he was overcome with despair on seeing that Yulia Sergeyevna was not alone, but walking with two ladies.

"It's awful, awful!" he whispered, feeling jealous. "It's awful!"

At the corner of the lane, she stopped to say goodbye to the ladies, and while doing so glanced at Laptev.

"I was coming to see you," he said. "I'm coming for a chat with your father. Is he at home?"

"Most likely," she answered. "It's early for him to have gone to the club."

There were gardens all along the lane, and a row of lime-trees growing by the fence cast a broad patch of shadow in the moonlight, so that the gate and the fences were completely plunged in darkness on one side, from which came the sounds of women whispering, smothered laughter, and someone playing softly on a balalaika. There was a fragrance of lime-flowers and of hay. This fragrance and the murmur of the unseen whispers worked upon Laptev. He was all at once overwhelmed with a passionate longing to throw his arms round his companion, to shower kisses on her face, her hands, her shoulders, to burst into sobs, to fall at her feet and to tell her how long he had been waiting for her. A faint scarcely perceptible scent of incense hung about her; and that scent reminded him of the time when he, too, believed in God and used to go to evening service, and when he used to dream so much of pure romantic love. And it seemed to him that, because this girl did not love him, all possibility of the happiness he had dreamed of then was lost to him forever.

She began speaking sympathetically of the illness of his sister, Nina Fyodorovna. Two months before his sister had undergone an operation for cancer, and now everyone was expecting a return of the disease.

"I went to see her this morning," said Yulia Sergeyevna, "and it seemed to me that during the last week she has, not exactly grown thin, but has, as it were, faded."

"Yes, yes," Laptev agreed. "There's no return of the symptoms, but every day I notice she grows weaker and weaker, and is wasting before my eyes. I don't understand what's the matter with her."

"Oh dear! And how strong she used to be, plump and rosy!" said Yulia Sergeyevna after a moment's silence. "Everyone here used to call her the Moscow lady. How she used to laugh! On holidays she used to dress up like a peasant girl, and it suited her so well."

Dr. Sergey Borisovitch was at home; he was a stout, red-faced man, wearing a long coat that reached below his knees, and looking as though he had short legs. He was pacing up and down his study, with his hands in his pockets, and humming to himself in an undertone, "Ru-ru-ru-ru." His grey whiskers looked unkempt, and his hair was unbrushed, as though he had just got out of bed. And his study with pillows on the sofa, with stacks of papers in the corners, and with a dirty invalid poodle lying under the table, produced the same impression of unkemptness and untidiness as himself.

"M. Laptev wants to see you," his daughter said to him, going into his study.

"Ru-ru-ru-ru," he hummed louder than ever, and turning into the drawing-room, gave his hand to Laptev, and asked: "What good news have you to tell me?"

It was dark in the drawing-room. Laptev, still standing with his hat in his hand, began apologizing for disturbing him; he asked what was to be done to make his sister sleep at night, and why she was growing so thin; and he was embarrassed by the thought that he had asked those very questions at his visit that morning.

"Tell me," he said, "wouldn't it be as well to send for some specialist on internal diseases from Moscow? What do you think of it?"

The doctor sighed, shrugged his shoulders, and made a vague gesture with his hands.

It was evident that he was offended. He was a very huffy man, prone to take offence, and always ready to suspect that people did not believe in him, that he was not recognized or properly respected, that his patients exploited him, and that his colleagues showed him ill-will. He was always jeering at himself, saying that fools like him were only made for the public to ride rough-shod over them.

Yulia Sergeyevna lighted the lamp. She was tired out with the service, and that was evident from her pale, exhausted face, and her weary step. She wanted to rest. She sat down on the sofa, put her hands on her lap, and sank into thought. Laptev knew that he was ugly, and now he felt as though he were conscious of his ugliness all over his body. He was short, thin, with ruddy cheeks, and his hair had grown so thin that his head felt cold. In his expression there was none of that refined simplicity which makes even rough, ugly faces attractive; in the society of women, he was awkward, over-talkative, affected. And now he almost despised himself for it. He must talk that Yulia Sergeyevna might not be bored in his company. But what about? About his sister's illness again?

And he began to talk about medicine, saying what is usually said. He approved of hygiene, and said that he had long ago wanted to found a night-refuge in Moscow — in fact, he had already calculated the cost of it. According to his plan the workmen who came in the evening to the night-refuge were to receive a supper of hot cabbage soup with bread, a warm, dry bed with a rug, and a place for drying their clothes and their boots.

Yulia Sergeyevna was usually silent in his presence, and in a strange way, perhaps by the instinct of a lover, he divined her thoughts and intentions. And now, from the fact that after the evening service she had not gone to her room to change her dress and drink tea, he deduced that she was going to pay some visit elsewhere.

"But I'm in no hurry with the night-refuge," he went on, speaking with vexation and irritability, and addressing the doctor, who looked at him, as it were, blankly and in perplexity, evidently unable to understand what induced him to raise the question of medicine and hygiene. "And most likely it will be a long time, too, before I make use of our estimate. I fear our night-shelter will fall into the hands of our pious humbugs and philanthropic ladies, who always ruin any undertaking."

Yulia Sergeyevna got up and held out her hand to Laptev.

"Excuse me," she said, "it's time for me to go. Please give my love to your sister."

"Ru-ru-ru-ru," hummed the doctor. "Ru-ru-ru-ru."

Yulia Sergeyevna went out, and after staying a little longer, Laptev said goodbye to the doctor and went home. When a man is dissatisfied and feels unhappy, how trivial seem to him the shapes of the lime-trees, the shadows, the clouds, all the beauties of nature, so complacent, so indifferent! By now the moon was high up in the sky, and the clouds were scudding quickly below. "But how naïve and provincial the moon is, how threadbare and paltry the clouds!" thought Laptev. He felt ashamed of the way he had talked just now about medicine, and the night-refuge. He felt with horror that next day he would not have will enough to resist trying to see her and talk to her again, and would again be convinced that he was nothing to her. And the day after – it would be the same. With what object? And how and when would it all end?

At home he went in to see his sister. Nina Fyodorovna still looked strong and gave the impression of being a well-built, vigorous woman, but her striking pallor made her look like a corpse, especially when, as now, she was lying on her back with her eyes closed; her eldest daughter Sasha, a girl of ten years old, was sitting beside her reading aloud from her reading-book.

"Alyosha has come," the invalid said softly to herself.

There had long been established between Sasha and her uncle a tacit compact, to take turns in sitting with the patient. On this occasion Sasha closed her reading-book, and without uttering a word, went softly out of the room. Laptev took an historical novel from the chest of drawers, and looking for the right page, sat down and began reading it aloud.

Nina Fyodorovna was born in Moscow of a merchant family. She and her two brothers had spent their childhood and early youth, living at home in Pyatnitsky Street. Their childhood was long and wearisome; her father treated her sternly, and had even on two or three occasions flogged her, and her mother had had a long illness and died. The servants were coarse, dirty, and hypocritical; the house was frequented by priests and monks, also hypocritical; they ate and drank and coarsely flattered her father, whom they did not like. The boys had the good-fortune to go to school, while Nina was left practically uneducated. All her life she wrote an illegible scrawl, and had read nothing but historical novels. Seventeen years ago, when she was twenty-two, on a summer holiday at Himki, she made the acquaintance of her present husband, a landowner called Panaurov, had fallen in love with him, and married him secretly against her father's will. Panaurov, a handsome, rather impudent fellow, who whistled and lighted his cigarette from the holy lamp, struck the father as an absolutely worthless person. And when the son-in-law began in his letters demanding a dowry, the old man wrote to his daughter that he would send her furs, silver, and various articles that had been left at her mother's death, as well as thirty thousand roubles, but without his paternal blessing. Later he sent another twenty thousand. This money, as well as the dowry, was spent; the estate had been sold and Panaurov moved with his family to the town and got a job in a provincial government office. In the town he formed another tie, and had a second family, and this was the subject of much talk, as his illicit family was not a secret.

Nina Fyodorovna adored her husband. And now, listening to the historical novel, she was thinking how much she had gone through in her life, how much she had suffered, and that if anyone were to describe her life it would make a very pathetic story. As the tumour was in her breast, she was persuaded that love and her domestic grief were the cause of her illness, and that jealousy and tears had brought her to her hopeless state.

At last Alexey Fyodorovitch closed the book and said:

"That's the end, and thank God for it. Tomorrow we'll begin a new one."

Nina Fyodorovna laughed. She had always been given to laughter, but of late Laptev had begun to notice that at moments her mind seemed weakened by illness, and she would laugh at the smallest trifle, and even without any cause at all.

"Yulia came before dinner while you were out," she said. "So far as I can see, she hasn't much faith in her papa. 'Let papa go on treating you,' she said, 'but write in secret to the holy elder to pray for you, too.' There is a holy man somewhere here. Yulia forgot her parasol here; you must take it to her tomorrow," she went on after a brief pause. "No, when the end comes, neither doctors nor holy men are any help."

"Nina, why can't you sleep at night?" Laptev asked, to change the subject.

"Oh, well, I don't go to sleep – that's all. I lie and think."

"What do you think about, dear?"

"About the children, about you . . . about my life. I've gone through a great deal, Alyosha, you know. When one begins to remember and remember. . . . My God!" She laughed. "It's no joke to have borne five children as I have, to have buried three . . . Sometimes I was expecting to be confined while my Grigory Nikolaitch would be sitting at that very time with another woman. There would be no one to send for the doctor or the midwife. I would go into the passage or the kitchen for the servant, and there Jews, tradesmen, moneylenders, would be waiting for him to come home. My head used to go round. . . . He did not love me, though he never said so openly. Now I've grown calmer – it doesn't weigh on my heart; but in old days, when I was younger, it hurt me – ach! how it hurt me, darling! Once – while we were still in the country – I found him in the garden with a lady, and I walked away . . . I walked on aimlessly, and I don't know how, but I found myself in the church porch. I fell on my knees: 'Queen of Heaven!' I said. And it was night, the moon was shining. . . ."

She was exhausted, she began gasping for breath. Then, after resting a little, she took her brother's hand and went on in a weak, toneless voice:

"How kind you are, Alyosha! . . . And how clever! . . . What a good man you've grown up into!"

At midnight Laptev said good-night to her, and as he went

away he took with him the parasol that Yulia Sergeyevna had forgotten. In spite of the late hour, the servants, male and female, were drinking tea in the dining-room. How disorderly! The children were not in bed, but were there in the dining-room, too. They were all talking softly in undertones, and had not noticed that the lamp was smoking and would soon go out. All these people, big and little, were disturbed by a whole succession of bad omens and were in an oppressed mood. The glass in the hall had been broken, the samovar had been buzzing every day, and, as though on purpose, was even buzzing now. They were describing how a mouse had jumped out of Nina Fyodorovna's boot when she was dressing. And the children were quite aware of the terrible significance of these omens. The elder girl, Sasha, a thin little brunette, was sitting motionless at the table, and her face looked scared and woebegone, while the younger, Lida, a chubby fair child of seven, stood beside her sister looking from under her brows at the light.

Laptev went downstairs to his own rooms in the lower storey, where under the low ceilings it was always close and smelt of geraniums. In his sitting-room, Panaurov, Nina Fyodorovna's husband, was sitting reading the newspaper. Laptev nodded to him and sat down opposite. Both sat still and said nothing. They used to spend whole evenings like this without speaking, and neither of them was in the least put out by this silence.

The little girls came down from upstairs to say good-night. Deliberately and in silence, Panaurov made the sign of the cross over them several times, and gave them his hand to kiss. They dropped curtsies, and then went up to Laptev, who had to make the sign of the cross and give them his hand to kiss also. This ceremony with the hand-kissing and curtsying was repeated every evening.

When the children had gone out Panaurov laid aside the newspaper and said:

"It's not very lively in our God-fearing town! I must confess, my dear fellow," he added with a sigh, "I'm very glad that at last you've found some distraction."

"What do you mean?" asked Laptev.

"I saw you coming out of Dr. Byelavin's just now. I expect you don't go there for the sake of the papa."

"Of course not," said Laptev, and he blushed.

"Well, of course not. And by the way, you wouldn't find such another old brute as that papa if you hunted by daylight with a candle. You can't imagine what a foul, stupid, clumsy beast he is! You cultured people in the capitals are still interested in the provinces only on the lyrical side, only from the *paysage* and *Poor Anton* point of view, but I can assure you, my boy, there's nothing logical about it; there's nothing but barbarism, meanness, and nastiness – that's all. Take the local devotees of science – the local intellectuals, so to speak. Can you imagine there are here in this town twenty-eight doctors? They've all made their fortunes, and they are living in houses of their own, and meanwhile the population is in just as helpless a condition as ever. Here, Nina had to have an operation, quite an ordinary one really, yet we were obliged to get a surgeon from Moscow; not one doctor here would undertake it. It's beyond all conception. They know nothing, they understand nothing. They take no interest in anything. Ask them, for instance, what cancer is – what it is, what it comes from."

And Panaurov began to explain what cancer was. He was a specialist on all scientific subjects, and explained from a scientific point of view everything that was discussed. But he explained it all in his own way. He had a theory of his own about the circulation of the blood, about chemistry, about astronomy. He talked slowly, softly, convincingly.

"It's beyond all conception," he pronounced in an imploring voice, screwing up his eyes, sighing languidly, and smiling as graciously as a king, and it was evident that he was very well satisfied with himself, and never gave a thought to the fact that he was fifty.

"I am rather hungry," said Laptev. "I should like something savoury."

"Well, that can easily be managed."

Not long afterwards Laptev and his brother-in-law were sitting upstairs in the dining-room having supper. Laptev had a glass of vodka, and then began drinking wine. Panaurov drank nothing. He never drank, and never gambled, yet in spite of that he had squandered all his own and his wife's property, and had accumulated debts. To squander so much in such a short time, one must have, not passions, but a special talent. Panaurov liked dainty fare, liked a handsome dinner service, liked music after dinner, speeches, bowing footmen, to whom he would carelessly fling tips of ten, even twenty-five roubles. He always took part in all lotteries and subscriptions, sent bouquets to ladies of his acquaintance on their birthdays, bought cups, stands for glasses, studs, ties, walking-sticks, scents, cigarette-holders, pipes, lap-dogs, parrots, Japanese bric-à-brac, antiques; he had silk nightshirts, and a bedstead made of ebony inlaid with mother-of-pearl. His dressing-gown was a genuine Bokhara, and everything was to correspond; and on all this there went every day, as he himself expressed, "a deluge" of money.

At supper he kept sighing and shaking his head.

"Yes, everything on this earth has an end," he said softly, screwing up his dark eyes. "You will fall in love and suffer. You will fall out of love; you'll be deceived, for there is no woman who will not deceive; you will suffer, will be brought to despair, and will be faithless too. But the time will come when all this will be a memory, and when you will reason about it coldly and look upon it as utterly trivial. . . ."

Laptev, tired, a little drunk, looked at his handsome head, his clipped black beard, and seemed to understand why women so loved this pampered, conceited, and physically handsome creature.

After supper Panaurov did not stay in the house, but went off to his other lodgings. Laptev went out to see him on his way.

Panaurov was the only man in the town who wore a top-hat, and his elegant, dandified figure, his top-hat and tan gloves, beside the grey fences, the pitiful little houses, with their three windows and the thickets of nettles, always made a strange and mournful impression.

After saying goodbye to him Laptev returned home without hurrying. The moon was shining brightly; one could distinguish every straw on the ground, and Laptev felt as though the moonlight were caressing his bare head, as though someone were passing a feather over his hair.

"I love!" he pronounced aloud, and he had a sudden longing to run to overtake Panaurov, to embrace him, to forgive him, to make him a present of a lot of money, and then to run off into the open country, into a wood, to run on and on without looking back.

At home he saw lying on the chair the parasol Yulia Sergeyevna had forgotten; he snatched it up and kissed it greedily. The parasol was a silk one, no longer new, tied round with old elastic. The handle was a cheap one, of white bone. Laptev opened it over him, and he felt as though there were the fragrance of happiness about him.

He settled himself more comfortably in his chair, and still keeping hold of the parasol, began writing to Moscow to one of his friends:

"DEAR PRECIOUS KOSTYA,

"Here is news for you: I'm in love again! I say *again*, because six years ago I fell in love with a Moscow actress, though I didn't even succeed in making her acquaintance, and for the last year and a half I have been living with a certain person you know — a woman neither young nor good-looking. Ah, my dear boy, how unlucky I am in love. I've never had any success with women, and if I say *again* it's simply because it's rather sad and mortifying to acknowledge even to myself that my youth has passed entirely without love, and that I'm in love in a real sense now for the first time in my life, at thirty-four. Let it stand that I love *again*.

"If only you knew what a girl she was! She couldn't be called a beauty — she has a broad face, she is very thin, but what a wonderful expression of goodness she has when she smiles! When she speaks, her voice is as clear as a bell. She never carries on a conversation with me — I don't know her; but when I'm beside her I feel she's a striking, exceptional creature, full of intelligence and lofty aspirations. She is religious, and you cannot imagine how deeply this touches me and exalts her in my eyes. On that point I am ready to argue with you endlessly. You may be right, to your thinking; but, still, I love to see her praying in church. She is a provincial, but she was educated in Moscow. She loves our Moscow; she dresses in the Moscow style, and I love her for that — love her, love her. . . . I see you frowning and getting up to read me a long lecture on what love is, and what sort of woman one can love, and what sort one cannot, and so on, and so on. But, dear Kostya, before I was in love I, too, knew quite well what love was.

"My sister thanks you for your message. She often recalls how she used to take Kostya Kotchevoy to the preparatory class, and never speaks of you except as *poor Kostya*, as she still thinks of you as the little orphan boy she remembers. And so, poor orphan, I'm in love. While it's a secret, don't say anything to a 'certain person'. I think it will all come right of itself, or, as the footman says in Tolstoy, will 'come round'."

When he had finished his letter Laptev went to bed. He was so tired that he couldn't keep his eyes open, but for some reason he could not get to sleep; the noise in the street seemed to prevent him. The cattle were driven by to the blowing of a horn, and soon afterwards the bells began ringing for early mass. At one minute a cart drove by creaking; at the next, he heard the voice of some woman going to market. And the sparrows twittered the whole time.

II

The next morning was a cheerful one; it was a holiday. At ten o'clock Nina Fyodorovna, wearing a brown dress and with her hair neatly arranged, was led into the drawing-room, supported on each side. There she walked about a little and stood by the open window, and her smile was broad and naïve, and, looking at her, one recalled a local artist, a great drunkard, who wanted her to sit to him for a picture of the Russian carnival. And all of them — the children, the servants, her brother, Alexey Fyodorovitch, and she herself — were suddenly convinced, that she was certainly going to get well. With shrieks of laughter the children ran after their uncle, chasing him and catching him, and filling the house with noise.

People called to ask how she was, brought her holy bread, told her that in almost all the churches they were offering up prayers for her that day. She had been conspicuous for her benevolence in the town, and was liked. She was very ready with her charity, like her brother Alexey, who gave away his money freely, without considering whether it was necessary to give it or not. Nina Fyodorovna used to pay the school fees for poor children; used to give away tea, sugar, and jam to old women; used to provide trousseaux for poor brides; and if she picked up a newspaper, she always looked first of all to see if there were any appeals for charity or a paragraph about somebody's being in a destitute condition.

She was holding now in her hand a bundle of notes, by means of which various poor people, her protégés, had procured goods from a grocer's shop.

They had been sent her the evening before by the shopkeeper with a request for the payment of the total — eighty-two roubles.

"My goodness, what a lot they've had! They've no

conscience!" she said, deciphering with difficulty her ugly hand-writing. "It's no joke! Eighty-two roubles! I declare I won't pay it."

"I'll pay it today," said Laptev.

"Why should you? Why should you?" cried Nina Fyodor-ovna in agitation. "It's quite enough for me to take two hundred and fifty every month from you and our brother. God bless you!" she added, speaking softly, so as not to be overheard by the servants.

"Well, but I spend two thousand five hundred a month," he said. "I tell you again, dear: you have just as much right to spend it as I or Fyodor. Do understand that, once for all. There are three of us, and of every three kopecks of our father's money, one belongs to you."

But Nina Fyodorovna did not understand, and her expression looked as though she were mentally solving some very difficult problem. And this lack of comprehension in pecuniary matters, always made Laptev feel uneasy and troubled. He suspected that she had private debts in addition which worried her and of which she scrupled to tell him.

Then came the sound of footsteps and heavy breathing; it was the doctor coming up the stairs, dishevelled and unkempt as usual.

"Ru-ru-ru," he was humming. "Ru-ru."

To avoid meeting him, Laptev went into the dining-room, and then went downstairs to his own room. It was clear to him that to get on with the doctor and to drop in at his house without formalities was impossible; and to meet the "old brute", as Panaurov called him, was distasteful. That was why he so rarely saw Yulia. He reflected now that the father was not at home, that if he were to take Yulia Sergeyevna her parasol, he would be sure to find her at home alone, and his heart ached with joy. Haste, haste!

He took the parasol and, violently agitated, flew on the wings of love. It was hot in the street. In the big courtyard of the doctor's house, overgrown with coarse grass and nettles, some twenty urchins were playing ball. These were all the children of working-class families who tenanted the three disreputable-looking lodges, which the doctor was always meaning to have done up, though he put it off from year to year. The yard resounded with ringing, healthy voices. At some distance on one side, Yulia Sergeyevna was standing at her porch, her hands folded, watching the game.

"Good morning!" Laptev called to her.

She looked round. Usually he saw her indifferent, cold, or tired as she had been the evening before. Now her face looked full of life and frolic, like the faces of the boys who were playing ball.

"Look, they never play so merrily in Moscow," she said, going to meet him. "There are no such big yards there, though; they've no place to run there. Papa has only just gone to you," she added, looking round at the children.

"I know; but I've not come to see him, but to see you," said Laptev, admiring her youthfulness, which he had not noticed till then, and seemed only that day to have discovered in her; it seemed to him as though he were seeing her slender white neck with the gold chain for the first time. "I've come to see you . . ." he repeated. "My sister has sent you your parasol; you forgot it yesterday."

She put out her hand to take the parasol, but he pressed it to his bosom and spoke passionately, without restraint, yielding again to the sweet ecstasy he had felt the night before, sitting under the parasol.

"I entreat you, give it me. I shall keep it in memory of you . . . of our acquaintance. It's so wonderful!"

"Take it," she said, and blushed; "but there's nothing wonderful about it."

He looked at her in ecstasy, in silence, not knowing what to say.

"Why am I keeping you here in the heat?" she said after a brief pause, laughing. "Let us go indoors."

"I am not disturbing you?"

They went into the hall. Yulia Sergeyevna ran upstairs, her white dress with blue flowers on it rustling as she went.

"I can't be disturbed," she answered, stopping on the landing. "I never do anything. Every day is a holiday for me, from morning till night."

"What you say is inconceivable to me," he said, going up to

her. "I grew up in a world in which everyone without exception, men and women alike, worked hard every day."

"But if one has nothing to do?" she asked.

"One has to arrange one's life under such conditions, that work is inevitable. There can be no clean and happy life without work."

Again he pressed the parasol to his bosom, and to his own surprise spoke softly, in a voice unlike his own:

"If you would consent to be my wife I would give everything — I would give everything. There's no price I would not pay, no sacrifice I would not make."

She started and looked at him with wonder and alarm.

"What are you saying!" she brought out, turning pale. "It's impossible, I assure you. Forgive me."

Then with the same rustle of her skirts she went up higher, and vanished through the doorway.

Laptev grasped what this meant, and his mood was transformed, completely, abruptly, as though a light in his soul had suddenly been extinguished. Filled with the shame of a man humiliated, of a man who is disdained, who is not liked, who is distasteful, perhaps disgusting, who is shunned, he walked out of the house.

"I would give everything," he thought, mimicking himself as he went home through the heat and recalled the details of his declaration. "I would give everything — like a regular tradesman. As though she wanted your *everything*!"

All he had just said seemed to him repulsively stupid. Why had he lied, saying that he had grown up in a world where everyone worked, without exception? Why had he talked to her in a lecturing tone about a clean and happy life? It was not clever, not interesting; it was false — false in the Moscow style. But by degrees there followed that mood of indifference into which criminals sink after a severe sentence. He began thinking that, thank God! everything was at an end and that the terrible uncertainty was over; that now there was no need to spend whole days in anticipation, in pining, in thinking always of the same thing. Now everything was clear; he must give up all hope of personal happiness, live without desires, without hopes, without dreams, or expectations, and to escape that dreary sadness which he was so sick of trying to soothe, he could busy himself with other people's affairs, other people's happiness, and old age would come on imperceptibly, and life would reach its end — and nothing more was wanted. He did not care, he wished for nothing, and could reason about it coolly, but there was a sort of heaviness in his face especially under his eyes, his forehead felt drawn tight like elastic — and tears were almost starting into his eyes. Feeling weak all over, he lay down on his bed, and in five minutes was sound asleep.

III

The proposal Laptev had made so suddenly threw Yulia Sergeyevna into despair.

She knew Laptev very little, had made his acquaintance by chance; he was a rich man, a partner in the well-known Moscow firm of "Fyodor Laptev and Sons"; always serious, apparently clever, and anxious about his sister's illness. It had seemed to her that he took no notice of her whatever, and she did not care about him in the least – and then all of a sudden that declaration on the stairs, that pitiful, ecstatic face. . . .

The offer had overwhelmed her by its suddenness and by the fact that the word "wife" had been uttered, and by the necessity of rejecting it. She could not remember what she had said to Laptev, but she still felt traces of the sudden, unpleasant feeling with which she had rejected him. He did not attract her; he looked like a shopman; he was not interesting; she could not have answered him except with a refusal, and yet she felt uncomfortable, as though she had done wrong.

"My God! without waiting to get into the room, on the stairs," she said to herself in despair, addressing the ikon which hung over her pillow; "and no courting beforehand, but so strangely, so oddly. . . ."

In her solitude her agitation grew more intense every hour, and it was beyond her strength to master this oppressive feeling alone. She needed someone to listen to her story and to tell her that she had done right. But she had no one to talk to. She had lost her mother long before; she thought her father a queer man, and could not talk to him seriously. He worried her with his whims, his extreme readiness to take offence, and his meaningless gestures; and as soon as one began to talk to him, he promptly turned the conversation on himself. And in her prayer she was not perfectly open, because she did not know for certain what she ought to pray for.

The samovar was brought in. Yulia Sergeyevna, very pale and tired, looking dejected, came into the dining-room to make tea – it was one of her duties – and poured out a glass for her father. Sergey Borisovitch, in his long coat that reached below his knees, with his red face and unkempt hair, walked up and down the room with his hands in his pockets, pacing, not from corner to corner, but backwards and forwards at random, like a wild beast in its cage. He would stand still by the table, sip his glass of tea with relish, and pace about again, lost in thought.

"Laptev made me an offer today," said Yulia Sergeyevna, and she flushed crimson.

The doctor looked at her and did not seem to understand.

"Laptev?" he queried. "Panaurov's brother-in-law?"

He was fond of his daughter; it was most likely that she would sooner or later be married, and leave him, but he tried not to think about that. He was afraid of being alone, and for some reason fancied, that if he were left alone in that great house, he would have an apoplectic stroke, but he did not like to speak of this directly.

"Well, I'm delighted to hear it," he said, shrugging his shoulders. "I congratulate you with all my heart. It offers you a splendid opportunity for leaving me, to your great satisfaction. And I quite understand your feelings. To live with an old father, an invalid, half crazy, must be very irksome at your age. I quite understand you. And the sooner I'm laid out and in the devil's clutches, the better everyone will be pleased. I congratulate you with all my heart."

"I refused him."

The doctor felt relieved, but he was unable to stop himself and went on:

"I wonder, I've long wondered, why I've not yet been put into a madhouse – why I'm still wearing this coat instead of a strait-waistcoat? I still have faith in justice, in goodness. I am a fool, an idealist, and nowadays that's insanity, isn't it? And how do they repay me for my honesty? They almost throw stones at me and ride rough-shod over me. And even my nearest kith and kin do nothing but try to get the better of me. It's high time the devil fetched an old fool like me. . . ."

"There's no talking to you like a rational being!" said Yulia.

She got up from the table impulsively, and went to her room in great wrath, remembering how often her father had been unjust to her. But a little while afterwards she felt sorry for her father, too, and when he was going to the club she went downstairs with him, and shut the door after him. It was a rough and stormy night; the door shook with the violence of the wind, and there were draughts in all directions in the passage, so that the candle was almost blown out. In her own domain upstairs Yulia Sergeyevna went the round of all the rooms, making the sign of the cross over every door and window; the wind howled, and it sounded as though someone were walking on the roof. Never had it been so dreary, never had she felt so lonely.

She asked herself whether she had done right in rejecting a man, simply because his appearance did not attract her. It was true he was a man she did not love, and to marry him would mean renouncing forever her dreams, her conceptions of happiness in married life, but would she ever meet the man of whom she dreamed, and would he love her? She was twenty-one already. There were no eligible young men in the town. She pictured all the men she knew – government clerks, schoolmasters, officers, and some of them were married already, and their domestic life was conspicuous for its dreariness and triviality; others were uninteresting, colourless, unintelligent, immoral. Laptev was, anyway, a Moscow man, had taken his degree at the university, spoke French. He lived in the capital, where there were lots of clever, noble, remarkable people; where there was noise and bustle, splendid theatres, musical evenings, first-rate dress-makers, confectioners. . . . In the Bible it was written that a wife must love her husband, and great importance was given to love in novels, but wasn't there exaggeration in it? Was it out of the question to enter upon married life without love? It was said, of course, that love soon passed away, and that nothing was left but habit, and that the object of married life was not to be found in love, nor in happiness, but in duties, such as the bringing up of one's children, the care of one's household, and so on. And perhaps what was meant in the Bible was love for one's husband as one's neighbour, respect for him, charity.

At night Yulia Sergeyevna read the evening prayers attentively, then knelt down, and pressing her hands to her bosom, gazing at the flame of the lamp before the ikon, said with feeling:

"Give me understanding, Holy Mother, our Defender! Give me understanding, O Lord!"

She had in the course of her life come across elderly maiden ladies, poor and of no consequence in the world, who bitterly repented and openly confessed their regret that they had refused suitors in the past. Would not the same thing happen to her? Had not she better go into a convent or become a Sister of Mercy?

She undressed and got into bed, crossing herself and crossing the air around her. Suddenly the bell rang sharply and plaintively in the corridor.

"Oh, my God!" she said, feeling a nervous irritation all over her at the sound. She lay still and kept thinking how poor this provincial life was in events, monotonous and yet not peaceful. One was constantly having to tremble, to feel apprehensive, angry or guilty, and in the end one's nerves were so strained, that one was afraid to peep out of the bedclothes.

A little while afterwards the bell rang just as sharply again. The servant must have been asleep and had not heard. Yulia Sergeyevna lighted a candle, and feeling vexed with the servant, began with a shiver to dress, and when she went out into the corridor, the maid was already closing the door downstairs.

"I thought it was the master, but it's someone from a patient," she said.

Yulia Sergeyevna went back to her room. She took a pack of cards out of the chest of drawers, and decided that if after shuffling the cards well and cutting, the bottom card turned out to be a red one, it would mean *yes* — that is, she would accept Laptev's offer; and that if it was a black, it would mean *no*. The card turned out to be the ten of spades.

That relieved her mind — she fell asleep; but in the morning, she was wavering again between *yes* and *no*, and she was dwelling on the thought that she could, if she chose, change her life. The thought harassed her, she felt exhausted and unwell; but yet, soon after eleven, she dressed and went to see Nina Fyodorovna. She wanted to see Laptev: perhaps now he would seem more attractive to her; perhaps she had been wrong about him hitherto. . . .

She found it hard to walk against the wind. She struggled along, holding her hat on with both hands, and could see nothing for the dust.

IV

Going into his sister's room, and seeing to his surprise Yulia Sergeyevna, Laptev had again the humiliating sensation of a man who feels himself an object of repulsion. He concluded that if after what had happened yesterday she could bring herself so easily to visit his sister and meet him, it must be because she was not concerned about him, and regarded him as a complete nonentity. But when he greeted her, and with a pale face and dust under her eyes she looked at him mournfully and remorsefully, he saw that she, too, was miserable.

She did not feel well. She only stayed ten minutes, and began saying goodbye. And as she went out she said to Laptev:

"Will you see me home, Alexey Fyodorovitch?"

They walked along the street in silence, holding their hats, and he, walking a little behind, tried to screen her from the wind. In the lane it was more sheltered, and they walked side by side.

"Forgive me if I was not nice yesterday;" and her voice quavered as though she were going to cry. "I was so wretched! I did not sleep all night."

"I slept well all night," said Laptev, without looking at her; "but that doesn't mean that I was happy. My life is broken. I'm deeply unhappy, and after your refusal yesterday I go about like a man poisoned. The most difficult thing was said yesterday. Today I feel no embarrassment and can talk to you frankly. I love you more than my sister, more than my dead mother. . . . I can live without my sister, and without my mother, and I have lived without them, but life without you – is meaningless to me; I can't face it. . . ."

And now too, as usual, he guessed her intention.

He realized that she wanted to go back to what had happened the day before, and with that object had asked him to accompany her, and now was taking him home with her. But what could she add to her refusal? What new idea had she in her head? From everything, from her glances, from her smile, and even from her tone, from the way she held her head and shoulders as she walked beside him, he saw that, as before, she did not love him, that he was a stranger to her. What more did she want to say?

Doctor Sergey Borisovitch was at home.

"You are very welcome. I'm always glad to see you, Fyodor Alexeyitch," he said, mixing up his Christian name and his father's. "Delighted, delighted!"

He had never been so polite before, and Laptev saw that he knew of his offer; he did not like that either. He was sitting now in the drawing-room, and the room impressed him strangely, with its poor, common decorations, its wretched pictures, and though there were arm-chairs in it, and a huge lamp with a shade over it, it still looked like an uninhabited place, a huge barn, and it was obvious that no one could feel at home in such a room, except a man like the doctor. The next room, almost twice as large, was called the reception-room, and in it there were only rows of chairs, as though for a dancing class. And while Laptev was sitting in the drawing-room talking to the doctor about his sister, he began to be tortured by a suspicion. Had not Yulia Sergeyevna been to his sister Nina's, and then brought him here to tell him that she would accept him? Oh, how awful it was! But the most awful thing of all was that his soul was capable of such a suspicion. And he imagined how the father and the daughter had spent the evening, and perhaps the night before, in prolonged consultation, perhaps dispute, and at last had come to the conclusion that Yulia had acted thoughtlessly in refusing a rich man. The words that parents use in such cases kept ringing in his ears:

"It is true you don't love him, but think what good you could do!"

The doctor was going out to see patients. Laptev would have gone with him, but Yulia Sergeyevna said:

"I beg you to stay."

She was distressed and dispirited, and told herself now that to refuse an honourable, good man who loved her, simply because he was not attractive, especially when marrying him would make it possible for her to change her mode of life, her cheerless, monotonous, idle life in which youth was passing with no prospect of anything better in the future – to refuse him under such circumstances was madness, caprice and folly, and that God might even punish her for it.

The father went out. When the sound of his steps had died

away, she suddenly stood up before Laptev and said resolutely, turning horribly white as she did so:

"I thought for a long time yesterday, Alexey Fyodorovitch. . . . I accept your offer."

He bent down and kissed her hand. She kissed him awkwardly on the head with cold lips.

He felt that in this love scene the chief thing – her love – was lacking, and that there was a great deal that was not wanted; and he longed to cry out, to run away, to go back to Moscow at once. But she was close to him, and she seemed to him so lovely, and he was suddenly overcome by passion. He reflected that it was too late for deliberation now; he embraced her passionately, and muttered some words, calling her *thou*; he kissed her on the neck, and then on the cheek, on the head. . . .

She walked away to the window, dismayed by these demonstrations, and both of them were already regretting what they had said and both were asking themselves in confusion:

"Why has this happened?"

"If only you knew how miserable I am!" she said, wringing her hands.

"What is it?" he said, going up to her, wringing his hands too. "My dear, for God's sake, tell me – what is it? Only tell the truth, I entreat you – nothing but the truth!"

"Don't pay any attention to it," she said, and forced herself to smile. "I promise you I'll be a faithful, devoted wife. . . . Come this evening."

Sitting afterwards with his sister and reading aloud an historical novel, he recalled it all and felt wounded that his splendid, pure, rich feeling was met with such a shallow response. He was not loved, but his offer had been accepted — in all probability because he was rich: that is, what was thought most of in him was what he valued least of all in himself. It was quite possible that Yulia, who was so pure and believed in God, had not once thought of his money; but she did not love him — did not love him, and evidently she had interested motives, vague, perhaps, and not fully thought out — still, it was so. The doctor's house with its common furniture was repulsive to him, and he looked upon the doctor himself as a wretched, greasy miser, a sort of operatic Gaspard from *Les Cloches de Corneville*. The very name "Yulia" had a vulgar sound. He imagined how he and his Yulia would stand at their wedding, in reality complete strangers to one another, without a trace of feeling on her side, just as though their marriage had been made by a professional matchmaker; and the only consolation left him now, as commonplace as the marriage itself, was the reflection that he was not the first, and would not be the last; that thousands of people were married like that; and that with time, when Yulia came to know him better, she would perhaps grow fond of him.

"Romeo and Juliet!" he said, as he shut the novel, and he laughed. "I am Romeo, Nina. You may congratulate me. I made an offer to Yulia Byelavin today."

348

Nina Fyodorovna thought he was joking, but when she believed it, she began to cry; she was not pleased at the news.

"Well, I congratulate you," she said. "But why is it so sudden?"

"No, it's not sudden. It's been going on since March, only you don't notice anything. . . . I fell in love with her last March when I made her acquaintance here, in your rooms."

"I thought you would marry someone in our Moscow set," said Nina Fyodorovna after a pause. "Girls in our set are simpler. But what matters, Alyosha, is that you should be happy – that matters most. My Grigory Nikolaitch did not love me, and there's no concealing it; you can see what our life is. Of course any woman may love you for your goodness and your brains, but, you see, Yulitchka is a girl of good family from a high-class boarding-school; goodness and brains are not enough for her. She is young, and, you, Alyosha, are not so young, and are not good-looking."

To soften the last words, she stroked his head and said:

"You're not good-looking, but you're a dear."

She was so agitated that a faint flush came into her cheeks, and she began discussing eagerly whether it would be the proper thing for her to bless Alyosha with the ikon at the wedding. She was, she reasoned, his elder sister, and took the place of his mother; and she kept trying to convince her dejected brother that the wedding must be celebrated in proper style, with pomp and gaiety, so that no one could find fault with it.

Then he began going to the Byelavins' as an accepted suitor, three or four times a day; and now he never had time to take Sasha's place and read aloud the historical novel. Yulia used to receive him in her two rooms, which were at a distance from the drawing-room and her father's study, and he liked them very much. The walls in them were dark; in the corner stood a case of ikons; and there was a smell of good scent and of the oil in the holy lamp. Her rooms were at the furthest end of the house; her bedstead and dressing-table were shut off by a screen. The doors of the bookcase were covered on the inside with a green curtain, and there were rugs on the floor, so that her footsteps were noiseless — and from this he concluded that she was of a reserved character, and that she liked a quiet, peaceful, secluded life. In her own home she was treated as though she were not quite grown up. She had no money of her own, and sometimes when they were out for walks together, she was overcome with confusion at not having a farthing. Her father allowed her very little for dress and books, hardly ten pounds a year. And, indeed, the doctor himself had not much money in spite of his good practice. He played cards every night at the club, and always lost. Moreover, he bought mortgaged houses through a building society, and let them. The tenants were irregular in paying the rent, but he was convinced that such speculations were profitable. He had mortgaged his own house in which he and his daughter were living, and with the money so raised had bought a piece of waste ground, and had already begun to build on it a large two-storey house, meaning to mortgage it, too, as soon as it was finished.

Laptev now lived in a sort of cloud, feeling as though he were not himself, but his double, and did many things which he would never have brought himself to do before. He went three or four times to the club with the doctor, had supper with him, and offered him money for house-building. He even visited Panaurov at his other establishment. It somehow happened that Panaurov invited him to dinner, and without thinking, Laptev accepted. He was received by a lady of five-and-thirty. She was tall and thin, with hair touched with grey, and black eyebrows, apparently not Russian. There were white patches of powder on her face. She gave him a honeyed smile and pressed his hand jerkily, so that the bracelets on her white hands tinkled. It seemed to Laptev that she smiled like that because she wanted to conceal from herself and from others that she was unhappy. He also saw two little girls, aged five and three, who had a marked likeness to Sasha. For dinner they had milk soup, cold veal, and chocolate. It was insipid and not good; but the table was splendid, with gold forks, bottles of Soyer, and cayenne pepper, an extraordinary bizarre cruet-stand, and a gold pepper-pot.

It was only as he was finishing the milk soup that Laptev realized how very inappropriate it was for him to be dining there. The lady was embarrassed, and kept smiling, showing her teeth. Panaurov expounded didactically what being in love was, and what it was due to.

"We have in it an example of the action of electricity," he said in French, addressing the lady. "Every man has in his skin microscopic glands which contain currents of electricity. If you meet with a person whose currents are parallel with your own, then you get love."

When Laptev went home and his sister asked him where he had been he felt awkward, and made no answer.

He felt himself in a false position right up to the time of the wedding. His love grew more intense every day, and Yulia seemed to him a poetic and exalted creature; but, all the same, there was no mutual love, and the truth was that he was buying her and she was selling herself. Sometimes, thinking things over, he fell into despair and asked himself: should he run away? He did not sleep for nights together, and kept thinking how he should meet in Moscow the lady whom he had called in his letters "a certain person", and what attitude his father and his brother, difficult people, would take towards his marriage and towards Yulia. He was afraid that his father would say something rude to Yulia at their first meeting. And something strange had happened of late to his brother Fyodor. In his long letters he had taken to writing of the importance of health, of the effect of illness on the mental condition, of the meaning of religion, but not a word about Moscow or business. These letters irritated Laptev, and he thought his brother's character was changing for the worse.

The wedding was in September. The ceremony took place at the Church of St. Peter and St. Paul, after mass, and the same day the young couple set off for Moscow. When Laptev and his wife, in a black dress with a long train, already looking not a girl but a married woman, said goodbye to Nina Fyodorovna, the invalid's face worked, but there was no tear in her dry eyes. She said:

"If – which God forbid – I should die, take care of my little girls."

"Oh, I promise!" answered Yulia Sergeyevna, and her lips and eyelids began quivering too.

"I shall come to see you in October," said Laptev, much moved. "You must get better, my darling."

They travelled in a special compartment. Both felt depressed and uncomfortable. She sat in the corner without taking off her hat, and made a show of dozing, and he lay on the seat opposite, and he was disturbed by various thoughts – of his father, of "a certain person", whether Yulia would like her Moscow flat. And looking at his wife, who did not love him, he wondered dejectedly "why this had happened".

V

The Laptevs had a wholesale business in Moscow, dealing in fancy goods: fringe, tape, trimmings, crochet cotton, buttons, and so on. The gross receipts reached two millions a year; what the net profit was, no one knew but the old father. The sons and the clerks estimated the profits at approximately three hundred thousand, and said that it would have been a hundred thousand more if the old man had not "been too free-handed" – that is, had not allowed credit indiscriminately. In the last ten years alone the bad debts had mounted up to the sum of a million; and when the subject was referred to, the senior clerk would wink slyly and deliver himself of sentences the meaning of which was not clear to everyone:

"The psychological sequences of the age."

Their chief commercial operations were conducted in the town market in a building which was called the warehouse. The entrance to the warehouse was in the yard, where it was always dark, and smelt of matting and where the dray-horses were always stamping their hoofs on the asphalt. A very humble-looking door, studded with iron, led from the yard into a room with walls discoloured by damp and scrawled over with charcoal, lighted up by a narrow window covered by an iron grating. Then on the left was another room larger and cleaner with an iron stove and a couple of chairs, though it, too, had a prison window: this was the office, and from it a narrow stone staircase led up to the second storey, where the principal room was. This was rather a large room, but owing to the perpetual darkness, the low-pitched ceiling, the piles of boxes and bales, and the numbers of men that kept flitting to and fro in it, it made as unpleasant an impression on a newcomer as the others. In the offices on the top storey the goods lay in bales, in bundles and in cardboard boxes on the shelves; there was no order nor neatness in the arrangement of it, and if crimson threads, tassels, ends of fringe, had not peeped out here and there from holes in the paper parcels, no one could have guessed what was being bought and sold here. And looking at these crumpled paper parcels and boxes, no one would have believed that a million was being made out of such trash, and that fifty men were employed every day in this warehouse, not counting the buyers.

When at midday, on the day after his arrival at Moscow, Laptev went into the warehouse, the workmen packing the goods were hammering so loudly that in the outer room and the office no one heard him come in. A postman he knew was coming down the stairs with a bundle of letters in his hand; he was wincing at the noise, and he did not notice Laptev either. The first person to meet him upstairs was his brother Fyodor Fyodorovitch, who was so like him that they passed for twins. This resemblance always reminded Laptev of his own personal appearance, and now, seeing before him a short, red-faced man with rather thin hair, with narrow plebeian hips, looking so uninteresting and so unintellectual, he asked himself: "Can I really look like that?"

"How glad I am to see you!" said Fyodor, kissing his brother and pressing his hand warmly. "I have been impatiently looking forward to seeing you every day, my dear fellow. When you wrote that you were getting married, I was tormented with curiosity, and I've missed you, too, brother. Only fancy, it's six months since we saw each other. Well? How goes it? Nina's very bad? Awfully bad?"

"Awfully bad."

"It's in God's hands," sighed Fyodor. "Well, what of your wife? She's a beauty, no doubt? I love her already. Of course, she is my little sister now. We'll make much of her between us."

Laptev saw the broad, bent back – so familiar to him – of his father, Fyodor Stepanovitch. The old man was sitting on a stool near the counter, talking to a customer.

"Father, God has sent us joy!" cried Fyodor. "Brother has come!"

Fyodor Stepanovitch was a tall man of exceptionally powerful build, so that, in spite of his wrinkles and eighty years, he still looked a hale and vigorous man. He spoke in a deep, rich, sonorous voice, that resounded from his broad chest as from a barrel. He wore no beard, but a short-clipped military moustache, and smoked cigars. As he was always too hot, he used all the year round to wear a canvas coat at home and at the warehouse. He had lately had an operation for cataract. His sight was bad, and he did nothing in the business but talk to the customers and have tea and jam with them.

Laptev bent down and kissed his head and then his lips.

"It's a good long time since we saw you, honoured sir," said the old man – "a good long time. Well, am I to congratulate you on entering the state of holy matrimony? Very well, then; I congratulate you."

And he put his lips out to be kissed. Laptev bent down and kissed him.

"Well, have you brought your young lady?" the old man asked, and without waiting for an answer, he said, addressing the customer: "'Herewith I beg to inform you, father, that I'm going to marry such and such a young lady.' Yes. But as for asking for his father's counsel or blessing, that's not in the rules nowadays. Now they go their own way. When I married I was over forty, but I went on my knees to my father and asked his advice. Nowadays we've none of that."

The old man was delighted to see his son, but thought it unseemly to show his affection or make any display of his joy. His voice and his manner of saying "your young lady" brought back to Laptev the depression he had always felt in the warehouse. Here every trifling detail reminded him of the past, when he used to be flogged and put on Lenten fare; he knew that even now boys were thrashed and punched in the face till their noses bled, and that when those boys grew up they would beat others. And before he had been five minutes in the warehouse, he always felt as though he were being scolded or punched in the face.

Fyodor slapped the customer on the shoulder and said to his brother:

"Here, Alyosha, I must introduce our Tambov benefactor, Grigory Timofeitch. He might serve as an example for the young men of the day; he's passed his fiftieth birthday, and he has tiny children."

The clerks laughed, and the customer, a lean old man with a pale face, laughed too.

"Nature above the normal capacity," observed the head-clerk, who was standing at the counter close by. "It always comes out when it's there."

The head-clerk — a tall man of fifty, in spectacles, with a dark beard, and a pencil behind his ear — usually expressed his ideas vaguely in roundabout hints, while his sly smile betrayed that he attached particular significance to his words. He liked to obscure his utterances with bookish words, which he understood in his own way, and many such words he used in a wrong sense. For instance, the word "except". When he had expressed some opinion positively and did not want to be contradicted, he would stretch out his hand and pronounce:

"Except!"

And what was most astonishing, the customers and the other clerks understood him perfectly. His name was Ivan Vassilitch Potchatkin, and he came from Kashira. Now, congratulating Laptev, he expressed himself as follows:

"It's the reward of valour, for the female heart is a strong opponent."

Another important person in the warehouse was a clerk called Makeitchev — a stout, solid, fair man with whiskers and a perfectly bald head. He went up to Laptev and congratulated him respectfully in a low voice:

"I have the honour, sir . . . The Lord has heard your parent's prayer. Thank God."

Then the other clerks began coming up to congratulate him on his marriage. They were all fashionably dressed, and looked like perfectly well-bred, educated men. Since between every two words they put in a "sir", their congratulations – something like "Best wishes, sir, for happiness, sir," uttered very rapidly in a low voice – sounded rather like the hiss of a whip in the air – "Shshsh-s s s s s!" Laptev was soon bored and longing to go home, but it was awkward to go away. He was obliged to stay at least two hours at the warehouse to keep up appearances. He walked away from the counter and began asking Makeitchev whether things had gone well while he was away, and whether anything new had turned up, and the clerk answered him respectfully, avoiding his eyes. A boy with a cropped head, wearing a grey blouse, handed Laptev a glass of tea without a saucer; not long afterwards another boy, passing by, stumbled over a box, and almost fell down, and Makeitchev's face looked suddenly spiteful and ferocious like a wild beast's, and he shouted at him:

"Keep on your feet!"

The clerks were pleased that their young master was married and had come back at last; they looked at him with curiosity and friendly feeling, and each one thought it his duty to say something agreeable when he passed him. But Laptev was convinced that it was not genuine, and that they were only flattering him because they were afraid of him. He never could forget how fifteen years before, a clerk, who was mentally deranged, had run out into the street with nothing on but his shirt and shaking his fists at the windows, shouted that he had been ill-treated; and how, when the poor fellow had recovered, the clerks had jeered at him for long afterwards, reminding him how he had called his employers "planters" instead of "exploiters". Altogether the employees at Laptevs' had a very poor time of it, and this fact was a subject of conversation for the whole market. The worst of it was that the old man, Fyodor Stepanovitch, maintained something of an Asiatic despotism in his attitude to them. Thus, no one knew what wages were paid to the old man's favourites, Potchatkin and Makeitchev. They received no more than three thousand a year, together with bonuses, but he made out that he paid them seven. The bonuses were given to all the clerks every year, but privately, so that the man who got little was bound from vanity to say he had got more. Not one boy knew when he would be promoted to be a clerk; not one of the men knew whether his employer was satisfied with him or not. Nothing was directly forbidden, and so the clerks never knew what was allowed, and what was not. They were not forbidden to marry, but they did not marry for fear of displeasing their employer and losing their place. They were allowed to have friends and pay visits, but the gates were shut at nine o'clock, and every morning the old man scanned them all suspiciously, and tried to detect any smell of vodka about them:

"Now then, breathe," he would say.

Every clerk was obliged to go to early service, and to stand in church in such a position that the old man could see them all. The fasts were strictly observed. On great occasions, such as the birthday of their employer or of any member of his family, the clerks had to subscribe and present a cake from Fley's, or an album. The clerks lived three or four in a room in the lower storey, and in the lodges of the house in Pyatnitsky Street, and at dinner ate from a common bowl, though there was a plate set before each of them. If one of the family came into the room while they were at dinner, they all stood up.

Laptev was conscious that only, perhaps, those among them who had been corrupted by the old man's training could seriously regard him as their benefactor; the others must have looked on him as an enemy and a "planter". Now, after six months' absence, he saw no change for the better; there was indeed something new which boded nothing good. His brother Fyodor, who had always been quiet, thoughtful, and extremely refined, was now running about the warehouse with a pencil behind his ear making a show of being very busy and businesslike, slapping customers on the shoulder and shouting "Friends!" to the clerks. Apparently he had taken up a new role, and Alexey did not recognize him in the part.

The old man's voice boomed unceasingly. Having nothing to do, he was laying down the law to a customer, telling him how he should order his life and his business, always holding himself up as an example. That boastfulness, that aggressive tone of authority,

Laptev had heard ten, fifteen, twenty years ago. The old man adored himself; from what he said it always appeared that he had made his wife and all her relations happy, that he had been munificent to his children, and a benefactor to his clerks and employees, and that everyone in the street and all his acquaintances remembered him in their prayers. Whatever he did was always right, and if things went wrong with people it was because they did not take his advice; without his advice nothing could succeed. In church he stood in the foremost place, and even made observations to the priests, if in his opinion they were not conducting the service properly, and believed that this was pleasing God because God loved him.

At two o'clock everyone in the warehouse was hard at work, except the old man, who still went on booming in his deep voice. To avoid standing idle, Laptev took some trimmings from a workgirl and let her go; then listened to a customer, a merchant from Vologda, and told a clerk to attend to him.

"T. V. A.!" resounded on all sides (prices were denoted by letters in the warehouse and goods by numbers). "R. I. T.!" As he went away, Laptev said goodbye to no one but Fyodor.

"I shall come to Pyatnitsky Street with my wife tomorrow," he said; "but I warn you, if father says a single rude thing to her, I shall not stay there another minute."

"You're the same as ever," sighed Fyodor. "Marriage has not changed you. You must be patient with the old man. So till eleven o'clock, then. We shall expect you impatiently. Come directly after mass, then."

"I don't go to mass."

"That does not matter. The great thing is not to be later than eleven, so you may be in time to pray to God and to lunch with us. Give my greetings to my little sister and kiss her hand for me. I have a presentiment that I shall like her," Fyodor added with perfect sincerity. "I envy you, brother!" he shouted after him as Alexey went downstairs.

"And why does he shrink into himself in that shy way as though he fancied he was naked?" thought Laptev, as he walked along Nikolsky Street, trying to understand the change that had come over his brother. "And his language is new, too: 'Brother, dear brother, God has sent us joy; to pray to God' – just like Iudushka in Shtchedrin."

VI

At eleven o'clock the next day, which was Sunday, he was driving with his wife along Pyatnitsky Street in a light, one-horse carriage. He was afraid of his father's doing something outrageous, and was already ill at ease. After two nights in her husband's house Yulia Sergeyevna considered her marriage a mistake and a calamity, and if she had had to live with her husband in any other town but Moscow, it seemed to her that she could not have endured the horror of it. Moscow entertained her – she was delighted with the streets, the churches; and if it had been possible to drive about Moscow in those splendid sledges with expensive horses, to drive the whole day from morning till night, and with the swift motion to feel the cold autumn air blowing upon her, she would perhaps not have felt herself so unhappy.

Near a white, lately stuccoed two-storey house the coachman pulled up his horse, and began to turn to the right. They were expected, and near the gate stood two policemen and the porter in a new full-skirted coat, high boots, and goloshes. The whole space, from the middle of the street to the gates and all over the yard from the porch, was strewn with fresh sand. The porter took off his hat, the policemen saluted. Near the entrance Fyodor met them with a very serious face.

"Very glad to make your acquaintance, little sister," he said, kissing Yulia's hand. "You're very welcome."

He led her upstairs on his arm, and then along a corridor through a crowd of men and women. The anteroom was crowded too, and smelt of incense.

"I will introduce you to our father directly," whispered Fyodor in the midst of a solemn, deathly silence. "A venerable old man, *pater-familias*."

In the big drawing-room, by a table prepared for service, Fyodor Stepanovitch stood, evidently waiting for them, and with him the priest in a calotte, and a deacon. The old man shook hands with Yulia without saying a word. Everyone was silent. Yulia was overcome with confusion.

The priest and the deacon began putting on their vestments.

A censer was brought in, giving off sparks and fumes of incense and charcoal. The candles were lighted. The clerks walked into the drawing-room on tiptoe and stood in two rows along the wall. There was perfect stillness, no one even coughed.

"The blessing of God," began the deacon. The service was read with great solemnity; nothing was left out and two canticles were sung — to sweetest Jesus and the most Holy Mother of God. The singers sang very slowly, holding up the music before them. Laptev noticed how confused his wife was. While they were singing the canticles, and the singers in different keys brought out "Lord have mercy on us", he kept expecting in nervous suspense that the old man would make some remark such as, "You don't know how to cross yourself," and he felt vexed. Why this crowd, and why this ceremony with priests and choristers? It was too bourgeois. But when she, like the old man, put her head under the gospel and afterwards several times dropped upon her knees, he realized that she liked it all, and was reassured.

At the end of the service, during "Many, many years", the priest gave the old man and Alexey the cross to kiss, but when Yulia went up, he put his hand over the cross, and showed he wanted to speak. Signs were made to the singers to stop.

"The prophet Samuel," began the priest, "went to Bethlehem at the bidding of the Lord, and there the elders of the town with fear and trembling asked him: 'Comest thou peaceably?' And the prophet answered: 'Peaceably: I am come to sacrifice unto

the Lord: sanctify yourselves and come with me to the sacrifice.'
Even so, Yulia, servant of God, shall we ask of thee, Dost thou
come bringing peace into this house?"

Yulia flushed with emotion. As he finished, the priest gave
her the cross to kiss, and said in quite a different tone of voice:

"Now Fyodor Fyodorovitch must be married; it's high time."

The choir began singing once more, people began moving,
and the room was noisy again. The old man, much touched,
with his eyes full of tears, kissed Yulia three times, made the
sign of the cross over her face, and said:

"This is your home. I'm an old man and need nothing."

The clerks congratulated her and said something, but the
choir was singing so loud that nothing else could be heard.
Then they had lunch and drank champagne. She sat beside the
old father, and he talked to her, saying that families ought not
to be parted but live together in one house; that separation and
disunion led to permanent rupture.

"I've made money and the children only do the spending of
it," he said. "Now, you live with me and save money. It's time
for an old man like me to rest."

Yulia had all the time a vision of Fyodor flitting about so
like her husband, but shyer and more restless; he fussed about
her and often kissed her hand.

"We are plain people, little sister," he said, and patches of
red came into his face as he spoke. "We live simply in Russian
style, like Christians, little sister."

As they went home, Laptev felt greatly relieved that everything had gone off so well, and that nothing outrageous had happened as he had expected. He said to his wife:

"You're surprised that such a stalwart, broad-shouldered father should have such stunted, narrow-chested sons as Fyodor and me. Yes; but it's easy to explain! My father married my mother when he was forty-five, and she was only seventeen. She turned pale and trembled in his presence. Nina was born first – born of a comparatively healthy mother, and so she was finer and sturdier than we were. Fyodor and I were begotten and born after mother had been worn out by terror. I can remember my father correcting me – or, to speak plainly, beating me – before I was five years old. He used to thrash me with a birch, pull my ears, hit me on the head, and every morning when I woke up my first thought was whether he would beat me that day. Play and childish mischief was forbidden us. We had to go to morning service and to early mass. When we met priests or monks we had to kiss their hands; at home we had to sing hymns. Here you are religious and love all that, but I'm afraid of religion, and when I pass a church I remember my childhood, and am overcome with horror. I was taken to the warehouse as soon as I was eight years old. I worked like a working boy, and it was bad for my health, for I used to be beaten there every day. Afterwards when I went to the high school, I used to go to school till dinner-time, and after dinner I had to sit in that warehouse till evening; and things went on like that till I was twenty-two, till I got to know Yartsev, and he persuaded me to leave my father's house. That Yartsev did a great deal for me. I tell you what," said Laptev, and he laughed with pleasure: "let us go and pay Yartsev a visit at once. He's a very fine fellow! How touched he will be!"

VII

On a Saturday in November Anton Rubinstein was conducting in a symphony concert. It was very hot and crowded. Laptev stood behind the columns, while his wife and Kostya Kotchevoy were sitting in the third or fourth row some distance in front. At the very beginning of an interval a "certain person", Polina Nikolaevna Razsudin, quite unexpectedly passed by him. He had often since his marriage thought with trepidation of a possible meeting with her. When now she looked at him openly and directly, he realized that he had all this time shirked having things out with her, or writing her two or three friendly lines, as though he had been hiding from her; he felt ashamed and flushed crimson. She pressed his hand tightly and impulsively and asked:

"Have you seen Yartsev?"

And without waiting for an answer she went striding on impetuously as though someone were pushing her on from behind.

She was very thin and plain, with a long nose; her face always looked tired, and exhausted, and it seemed as though it were an effort to her to keep her eyes open, and not to fall down. She had fine, dark eyes, and an intelligent, kind, sincere expression, but her movements were awkward and abrupt. It was hard to talk to her, because she could not talk or listen quietly. Loving her was not easy. Sometimes when she was alone with Laptev she would go on laughing for a long time, hiding her face in her hands, and would declare that love was not the chief thing in life for her, and would be as whimsical as a girl of seventeen; and before kissing her he would have to put out all the candles. She was thirty. She was married to a schoolmaster, but had not lived with her husband for years. She earned her living by giving music lessons and playing in quartettes.

During the ninth symphony she passed again as though by accident, but the crowd of men standing like a thick wall behind the columns prevented her going further, and she remained beside him. Laptev saw that she was wearing the same little velvet blouse she had worn at concerts last year and the year before. Her gloves were new, and her fan, too, was new, but it was a common one. She was fond of fine clothes, but she did not know how to dress, and grudged spending money on it. She dressed so badly and untidily that when she was going to her lessons striding hurriedly down the street, she might easily have been taken for a young monk.

The public applauded and shouted encore.

"You'll spend the evening with me," said Polina Nikolaevna,

369

going up to Laptev and looking at him severely. "When this is over we'll go and have tea. Do you hear? I insist on it. You owe me a great deal, and haven't the moral right to refuse me such a trifle."

"Very well; let us go," Laptev assented.

Endless calls followed the conclusion of the concert. The audience got up from their seats and went out very slowly, and Laptev could not go away without telling his wife. He had to stand at the door and wait.

"I'm dying for some tea," Polina Nikolaevna said plaintively. "My very soul is parched."

"You can get something to drink here," said Laptev. "Let's go to the buffet."

"Oh, I've no money to fling away on waiters. I'm not a shopkeeper."

He offered her his arm; she refused, in a long, wearisome sentence which he had heard many times, to the effect that she did not class herself with the feebler fair sex, and did not depend on the services of gentlemen.

As she talked to him she kept looking about at the audience and greeting acquaintances; they were her fellow-students at the higher courses and at the conservatorium, and her pupils. She gripped their hands abruptly, as though she were tugging at them. But then she began twitching her shoulders, and trembling as though she were in a fever, and at last said softly, looking at Laptev with horror:

"Who is it you've married? Where were your eyes, you mad fellow? What did you see in that stupid, insignificant girl? Why, I loved you for your mind, for your soul, but that china doll wants nothing but your money!"

"Let us drop that, Polina," he said in a voice of supplication. "All that you can say to me about my marriage I've said to myself many times already. Don't cause me unnecessary pain."

Yulia Sergeyevna made her appearance, wearing a black dress with a big diamond brooch, which her father-in-law had sent her after the service. She was followed by her suite – Kotchevoy, two doctors of their acquaintance, an officer, and a stout young man in student's uniform, called Kish.

"You go on with Kostya," Laptev said to his wife. "I'm coming later."

Yulia nodded and went on. Polina Nikolaevna gazed after her, quivering all over and twitching nervously, and in her eyes there was a look of repulsion, hatred, and pain.

Laptev was afraid to go home with her, foreseeing an unpleasant discussion, cutting words, and tears, and he suggested that they should go and have tea at a restaurant. But she said:

"No, no. I want to go home. Don't dare to talk to me of restaurants."

She did not like being in a restaurant, because the atmosphere of restaurants seemed to her poisoned by tobacco smoke and the breath of men. Against all men she did not know she cherished a strange prejudice, regarding them all as immoral rakes, capable of attacking her at any moment. Besides, the music played at restaurants jarred on her nerves and gave her a headache.

Coming out of the Hall of Nobility, they took a sledge in Ostozhenka and drove to Savelovsky Lane, where she lodged. All the way Laptev thought about her. It was true that he owed her a great deal. He had made her acquaintance at the flat of his friend Yartsev, to whom she was giving lessons in harmony. Her love for him was deep and perfectly disinterested, and her relations with him did not alter her habits; she went on giving her lessons and wearing herself out with work as before. Through her he came to understand and love music, which he had scarcely cared for till then.

"Half my kingdom for a cup of tea!" she pronounced in a hollow voice, covering her mouth with her muff that she might not catch cold. "I've given five lessons, confound them! My pupils are as stupid as posts; I nearly died of exasperation. I don't know how long this slavery can go on. I'm worn out. As soon as I can scrape together three hundred roubles, I shall throw it all up and go to the Crimea, to lie on the beach and drink in ozone. How I love the sea – oh, how I love the sea!"

"You'll never go," said Laptev. "To begin with, you'll never save the money; and, besides, you'd grudge spending it. Forgive me, I repeat again: surely it's quite as humiliating to collect the money by farthings from idle people who have music lessons to while away their time, as to borrow it from your friends."

"I haven't any friends," she said irritably. "And please don't talk nonsense. The working class to which I belong has one privilege: the consciousness of being incorruptible – the right to refuse to be indebted to wretched little shopkeepers, and to treat them with scorn. No, indeed, you don't buy me! I'm not a Yulitchka!"

Laptev did not attempt to pay the driver, knowing that it would call forth a perfect torrent of words, such as he had often heard before. She paid herself.

She had a little furnished room in the flat of a solitary lady who provided her meals. Her big Becker piano was for the time at Yartsev's in Great Nikitsky Street, and she went there every day to play on it. In her room there were armchairs in loose covers, a bed with a white summer quilt, and flowers belonging to the landlady; there were oleographs on the walls, and there was nothing that would have suggested that there was a woman, and a woman of university education, living in it. There was no toilet table; there were no books; there was not even a writing-table. It was evident that she went to bed as soon as she got home, and went out as soon as she got up in the morning.

The cook brought in the samovar. Polina Nikolaevna made tea, and, still shivering – the room was cold – began abusing the singers who had sung in the ninth symphony. She was so tired she could hardly keep her eyes open. She drank one glass of tea, then a second, and then a third.

"And so you are married," she said. "But don't be uneasy; I'm not going to pine away. I shall be able to tear you out of my heart. Only it's annoying and bitter to me that you are just as contemptible as everyone else; that what you want in a woman is not brains or intellect, but simply a body, good looks, and youth. . . . Youth!" she pronounced through her nose, as though mimicking some one, and she laughed. "Youth! You must have purity, *Reinheit! Reinheit!* " she laughed, throwing herself back in her chair. *"Reinheit!"*

When she left off laughing her eyes were wet with tears.

"You're happy, at any rate?" she asked.

"No."

"Does she love you?"

Laptev, agitated, and feeling miserable, stood up and began walking about the room.

"No," he repeated. "If you want to know, Polina, I'm very unhappy. There's no help for it; I've done the stupid thing, and there's no correcting it now. I must look at it philosophically. She married me without love, stupidly, perhaps with mercenary motives, but without understanding, and now she evidently sees her mistake and is miserable. I see it. At night we sleep together, but by day she is afraid to be left alone with me for five minutes, and tries to find distraction, society. With me she feels ashamed and frightened."

"And yet she takes money from you?"

"That's stupid, Polina!" cried Laptev. "She takes money from me because it makes absolutely no difference to her whether she has it or not. She is an honest, pure girl. She married me simply because she wanted to get away from her father, that's all."

"And are you sure she would have married you if you had not been rich?" asked Polina.

"I'm not sure of anything," said Laptev dejectedly. "Not of anything. I don't understand anything. For God's sake, Polina, don't let us talk about it."

"Do you love her?"

"Desperately."

A silence followed. She drank a fourth glass, while he paced up and down, thinking that by now his wife was probably having supper at the doctors' club.

"But is it possible to love without knowing why?" asked Polina, shrugging her shoulders. "No; it's the promptings of animal passion! You are poisoned, intoxicated by that beautiful body, that *Reinheit*! Go away from me; you are unclean! Go to her!"

She brandished her hand at him, then took up his hat and hurled it at him. He put on his fur coat without speaking and went out, but she ran after him into the passage, clutched his arm above the elbow, and broke into sobs.

"Hush, Polina! Don't!" he said, and could not unclasp her fingers. "Calm yourself, I entreat you."

She shut her eyes and turned pale, and her long nose became an unpleasant waxy colour like a corpse's, and Laptev still could not unclasp her fingers. She had fainted. He lifted her up carefully, laid her on her bed, and sat by her for ten minutes till she came to herself. Her hands were cold, her pulse was weak and uneven.

"Go home," she said, opening her eyes. "Go away, or I shall begin howling again. I must take myself in hand."

When he came out, instead of going to the doctors' club where his friends were expecting him, he went home. All the way home he was asking himself reproachfully why he had not settled down to married life with that woman who loved him so much, and was in reality his wife and friend. She was the one human being who was devoted to him; and, besides, would it not have been a grateful and worthy task to give happiness, peace, and a home to that proud, clever, overworked creature? Was it for him, he asked himself, to lay claim to youth and beauty, to that happiness which could not be, and which, as though in punishment or mockery, had kept him for the last three months in a state of gloom and oppression. The honeymoon was long over, and he still, absurd to say, did not know what sort of person his wife was. To her school friends and her father she wrote long letters of five sheets, and was never at a loss for something to say to them, but to him she never spoke except about the weather or to tell him that dinner was ready, or that it was supper-time. When at night she said her lengthy prayers and then kissed her crosses and ikons, he thought, watching her with hatred, "Here she's praying. What's she praying about? What about?" In his thoughts he showered insults on himself and her, telling himself that when he got into bed and took her into his arms, he was taking what he had paid for; but it was horrible. If only it had been a healthy, reckless, sinful woman; but here he had youth, piety, meekness, the pure eyes of innocence. . . . While they were engaged her piety had touched him; now the conventional definiteness of her views and convictions seemed to him a barrier, behind which the real truth could not be seen. Already everything in his married life was agonizing. When his wife, sitting beside him in the theatre, sighed or laughed spontaneously, it was bitter to him that she enjoyed herself alone and would not share her delight with him. And it was remarkable that she was friendly with all his friends, and they all knew what she was like already, while he knew nothing about her, and only moped and was dumbly jealous.

When he got home Laptev put on his dressing-gown and slippers, and sat down in his study to read a novel. His wife was not at home. But within half an hour there was a ring at the hall door, and he heard the muffled footsteps of Pyotr running to open it. It was Yulia. She walked into the study in her fur coat, her cheeks rosy with the frost.

"There's a great fire in Pryesnya," she said breathlessly. "There's a tremendous glow. I'm going to see it with Konstantin Ivanovitch."

"Well, do, dear!"

The sight of her health, her freshness, and the childish horror in her eyes, reassured Laptev. He read for another half-hour and went to bed.

Next day Polina Nikolaevna sent to the warehouse two books

she had borrowed from him, all his letters and his photographs; with them was a note consisting of one word — "*basta.*"

VIII

Towards the end of October Nina Fyodorovna had unmistakable symptoms of a relapse. There was a change in her face, and she grew rapidly thinner. In spite of acute pain she still imagined that she was getting better, and got up and dressed every morning as though she were well, and then lay on her bed, fully dressed, for the rest of the day. And towards the end she became very talkative. She would lie on her back and talk in a low voice, speaking with an effort and breathing painfully. She died suddenly under the following circumstances.

It was a clear moonlight evening. In the street people were tobogganing in the fresh snow, and their clamour floated in at the window. Nina Fyodorovna was lying on her back in bed, and Sasha, who had no one to take turns with her now, was sitting beside her half asleep.

"I don't remember his father's name," Nina Fyodorovna was saying softly, "but his name was Ivan Kotchevoy — a poor clerk. He was a sad drunkard, the Kingdom of Heaven be his! He used to come to us, and every month we used to give him a pound of sugar and two ounces of tea. And money, too, sometimes, of course. Yes. . . . And then, this is what happened. Our

Kotchevoy began drinking heavily and died, consumed by vodka. He left a little son, a boy of seven. Poor little orphan! . . . We took him and hid him in the clerk's quarters, and he lived there for a whole year, without father's knowing. And when father did see him, he only waved his hand and said nothing. When Kostya, the little orphan, was nine years old – by that time I was engaged to be married – I took him round to all the day schools. I went from one to the other, and no one would take him. And he cried. . . . 'What are you crying for, little silly?' I said. I took him to Razgulyay to the second school, where – God bless them for it! – they took him, and the boy began going every day on foot from Pyatnitsky Street to Razgulyay Street and back again. . . . Alyosha paid for him. . . . By God's grace the boy got on, was good at his lessons, and turned out well. . . . He's a lawyer now in Moscow, a friend of Alyosha's, and so good in science. Yes, we had compassion on a fellow-creature and took him into our house, and now I daresay, he remembers us in his prayers . . . Yes. . . ."

Nina Fyodorovna spoke more and more slowly with long pauses, then after a brief silence she suddenly raised herself and sat up.

"There's something the matter with me . . . something seems wrong," she said. "Lord have mercy on me! Oh, I can't breathe!"

Sasha knew that her mother would soon die; seeing now how suddenly her face looked drawn, she guessed that it was the end, and she was frightened.

"Mother, you mustn't!" she began sobbing. "You mustn't."

"Run to the kitchen; let them go for father. I am very ill indeed."

Sasha ran through all the rooms calling, but there were none of the servants in the house, and the only person she found was Lida asleep on a chest in the dining-room with her clothes on and without a pillow. Sasha ran into the yard just as she was without her goloshes, and then into the street. On a bench at the gate her nurse was sitting watching the tobogganing. From beyond the river, where the tobogganing slope was, came the strains of a military band.

"Nurse, mother's dying!" sobbed Sasha. "You must go for father! . . ."

The nurse went upstairs, and, glancing at the sick woman, thrust a lighted wax candle into her hand. Sasha rushed about in terror and besought someone to go for her father, then she put on a coat and a kerchief, and ran into the street. From the servants she knew already that her father had another wife and two children with whom he lived in Bazarny Street. She ran out of the gate and turned to the left, crying, and frightened of unknown people. She soon began to sink into the snow and grew numb with cold.

She met an empty sledge, but she did not take it: perhaps, she thought, the man would drive her out of town, rob her, and throw her into the cemetery (the servants had talked of such a case at tea). She went on and on, sobbing and panting with exhaustion. When she got into Bazarny Street, she inquired where M. Panaurov lived. An unknown woman spent a long time directing her, and seeing that she did not understand, took her by the hand and led her to a house of one storey that stood back from the street. The door stood open. Sasha ran through the entry, along the corridor, and found herself at last in a warm, lighted room where her father was sitting by the samovar with a lady and two children. But by now she was unable to utter a word, and could only sob. Panaurov understood.

"Mother's worse?" he asked. "Tell me, child: is mother worse?"

He was alarmed and sent for a sledge.

When they got home, Nina Fyodorovna was sitting propped up with pillows, with a candle in her hand. Her face looked dark and her eyes were closed. Crowding in the doorway stood the nurse, the cook, the housemaid, a peasant called Prokofy and a few persons of the humbler class, who were complete strangers. The nurse was giving them orders in a whisper, and they did not understand. Inside the room at the window stood Lida, with a pale and sleepy face, gazing severely at her mother.

Panaurov took the candle out of Nina Fyodorovna's hand, and, frowning contemptuously, flung it on the chest of drawers.

"This is awful!" he said, and his shoulders quivered. "Nina, you must lie down," he said affectionately. "Lie down, dear."

She looked at him, but did not know him. They laid her down on her back.

When the priest and the doctor, Sergey Borisovitch, arrived, the servants crossed themselves devoutly and prayed for her.

"What a sad business!" said the doctor thoughtfully, coming out into the drawing-room. "Why, she was still young – not yet forty."

They heard the loud sobbing of the little girls. Panaurov, with a pale face and moist eyes, went up to the doctor and said in a faint, weak voice:

"Do me a favour, my dear fellow. Send a telegram to Moscow. I'm not equal to it."

The doctor fetched the ink and wrote the following telegram to his daughter:

"Madame Panaurov died at eight o'clock this evening. Tell your husband: a mortgaged house for sale in Dvoryansky Street, nine thousand cash. Auction on twelfth. Advise him not miss opportunity."

IX

Laptev lived in one of the turnings out of Little Dmitrovka. Besides the big house facing the street, he rented also a two-storey lodge in the yard at the back of his friend Kotchevoy, a lawyer's assistant whom all the Laptevs called Kostya, because he had grown up under their eyes. Facing this lodge stood another, also of two storeys, inhabited by a French family consisting of a husband and wife and five daughters.

There was a frost of twenty degrees. The windows were frozen over. Waking up in the morning, Kostya, with an anxious face, took twenty drops of a medicine; then, taking two dumb-bells out of the bookcase, he did gymnastic exercises. He was tall and thin, with big reddish moustaches; but what was most noticeable in his appearance was the length of his legs.

Pyotr, a middle-aged peasant in a reefer jacket and cotton breeches tucked into his high boots, brought in the samovar and made the tea.

"It's very nice weather now, Konstantin Ivanovitch," he said.

"It is, but I tell you what, brother, it's a pity we can't get on, you and I, without such exclamations."

Pyotr sighed from politeness.

"What are the little girls doing?" asked Kotchevoy.

"The priest has not come. Alexey Fyodorovitch is giving them their lesson himself."

Kostya found a spot in the window that was not covered with frost, and began looking through a field-glass at the windows of the house where the French family lived.

"There's no seeing," he said.

Meanwhile Alexey Fyodorovitch was giving Sasha and Lida a Scripture lesson below. For the last six weeks they had been living in Moscow, and were installed with their governess in the lower storey of the lodge. And three times a week a teacher from a school in the town, and a priest, came to give them lessons. Sasha was going through the New Testament and Lida was going through the Old. The time before Lida had been set the story up to Abraham to learn by heart.

"And so Adam and Eve had two sons," said Laptev. "Very good. But what were they called? Try to remember them!"

Lida, still with the same severe face, gazed dumbly at the table. She moved her lips, but without speaking; and the elder girl, Sasha, looked into her face, frowning.

"You know it very well, only you mustn't be nervous," said Laptev. "Come, what were Adam's sons called?"

"Abel and Canel," Lida whispered.

"Cain and Abel," Laptev corrected her.

A big tear rolled down Lida's cheek and dropped on the book. Sasha looked down and turned red, and she, too, was on the point of tears. Laptev felt a lump in his throat, and was so sorry for them he could not speak. He got up from the table and lighted a cigarette. At that moment Kotchevoy came down the stairs with a paper in his hand. The little girls stood up, and without looking at him, made curtsies.

"For God's sake, Kostya, give them their lessons," said Laptev, turning to him. "I'm afraid I shall cry, too, and I have to go to the warehouse before dinner."

"All right."

Alexey Fyodorovitch went away. Kostya, with a very serious

face, sat down to the table and drew the Scripture history towards him.

"Well," he said; "where have you got to?"

"She knows about the Flood," said Sasha.

"The Flood? All right. Let's peg in at the Flood. Fire away about the Flood." Kostya skimmed through a brief description of the Flood in the book, and said: "I must remark that there really never was a flood such as is described here. And there was no such person as Noah. Some thousands of years before the birth of Christ, there was an extraordinary inundation of the earth, and that's not only mentioned in the Jewish Bible, but in the books of other ancient peoples: the Greeks, the Chaldeans, the Hindoos. But whatever the inundation may have been, it couldn't have covered the whole earth. It may have flooded the plains, but the mountains must have remained. You can read this book, of course, but don't put too much faith in it."

Tears trickled down Lida's face again. She turned away and suddenly burst into such loud sobs, that Kostya started and jumped up from his seat in great confusion.

"I want to go home," she said, "to papa and to nurse."

Sasha cried too. Kostya went upstairs to his own room, and spoke on the telephone to Yulia Sergeyevna.

"My dear soul," he said, "the little girls are crying again; there's no doing anything with them."

Yulia Sergeyevna ran across from the big house in her indoor dress, with only a knitted shawl over her shoulders, and chilled through by the frost, began comforting the children.

"Do believe me, do believe me," she said in an imploring voice, hugging first one and then the other. "Your papa's coming today; he has sent a telegram. You're grieving for mother, and I grieve too. My heart's torn, but what can we do? We must bow to God's will!"

When they left off crying, she wrapped them up and took them out for a drive. They stopped near the Iverskoy chapel, put up candles at the shrine, and, kneeling down, prayed. On the way back they went in Filippov's, and had cakes sprinkled with poppy-seeds.

The Laptevs had dinner between two and three. Pyotr handed the dishes. This Pyotr waited on the family, and by day ran to the post, to the warehouse, to the law courts for Kostya; he spent his evenings making cigarettes, ran to open the door at night, and before five o'clock in the morning was up lighting the stoves, and no one knew where he slept. He was very fond of opening seltzer-water bottles and did it easily, without a bang and without spilling a drop.

"With God's blessing," said Kostya, drinking off a glass of vodka before the soup.

At first Yulia Sergeyevna did not like Kostya; his bass voice, his phrases such as "Landed him one on the beak", "filth", "produce the samovar", etc., his habit of clinking glasses and making sentimental speeches, seemed to her trivial. But as she got to know him better, she began to feel very much at home with him. He was open with her; he liked talking to her in a low voice in the evening, and even gave her novels of his own composition to read, though these had been kept a secret even from such friends as Laptev and Yartsev. She read these novels and praised them, so that she might not disappoint him, and he was delighted because he hoped sooner or later to become a distinguished author.

In his novels he described nothing but country-house life, though he had only seen the country on rare occasions when visiting friends at a summer villa, and had only been in a real country-house once in his life, when he had been to Volokolamsk on law business. He avoided any love interest as though he were ashamed of it; he put in frequent descriptions of nature, and in them was fond of using such expressions as "the capricious lines of the mountains, the miraculous forms of the clouds, the harmony of mysterious rhythms . . ." His novels had never been published, and this he attributed to the censorship.

He liked the duties of a lawyer, but yet he considered that his most important pursuit was not the law but these novels. He believed that he had a subtle, aesthetic temperament, and he always had leanings towards art. He neither sang nor played on any musical instrument, and was absolutely without an ear for music, but he attended all the symphony and philharmonic concerts, got up concerts for charitable objects, and made the acquaintance of singers. . . .

They used to talk at dinner.

"It's a strange thing," said Laptev, "my Fyodor took my breath away again! He said we must find out the date of the centenary of our firm, so as to try and get raised to noble rank; and he said it quite seriously. What can be the matter with him? I confess I begin to feel worried about him."

They talked of Fyodor, and of its being the fashion now-adays to adopt some pose or other. Fyodor, for instance, tried to appear like a plain merchant, though he had ceased to be one; and when the teacher came from the school, of which old Laptev was the patron, to ask Fyodor for his salary, the latter changed his voice and deportment, and behaved with the teacher as though he were someone in authority.

There was nothing to be done; after dinner they went into the study. They talked about the decadents, about *The Maid of Orleans*, and Kostya delivered a regular monologue; he fancied that he was very successful in imitating Ermolova. Then they sat down and played whist. The little girls had not gone back to the lodge but were sitting together in one arm-chair, with pale and mournful faces, and were listening to every noise in the street, wondering whether it was their father coming. In the evening when it was dark and the candles were lighted, they felt deeply dejected. The talk over the whist, the footsteps of Pyotr, the crackling in the fireplace, jarred on their nerves, and they did not like to look at the fire. In the evenings they did not want to cry, but they felt strange, and there was a load on their hearts. They could not understand how people could talk and laugh when their mother was dead.

"What did you see through the field-glasses today?" Yulia Sergeyevna asked Kostya.

"Nothing today, but yesterday I saw the old Frenchman having his bath."

At seven o'clock Yulia and Kostya went to the Little Theatre. Laptev was left with the little girls.

"It's time your father was here," he said, looking at his watch. "The train must be late."

The children sat in their arm-chair dumb and huddling together like animals when they are cold, while he walked about the room looking impatiently at his watch. It was quiet in the house. But just before nine o'clock someone rang at the bell. Pyotr went to open the door.

Hearing a familiar voice, the children shrieked, burst into sobs, and ran into the hall. Panaurov was wearing a sumptuous coat of antelope skin, and his head and moustaches were white with hoar-frost. "In a minute, in a minute," he muttered, while Sasha and Lida, sobbing and laughing, kissed his cold hands, his hat, his antelope coat. With the languor of a handsome man spoilt by too much love, he fondled the children without haste, then went into the study and said, rubbing his hands:

"I've not come to stay long, my friends. I'm going to Petersburg tomorrow. They've promised to transfer me to another town."

He was staying at the Dresden Hotel.

X

A friend who was often at the Laptevs' was Ivan Gavrilitch Yartsev. He was a strong, healthy man with black hair and a clever, pleasant face. He was considered to be handsome, but of late he had begun to grow stout, and that rather spoilt his face and figure; another thing that spoilt him was that he wore his hair cut so close that the skin showed through.

At the University his tall figure and physical strength had won him the nickname of "the pounder" among the students. He had taken his degree with the Laptev brothers in the faculty of philology – then he went in for science and now had the degree of *magister* in chemistry. But he had never given a lecture or even been a demonstrator. He taught physics and natural history in the modern school, and in two girls' high schools. He was enthusiastic over his pupils, especially the girls, and used to maintain that a remarkable generation was growing up. At home he spent his time studying sociology and Russian history, as well as chemistry, and he sometimes published brief notes in the newspapers and magazines, signing them "Y." When he talked of some botanical or zoological subject, he spoke like an historian; when he was discussing some historical question, he approached it as a man of science.

Kish, nicknamed "the eternal student", was also like one of the family at the Laptevs'. He had been for three years studying medicine. Then he took up mathematics, and spent two years over each year's course. His father, a provincial druggist, used to send him forty roubles a month, to which his mother, without his father's knowledge, added another ten. And this sum was not only sufficient for his board and lodging, but even for such luxuries as an overcoat lined with Polish beaver, gloves, scent, and photographs (he often had photographs taken of himself and used to distribute them among his friends). He was neat and demure, slightly bald, with golden side-whiskers, and he had the air of a man nearly always ready to oblige. He was always busy looking after other people's affairs. At one time he would be rushing about with a subscription list; at another time he would be freezing in the early morning at a ticket office to buy tickets for ladies of his acquaintance, or at somebody's request would be ordering a wreath or a bouquet. People simply said of him: "Kish will go, Kish will do it, Kish will buy it." He was usually unsuccessful in carrying out his commissions. Reproaches were showered upon him, people frequently forgot to pay him for the things he bought, but he simply sighed in hard cases and never protested. He was never particularly delighted nor disappointed; his stories were always long and boring; and his jokes invariably provoked laughter just because they were not funny. Thus, one day, for instance, intending to make a joke, he said to Pyotr: "Pyotr, you're not a sturgeon"; and this aroused a general laugh, and he, too, laughed for a long time, much pleased at having made such a successful jest. Whenever one of the professors was buried, he walked in front with the mutes.

Yartsev and Kish usually came in the evening to tea. If the Laptevs were not going to the theatre or a concert, the evening tea lingered on till supper. One evening in February the following conversation took place:

"A work of art is only significant and valuable when there are some serious social problems contained in its central idea," said Kostya, looking wrathfully at Yartsev. "If there is in the work a protest against serfdom, or the author takes up arms against the vulgarity of aristocratic society, the work is significant and valuable. The novels that are taken up with 'Ach!' and 'Och!' and 'she loved him, while he ceased to love her', I tell you, are worthless, and damn them all, I say!"

"I agree with you, Konstantin Ivanovitch," said Yulia Sergeyevna. "One describes a love scene; another, a betrayal; and the third, meeting again after separation. Are there no other subjects? Why, there are many people sick, unhappy, harassed by poverty, to whom reading all that must be distasteful."

It was disagreeable to Laptev to hear his wife, not yet twenty-two, speaking so seriously and coldly about love. He understood why this was so.

"If poetry does not solve questions that seem so important," said Yartsev, "you should turn to works on technical subjects, criminal law, or finance, read scientific pamphlets. What need is there to discuss in *Romeo and Juliet* liberty of speech, or the disinfecting of prisons, instead of love, when you can find all that in special articles and textbooks?"

"That's pushing it to the extreme," Kostya interrupted. "We are not talking of giants like Shakespeare or Goethe; we are talking of the hundreds of talented mediocre writers, who would be infinitely more valuable if they would let love alone, and would employ themselves in spreading knowledge and humane ideas among the masses."

Kish, lisping and speaking a little through his nose, began telling the story of a novel he had lately been reading. He spoke circumstantially and without haste. Three minutes passed, then five, then ten, and no one could make out what he was talking about, and his face grew more and more indifferent, and his eyes more and more blank.

"Kish, do be quick over it," Yulia Sergeyevna could not resist saying; "it's really agonizing!"

"Shut up, Kish!" Kostya shouted to him.

They all laughed, and Kish with them.

Fyodor came in. Flushing red in patches, he greeted them all in a nervous flurry, and led his brother away into the study. Of late he had taken to avoiding the company of more than one person at once.

"Let the young people laugh, while we speak from the heart in here," he said, settling himself in a deep arm-chair at a distance from the lamp. "It's a long time, my dear brother, since we've seen each other. How long is it since you were at the warehouse? I think it must be a week."

"Yes, there's nothing for me to do there. And I must confess that the old man wearies me."

"Of course, they could get on at the warehouse without you and me, but one must have some occupation. 'In the sweat of thy brow thou shalt eat bread,' as it is written. God loves work."

Pyotr brought in a glass of tea on a tray. Fyodor drank it without sugar, and asked for more. He drank a great deal of tea, and could get through as many as ten glasses in the evening.

"I tell you what, brother," he said, getting up and going to his brother. "Laying aside philosophic subtleties, you must get elected on to the town council, and little by little we will get you on to the local Board, and then to be an alderman. And as time goes on — you are a clever man and well-educated — you will be noticed in Petersburg and asked to go there — active men on the provincial assemblies and town councils are all the fashion there now — and before you are fifty you'll be a privy councillor, and have a ribbon across your shoulders."

Laptev made no answer; he knew that all this — being a privy councillor and having a ribbon over his shoulder — was what Fyodor desired for himself, and he did not know what to say.

The brothers sat still and said nothing. Fyodor opened his

watch and for a long, long time gazed into it with strained attention, as though he wanted to detect the motion of the hand, and the expression of his face struck Laptev as strange.

They were summoned to supper. Laptev went into the dining-room, while Fyodor remained in the study. The argument was over and Yartsev was speaking in the tones of a professor giving a lecture:

"Owing to differences of climate, of energy, of tastes, of age, equality among men is physically impossible. But civilized man can make this inequality innocuous, as he has already done with bogs and bears. A learned man succeeded in making a cat, a mouse, a falcon, a sparrow, all eat out of one plate; and education, one must hope, will do the same thing with men. Life continually progresses, civilization makes enormous advances before our eyes, and obviously a time will come when we shall think, for instance, the present condition of the factory population as absurd as we now do the state of serfdom, in which girls were exchanged for dogs."

"That won't be for a long while, a very long while," said Kostya, with a laugh, "not till Rothschild thinks his cellars full of gold absurd, and till then the workers may bend their backs and die of hunger. No; that's not it. We mustn't wait for it; we must struggle for it. Do you suppose because the cat eats out of the same saucer as the mouse – do you suppose that she is influenced by a sense of conscious intelligence? Not a bit of it! She's made to do it by force."

"Fyodor and I are rich; our father's a capitalist, a millionaire. You will have to struggle with us," said Laptev, rubbing his forehead with his hand. "Struggle with me is an idea I cannot grasp. I am rich, but what has money given me so far? What has this power given me? In what way am I happier than you? My childhood was slavery, and money did not save me from the birch. When Nina was ill and died, my money did not help her. If people don't care for me, I can't make them like me if I spend a hundred million."

"But you can do a great deal of good," said Kish.

"Good, indeed! You spoke to me yesterday of a mathematical man who is looking for a job. Believe me, I can do as little for him as you can. I can give money, but that's not what he wants — I asked a well-known musician to help a poor violinist, and this is what he answered: 'You apply to me just because you are not a musician yourself.' In the same way I say to you that you apply for help to me so confidently because you've never been in the position of a rich man."

"Why you bring in the comparison with a well-known musician I don't understand!" said Yulia Sergeyevna, and she flushed crimson. "What has the well-known musician to do with it!"

Her face was quivering with hatred, and she dropped her eyes to conceal the feeling. And not only her husband, but all the men sitting at the table, knew what the look in her face meant.

"What has the well-known musician got to do with it?" she said slowly. "Why, nothing's easier than helping someone poor."

Silence followed. Pyotr handed the woodcock, but they all refused it, and ate nothing but salad. Laptev did not remember what he had said, but it was clear to him that it was not his words that were hateful, but the fact of his meddling in the conversation at all.

After supper he went into his study; intently, with a beating heart, expecting further humiliation, he listened to what was going on in the hall. An argument had sprung up there again. Then Yartsev sat down to the piano and played a sentimental song. He was a man of varied accomplishments; he could play and sing, and even perform conjuring tricks.

"You may please yourselves, my friends, but I'm not going to stay at home," said Yulia. "We must go somewhere."

They decided to drive out of town, and sent Kish to the merchant's club to order a three-horse sledge. They did not ask Laptev to go with them because he did not usually join these expeditions, and because his brother was sitting with him; but he took it to mean that his society bored them, and that he was not wanted in their light-hearted youthful company. And his vexation, his bitter feeling, was so intense that he almost shed tears. He was positively glad that he was treated so ungraciously, that he was scorned, that he was a stupid, dull husband, a money-bag; and it seemed to him, that he would have been even more glad if his wife were to deceive him that night with his best friend, and were afterwards to acknowledge it, looking at him with hatred. . . . He was jealous on her account of their student friends, of actors, of singers, of Yartsev, even of casual acquaintances; and now he had a passionate longing for her really to be unfaithful to him. He longed to find her in another man's arms, and to be rid of this nightmare forever. Fyodor was drinking tea, gulping it noisily. But he, too, got up to go.

"Our old father must have got cataract," he said, as he put on his fur coat. "His sight has become very poor."

Laptev put on his coat, too, and went out. After seeing his brother part of the way home, he took a sledge and drove to Yar's.

"And this is family happiness!" he said, jeering at himself. "This is love!"

His teeth were chattering, and he did not know if it were jealousy or something else. He walked about near the tables; listened to a comic singer in the hall. He had not a single phrase ready if he should meet his own party; and he felt sure beforehand that if he met his wife, he would only smile pitifully and not cleverly, and that everyone would understand what feeling had induced him to come here. He was bewildered by the electric light, the loud music, the smell of powder, and the fact that the ladies he met looked at him. He stood at the doors trying to see and to hear what was going on in the private rooms, and it seemed to him that he was somehow playing a mean, contemptible part on a level with the comic singers and those ladies. Then he went to Strelna, but he found none of his circle there, either; and only when on the way home he was again driving up to Yar's, a three-horse sledge noisily overtook him. The driver was drunk and shouting, and he could hear Yartsev laughing: "Ha, ha, ha!"

Laptev returned home between three and four. Yulia Sergeyevna was in bed. Noticing that she was not asleep, he went up to her and said sharply:

"I understand your repulsion, your hatred, but you might spare me before other people; you might conceal your feelings."

She got up and sat on the bed with her legs dangling. Her eyes looked big and black in the lamplight.

"I beg your pardon," she said.

He could not utter a single word from excitement and the trembling of his whole body; he stood facing her and was dumb. She trembled, too, and sat with the air of a criminal waiting for explanations.

"How I suffer!" he said at last, and he clutched his head. "I'm in hell, and I'm out of my mind."

"And do you suppose it's easy for me?" she asked, with a quiver in her voice. "God alone knows what I go through."

"You've been my wife for six months, but you haven't a spark of love for me in your heart. There's no hope, not one ray of light! Why did you marry me?" Laptev went on with despair. "Why? What demon thrust you into my arms? What did you hope for? What did you want?"

She looked at him with terror, as though she were afraid he would kill her.

"Did I attract you? Did you like me?" he went on, gasping

for breath. "No. Then what? What? Tell me what?" he cried. "Oh, the cursed money! The cursed money!"

"I swear to God, no!" she cried, and she crossed herself. She seemed to shrink under the insult, and for the first time he heard her crying. "I swear to God, no!" she repeated. "I didn't think about your money; I didn't want it. I simply thought I should do wrong if I refused you. I was afraid of spoiling your life and mine. And now I am suffering for my mistake. I'm suffering unbearably!"

She sobbed bitterly, and he saw that she was hurt; and not knowing what to say, dropped down on the carpet before her.

"That's enough; that's enough," he muttered. "I insulted you because I love you madly." He suddenly kissed her foot and passionately hugged it. "If only a spark of love," he muttered. "Come, lie to me; tell me a lie! Don't say it's a mistake! . . ."

But she went on crying, and he felt that she was only enduring his caresses as an inevitable consequence of her mistake. And the foot he had kissed she drew under her like a bird. He felt sorry for her.

She got into bed and covered her head over; he undressed and got into bed, too. In the morning they both felt confused and did not know what to talk about, and he even fancied she walked unsteadily on the foot he had kissed.

Before dinner Panaurov came to say goodbye. Yulia had an irresistible desire to go to her own home; it would be nice, she thought, to go away and have a rest from married life, from the embarrassment and the continual consciousness that she had done wrong. It was decided at dinner that she should set off with Panaurov, and stay with her father for two or three weeks until she was tired of it.

XI

She travelled with Panaurov in a reserved compartment; he had on his head an astrakhan cap of peculiar shape.

"Yes, Petersburg did not satisfy me," he said, drawling, with a sigh. "They promise much, but nothing definite. Yes, my dear girl. I have been a Justice of the Peace, a member of the local Board, chairman of the Board of Magistrates, and finally councillor of the provincial administration. I think I have served my country and have earned the right to receive attention; but – would you believe it? – I can never succeed in wringing from the authorities a post in another town. . . ."

Panaurov closed his eyes and shook his head.

"They don't recognize me," he went on, as though dropping asleep. "Of course I'm not an administrator of genius, but, on the other hand, I'm a decent, honest man, and nowadays even that's something rare. I regret to say I have not been always quite straightforward with women, but in my relations with the Russian government I've always been a gentleman. But enough of that," he said, opening his eyes; "let us talk of you. What put it into your head to visit your papa so suddenly?"

"Well. . . . I had a little misunderstanding with my husband," said Yulia, looking at his cap.

"Yes. What a queer fellow he is! All the Laptevs are queer. Your husband's all right – he's nothing out of the way, but his brother Fyodor is a perfect fool."

Panaurov sighed and asked seriously:

"And have you a lover yet?"

Yulia looked at him in amazement and laughed.

"Goodness knows what you're talking about."

It was past ten o'clock when they got out at a big station and had supper. When the train went on again Panaurov took off his greatcoat and his cap, and sat down beside Yulia.

"You are very charming, I must tell you," he began. "Excuse me for the eating-house comparison, but you remind me of fresh salted cucumber; it still smells of the hotbed, so to speak, and yet has a smack of the salt and a scent of fennel about it. As time goes on you will make a magnificent woman, a wonderful, exquisite woman. If this trip of ours had happened five years ago," he sighed, "I should have felt it my duty to join the ranks of your adorers, but now, alas, I'm a veteran on the retired list."

He smiled mournfully, but at the same time graciously, and put his arm round her waist.

"You must be mad!" she said; she flushed crimson and was so frightened that her hands and feet turned cold.

"Leave off, Grigory Nikolaevitch!"

"What are you afraid of, dear?" he asked softly. "What is there dreadful about it? It's simply that you're not used to it."

If a woman protested he always interpreted it as a sign that he had made an impression on her and attracted her. Holding Yulia round the waist, he kissed her firmly on the cheek, then on the lips, in the full conviction that he was giving her intense gratification. Yulia recovered from her alarm and confusion, and began laughing. He kissed her once more and said, as he put on his ridiculous cap:

"That is all that the old veteran can give you. A Turkish Pasha, a kind-hearted old fellow, was presented by someone – or inherited, I fancy it was – a whole harem. When his beautiful young wives drew up in a row before him, he walked round them, kissed each one of them, and said: 'That is all that I am equal to giving you.' And that's just what I say, too."

All this struck her as stupid and extraordinary, and amused her. She felt mischievous. Standing up on the seat and humming, she got a box of sweets from the shelf, and throwing him a piece of chocolate, shouted:

"Catch!"

He caught it. With a loud laugh she threw him another sweet, then a third, and he kept catching them and putting them into his mouth, looking at her with imploring eyes; and it seemed to her that in his face, his features, his expression, there was a great deal that was feminine and childlike. And when, out of breath, she sat down on the seat and looked at him, laughing, he tapped her cheek with two fingers, and said as though he were vexed:

"Naughty girl!"

"Take it," she said, giving him the box. "I don't care for sweet things."

He ate up the sweets — every one of them, and locked the empty box in his trunk; he liked boxes with pictures on them.

"That's mischief enough, though," he said. "It's time for the veteran to go bye-bye."

He took out of his hold-all a Bokhara dressing-gown and a pillow, lay down, and covered himself with the dressing-gown.

"Good-night, darling!" he said softly, and sighed as though his whole body ached.

And soon a snore was heard. Without the slightest feeling of constraint, she, too, lay down and went to sleep.

When next morning she drove through her native town from the station homewards, the streets seemed to her empty and deserted. The snow looked grey, and the houses small, as though someone had squashed them. She was met by a funeral procession: the dead body was carried in an open coffin with banners.

"Meeting a funeral, they say, is lucky," she thought.

There were white bills pasted in the windows of the house where Nina Fyodorovna used to live.

With a sinking at her heart she drove into her own courtyard and rang at the door. It was opened by a servant she did not know – a plump, sleepy-looking girl wearing a warm wadded jacket. As she went upstairs Yulia remembered how Laptev had declared his love there, but now the staircase was unscrubbed, covered with foot-marks. Upstairs in the cold passage patients were waiting in their out-door coats. And for some reason her heart beat violently, and she was so excited she could scarcely walk.

The doctor, who had grown even stouter, was sitting with a brick-red face and dishevelled hair, drinking tea. Seeing his daughter, he was greatly delighted, and even lachrymose. She thought that she was the only joy in this old man's life, and much moved, she embraced him warmly, and told him she would stay a long time – till Easter. After taking off her things in her own room, she went back to the dining-room to have tea with him. He was pacing up and down with his hands in his pockets, humming, "Ru-ru-ru"; this meant that he was dissatisfied with something.

"You have a gay time of it in Moscow," he said. "I am very glad for your sake. . . . I'm an old man and I need nothing. I shall soon give up the ghost and set you all free. And the wonder is that my hide is so tough, that I'm alive still! It's amazing!"

He said that he was a tough old ass that everyone rode on. They had thrust on him the care of Nina Fyodorovna, the worry of her children, and of her burial; and that coxcomb Panaurov would not trouble himself about it, and had even borrowed a hundred roubles from him and had never paid it back.

"Take me to Moscow and put me in a madhouse," said the doctor. "I'm mad; I'm a simple child, as I still put faith in truth and justice."

Then he found fault with her husband for his short-sightedness in not buying houses that were being sold so cheaply. And now it seemed to Yulia that she was not the one joy in this old man's life. While he was seeing his patients, and afterwards going his rounds, she walked through all the rooms, not knowing what to do or what to think about. She had already grown strange to her own town and her own home. She felt no inclination to go into the streets or see her friends; and at the thought of her old friends and her life as a girl, she felt no sadness nor regret for the past.

In the evening she dressed a little more smartly and went to the evening service. But there were only poor people in the church, and her splendid fur coat and hat made no impression. And it seemed to her that there was some change in the church as well as in herself. In old days she had loved it when they read the prayers for the day at evening service, and the choir sang anthems such as "I will open my lips". She liked moving slowly in the crowd to the priest who stood in the middle of the church, and then to feel the holy oil on her forehead; now she only waited for the service to be over. And now, going out of the church, she was only afraid that beggars would ask for alms; it was such a bore to have to stop and feel for her pockets; besides, she had no coppers in her pocket now – nothing but roubles.

She went to bed early, and was a long time in going to sleep. She kept dreaming of portraits of some sort, and of the funeral procession she had met that morning. The open coffin with the dead body was carried into the yard, and brought to a standstill at the door; then the coffin was swung backwards and forwards on a sheet, and dashed violently against the door. Yulia woke and jumped up in alarm. There really was a bang at the door, and the wire of the bell rustled against the wall, though no ring was to be heard.

The doctor coughed. Then she heard the servant go downstairs, and then come back.

"Madam!" she said, and knocked at the door. "Madam!"

"What is it?" said Yulia.

"A telegram for you!"

Yulia went out to her with a candle. Behind the servant stood the doctor, in his night-clothes and greatcoat, and he, too, had a candle in his hand. "Our bell is broken," he said, yawning sleepily. "It ought to have been mended long ago."

Yulia broke open the telegram and read:

"We drink to your health. – YARTSEV, KOTCHEVOY."

"Ah, what idiots!" she said, and burst out laughing; and her heart felt light and gay.

Going back into her room, she quietly washed and dressed, then she spent a long time in packing her things, until it was daylight, and at midday she set off for Moscow.

XII

In Holy Week the Laptevs went to an exhibition of pictures in the school of painting. The whole family went together in the Moscow fashion, the little girls, the governess, Kostya, and all.

Laptev knew the names of all the well-known painters, and never missed an exhibition. He used sometimes to paint little landscape paintings when he was in the country in the summer, and he fancied he had a good deal of taste, and that if he had studied he might have made a good painter. When he was abroad he sometimes used to go to curio shops, examining the antiques with the air of a connoisseur and giving his opinion on them. When he bought any article he gave just what the shopkeeper liked to ask for it and his purchase remained afterwards in a box in the coach-house till it disappeared altogether. Or going into a print shop, he would slowly and attentively examine the engravings and the bronzes, making various remarks on them, and would buy a common frame or a box of wretched prints. At home he had pictures always of large dimensions but of inferior quality; the best among them were badly hung. It had happened to him more than once to pay large sums for things which had afterwards turned out to be forgeries of the grossest kind. And it was remarkable that, though as a rule timid in the affairs of life, he was exceedingly bold and self-confident at a picture exhibition. Why?

Yulia Sergeyevna looked at the pictures as her husband did, through her open fist or an opera-glass, and was surprised that the people in the pictures were like live people, and the trees like real trees. But she did not understand art, and it seemed to her that many pictures in the exhibition were alike, and she imagined that the whole object in painting was that the figures and objects should stand out as though they were real, when you looked at the picture through your open fist.

"That forest is Shiskin's," her husband explained to her. "He always paints the same thing. . . . But notice snow's never such a lilac colour as that. . . . And that boy's left arm is shorter than his right."

When they were all tired and Laptev had gone to look for Kostya, that they might go home, Yulia stopped indifferently before a small landscape. In the foreground was a stream, over it a little wooden bridge; on the further side a path that disappeared in the dark grass; a field on the right; a copse; near it a camp-fire – no doubt of watchers by night; and in the distance there was a glow of the evening sunset.

Yulia imagined walking herself along the little bridge, and then along the little path further and further, while all round was stillness, the drowsy landrails calling and the fire flickering in the distance. And for some reason she suddenly began to feel that she had seen those very clouds that stretched across the red part of the sky, and that copse, and that field before, many times before. She felt lonely, and longed to walk on and on along the path; and there, in the glow of sunset was the calm reflection of something unearthly, eternal.

"How finely that's painted!" she said, surprised that the picture had suddenly become intelligible to her.

"Look, Alyosha! Do you see how peaceful it is?"

She began trying to explain why she liked the landscape so much, but neither Kostya nor her husband understood her. She kept looking at the picture with a mournful smile, and the fact that the others saw nothing special in it troubled her. Then she began walking through the rooms and looking at the pictures again. She tried to understand them and no longer thought that a great many of them were alike. When, on returning home, for the first time she looked attentively at the big picture that hung over the piano in the drawing-room, she felt a dislike for it, and said:

"What an idea to have pictures like that!"

And after that the gilt cornices, the Venetian looking-glasses with flowers on them, the pictures of the same sort as the one that hung over the piano, and also her husband's and Kostya's reflections upon art, aroused in her a feeling of dreariness and vexation, even of hatred.

Life went on its ordinary course from day to day with no promise of anything special. The theatrical season was over, the warm days had come. There was a long spell of glorious weather. One morning the Laptevs attended the district court to hear Kostya, who had been appointed by the court to defend someone. They were late in starting, and reached the court after the examination of the witnesses had begun. A soldier in the reserve was accused of theft and housebreaking. There were a great number of witnesses, washerwomen; they all testified that the accused was often in the house of their employer – a woman who kept a laundry. At the Feast of the Exaltation of the Cross he came late in the evening and began asking for money; he wanted a pick-me-up, as he had been drinking, but no one gave him anything. Then he went away, but an hour afterwards he came back, and brought with him some beer and a soft gingerbread cake for the little girl. They drank and sang songs almost till daybreak, and when in the morning they looked about, the lock of the door leading up into the attic was broken, and of the linen three men's shirts, a petticoat, and two sheets were missing. Kostya asked each witness sarcastically whether she had not drunk the beer the accused had brought. Evidently he was insinuating that the washerwomen had stolen the linen themselves. He delivered his speech without the slightest nervousness, looking angrily at the jury.

He explained what robbery with housebreaking meant, and the difference between that and simple theft. He spoke very circumstantially and convincingly, displaying an unusual talent for speaking at length and in a serious tone about what had been known to everyone long before. And it was difficult to make out exactly what he was aiming at. From his long speech the foreman of the jury could only have deduced "that it was housebreaking but not robbery, as the washerwomen had sold the linen for drink themselves; or, if there had been robbery, there had not been housebreaking". But obviously, he said just what was wanted, as his speech moved the jury and the audience, and was very much liked. When they gave a verdict of acquittal, Yulia nodded to Kostya, and afterwards pressed his hand warmly.

In May the Laptevs moved to a country villa at Sokolniki. By that time Yulia was expecting a baby.

XIII

More than a year had passed. Yulia and Yartsev were lying on the grass at Sokolniki not far from the embankment of the Yaroslav railway; a little distance away Kotchevoy was lying with hands under his head, looking at the sky. All three had been for a walk, and were waiting for the six o'clock train to pass to go home to tea.

"Mothers see something extraordinary in their children, that is ordained by nature," said Yulia. "A mother will stand for hours together by the baby's cot looking at its little ears and eyes and nose, and fascinated by them. If anyone else kisses her baby the poor thing imagines that it gives him immense pleasure. And a mother talks of nothing but her baby. I know that weakness in mothers, and I keep watch over myself, but my Olga really is exceptional. How she looks at me when I'm nursing her! How she laughs! She's only eight months old, but, upon my word, I've never seen such intelligent eyes in a child of three."

"Tell me, by the way," asked Yartsev: "which do you love most – your husband or your baby?"

Yulia shrugged her shoulders.

"I don't know," she said. "I never was so very fond of my husband, and Olga is in reality my first love. You know that I did not marry Alexey for love. In old days I was foolish and miserable, and thought that I had ruined my life and his, and now I see that love is not necessary – that it is all nonsense."

"But if it is not love, what feeling is it that binds you to your husband? Why do you go on living with him?"

"I don't know. . . . I suppose it must be habit. I respect him, I miss him when he's away for long, but that's – not love. He is a clever, honest man, and that's enough to make me happy. He is very kind and good-hearted. . . ."

"Alyosha's intelligent, Alyosha's good," said Kostya, raising his head lazily; "but, my dear girl, to find out that he is intelligent, good, and interesting, you have to eat a hundredweight of salt with him. . . . And what's the use of his goodness and intelligence? He can fork out money as much as you want, but when character is needed to resist insolence or aggressiveness, he is faint-hearted and overcome with nervousness. People like your amiable Alyosha are splendid people, but they are no use at all for fighting. In fact, they are no use for anything."

At last the train came in sight. Coils of perfectly pink smoke from the funnels floated over the copse, and two windows in the last compartment flashed so brilliantly in the sun, that it hurt their eyes to look at it.

"Tea-time!" said Yulia Sergeyevna, getting up.

She had grown somewhat stouter of late, and her movements were already a little matronly, a little indolent.

"It's bad to be without love though," said Yartsev, walking behind her. "We talk and read of nothing else but love, but we do very little loving ourselves, and that's really bad."

"All that's nonsense, Ivan Gavrilitch," said Yulia. "That's not what gives happiness."

They had tea in the little garden, where mignonette, stocks, and tobacco plants were in flower, and spikes of early gladiolus were just opening. Yartsev and Kotchevoy could see from Yulia's face that she was passing through a happy period of inward peace and serenity, that she wanted nothing but what she had, and they, too, had a feeling of peace and comfort in their hearts. Whatever was said sounded apt and clever; the pines were lovely — the fragrance of them was exquisite as it had never been before; and the cream was very nice; and Sasha was a good, intelligent child.

After tea Yartsev sang songs, accompanying himself on the piano, while Yulia and Kotchevoy sat listening in silence, though Yulia got up from time to time, and went softly indoors, to take a look at the baby and at Lida, who had been in bed for the last two days feverish and eating nothing.

"My friend, my tender friend," sang Yartsev. "No, my friends,

I'll be hanged if I understand why you are all so against love!" he said, flinging back his head. "If I weren't busy for fifteen hours of the twenty-four, I should certainly fall in love."

Supper was served on the verandah; it was warm and still, but Yulia wrapped herself in a shawl and complained of the damp. When it got dark, she seemed not quite herself; she kept shivering and begging her visitors to stay a little longer. She regaled them with wine, and after supper ordered brandy to keep them from going. She didn't want to be left alone with the children and the servants.

"We summer visitors are getting up a performance for the children," she said. "We have got everything – a stage and actors; we are only at a loss for a play. Two dozen plays of different sorts have been sent us, but there isn't one that is suitable. Now, you are fond of the theatre, and are so good at history," she said, addressing Yartsev. "Write an historical play for us."

"Well, I might."

The men drank up all the brandy, and prepared to go.

It was past ten, and for summer-villa people that was late.

"How dark it is! One can't see a bit," said Yulia, as she went with them to the gate. "I don't know how you'll find your way. But, isn't it cold?"

She wrapped herself up more closely and walked back to the porch.

"I suppose my Alexey's playing cards somewhere," she called to them. "Good-night!"

After the lighted rooms nothing could be seen. Yartsev and Kostya groped their way like blind men to the railway embankment and crossed it.

"One can't see a thing," said Kostya in his bass voice, standing still and gazing at the sky. "And the stars, the stars, they are like new three-penny-bits. Gavrilitch!"

"Ah?" Yartsev responded somewhere in the darkness.

"I say, one can't see a thing. Where are you?"

Yartsev went up to him whistling, and took his arm.

"Hi, there, you summer visitors!" Kostya shouted at the top of his voice. "We've caught a socialist."

When he was exhilarated he was always very rowdy, shouting, wrangling with policemen and cab-drivers, singing, and laughing violently.

"Nature be damned," he shouted.

"Come, come," said Yartsev, trying to pacify him. "You mustn't. Please don't."

Soon the friends grew accustomed to the darkness, and were able to distinguish the outlines of the tall pines and telegraph posts. From time to time the sound of whistles reached them from the station and the telegraph wires hummed plaintively. From the copse itself there came no sound, and there was a feeling of pride, strength, and mystery in its silence, and on the right it seemed that the tops of the pines were almost touching the sky. The friends found their path and walked along it. There it was quite dark, and it was only from the long strip of sky dotted with stars, and from the firmly trodden earth under their feet, that they could tell they were walking along a path. They walked along side by side in silence, and it seemed to both of them that people were coming to meet them. Their tipsy exhilaration passed off. The fancy came into Yartsev's mind that perhaps that copse was haunted by the spirits of the Muscovite Tsars, boyars, and patriarchs, and he was on the point of telling Kostya about it, but he checked himself.

When they reached the town gate there was a faint light of dawn in the sky. Still in silence, Yartsev and Kotchevoy walked along the wooden pavement, by the cheap summer cottages, eating-houses, timber-stacks. Under the arch of inter-lacing branches, the damp air was fragrant of lime-trees, and then a broad, long street opened before them, and on it not a soul, not a light. . . . When they reached the Red Pond, it was daylight.

"Moscow — it's a town that will have to suffer a great deal more," said Yartsev, looking at the Alexyevsky Monastery.

"What put that into your head?"

"I don't know. I love Moscow."

Both Yartsev and Kostya had been born in Moscow, and adored the town, and felt for some reason antagonistic to every other town. Both were convinced that Moscow was a remarkable town, and Russia a remarkable country. In the Crimea, in the Caucasus, and abroad, they felt dull, uncomfortable, and ill at ease, and they thought their grey Moscow weather very pleasant and healthy. And when the rain lashed at the window-panes and it got dark early, and when the walls of the churches and houses looked a drab, dismal colour, days when one doesn't know what to put on when one is going out — such days excited them agreeably.

At last near the station they took a cab.

"It really would be nice to write an historical play," said Yartsev, "but not about the Lyapunovs or the Godunovs, but of the times of Yaroslav or of Monomach. . . . I hate all historical plays except the monologue of Pimen. When you have to do with some historical authority or even read a textbook of Russian history, you feel that everyone in Russia is exceptionally talented, gifted, and interesting; but when I see an historical play at the theatre, Russian life begins to seem stupid, morbid, and not original."

Near Dmitrovka the friends separated, and Yartsev went on to his lodging in Nikitsky Street. He sat half dozing, swaying from side to side, and pondering on the play. He suddenly imagined a terrible din, a clanging noise, and shouts in some unknown language, that might have been Kalmuck, and a village wrapped in flames, and forests near covered with hoar-frost and soft pink in the glow of the fire, visible for miles around, and so clearly that every little fir-tree could be distinguished, and savage men darting about the village on horseback and on foot, and as red as the glow in the sky.

"The Polovtsy," thought Yartsev.

One of them, a terrible old man with a bloodstained face all scorched from the fire, binds to his saddle a young girl with a white Russian face, and the girl looks sorrowful, understanding. Yartsev flung back his head and woke up.

"My friend, my tender friend . . ." he hummed.

As he paid the cabman and went up his stairs, he could not shake off his dreaminess; he saw the flames catching the village, and the forest beginning to crackle and smoke. A huge, wild bear frantic with terror rushed through the village. . . . And the girl tied to the saddle was still looking.

When at last he went into his room it was broad daylight. Two candles were burning by some open music on the piano. On the sofa lay Polina Razsudin wearing a black dress and a sash, with a newspaper in her hand, fast asleep. She must have been playing late, waiting for Yartsev to come home, and, tired of waiting, fell asleep.

"Hullo, she's worn out," he thought.

Carefully taking the newspaper out of her hands, he covered her with a rug. He put out the candles and went into his bedroom. As he got into bed, he still thought of his historical play, and the tune of "My friend, my tender friend" was still ringing in his head. . . .

Two days later Laptev looked in upon him for a moment to tell him that Lida was ill with diphtheria, and that Yulia Sergeyevna and her baby had caught it from her, and five days later came the news that Lida and Yulia were recovering, but the baby was dead, and that the Laptevs had left their villa at Sokolniki and had hastened back to Moscow.

XIV

It had become distasteful to Laptev to be long at home. His wife was constantly away in the lodge declaring that she had to look after the little girls, but he knew that she did not go to the lodge to give them lessons but to cry in Kostya's room. The ninth day came, then the twentieth, and then the fortieth, and still he had to go to the cemetery to listen to the requiem, and then to wear himself out for a whole day and night thinking of nothing but that unhappy baby, and trying to comfort his wife with all sorts of commonplace expressions. He went rarely to the warehouse now, and spent most of his time in charitable work, seizing upon every pretext requiring his attention, and he was glad when he had for some trivial reason to be out for the whole day. He had been intending of late to go abroad, to study night-refuges, and that idea attracted him now.

It was an autumn day. Yulia had just gone to the lodge to cry, while Laptev lay on a sofa in the study thinking where he could go. Just at that moment Pyotr announced Polina Razsudin. Laptev was delighted; he leaped up and went to meet the unexpected visitor, who had been his closest friend, though he had almost begun to forget her. She had not changed in the least since that evening when he had seen her for the last time, and was just the same as ever.

"Polina," he said, holding out both hands to her. "What ages! If you only knew how glad I am to see you! Do come in!"

Polina greeted him, jerked him by the hand, and without taking off her coat and hat, went into the study and sat down.

"I've come to you for one minute," she said. "I haven't time to talk of any nonsense. Sit down and listen. Whether you are glad to see me or not is absolutely nothing to me, for I don't care a straw for the gracious attentions of you lords of creation. I've only come to you because I've been to five other places already today, and everywhere I was met with a refusal, and it's a matter that can't be put off. Listen," she went on, looking into his face. "Five students of my acquaintance, stupid, unintelligent people, but certainly poor, have neglected to pay their fees, and are being excluded from the university. Your wealth makes it your duty to go straight to the university and pay for them."

"With pleasure, Polina."

"Here are their names," she said, giving him a list. "Go this minute; you'll have plenty of time to enjoy your domestic happiness afterwards."

At that moment a rustle was heard through the door that led into the drawing-room; probably the dog was scratching itself. Polina turned crimson and jumped up.

"Your Dulcinea's eavesdropping," she said. "That's horrid!"

Laptev was offended at this insult to Yulia.

"She's not here; she's in the lodge," he said. "And don't speak of her like that. Our child is dead, and she is in great distress."

"You can console her," Polina scoffed, sitting down again; "she'll have another dozen. You don't need much sense to bring children into the world."

Laptev remembered that he had heard this, or something very like it, many times in old days, and it brought back a whiff of the romance of the past, of solitary freedom, of his bachelor life, when he was young and thought he could do anything he chose, when he had neither love for his wife nor memory of his baby.

"Let us go together," he said, stretching.

When they reached the university Polina waited at the gate, while Laptev went into the office; he came back soon afterwards and handed Polina five receipts.

"Where are you going now?" he asked.

"To Yartsev's."

"I'll come with you."

"But you'll prevent him from writing."

"No, I assure you I won't," he said, and looked at her imploringly.

She had on a black hat trimmed with crape, as though she were in mourning, and a short, shabby coat, the pockets of which stuck out. Her nose looked longer than it used to be, and her face looked bloodless in spite of the cold. Laptev liked walking with her, doing what she told him, and listening to her grumbling. He walked along thinking about her, what inward strength there must be in this woman, since, though she was so ugly, so angular, so restless, though she did not know how to dress, and always had untidy hair, and was always somehow out of harmony, she was yet so fascinating.

They went into Yartsev's flat by the back way through the kitchen, where they were met by the cook, a clean little old woman with grey curls; she was overcome with embarrassment, and with a honeyed smile which made her little face look like a pie, said:

"Please walk in."

Yartsev was not at home. Polina sat down to the piano, and beginning upon a tedious, difficult exercise, told Laptev not to hinder her. And without distracting her attention by conversation, he sat on one side and began turning over the pages of a *The Messenger of Europe*. After practising for two hours – it was the task she set herself every day – she ate something in the kitchen and went out to her lessons. Laptev read the continuation of a story, then sat for a long time without reading and without being bored, glad to think that he was too late for dinner at home.

"Ha, ha, ha!" came Yartsev's laugh, and he walked in with ruddy cheeks, looking strong and healthy, wearing a new coat with bright buttons. "Ha, ha, ha!"

The friends dined together. Then Laptev lay on the sofa while Yartsev sat near and lighted a cigar. It got dark.

"I must be getting old," said Laptev. "Ever since my sister Nina died, I've taken to constantly thinking of death."

They began talking of death, of the immortality of the soul, of how nice it would be to rise again and fly off somewhere to Mars, to be always idle and happy, and, above all, to think in a new special way, not as on earth.

"One doesn't want to die," said Yartsev softly. "No sort of philosophy can reconcile me to death, and I look on it simply as annihilation. One wants to live."

"You love life, Gavrilitch?"

"Yes, I love it."

"Do you know, I can never understand myself about that. I'm always in a gloomy mood or else indifferent. I'm timid, without self-confidence; I have a cowardly conscience; I never can adapt myself to life, or become its master. Some people talk nonsense or cheat, and even so enjoy life, while I consciously do good, and feel nothing but uneasiness or complete indifference. I explain all that, Gavrilitch, by my being a slave, the grandson of a serf. Before we plebeians fight our way into the true path, many of our sort will perish on the way."

"That's all quite right, my dear fellow," said Yartsev, and he sighed. "That only proves once again how rich and varied Russian life is. Ah, how rich it is! Do you know, I feel more convinced every day that we are on the eve of the greatest triumph, and I should like to live to take part in it. Whether you like to believe it or not, to my thinking a remarkable generation is growing up. It gives me great enjoyment to teach the children, especially the girls. They are wonderful children!"

Yartsev went to the piano and struck a chord.

"I'm a chemist, I think in chemical terms, and I shall die a chemist," he went on. "But I am greedy, and I am afraid of dying unsatisfied; and chemistry is not enough for me, and I seize upon Russian history, history of art, the science of teaching music. . . . Your wife asked me in the summer to write an historical play, and now I'm longing to write and write. I feel as though I could sit for three days and three nights without moving, writing all the time. I am worn out with ideas – my brain's crowded with them, and I feel as though there were a pulse throbbing in my head. I don't in the least want to become anything special, to create something great. I simply want to live, to dream, to hope, to be in the midst of everything. . . . Life is short, my dear fellow, and one must make the most of everything."

After this friendly talk, which was not over till midnight, Laptev took to coming to see Yartsev almost every day. He felt drawn to him. As a rule he came towards evening, lay down on the sofa, and waited patiently for Yartsev to come in, without feeling in the least bored. When Yartsev came back from his work, he had dinner, and sat down to work; but Laptev would ask him a question, a conversation would spring up, and there was no more thought of work and at midnight the friends parted very well pleased with one another.

But this did not last long. Arriving one day at Yartsev's,

Laptev found no one there but Polina, who was sitting at the piano practising her exercises. She looked at him with a cold, almost hostile expression, and asked without shaking hands:

"Tell me, please: how much longer is this going on?"

"This? What?" asked Laptev, not understanding.

"You come here every day and hinder Yartsev from working. Yartsev is not a tradesman; he is a scientific man, and every moment of his life is precious. You ought to understand and to have some little delicacy!"

"If you think that I hinder him," said Laptev, mildly, disconcerted, "I will give up my visits."

"Quite right, too. You had better go, or he may be home in a minute and find you here."

The tone in which this was said, and the indifference in Polina's eyes, completely disconcerted him. She had absolutely no sort of feeling for him now, except the desire that he should go as soon as possible – and what a contrast it was to her old love for him! He went out without shaking hands with her, and he fancied she would call out to him, bring him back, but he heard the scales again, and as he slowly went down the stairs he realized that he had become a stranger to her now.

Three days later Yartsev came to spend the evening with him.

"I have news," he said, laughing. "Polina Nikolaevna has moved into my rooms altogether." He was a little confused, and went on in a low voice: "Well, we are not in love with each other, of course, but I suppose that . . . that doesn't matter. I am glad I can give her a refuge and peace and quiet, and make it possible for her not to work if she's ill. She fancies that her coming to live with me will make things more orderly, and that under her influence I shall become a great scientist. That's what she fancies. And let her fancy it. In the South they have a saying: 'Fancy makes the fool a rich man.' Ha, ha, ha!"

Laptev said nothing. Yartsev walked up and down the study, looking at the pictures he had seen so many times before, and said with a sigh:

"Yes, my dear fellow, I am three years older than you are, and it's too late for me to think of real love, and in reality a woman like Polina Nikolaevna is a godsend to me, and, of course, I shall get on capitally with her till we're both old people; but, goodness knows why, one still regrets something, one still longs for something, and I still feel as though I am lying in the Vale of Daghestan and dreaming of a ball. In short, man's never satisfied with what he has."

He went into the drawing-room and began singing as though nothing had happened, and Laptev sat in his study with his eyes shut, and tried to understand why Polina had gone to live with Yartsev. And then he felt sad that there were no lasting, permanent attachments. And he felt vexed that Polina Nikolaevna had gone to live with Yartsev, and vexed with himself that his feeling for his wife was not what it had been.

XV

Laptev sat reading and swaying to and fro in a rocking-chair;
Yulia was in the study, and she, too, was reading. It seemed there
was nothing to talk about; they had both been silent all day. From
time to time he looked at her from over his book and thought:
"Whether one marries from passionate love, or without love at
all, doesn't it come to the same thing?" And the time when he
used to be jealous, troubled, distressed, seemed to him far away.
He had succeeded in going abroad, and now he was resting after
the journey and looking forward to another visit in the spring
to England, which he had very much liked.

And Yulia Sergeyevna had grown used to her sorrow, and
had left off going to the lodge to cry. That winter she had given
up driving out shopping, had given up the theatres and concerts,
and had stayed at home. She never cared for big rooms, and
always sat in her husband's study or in her own room, where
she had shrines of ikons that had come to her on her marriage,
and where there hung on the wall the landscape that had pleased
her so much at the exhibition. She spent hardly any money on
herself, and was almost as frugal now as she had been in her
father's house.

The winter passed cheerlessly. Card-playing was the
rule everywhere in Moscow, and if any other recreation was
attempted, such as singing, reading, drawing, the result was

even more tedious. And since there were few talented people in Moscow, and the same singers and reciters performed at every entertainment, even the enjoyment of art gradually palled and became for many people a tiresome and monotonous social duty.

Moreover, the Laptevs never had a day without something vexatious happening. Old Laptev's eyesight was failing; he no longer went to the warehouse, and the oculist told them that he would soon be blind. Fyodor had for some reason given up going to the warehouse and spent his time sitting at home writing something. Panaurov had got a post in another town, and had been promoted an actual civil councillor, and was now staying at the Dresden. He came to the Laptevs' almost every day to ask for money. Kish had finished his studies at last, and while waiting for Laptev to find him a job, used to spend whole days at a time with them, telling them long, tedious stories. All this was irritating and exhausting, and made daily life unpleasant.

Pyotr came into the study, and announced an unknown lady. On the card he brought in was the name "Josephina Iosefovna Milan".

Yulia Sergeyevna got up languidly and went out limping slightly, as her foot had gone to sleep. In the doorway appeared a pale, thin lady with dark eyebrows, dressed altogether in black. She clasped her hands on her bosom and said supplicatingly

"M. Laptev, save my children!"

The jingle of her bracelets sounded familiar to him, and he knew the face with patches of powder on it; he recognized her as the lady with whom he had once so inappropriately dined before his marriage. It was Panaurov's second wife.

"Save my children," she repeated, and her face suddenly quivered and looked old and pitiful. "You alone can save us, and I have spent my last penny coming to Moscow to see you! My children are starving!"

She made a motion as though she were going to fall on her knees. Laptev was alarmed, and clutched her by the arm.

"Sit down, sit down . . ." he muttered, making her sit down. "I beg you to be seated."

"We have no money to buy bread," she said. "Grigory Nikolaevitch is going away to a new post, but he will not take the children and me with him, and the money which you so generously send us he spends only on himself. What are we to do? What? My poor, unhappy children!"

"Calm yourself, I beg. I will give orders that that money shall be made payable to you."

She began sobbing, and then grew calmer, and he noticed that the tears had made little pathways through the powder on her cheeks, and that she was growing a moustache.

"You are infinitely generous, M. Laptev. But be our guardian angel, our good fairy, persuade Grigory Nikolaevitch not to abandon me, but to take me with him. You know I love him – I love him insanely; he's the comfort of my life."

Laptev gave her a hundred roubles, and promised to talk to Panaurov, and saw her out to the hall in trepidation the whole time, for fear she should break into sobs or fall on her knees.

After her, Kish made his appearance. Then Kostya came in with his photographic apparatus. Of late he had been attracted by photography and took photographs of everyone in the house several times a day. This new pursuit caused him many disappointments, and he had actually grown thinner.

Before evening tea Fyodor arrived. Sitting in a corner in the study, he opened a book and stared for a long time at a page, obviously not reading. Then he spent a long time drinking tea; his face turned red. In his presence Laptev felt a load on his heart; even his silence was irksome to him.

"Russia may be congratulated on the appearance of a new author," said Fyodor. "Joking apart, though, brother, I have turned out a little article – the first fruits of my pen, so to say – and I've brought it to show you. Read it, dear boy, and tell me your opinion – but sincerely."

He took a manuscript out of his pocket and gave it to his brother. The article was called "The Russian Soul"; it was written tediously, in the colourless style in which people with no talent, but full of secret vanity, usually write. The leading idea of it was that the intellectual man has the right to disbelieve in the supernatural, but it is his duty to conceal his lack of faith, that he may not be a stumbling-block and shake the faith of others. Without faith there is no idealism, and idealism is destined to save Europe and guide humanity into the true path.

"But you don't say what Europe has to be saved from," said Laptev.

"That's intelligible of itself."

"Nothing is intelligible," said Laptev, and he walked about the room in agitation. "It's not intelligible to me why you wrote it. But that's your business."

"I want to publish it in pamphlet form."

"That's your affair."

They were silent for a minute. Fyodor sighed and said:

"It's an immense regret to me, dear brother, that we think differently. Oh, Alyosha, Alyosha, my darling brother! You and I are true Russians, true believers, men of broad nature; all of these German and Jewish crochets are not for us. You and I are not wretched upstarts, you know, but representatives of a distinguished merchant family."

"What do you mean by a distinguished family?" said Laptev, restraining his irritation. "A distinguished family! The landowners beat our grandfather and every low little government clerk punched him in the face. Our grandfather thrashed our father, and our father thrashed us. What has your distinguished family done for us? What sort of nerves, what sort of blood, have we inherited? For nearly three years you've been arguing like an ignorant deacon, and talking all sorts of nonsense, and now you've written – this slavish drivel here! While I, while I! Look at me. . . . No elasticity, no boldness, no strength of will; I tremble over every step I take as though I should be flogged for it. I am timid before nonentities, idiots, brutes, who are immeasurably my inferiors mentally and morally; I am afraid of porters, doorkeepers, policemen, gendarmes. I am afraid of everyone, because I was born of a mother who was terrified, and because from a child I was beaten and frightened! . . . You and I will do well to have no children. Oh, God, grant that this distinguished merchant family may die with us!"

Yulia Sergeyevna came into the study and sat down at the table.

"Are you arguing about something here?" she asked. "Am I interrupting?"

"No, little sister," answered Fyodor. "Our discussion was of principles. Here, you are abusing the family," he added, turning to his brother. "That family has created a business worth a million, though. That stands for something, anyway!"

"A great distinction — a business worth a million! A man with no particular brains, without abilities, by chance becomes a trader, and then when he has grown rich he goes on trading from day to day, with no sort of system, with no aim, without having any particular greed for money. He trades mechanically, and money comes to him of itself, without his going to meet it. He sits all his life at his work, likes it only because he can domineer over his clerks and get the better of his customers. He's a churchwarden because he can domineer over the choristers and keep them under his thumb; he's the patron of a school because he likes to feel the teacher is his subordinate and enjoys lording it over him. The merchant does not love trading, he loves dominating, and your warehouse is not so much a commercial establishment as a torture chamber! And for a business like yours, you want clerks who have been deprived of individual character and personal life – and you make them such by forcing them in childhood to lick the dust for a crust of bread, and you've trained them from childhood to believe that you are their benefactors. No fear of your taking a university man into your warehouse!"

"University men are not suitable for our business."

"That's not true," cried Laptev. "It's a lie!"

"Excuse me, it seems to me you spit into the well from which you drink yourself," said Fyodor, and he got up. "Our business is hateful to you, yet you make use of the income from it."

"Aha! We've spoken our minds," said Laptev, and he laughed, looking angrily at his brother. "Yes, if I didn't belong to your distinguished family – if I had an ounce of will and courage, I should long ago have flung away that income, and have gone to work for my living. But in your warehouse you've destroyed all character in me from a child! I'm your product."

Fyodor looked at the clock and began hurriedly saying goodbye. He kissed Yulia's hand and went out, but instead of going into the hall, walked into the drawing-room, then into the bedroom.

"I've forgotten how the rooms go," he said in extreme confusion. "It's a strange house. Isn't it a strange house!"

He seemed utterly overcome as he put on his coat, and there

was a look of pain on his face. Laptev felt no more anger; he was frightened, and at the same time felt sorry for Fyodor, and the warm, true love for his brother, which seemed to have died down in his heart during those three years, awoke, and he felt an intense desire to express that love.

"Come to dinner with us tomorrow, Fyodor," he said, and stroked him on the shoulder. "Will you come?"

"Yes, yes; but give me some water."

Laptev ran himself to the dining-room to take the first thing he could get from the sideboard. This was a tall beer-jug. He poured water into it and brought it to his brother. Fyodor began drinking, but bit a piece out of the jug; they heard a crunch, and then sobs. The water ran over his fur coat and his jacket, and Laptev, who had never seen men cry, stood in confusion and dismay, not knowing what to do. He looked on helplessly while Yulia and the servant took off Fyodor's coat and helped him back again into the room, and went with him, feeling guilty.

Yulia made Fyodor lie down on the sofa and knelt beside him.

"It's nothing," she said, trying to comfort him. "It's your nerves. . . ."

"I'm so miserable, my dear!" he said. "I am so unhappy, unhappy . . . but all the time I've been hiding it, I've been hiding it!"

He put his arm round her neck and whispered in her ear:

"Every night I see my sister Nina. She comes and sits in the chair near my bed. . . ."

When, an hour later, he put on his fur coat in the hall, he was smiling again and ashamed to face the servant. Laptev went with him to Pyatnitsky Street.

"Come and have dinner with us tomorrow," he said on the way, holding him by the arm, "and at Easter we'll go abroad together. You absolutely must have a change, or you'll be getting quite morbid."

When he got home Laptev found his wife in a state of great nervous agitation. The scene with Fyodor had upset her, and she could not recover her composure. She wasn't crying but kept tossing on the bed, clutching with cold fingers at the quilt, at the pillows, at her husband's hands. Her eyes looked big and frightened.

"Don't go away from me, don't go away," she said to her husband. "Tell me, Alyosha, why have I left off saying my prayers? What has become of my faith? Oh, why did you talk of religion before me? You've shaken my faith, you and your friends. I never pray now."

He put compresses on her forehead, chafed her hands, gave her tea to drink, while she huddled up to him in terror. . . ."

Towards morning she was worn out and fell asleep, while Laptev sat beside her and held her hand. So that he could get no sleep. The whole day afterwards he felt shattered and dull, and wandered listlessly about the rooms without a thought in his head.

XVI

The doctor said that Fyodor's mind was affected. Laptev did not know what to do in his father's house, while the dark warehouse in which neither his father nor Fyodor ever appeared now seemed to him like a sepulchre. When his wife told him that he absolutely must go every day to the warehouse and also to his father's, he either said nothing, or began talking irritably of his childhood, saying that it was beyond his power to forgive his father for his past, that the warehouse and the house in Pyatnitsky Street were hateful to him, and so on.

One Sunday morning Yulia went herself to Pyatnitsky Street. She found old Fyodor Stepanovitch in the same big drawing-room in which the service had been held on her first arrival. Wearing slippers, and without a cravat, he was sitting motionless in his arm-chair, blinking with his sightless eyes.

"It's I – your daughter-in-law," she said, going up to him. "I've come to see how you are."

He began breathing heavily with excitement.

Touched by his affliction and his loneliness, she kissed his hand; and he passed his hand over her face and head, and having satisfied himself that it was she, made the sign of the cross over her.

"Thank you, thank you," he said. "You know I've lost my eyes and can see nothing. . . . I can dimly see the window and the fire, but people and things I cannot see at all. Yes, I'm going blind, and Fyodor has fallen ill, and without the master's eye things are in a bad way now. If there is any irregularity there's no one to look into it; and folks soon get spoiled. And why is it Fyodor has fallen ill? Did he catch cold? Here I have never ailed in my life and never taken medicine. I never saw anything of doctors."

And, as he always did, the old man began boasting. Meanwhile the servants hurriedly laid the table and brought in lunch and bottles of wine.

Ten bottles were put on the table; one of them was in the shape of the Eiffel Tower. There was a whole dish of hot pies smelling of jam, rice, and fish.

"I beg my dear guest to have lunch," said the old man.

She took him by the arm, led him to the table, and poured him out a glass of vodka.

"I will come to you again tomorrow," she said, "and I'll bring your grandchildren, Sasha and Lida. They will be sorry for you, and fondle you."

"There's no need. Don't bring them. They are illegitimate."

"Why are they illegitimate? Why, their father and mother were married."

"Without my permission. I do not bless them, and I don't want to know them. Let them be."

"You speak strangely, Fyodor Stepanovitch," said Yulia, with a sigh.

"It is written in the Gospel: children must fear and honour their parents."

"Nothing of the sort. The Gospel tells us that we must forgive even our enemies."

"One can't forgive in our business. If you were to forgive everyone, you would come to ruin in three years."

"But to forgive, to say a kind, friendly word to anyone, even a sinner, is something far above business, far above wealth."

Yulia longed to soften the old man, to awaken a feeling of compassion in him, to move him to repentance; but he only listened condescendingly to all she said, as a grown-up person listens to a child.

"Fyodor Stepanovitch," said Yulia resolutely, "you are an old man, and God soon will call you to Himself. He won't ask you how you managed your business, and whether you were successful in it, but whether you were gracious to people; or whether you were harsh to those who were weaker than you, such as your servants, your clerks."

"I was always the benefactor of those that served me; they ought to remember me in their prayers forever," said the old man, with conviction, but touched by Yulia's tone of sincerity, and anxious to give her pleasure, he said: "Very well; bring my grandchildren tomorrow. I will tell them to buy me some little presents for them."

The old man was slovenly in his dress, and there was cigar

ash on his breast and on his knees; apparently no one cleaned his boots, or brushed his clothes. The rice in the pies was half cooked, the tablecloth smelt of soap, the servants tramped noisily about the room. And the old man and the whole house had a neglected look, and Yulia, who felt this, was ashamed of herself and of her husband.

"I will be sure to come and see you tomorrow," she said.

She walked through the rooms, and gave orders for the old man's bedroom to be set to rights, and the lamp to be lighted under the ikons in it. Fyodor, sitting in his own room, was looking at an open book without reading it. Yulia talked to him and told the servants to tidy his room, too; then she went downstairs to the clerks. In the middle of the room where the clerks used to dine, there was an unpainted wooden post to support the ceiling and to prevent its coming down. The ceilings in the basement were low, the walls covered with cheap paper, and there was a smell of charcoal fumes and cooking. As it was a holiday, all the clerks were at home, sitting on their bedsteads waiting for dinner. When Yulia went in they jumped up, and answered her questions timidly, looking up at her from under their brows like convicts.

"Good heavens! What a horrid room you have!" she said, throwing up her hands. "Aren't you crowded here?"

"Crowded, but not aggrieved," said Makeitchev. "We are greatly indebted to you, and will offer up our prayers for you to our Heavenly Father."

"The congruity of life with the conceit of the personality," said Potchatkin.

And noticing that Yulia did not understand Potchatkin, Makeitchev hastened to explain:

"We are humble people and must live according to our position."

She inspected the boys' quarters, and then the kitchen, made acquaintance with the housekeeper, and was thoroughly dissatisfied.

When she got home she said to her husband:

"We ought to move into your father's house and settle there for good as soon as possible. And you will go every day to the warehouse."

Then they both sat side by side in the study without speaking. His heart was heavy, and he did not want to move into Pyatnitsky Street or to go into the warehouse; but he guessed what his wife was thinking, and could not oppose her. He stroked her cheek and said:

"I feel as though our life is already over, and that a grey half-life is beginning for us. When I knew that my brother Fyodor was hopelessly ill, I shed tears; we spent our childhood and youth together, when I loved him with my whole soul. And now this catastrophe has come, and it seems, too, as though, losing him, I am finally cut away from my past. And when you said just now that we must move into the house in Pyatnitsky

Street, to that prison, it began to seem to me that there was no future for me either."

He got up and walked to the window.

"However that may be, one has to give up all thoughts of happiness," he said, looking out into the street. "There is none. I never have had any, and I suppose it doesn't exist at all. I was happy once in my life, though, when I sat at night under your parasol. Do you remember how you left your parasol at Nina's?" he asked, turning to his wife. "I was in love with you then, and I remember I spent all night sitting under your parasol, and was perfectly blissful."

Near the book-case in the study stood a mahogany chest with bronze fittings where Laptev kept various useless things, including the parasol. He took it out and handed it to his wife.

"Here it is."

Yulia looked for a minute at the parasol, recognized it, and smiled mournfully.

"I remember," she said. "When you proposed to me you held it in your hand." And seeing that he was preparing to go out, she said: "Please come back early if you can. I am dull without you."

And then she went into her own room, and gazed for a long time at the parasol.

XVII

In spite of the complexity of the business and the immense turnover, there were no bookkeepers in the warehouse, and it was impossible to make anything out of the books kept by the cashier in the office. Every day the warehouse was visited by agents, German and English, with whom the clerks talked politics and religion. A man of noble birth, ruined by drink, an ailing, pitiable creature, used to come to translate the foreign correspondence in the office; the clerks used to call him a midge, and put salt in his tea. And altogether the whole concern struck Laptev as a very queer business.

He went to the warehouse every day and tried to establish a new order of things; he forbade them to thrash the boys and to jeer at the buyers, and was violently angry when the clerks gleefully despatched to the provinces worthless shop-soiled goods as though they were new and fashionable. Now he was the chief person in the warehouse, but still, as before, he did not know how large his fortune was, whether his business was doing well, how much the senior clerks were paid, and so on. Potchatkin and Makeitchev looked upon him as young and inexperienced, concealed a great deal from him, and whispered mysteriously every evening with his blind old father.

It somehow happened at the beginning of June that Laptev went into the Bubnovsky restaurant with Potchatkin to talk business with him over lunch. Potchatkin had been with the Laptevs a long while, and had entered their service at eight years old. He seemed to belong to them – they trusted him fully; and when on leaving the warehouse he gathered up all the takings from the till and thrust them into his pocket, it never aroused the slightest suspicion. He was the head man in the business and in the house, and also in the church, where he performed the duties of churchwarden in place of his old master. He was nicknamed Malyuta Skuratov on account of his cruel treatment of the boys and clerks under him.

When they went into the restaurant he nodded to a waiter and said:

"Bring us, my lad, half a bodkin and twenty-four unsavouries."

After a brief pause the waiter brought on a tray half a bottle of vodka and some plates of various kinds of savouries.

"Look here, my good fellow," said Potchatkin. "Give us a plateful of the source of all slander and evil-speaking, with mashed potatoes."

The waiter did not understand; he was puzzled, and would have said something, but Potchatkin looked at him sternly and said:

"Except."

The waiter thought intently, then went to consult with his colleagues, and in the end guessing what was meant, brought a plateful of tongue. When they had drunk a couple of glasses and had had lunch, Laptev asked:

444

"Tell me, Ivan Vassilitch, is it true that our business has been dropping off for the last year?"

"Not a bit of it."

"Tell me frankly and honestly what income we have been making and are making, and what our profits are. We can't go on in the dark. We had a balancing of the accounts at the warehouse lately, but, excuse me, I don't believe in it; you think fit to conceal something from me and only tell the truth to my father. You have been used to being diplomatic from your childhood, and now you can't get on without it. And what's the use of it? So I beg you to be open. What is our position?"

"It all depends upon the fluctuation of credit," Potchatkin answered after a moment's pause.

"What do you understand by the fluctuation of credit?"

Potchatkin began explaining, but Laptev could make nothing of it, and sent for Makeitchev. The latter promptly made his appearance, had some lunch after saying grace, and in his sedate, mellow baritone began saying first of all that the clerks were in duty bound to pray night and day for their benefactors.

"By all means, only allow me not to consider myself your benefactor," said Laptev.

"Every man ought to remember what he is, and to be conscious of his station. By the grace of God you are a father and benefactor to us, and we are your slaves."

"I am sick of all that!" said Laptev, getting angry. "Please be a benefactor to me now. Please explain the position of our business. Give up looking upon me as a boy, or tomorrow I shall close the business. My father is blind, my brother is in the asylum, my nieces are only children. I hate the business; I should be glad to go away, but there's no one to take my place, as you know. For goodness' sake, drop your diplomacy!"

They went to the warehouse to go into the accounts; then they went on with them at home in the evening, the old father himself assisting. Initiating his son into his commercial secrets, the old man spoke as though he were engaged, not in trade, but in sorcery. It appeared that the profits of the business were increasing approximately ten per cent per annum, and that the Laptevs' fortune, reckoning only money and paper securities, amounted to six million roubles.

When at one o'clock at night, after balancing the accounts, Laptev went out into the open air, he was still under the spell of those figures. It was a still, sultry, moonlight night. The white walls of the houses beyond the river, the heavy barred gates, the stillness and the black shadows, combined to give the impression of a fortress, and nothing was wanting to complete the picture but a sentinel with a gun. Laptev went into the garden and sat down on a seat near the fence, which divided them from the neighbour's yard, where there was a garden, too. The bird-cherry was in bloom. Laptev remembered that the tree had been just as gnarled and just as big when he was a child, and had not changed at all since then. Every corner of the garden and of the yard recalled the far-away past. And in his childhood, too, just as now, the whole yard bathed in moonlight could be seen through the sparse trees, the shadows had been mysterious and forbidding, a black dog had lain in the middle of the yard, and the clerks' windows had stood wide open. And all these were cheerless memories.

The other side of the fence, in the neighbour's yard, there was a sound of light steps.

"My sweet, my precious . . ." said a man's voice so near the fence that Laptev could hear the man's breathing.

Now they were kissing. Laptev was convinced that the millions and the business which was so distasteful to him were ruining his life, and would make him a complete slave. He imagined how, little by little, he would grow accustomed to his position; would, little by little, enter into the part of the head of a great firm; would begin to grow dull and old, die in the end, as the average man usually does die, in a decrepit, soured old age, making everyone about him miserable and depressed. But what hindered him from giving up those millions and that business, and leaving that yard and garden which had been hateful to him from his childhood?

The whispering and kisses the other side of the fence disturbed him. He moved into the middle of the yard, and, unbuttoning his shirt over his chest, looked at the moon, and it seemed to him that he would order the gate to be unlocked, and would go out and never come back again. His heart ached sweetly with the foretaste of freedom; he laughed joyously, and pictured how exquisite, poetical, and even holy, life might be. . . .

But he still stood and did not go away, and kept asking himself: "What keeps me here?" And he felt angry with himself and with the black dog, which still lay stretched on the stone yard, instead of running off to the open country, to the woods, where it would have been free and happy. It was clear that that dog and he were prevented from leaving the yard by the same thing; the habit of bondage, of servitude. . . .

At midday next morning he went to see his wife, and that he might not be dull, asked Yartsev to go with him. Yulia Sergeyevna was staying in a summer villa at Butovo, and he had not been to see her for five days. When they reached the station the friends got into a carriage, and all the way there Yartsev was singing and in raptures over the exquisite weather. The villa was in a great park not far from the station. At the beginning of an avenue, about twenty paces from the gates, Yulia Sergeyevna was sitting under a broad, spreading poplar, waiting for her guests. She had on a light, elegant dress of a pale cream colour trimmed with lace, and in her hand she had the old familiar parasol. Yartsev greeted her and went on to the villa from which came the sound of Sasha's and Lida's voices, while Laptev sat down beside her to talk of business matters.

"Why is it you haven't been for so long?" she said, keeping his hand in hers. "I have been sitting here for days watching for you to come. I miss you so when you are away!"

She stood up and passed her hand over his hair, and scanned his face, his shoulders, his hat, with interest.

"You know I love you," she said, and flushed crimson. "You are precious to me. Here you've come. I see you, and I'm so happy I can't tell you. Well, let us talk. Tell me something."

She had told him she loved him, and he could only feel as though he had been married to her for ten years, and that he was hungry for his lunch. She had put her arm round his neck, tickling his cheek with the silk of her dress; he cautiously removed her hand, stood up, and without uttering a single word, walked to the villa. The little girls ran to meet him.

"How they have grown!" he thought. "And what changes in these three years. . . . But one may have to live another thirteen years, another thirty years. . . . What is there in store for us in the future? If we live, we shall see."

He embraced Sasha and Lida, who hung upon his neck, and said:

"Grandpapa sends his love. . . . Uncle Fyodor is dying. Uncle Kostya has sent a letter from America and sends you his love in it. He's bored at the exhibition and will soon be back. And Uncle Alyosha is hungry."

Then he sat on the verandah and saw his wife walking slowly along the avenue towards the house. She was deep in thought; there was a mournful, charming expression in her face, and her eyes were bright with tears. She was not now the slender, fragile, pale-faced girl she used to be; she was a mature, beautiful, vigorous woman. And Laptev saw the enthusiasm with which Yartsev looked at her when he met her, and the way her new, lovely expression was reflected in his face, which looked mournful and ecstatic too. One would have thought that he was seeing her for the first time in his life. And while they were at lunch on the verandah, Yartsev smiled with a sort of joyous shyness, and kept gazing at Yulia and at her beautiful neck. Laptev could not help watching them while he thought that he had perhaps another thirteen, another thirty years of life before him. . . . And what would he have to live through in that time? What is in store for us in the future?

And he thought:

"Let us live, and we shall see."